D0442547

Bakhita

ALSO BY VÉRONIQUE OLMI

Beside the Sea

Bakhita

A Novel of the Saint of Sudan

VÉRONIQUE OLMI

translated from the French
by Adriana Hunter

OTHER PRESS
NEW YORK

Originally published in French as *Bakhita* in 2017
by Éditions Albin Michel, Paris

Production editor: Yvonne E. Cárdenas
Text designer: Jennifer Daddio
This book was set in Centaur MT by
Alpha Design & Composition of Pittsfield, NH

1 3 5 7 9 10 8 6 4 2

 Printed in the United States of America on acid-free paper. For information write to Other Press LLC, 267 Fifth Avenue, 6th Floor, New York, NY 10016. Or visit our Web site: www.otherpress.com

LIBRARY OF CONGRESS
CATALOGING-IN-PUBLICATION DATA

Names: Olmi, Véronique, author. |
Hunter, Adriana, translator.
Title: Bakhita : a novel of the Saint of Sudan /
Véronique Olmi ; translated from the French
by Adriana Hunter
Other titles: Bakhita. English
Description: New York : Other Press, [2019]
Identifiers: LCCN 2018036541 (print) | LCCN
2018051471 (ebook) | ISBN 9781590519783
(ebook) | ISBN 9781590519776 (hardcover)
Subjects: LCSH: Bakhita, mère,
1869-1947--Fiction. | Christian saints--Fiction. |
GSAFD: Biographical fiction.
Classification: LCC PQ2675.L48 (ebook) |
LCC PQ2675.L48 B3413 2019 (print) |
DDC 843/.914--dc23
LC record available at
http://lccn.loc.gov/2018036541

Publisher's Note: This is a work of fiction. Names, characters, places, and incidents either are the product of the author's imagination or are used fictitiously.

FOR

Louis

FOR

Bonnie

They will even take away our name: and if we want to keep it,
we will have to find in ourselves the strength to do so, to
manage somehow so that behind the name something
of us, of us as we were, still remains.

—PRIMO LEVI, *IF THIS IS A MAN*

ONE

From Slavery to Freedom

She does not know her name. Does not know in what language she dreams. Remembers words in Arabic, Turkish, and Italian, and speaks various dialects. Several are from Sudan, another from Veneto. People call it "a jumble." *She speaks a jumble of languages and is hard to understand. You have to say it all again, using different words. Which she doesn't know.* With slow, passionate application she can read Italian, and she signs things with wobbly, almost childlike writing. She knows three prayers in Latin. Religious incantations that she sings in a deep powerful voice.

She has often been asked to tell the story of her life, and has told it again and again, from the beginning. It is the beginning they are interested to hear, so terrible. In her *jumble,* she has told her story, and that is how her memories have returned. By relating in chronological order the events from so long ago, so painful. *Storia Meravigliosa.* That is the title of her life story. A serialization in a periodical, and later a book. She has never read it. Her life as told to them. She was proud and ashamed of it. Was afraid of how people might react, and loved being loved for this story, for what she dared to say and what she left unsaid, things they would not have wanted to hear, would not have understood, and that she has never actually told anyone. *A wonderful story.* In the telling of it, her memory came back. And yet she has never remembered her name. Has never known what she was called. But that is not what matters. Because who she was as a child, in the days when she went by the name her father gave her—that she has not forgotten. Like an homage to childhood, she still harbors within her the little girl she once was. The child who should have died in slavery but survived; that child was and still is what no one has ever succeeded in taking from her.

When she was born, there were two of them. Two identical little girls. And she was always her twin's double. Even though she did not know where she was, she lived with her. They were separated, but together. They grew up and grew old far apart, yet alike. At night she was particularly aware of her presence, sensed the body that should have been next to hers, its breathing. Their father was the village chief's brother, in Olgossa in Darfur. The name of her village and the region were supplied by other people, when she told them her story and they cross-referenced maps, dates, and events. So it was in Olgossa that her father bared them, her twin and her, to the moon in order to protect them; and it was to the moon that he first spoke their names, which were reminders for all time of how they had come into the world, so that for all time the world would remember them. She knows this is how it happened, she knows it infallibly and for all time. When she looks at the darkness of night, she often thinks of her father's hands, and wonders in what corner of this vastness her name lives on.

In Olgossa in the evenings, when the sun had slipped behind the rocky uplands, when the men and their flocks had come home and the goats were lying under the trees, when the donkey's braying sounded out its tuneless music and the ground had not yet cooled, the people of her village gathered around the fire. They talked loudly like the crowds in small markets. She sat on her father's knee and rested her head against his shoulder. When he spoke, his voice made her skin tingle. A prolonged shiver, a shiver that had a smell, a melody, and a warmth all its own. Her twin would sit on his other knee and felt the same fear as she did in the gathering darkness. She thought so often of those evenings, of the sweet sensation of their protected fears. She closed her eyes on the recollection. And kept to herself her indefinable sadness, a sadness she could not possibly explain. She did not have the vocabulary to describe it; the words she knew were concrete and rough-hewn, they each identified an image or a shape but could not represent the elusive or the ever-present. It was only in the expression in her eyes that you could see the contrast between her strength and her innocence; in her expression too that you could see what she had lost and what her inner life had allowed her to reclaim. Her life. Which she protected like a gift.

Her mother's face must have been beautiful, because she herself was beautiful. Because she was always chosen for this, her beauty. Her mother must have been tall with high cheekbones, a wide forehead, and black eyes with that blue starlike spark at the center of them. Just like hers. Her mother smelled of grilled millet, the bitter sugar of sweat, and milk; smelled of the things she gave to others. She knows her mother smelled like this because she has come across this combination several times, and it knocked the breath out of her. It was terrible not being able to hold on to it, suffering the shock of it without savoring its comforts. It was terrible, but it also felt good being jolted like this, a few seconds she simply had to accept, like a painless mystery. Of the eleven children her mother had brought into the world, four died. Two were abducted.

She was five when it happened for the first time. Five, six, or seven, how to know? She was born in 1869. Perhaps a little earlier. Or a little later, she does not know. Time has no name for her, she does not like writing numbers, cannot tell the time from a clock, only from the shadows cast by trees. People who asked her to tell her story *from the beginning* calculated her age in relation to wars in her native Sudan, that species of violence she would meet again elsewhere, because every part of the world is the same, born of chaos and explosions, falling apart as it moves forward.

She is about five, and it is the end of the world. This particular afternoon bears a light never seen since, a peaceful happiness, resonant and yet unnoticed. No one knows it is there. People live within this happiness like busy little birds, and on this afternoon the children in her village play in the shade of the great baobab, and the tree is like someone they trust. It is a center and an ancestor, a source of shade and an immutable point. The elderly are asleep at this time of day. The men are harvesting watermelons in the fields. On the edge of the village the women beat sorghum, the soft music of a peaceful village that tends its fields, an image of a lost paradise that she will nurture to convince herself it existed. She is from this place, this site of massacred innocence, of goodness and rest. That is what she wants. To come from a fair life. As every life is before it is acquainted with evil.

Her older sister, Kishmet, has come over from her husband's village to spend the afternoon at home with them. She is fourteen, or thereabouts. She has not brought her baby, her mother-in-law is looking after the child, who has a slight fever, and so, for a few hours, she can be her parents' daughter again. She is having an afternoon nap with the twin in the women's hut. She is sad that she lives in another village, that she belongs to her husband now, not to her father, but she is proud to have a child. Her breasts are full; before falling asleep the twins drank a little of her milk, it soothed them both.

The women's humming as they beat sorghum is like the buzz of insects. She is five years old and she is at her mother's side, playing with her small pebbles. Doing what all children do, being inventive, bringing to life inanimate objects, stones, plants, orchestrating and imagining. These are her very last moments of innocence. Awareness is about to strike her down in a single blow and turn her life inside out like a glove. Her mother sings a little more slowly than the other women, she can hear this discrepancy, her mother's thoughts are elsewhere, because her eldest daughter has come for the afternoon. Soon she will be a grown woman. She already has a baby. Will have another. And then another. A married woman's life. Her mother's slower singing betrays pride, quiet concern. And tenderness.

She is five years old and she is afraid of snakes. Her older brother often draws long ribbon shapes in the sand with the end of a stick. He laughs when she screams, it's a game, a big brother's joke, and she will always associate her brother with snakes. She will miss this unequal game, her brother waiting eagerly for her fear, his eyes laughing in anticipation, the taunting look he gives her, granting her a fleeting importance. On this particular afternoon, it is just when she sees some snake tracks—tracks her brother may not have drawn—that she hears something appallingly loud. Unfamiliar. She doesn't understand it, but the women immediately stop beating their sorghum, they look up, scream as if calamity were already upon them, and they run to catch up with the sound. Her mother grabs her without even looking, as if she were a bundle of clothes, snatches her up like an armful of dry grass, and then drops her, runs off screaming. Forgetting her. Leaves her there, suddenly, in the disfigured village, surrounded by flames, and races into the hut where Kishmet and the twin were sleeping. Now she is alone. Surrounded by fire and dead bodies. A terror of abandonment takes root within her. She calls for her mother. Shrieks her name, but her cries are lost in the furious roar of the fire, the thudding sounds as the men beat it down with pitchforks. They pour buckets of water over it, smoke shrouds the village, chokes it. The child coughs and calls her mother, but neither her sobs nor her outstretched arms are answered.

When her mother reaches the women's hut, she looks for Kishmet but finds only the twin. Alone and alive. She shakes her. Kisses her.

Pushes her away. Then hugs her close. Panicky, incoherent behavior. *Tell me what you saw!* She screams at the child. Saying it again and again in a shrill voice, repeating her demand through hysterical sobs: *Tell me what you saw!* The child does not utter a word. The mother knows what happened. She herself was born in a time of war, she knows how slavery works, knows why her daughter has been taken and what she will be used for. What she wants from the young twin is one last image of Kishmet. *Tell me what you saw!* means: *Tell me you still see her!* But the child does not move. She is silent. Her face has changed, expresses a new awareness, one she does not yet have the words to communicate.

The abductors stormed in at a gallop that afternoon, with fire, rifles, chains, yokes, and horses, and they took everyone they could. The young, mostly. Boys to make soldiers of them, girls for pleasure and servitude. They worked quickly, this was routine for them. They knew the village, informed by allies who had told them how to get there and who may have been from the neighboring village. They knew what they would find there.

The men and women of Olgossa have arrived home too late. Their sons and daughters tried to run away, to hide, but they were taken, wounded, killed, and their voices were smothered in the great blast of the flames. There are bodies on the ground, dismembered, burned, groaning as the life ebbs out of them in large pools of blood. There are stray goats, whimpering dogs, and birds fallen silent. There are destroyed huts and broken slave yokes, evidence that the raiders have been here. The fire is still spreading from one point to another. The familiar signature left by slave traders.

The village is in disarray for several days, like a field after a storm. She does not recognize her own twin, does not recognize the place where she lives. Olgossa is filled with the moaning of the injured, on and on it goes, a constant repetition of suffering, like an endless round of slow, despairing supplications. She does not recognize the people with whom she lives. The villagers have gathered up the dead and counted the missing. They found decapitated old men, children with amputated limbs. Found devastation and pillage, ravaged fields, dying cows, the river water tainted by bloated corpses, every sign of life wiped out. And the women clutched and scratched at their own bodies till they drew blood, beat their foreheads on the ground, howling sounds the child had never heard. The men took up their lances and tom-toms, and set off into the night. The witch doctor came and made sacrifices. After many days and nights, the men returned. But did not meet their womenfolk's eyes. In front of their sons too they looked away. Confronted with rifles and gunpowder, their bows and arrows served only to indicate their impotent presence. Such irony.

For a long time the smell of bodies and burned straw hung over the village, and ash flittered about for several days before disappearing on the wind. And when the ash had gone, it was all truly over. But in the sand outside the women's hut, her older sister's body had left a snake trail as wide as a baobab branch. She still sees it. Even when others have walked over it. Even when the rain changes the red earth into clods of mud. She sees this image of her brutal, mute absence. A warning. And she still harbors that naked fear, the fear of her own screams that her mother did not hear. This is a new danger: Losing her mother's protection. A mother she no longer recognizes. An anxious, nervous, sleepless woman.

Of course the inhabitants of Olgassa considered leaving the village, because it was now known to the traders and their agents would surely come back. And then they thought of those who had done so before them, who had fled their ransacked villages, abandoned their crops, lost their flocks, had left for another place that they never actually reached. They had been found starved to death at the foot of hills, on plains, and in forests. And so the inhabitants of Olgossa stayed. Living in fear of going to fetch firewood, going to fetch water, fear of seeing their children stray away, their women grow too beautiful, fear that rifles and gunpowder should come galloping back. At any moment. By day. Or by night. And their happiness became a faltering thing, muddied by grief and powerlessness, and by this newfound wariness of strangers, but also, and most important, of those who were not strangers and had readily explained where they could be found.

Her mother had so many children. That is how she always remembers her, with children clutching her hands, her legs, swelling her belly, suckling at her breasts, sleeping against her back. A tree with its branches. That is her mother. Mother to all children, a universal loving mother, a reflection of every woman who has brought life into the world, she is forever loving and powerful, she is unconditional love, absolute self-sacrificing love. A mater dolorosa.

She has tried to cling to these appealing images of her mother, images from before the raid. The feast day when she saw her body painted red, gleaming with oil, looking like a flame rearing up from the sand. She was as beautiful as a stranger. Her children followed her, hand in hand, giggling shyly. The village was always full of children. You grew up with a child in your arms. On your hip. On your back. Holding your hand. You grew up accepting all the children that came after you, you grew up so that you could help carry them, and so on ad infinitum. Children snuck out of their huts, scattered, ran naked and free, screeching, laughing, and, only briefly, crying. And others were already being born.

For that feast day, the child remembers, her mother took her to one side and braided her hair with tiny red, yellow, and blue beads. She strung around her girlish waist and wrists the same red, yellow, and blue beads; they had belonged to her ancestors and were the symbol of their tribe, their distinguishing feature, like patterns painted on bodies and faces, tattoos on eyelids, like their hairstyles and finery. These colors come back to her, fragments of childhood that resurface and in which she longs to believe. On that feast day, her mother had devoted time to her alone, and when she had finished she told her, *You look beautiful.* And the child thought her mother was her own precious jewel, and swore to herself that when she grew up she would be like her, be like this red flame that children followed.

In the two years after the raid she believed that she would be married, she would have children and fill the great chasm left by her older sister. She would repair the sorrow. That's what she would be. A repairer of sorrow. So that her mother could stop being this woman who stumbles, this constantly wary woman who tells them ten times a day not to stray too far, never to talk to strangers, never to follow people who are not from the village, even women, even youngsters, it has become a litany she no longer hears, her mother's new form of song.

She is seven now, and knows that beyond the hills her older sister and other girls and other boys have vanished and become slaves. Slave, she doesn't really know what it means. It's a word for absence, for a village set alight, the word after which there is nothing left. She learned it, and then she went on living, just as little children do, little children who play without realizing they are busy growing up and learning.

She is seven, she takes the cows down to the river, never goes alone, never strays, ever, but she is needed and she likes that. She has her place. And her own personality too. They say she is a happy child, always cheerful, that she never sits still for a moment. Her mother says she is "gentle and good," so even when she is angry, even when she is furious, she tries to be as her mother describes her, "gentle and good," it contains her a little, brings her back to a more reasonable state, this child with so much imagination who invents new stories every day and tells them to the little ones, stories she acts out to bring them more fully to life. She likes doing this, likes the kids' eyes gleaming in anticipation of the rest of the story, the squeals of pretend terror, their hands covering their mouths, the laughter of their relief. She enjoys giving them these moments of fantasy, the pride she feels in eliciting hidden emotions: Fear and hope.

She is seven and she obeys her mother, who asks her one day to go pick grass on the edge of the village. She is not entirely alone, she is with her friend who is called Sira, she remembers a sweet name, so why not Sira. She strides out, swinging her hands and singing her funny song, "When children were born to the lioness," a song she made up and sings to the little ones. It is about an old woman who remembers a time when children were born covered in fur and armed with teeth that they then lost as they grew up and became real humans. When she dreams things up, she sees herself as a spirit, a lost child, a warrior animal. Her own fear always subsides with the story's happy ending.

On this particular afternoon she walks side by side with Sira, they dawdle on their way to fetch the grass her mother wants, there is something indolent in the air, the wind is dropping, the sun has lost its hard edge, and it is perhaps this balminess that makes Sira and her so carefree and dreamy. They see the two men and are not suspicious. No powder, no rifles, no horses, just two men from a nearby village. Neighbors.

They too have suffered raids. They lost everything. Perhaps they want to exchange one of these children for one that the slave traders took from them and whom they hope to recover. Perhaps they have become slave dealers themselves. Escapees from a raided village, trying to find a way to survive. And the two girls are alone. So young. Little girls command the highest price, better even than young boys. Children aged seven to ten are the most highly prized, and with this one, they can see she's already beautiful, they can see it, she's a beauty who will blossom and fetch a high price. A beauty worthy of a harem. They smile. Say hello, in a dialect not very unlike the girls', wait a while, wait despite their impatience, then confer quietly and agree on how to go about this, they'll take only one, they're no longer young men and the girls already look sturdy, they can probably defend themselves like lions, just one would be less risky, the more beautiful one of course. Only one of the men speaks to her, so as not to frighten her, the other stands nearby, ready to intervene if there is any resistance.

The man asks Sira to walk away. Walk a little way away. A little farther. Farther down there. Sira steps back, not looking behind her, steps back again. He keeps waving his hands, and she obeys. She stops near the river. The men are amazed at how easy it is, the girls make no protest, they are not far from the village, just one scream and they would have fled instantly. Then the man turns to her and tells her to walk in the opposite direction, toward the banana palm. She does not move. Looks disoriented, almost a half-wit. He points to the banana palm, tells her she must go fetch a bundle, she does not understand. She looks at the tree. And then at her friend. Sira is hopping from one foot to the other, on and on, and her eyes are huge. The man raises his voice now. "He's not from our village, a stranger." She thinks this, the thought like an arrow. Her friend jigs faster from one foot to the other, and her wide eyes stare at her, spilling tears. She can smell fear. Is caught in the web of fear communicated from the men to Sira and from Sira to her. Her ears buzz and her vision blurs. The man grins, she can see his yellow teeth, the impatience in his smile, and the other man, still with one hand on his hip, breathes heavily, irritably. The man keeps his eyes open, the village is close by, someone could walk past, it is the end of the afternoon, they'll be bringing in the flocks, this kid is beautiful but stupid. She can feel time distorting and weighing heavily. She can't see the bundle. Can't speak. Doesn't want to scream. Doesn't try to run away. She can tell she's slipping, falling in some way. But doesn't know how. Sira is now bent double with both fists rammed in her mouth, watching her, her body looks as if it might sink into the ground. The world is silent and furious. The wind has dropped, the white sky is overtaken by a single cloud, vast and motionless. The man gestures again. She looks at the tree he wants her to go to. Without knowing why, she complies. Walks toward the tree. Both men follow her, they join her cautiously under the banana palm. The sound of her heart. Like a tom-tom calling for a gathering. The man who had his hand on his hip takes out a dagger and puts it to her throat, covers her mouth with his other hand, "If you scream, I'll kill you!," it's such a big hand, it covers her whole face, it smells bad, and the tom-tom is hammering inside her head, her chest, her stomach, and her legs are shaking. She doesn't know what made the men so angry. They're now shouting in their dialect, and the dagger is pressing hard against her neck, she thinks maybe they eat little girls just like people in her village eat gazelles. They drag her like a dead gazelle, she's naked, like all children in her village. They walk away, dragging her behind them. Olgossa grows farther and farther away. Collapsing even more quickly than it did in the flames.

She walked with them until it was dark. Did not hear people from her village come after them. Did not hear the bush drums beat. Did not see her father loom out of nowhere, powerful and fearsome. She kept on walking for a long time, the day dwindled, and still she waited for them. They would be worried, they would walk quickly, they would run to find her. But they did not come, and so there was the sudden terror, the realization of what she had set in motion. She pictured her village in flames. Thought that was why they hadn't come to rescue her. A child is taken and the village burns and the inhabitants are busy fighting the destruction. That's what she had done. She had disobeyed, had triggered catastrophe, and now calling for her mother, reaching out her arms was, once again, pointless. No one would hear her now.

She waited. Did a lot of waiting. And a lot of walking. Night fell, and then... What happened then she has never told anyone. As if she has never managed to remember it. As if it never happened. It is not a wonderful story. *Storia Meravigliosa.* For a story to be wonderful, the beginning has to be terrible, of course, but the misery must be acceptable, and no one can emerge from it tainted, neither the storyteller nor those listening.

Night fell. She was alone with her abductors. How to describe what she wishes she had never experienced?

The walking went on for two days and two nights. She did not know where the big river was, or the villages, what lay on the far side of the hill, the far side of the trees, and the far side of the stars. But she tried to remember, so that she could retrace the route and go back home. She was afraid and she remembered. Was lost and she recited: The little stream. The pen with four goats. The dune. The bushes. The wells. The banana palms. Some thornbushes. A yellow dog. A donkey. Two donkeys. A dwarf palm. An old man sitting on the ground. Acacia trees. The dune. A field of millet. She hears the hyenas' shrill calls. The heat has turned to ice in the gathering dark, the wind is quick and cold. The countryside fades. She is in the middle of this invisibility.

The outskirts of a village. A small beaten-earth path, a few huts, skinny dogs, and the echoes of a far-off life. There are men here, talking among themselves, halfheartedly, without passion. They greet her two abductors and go back to their meandering discussion. They are accustomed to stolen children, see them everywhere, all the time, always have. They do not look at the little girl, there is neither pity nor curiosity. Just an ordinary evening.

Her captors open a door. They throw her in. She falls. Onto hard, ice-cold ground. They close the door with a large key. She is terrified, and the word "mama" is all she can remember, the only thing that really exists. The word inhabits her head, her chest, her whole body. It blends with her pain, her huge fear at what was done to her, at what she doesn't understand, it is the only name that stays with her. Another has gone missing: her own. On that first night the two men asked what her name was. She was too afraid to look at them. Eyes lowered, she could see the dagger. Gleaming and cold. What was her name. What did her mama call her. What was her name. What did her father call her when he talked to the moon. One of the men put his hand on her thin legs scratched by acacia thorns on their journey. What was her name. She left her name beside the river. She left it under the banana palm. It described how she came into the world. But she doesn't remember how she came into the world. She cries in panic. Only her mother's name remains. It is all around her. And it can do nothing for her.

There is no daylight in the locked room where they have thrown her, and night never falls. There is no sun. No moon. And no stars. The outside world appears feebly, through a hole gouged at the top of the wall. She stays there a long time. Perhaps a month. A time with no rhythm to it, a time paired inextricably with dread. She calls for her mother and her mother does not come. She begs her so tenderly. Asks to be forgiven: Sorry, I shouldn't have, sorry, I won't do it again, punish me, take me back, I'm sorry. Occasionally her mother appears in her dreams and her delirium, apparitions that connect her to her family. Does her mother get up in the night to listen for her? Does she beg her father to go find her? Does she curse her for digging farther into the deep wound of her sorrow?

She sometimes thinks she will stay here her whole life, kept by the two captors who come every evening with some bread and water, and their violence, too. She will grow up like this. Is that possible? Does that happen? Being forgotten by everyone, except these two men? Existing only for them?

She is in the dark of night, and there is nothing after this night but the start of this same night all over again. She smells the rats, feels the nits in her hair, everything is invisible and threatening, she is dirty and assaulted on all sides, she wears a new body, full of pain and shame. Now no one comes near her other than to hurt her. Any presence is a threat. It will be a long time before she learns not to start if someone comes close to her, before she stops being afraid of an outstretched hand, an overconfident eye. A long time before she calms the instinct of a prey animal on the alert, even in moments of joy or in her sleep.

She sleeps curled like an unborn child, sucks her thumb, and sometimes sings her song "When children were born to the lioness," resting her hand on her chest, to feel her skin reverberate as her father's used to. Her voice quavers like the air in the midday sun, and her skin rips. Cockroach stings and mouse bites draw burning ideograms that she traces with her fingers.

One morning she decides to escape. Finds within her the strength to hope, to believe in something, and to disobey. For days on end she scratches at the ground, and at the clayey hole at the top of the wall. Standing on tiptoe, straining up, she claws as best she can. She is small, she is thin, but she decides to scratch away at it all the time, every day, and then the hole will grow, and she will go home. She discovers she has a stubborn, dogged strength, a will to live, what is called the survival instinct. There are always two people in her: one at the mercy of the men's violence and the other, strangely spared, who refuses this fate. Her life deserves something different. She knows this.

Every day she scratches and says "Mama Mama" over and over, the name contains her, she is held within the tempo of this repeated word and it becomes an order. Very soon her fingers bleed. Scabs form and then are torn open, how to make the hole bigger, with what? One morning she throws mice up at it, to get them to help her. But those that don't fall back down, slip out through the hole without nibbling at it. Those that fall squeak shrilly and this calms her fear. Make me tiny! she asks the moon one evening, even though she cannot see it, Get me out! She cries and can feel herself disappearing, can feel life abandoning her. Then she sits herself up again. Something draws her, wakes her from her despair. She looks at the hole and speaks to it. It becomes her friend. Her enemy. An animal to be tamed. A spirit to placate. She keeps her eyes trained on it even when they are closed. Keeps her mind trained on it even when she sleeps. For a whole day she rubs at it with her hair. Her hair shreds. The hole grows no bigger. Every day, standing on tiptoe, she measures it with her outstretched hands. It is three hands wide. And never more.

So then she finds another means of escape. It is now to herself that she tells her stories. She sometimes imagines the little ones listening to her, remembers their eyes gleaming with fear and hope, she starts the story and never finishes it, doesn't know where it ends, everything slips through her fingers, she is gripped by fever and is suddenly immersed in her former life, immersed in a time when she heard calls to bring the flocks in for the evening. Her mother's calls when it was time to eat. The old women's croaky voices as they chatted in the sinking sunlight. She can hear and see it all. She sets it all out around her, turns the scorpions, rats, and ants into people she loves, names them, and watches them live. For a time this alternative reality saves her. And then the despair returns. She sees where she really is. Knows she is no one now. Howls like an abandoned animal. Screams and cries in a half-dream, half-waking state, journeying between the imaginary and the real, between childhood and the end of childhood. She balls her fists. The hole in the clay is an eye watching her. It is high up. It does not deliver her.

One morning one of her captors opens the door and drags her out, the light is like a knife. There are voices. There are men. A dense hubbub in a language that is not her tribe's. She immediately grasps that the people who have come are not from her village. Her disappointment is as violent as the sunlight. She feels the men's hands on her and opens her eyes, white needles dancing, nothing else. One of the men opens her eyelids and says she is sick. Then the captor takes her chin in his hand and forces her to open her mouth and show her teeth. Someone throws a stick for her to run and fetch, at first she does not understand. Does not fetch it. He slaps her and throws the stick again. She runs. The man spits when she falls. Her legs cannot carry her, she is supported by two gnarled pieces of wood. She does not understand what is expected of her. Is panic-stricken. Does not know what they want. She is inspected. All over. It hurts and she cannot understand why people keep wanting to hurt her. She cries because she doesn't understand, cries with dejection, and this infuriates her captor, he shows the dealer her muscles, her calves, her arms, and most of all keeps saying that she is beautiful. *Djamila*. This is the word that refers to her. *Djamila*. The discussions start, the arguing and the laughter freighted with scorn. Her eyes grow accustomed to the light. Behind the haggling she can see some men and women. A small group waiting. For what she does not know. She listens to the negotiations in an unintelligible language. Will she be sent back into the hole? She has a fleeting hope that these men were sent by her father, then she sees money passed from their hands to the captor's. Clearly sees the coins. She does not want to go back in the hole, to stay with her captors, would rather leave here with these people, *wants* to leave with them. She listens and understands a few words, saying she is *about seven years old*, saying her name is *Bakhita*. The captor puts the money in a small pouch and pushes her toward the waiting group. She is terrified but leaves her prison. She does not know that *Bakhita,* her new name, means "Lucky One." Does not know she has been sold to Muslim slave dealers. The truth is, she knows nothing about what all this means.

They are chained to each other. Men in front. Three of them. With chains around their necks, linked to the other two men's necks. Women behind. Three of them. With chains around their necks. Linked to the other two women's necks. They are all naked, like her. There is also a little girl, scarcely older than she is. The girl is not chained, and the two children are put side by side, between two guards, bringing up the rear. She watches this procession, the guards have whips and rifles, the chained walk on, uncomplaining, they have not looked at her, will not look at her. And yet all through her life she will seek out eye contact with those who have been mistreated, by life, work or their masters. She is stepping into the world of organized violence and obedience, she is seven years old and, despite her fear, she watches attentively. She did not know people could walk in chains under the lash of whips. Did not know this was done to humans. And does not know what this is called. So she asks the other child what this is.

"Shhh..." the girl replies.

"Who are they?" she says again, more quietly. But the child indicates that she doesn't understand. Doesn't speak her dialect.

"Them!" she says, pointing to the young men walking ahead of them. "Who?"

The other girl screws up her eyes, trying to understand. "*Abid,*" she says suddenly, then points to her. "You: *abda.*"

A feeling of dread strikes her like a physical blow. *Abda*. Her sister. That's what this is. What happened to her. *Abda,* slave, it's the worst that could happen, it's Kishmet and it's Bakhita herself. And all of a sudden it is real, it comes to life in front of her, right there, before her eyes, and for the first time she wonders: "Is Kishmet here?" She will never stop asking herself this question.

She can remember being lost in the smoke in her village, calling to her mother who could not hear her. She looks at these young girls in chains, can still hear her mother screaming, *Tell me what you saw!* And now she is the one her mother orders to see. So she looks, young bodies already stooped, scars on their backs, their feet torn to shreds, and the word "slave," that word full of terror walking ahead of her. The child next to her points to her own chest and says very quietly, "Binah. Bi-nah." Then points to her and asks a question she does not understand but guesses. She would like to reply but does not know how to. It is a long time since anyone has spoken to her, and every language is now foreign to her. She hesitates. Looks at the slaves. Then rubs her tear-filled eyes with her fingers, wipes the mucus from her face with her filthy arm, and utters the word for the first time, points to herself and says, "Bakhita."

In the days after that she feels she is crossing the whole world. Plains and deserts, forests, dry riverbeds, stinking swamps. They step over crevasses, furrows in wearied soil. They climb mountains. With burning hot stones that shift underfoot and bring down men laden like donkeys, stones hiding snakes that rear up their heads and hiss. She repeats her name to herself, this name she loathes. Tries to get to know herself: "Bakhita doesn't scream when she sees the snake's dancing tongue," "Bakhita doesn't grasp Binah's hand when she falls on the stones..." With this new name, she is afraid the sun and moon will not recognize her. She tries to find her bearings in this new life, but she has no idea where she is going or what will happen. She knows her village is getting farther and farther away, does not recognize this landscape, everything she sees, she sees for the first time. The wind is hot, it whips her legs with fistfuls of sand, and its sting stays on her skin a long time, like the bites of the mosquitoes she never sees. There are days when the sky fills with water, a huge gray belly overhead, but no one talks of rain, no one says prayers or sings the songs that make the rains come, and so they stay there with their thirst, separated from the sky.

She is no longer in prison but is in the vast ever-changing world, and she watches, exhausted but avid too. She sees birds with red-and-blue wings, they call to one another across great distances, then suddenly disappear, as if wiped from the sky in an instant. Will these birds fly to where her mother is? Can they both see the same things? Can she send her thoughts to her? She looks for her in everything she sees. Very early one morning she sees a falcon gliding in the sky, its wings open like a hand at rest, and the calm of it makes her weep. It is so like her mother, before the great sorrow. She sees flowers that nod in the wind, and wonders what their dance is trying to tell her but cannot make it out. Her mother would know. Her mother can read the landscape. She sees a fallen tree, knocked down by wild animals, its branches driven into the earth like claws, and remembers the trunk of the fallen baobab on which children play in her village, and where her mother sits to watch the morning sun rise. She hears animals running, hears them but does not see them, their footfalls rumble beneath her feet, she thinks of her mother dancing, she never leaves her, but over and above all her thoughts are exhaustion and pain. Thirst tormenting her. And her tears when she looks at the chained women, who are not her older sister. They make a watery sound in their throats, coughs kept inside. They groan and trip, their hands constantly on the move, their fingers quivering on outstretched arms. Their necks are cut and swollen, sometimes they try to ease the chains off their wounds, an endlessly repeated hand gesture, it has no effect, so they stop. And then they start again. This makes the guards laugh. Irritates them too, they say the women are lucky their hands are free, it won't always be like that, and then they use their whips, their sticks, or their daggers, brandish their rifles. The women are frightened, and when one of them falls, it brings down the others, and everything is in disarray, the chains strangle them a little tighter, there are screams and sobs, they have to think about the others chained to them all the time, but she, no, she thinks of her older sister. Was this done to her?

She realizes she has traveled a long way since being captured, she has walked very far and no longer even tries to remember landmarks: the hills, mountains, dunes, plains, and forests, she can't learn all of it. This is the world, she is discovering it, the dialects change along with the landscape, the shape of the huts, the animals kept in pens and those on the plains, the people's faces, the marks on their skin, the black of their skin, some are tattooed, others scarified, she has never seen this before, it is beautiful and terrifying. Some are as tall and narrow as grass stalks, others short like aged children, and all are accustomed to passing caravans. Their villages are on the slave route, which runs from zareba to zareba, centers scattered all over the land, places where slaves are gathered, guarded, and selected for the important traders to whom they belong, traders in ivory and captives. Later they will be taken to large markets. In the villages through which they pass, impromptu deals are sometimes struck. Those who have no slaves to offer sell someone they have stolen or a member of their own family. Bakhita saw this once, in a village ravaged by famine, a skeletal young man offering a little girl disfigured by starvation. The guards spat on the ground, who did he think they were? They lashed the girl with a whip and she collapsed instantly, proof she was worthless. Bakhita did not realize she was the boy's sister, Binah explained this to her, insisting she must believe it. Bakhita blocked her ears. Sometimes knowledge of the world is terribly wearying. And then a moment later it is the very opposite. She wants to see everything, hear everything. Even what she does not understand. She wants to remember words in Arabic, remember what she sees, what hunger and poverty can do to people. She sees fear that gives rise to anger, and despair that gives rise to hatred. She acknowledges all of this but cannot put a name to it. The spectacle of humankind. The battle destroying them all.

She learns that everyone buys and sells slaves, it is the most abject penury not to own just one or two. She sees slaves in the fields and in houses, blacksmiths, militiamen, farmhands, they are everywhere, an epidemic of slaves. When her guards buy more, and they always choose the young, they go through the same process every time: Before buying them, they check their teeth, eyes, skin, inside, outside, their muscles and bones, they throw the stick, make them turn around, jump, raise their arms, and talk too, occasionally. They beat any women who weep. Who wail when they are separated from their children, or stop wailing. The women open their mouths and their voices are hunkered deep in their stomachs, in icy silence. Bakhita watches them and thinks about Kishmet's baby, was it a girl or a boy? She is dazed, giddy with so much heartbreak. She is part of this story, *abda*, and cannot escape it, cannot escape this terrifying story. She keeps going. And is frightened too. Because the trader not only buys, he also abandons. Abandons those too tired to continue, those who cough or limp, those who bleed or fall, but he keeps Binah and her. She wants him to keep them. Because it would be worse without him, she knows. Being abandoned by the guards does not mean being free, quite the opposite. Ever since she was captured she has known that other men could take her, keep her, and sell her. So she is afraid of being injured. Being ill. Showing that she is tired or thirsty. She follows the caravan, men in front, women behind,

Binah and herself between the two guards. A long line of despairing naked figures, traveling across a supremely indifferent world. She whose father presented her before the moon, she who knew herself to be a guest of this world, now finds the universe no longer protects her. Slaves pass by and live nowhere. Their people do not exist. They are a part of this dispersal, this martyrdom, men and women far from their own lands, who keep walking and often die along the way.

At night, before it is time to sleep, the guards remove the chains and padlocks from around the men and women's necks, and put them on their feet. Two by two they are chained. The same is done to Bakhita and Binah. They are chained together, by their feet, and they do everything together. Filled with shame. At first they dare not look at each other and barely speak. One evening their embarrassment makes them laugh, so they hold on to this laughter and on subsequent evenings they laugh in anticipation of what they must do together, in the ground, and even if their laughter is more forced than heartfelt, it lends a little dignity to their shame. Bakhita learns this and will keep it her whole life, an enduring nicety: humor, a way of indicating her presence, and her tenderness too.

She and Binah try to blend their dialects, and it is hard. They add in some words of Arabic, but the few Arabic words they know are harsh and coarse, unfit for what they want to say to each other. They want to describe their lives before. Tell each other what it was like then, when they were young (or even younger), and in so doing stay connected to those lives, to their own stories, to their living and their dead. Bakhita learns that Binah was taken shortly before she was. She too wants to find her mother. She says that her older sister was not taken by slave traders but died bringing a baby boy into the world. To explain her words, she mimes childbirth, the baby, and dying. Bakhita does not understand all of it. She looks at her little friend and remembers the children who once listened to her stories, there is the same expectation in Binah's eyes. She decides against telling Binah about her twin, her father, the herd of cows she took down to the stream, and her brother who drew snake trails in the sand. And when Binah asks what her real name is, her mouth twists out of shape and she pinches her arm to stop herself from crying. Binah on the other hand knows her name. Her name is Awadir. She says it to Bakhita, like a secret she must never pass on, ever. The following night, they sleep holding hands. And Bakhita feels an unexpected strength, a powerful current, and this too is new: sharing feelings of love with a stranger when they can no longer be given to someone who is not there.

One day, under the violent onslaught of a white sun, the caravan reaches Taweisha. This caravan is no longer quite what it was—some slaves have been bought and others have died—and all along the way it has been followed by hyenas and vultures waiting to feed on slaves. The sick whom the guards unchained and left to die under the sky. Those who simply stopped breathing and suddenly collapsed. Those who begged for respite, and whom the guards struck to the ground with their sticks, then left there. The route taken by the caravan is marked by broken skeletons like bundles of wood, picked clean and bleached white. Bakhita has come to know a death with no rituals or grave, a death that goes beyond death, associated not with people dying but a system living. She is afraid of the hyenas' cries and the vultures' flight, and does not know that on routes traveled by larger caravans, these animals, overfed, no longer hover. Slaves die and simply stay there in the vast silence of those roads that are like mass graves.

Taweisha, the central station they finally reach after walking for thirty days, is the last frontier town between Darfur and Kordofan. This zareba is where the slave drivers bring captives they do not intend to take to the coast themselves. A town for every kind of trade and contraband. Trade in eunuchs. Trade in slaves who are exchanged or sold to middlemen. Contraband such as ivory, lead, mirrors, perfumes. Caravans large and small come together here, powerful dealers and small-time crooks, and everything is appraised, gauged, given a price.

Straw huts and stone shacks cling to the hillside, in the area where the locals live. For the slaves there are large windowless sheds at the foot of the hill. When Bakhita reaches Taweisha, she does not know that she is now entering the implacable machinery of slavery. Her caravan is immediately inspected by two *faroucs,* as black as ebony, as black as she is, as black as her captors, but also slaves themselves. They run the camp, military men without whom nothing happens. They are envied and protected, they have farms in Taweisha, and wives and children, and slaves of their own, very young boys who were captured or volunteered to serve them and whose gratitude is unbounded, child soldiers, saved from destitution. The faroucs talk to Bakhita's guards, they know them well, everything is based on trust, organization, and hierarchy. A few of the locals come down the hillside to have a look at them and to make comments in a language Bakhita does not understand, children gaze at them, unsurprised because this happens all the time, slaves that need grading before heading off to the big market. And all at once there is silence, people straighten and then bow, the Muslim cleric, the *faki,* has just arrived. Bakhita is meant to look humbly at the ground but she does not, she is suddenly drawn to a tiny baby sleeping in its mother's arms, a local woman's arms. She wants to touch the baby's feet. In her mind's eye, she steps out from the rows of slaves, leaves behind everything sordid, and makes for the newest, most fragile life. She hardly notices the faki, this feared, venerated man, dressed entirely in black, his long beard hanging down his chest, this man who has come for little boys. In the rows of slaves there are cries and sobs, whip cracks and pleas, fear travels through them like a breath of wind. Bakhita loses herself in contemplating the baby's feet, they are so small, she had forgotten how beautiful a foot could be, with its tiny toes and almost transparent nails, its creases, the curve of it, the fine skin, she had forgotten a child's foot, a foot that has never walked. The faki continues with his selection, he knows that of the twenty little boys he chooses, only two will survive emasculation. It is precisely this rarity that confers their value, and nothing fetches a higher price than a eunuch. The air is heavy, the breeze lifts the dry soil sluggishly, lazily. Bakhita reaches her hand toward the baby's feet, the mother recoils, screaming, a guard strikes Bakhita with a whip, there is a brief silence before she cries, and the baby cries too, woken by its mother's scream. Bakhita is not crying about the whipping alone, the searing shock of it, she is crying for the babies in her village, for Kishmet's baby, and for the baby she once was but who is now lost. It is an inconsolable distress. The mother walks away with her child. The twenty little boys follow the faki, he will castrate them himself, a distinction in which he takes pride, because this procedure that no Muslim is meant to undertake is usually entrusted to the Jews, but eunuchs are growing scarce and Darfur's fakis do their bit. Darfur, to the west of Sudan, is the new location for human trafficking, an asylum for all wrongdoers, for brutality in brutality, and inhumanity in inhumanity.

Bakhita sobs and through the tears that scald her dust-filled eyes, she sees a young slave woman tearing out her own hair and screaming. "Her little brother," Binah explains. "Brother. Of hers." She shows Bakhita the string of boys following the important cleric. They are not chained but walk calmly away, holding hands, the faki told them he has selected them for a very special life, they are the chosen ones. They do not understand Arabic. But they go meekly to their fate, they have seen the punishments handed out to anyone who disobeys so they are careful to be well behaved. One of them turns momentarily to look at the girl gesticulating dementedly, just a look, filled with detached affection.

After this the slaves become agitated and start to shake with exhaustion under the white sky, they start leaning on each other, hurting each other, pulling at each other's necks. The guards are worried the goods will be damaged, they unlock the padlocks to move the chains from the slaves' necks to their ankles, then they open the gate to the large round huts, and chivy the women into one hut and the men into another. No fornication, they say. The slaves do not understand these words, but who would have the heart for intimacy, which of them would have the strength for coupling? This is not life. It is survival.

Bakhita quickly realizes that being in the hut is worse than being outside. She rediscovers the oppression of her time in the hole where she was locked away by her captors, and here the scorpions are as big as a hand, the rats like small foxes. She drags Binah to the far end of the hut, they cling together and she sings her funny song "When children were born to the lioness," not really saying the words, only the melody trickles from her dry lips. She goes on and on singing the same notes, trying to escape inside her own head again, but all about her there is wailing and groaning, the world around her is stronger, she cannot remove herself from it. She feels Binah next to her, bone-tired, silent, resting her head on her shoulder and saying, "I like your little song." Bakhita does not understand the words but grasps the gist. And this is how she will go through life now. Connected to other people by intuition, sensing what emanates from them by their voice, their stride, the look in their eye, sometimes a gesture.

She watches. The women with whom she lives. Those who were here before and the newcomers, like herself. They are young mostly, there are other little girls, who eye each other, seek out their own kind, ask for news in a mixture of dialects and Arabic, and then, weary and disappointed, return to their fate as girls for sale. The place smells of vomit and shit, sweat, pus and urine, menstrual blood, they all sleep on the bare earth, when and if they sleep. Where will they all go? What will be done to them? How long will this last? They don't know. Guards come to fetch the sick, they are taken away and never seen again. Some adolescent girls are called out for a few hours, and when they return they stumble like drunkards and talk of killing themselves. Others tell terrible stories that no one wants to understand, and if they do understand, they choose not to believe them. Bakhita hears the story of the slave woman who could no longer keep up with her caravan, and her dealer hung her from a tree by her neck, to be sure that she had no rest, sure that she died and no one else could profit from her. She does not catch the young slave woman's name but thinks of her sister, and knows that she too was rebaptized, what is her name now? A Muslim name to make a Muslim woman of her, but also so that they can all be mistaken for one another, so no one can ever find anyone, the facts are scrambled, they are part of the big herd. There is talk of slaves abandoned, still yoked about the neck, by buyers who can no longer afford to feed them; slaves stabbed to death or shot; there is talk of the woman whose baby was thrown to the crocodiles and who threw herself into the river to join him, and of the woman whose pregnant belly was split right open because her captors had laid bets on the baby's sex. Bakhita does not want to hear these tales that she struggles to understand. Above and beyond the overriding mistrust in the hut, the loathing and the madness taking hold among the women, there is her love for Kishmet, and for one fleeting moment, all the captives look like her. The woman scratching her cheeks till they bleed. The one knocking her head against the mud walls. The one who has stopped talking but just grunts and moans. The one praying. The one snoring. The one laughing and crying at once. And this tiny little girl who has come to huddle against her, who refuses to speak and keeps her eyes closed. Bakhita can feel the child's heartbeat, notices her habit of patting her arm with one finger, perhaps she is lulling herself, perhaps she is marking out time to a story, perhaps she is losing her mind, how to know. She is like a baby bird held on a scrap of straw, a tiny place of warmth in which to find rest, her eyes closed against Bakhita, her breathing outside any notion of fear. Bakhita does not know her. Not her name, where she is from, or how she came here. She is four years old, maybe five. Bakhita senses that every one of these imprisoned women would like to do what this little girl is doing. She puts her hand on the child's head and can feel her pulse against her palm. She in turn is soothed. She dares to think about what is precious to her, dares to conjure her mother's face. Her laugh. Her voice. Her smell. That other life. When her name was... When her name was... What was her name? And her twin's? And her older brother's? And her friend's? What were all their names? She tries to remember, then falls asleep with the little girl next to her dribbling and heaving deep sighs.

She wakes with a start in the morning. The rooster has just crowed for the first time. She hears the call to prayer. Is snapped out of a colorful, violent, incoherent dream. She is sweating and her heartbeat thumps in her throat. The little girl has intertwined her legs with hers, two skinny scarred legs. The child is frowning, pursing her lips, brittle as dried grass. She too must have a Muslim name. A name that does not speak of what the world was like the day she was born. But neither of their fathers made their pledges to the moon in vain. Their fathers are powerful and kind. And she knows with certainty that her forgotten name lives on somewhere, protected. She can make out the sleeping bodies amid the foul stench and intimate noises, and decides she is happy to be called Bakhita. She makes this decision, accepts it. Bakhita. *Abda.* Slave. Like the other women and the little girl in her arms. She says *yes.* And then goes back to sleep. Slips into a dream in which her mother holds her close. Tries to find the words to tell her that she loves her, to reassure her, but she loves her so much she cannot find the words. For a love like that there are none.

After a few days they are herded out of the hut. Not only to work and serve men's pleasure. They are all herded out. Men, women. Adolescents, little children. Out they go. The dead have been discarded, the sick sold off to passing peddlers before they lost all their value, leaving the prime choice, strong healthy young people and children. They come outside and discover daylight once more. The smell of baked bread, grilled corn. Barking, goats bleating, donkeys braying, the calling and chatter of the village, this is life, and it is unbearably beautiful. Bakhita hears the wind in the leaves of a baobab, loud and so familiar it brings tears to her eyes. She does not know why something beautiful grieves her so much, why the chaotic sway of these leaves constricts her heart. They are shoved around, lined up in rows, and fear instantly has them in its grip. A little way in front of her she hears the child who slept in her arms crying. Over her lament is the sound of the wind in the baobab leaves. A swelling, discordant music. It is already hot, and in every slave's mind there is the same terrible dejection at the thought of setting off again, walking and managing not to die.

The faroucs must decide which of them will be sent to the coast, to the huge market, to Khartoum, the home of the three great traders who between them run the slave trade. So far the slaves have simply passed from hand to hand, middleman to middleman, now the final destination is drawing near. They are inspected again, evaluated, and divided into groups, the faroucs manage this process and the faki is there too. Deliberation, discussion, endless debate. Bakhita knows she must not open her eyes wide, must walk gently to get used to it again, knows she must not touch babies' feet, look adults in the eye, talk to Binah, show signs of exhaustion, or ask for water, knows how she must behave but she is so afraid of being separated from Binah that her legs shake. Every now and then their fingers brush against each other's and say, *I won't let go your hand,* but they see young men and women leave, one after another, forming a caravan, they leave and it is starting all over again, the keys and padlocks, the chains, one after another they are chosen, and she thinks that if she and Binah are separated she will go mad, like the women she saw in the hut, and she thinks of her mother again, "My little daughter is gentle and good." She is still her mother's little daughter. Is still gentle and good. Has not gone mad. And she will not. She sees the tiny child who slept in her arms stumble and set off, her face turned up, eyes searching helplessly for a woman to latch on to. The group moves away, a cloud of dust captured in the blinding light.

When the cacophony of ironwork, whips, and orders has dwindled, when she can hear only the barks of dogs following them, and then the barks of dogs returning, there are not many slaves left at the zareba, and she and Binah are among them. Together once more, maybe only for a day or two, but together. Perhaps there were too many children in the caravan that has just left, it's tricky, this precious merchandise that slows down consignments. They have been set aside for another convoy. This is an unbelievable gift, pure chance and such a joy, the urge to whoop and clap their hands, the urge to jump up and down, to throw themselves into each other's arms and feel against her own body her friend's thin body, her little-girl bones, her smell of damp, urine, and dust, her smell of old age that belies the power of this brief happiness. Of course they do none of this. They take the risk of becoming attached to each other but with no outward signs of this affection, no accesses of human emotion.

The guard chains them together and shuts them in again, and they talk. Without understanding each other's dialect, they understand their suffering. Without really following each other's words, they describe their misdemeanors, their villages, their parents, grandparents, brothers and sisters, cousins, ancestors, those who have died and those who still wait for them, and it all becomes real again, and never-ending too, as if they already have long lives behind them. They assimilate each other's words, sometimes the process is disheartening and incomprehensible, sometimes it falls into place, the words fly, then they repeat these foreign words over and over, and when they fall silent and are left alone with everything they have disclosed, sorrow washes over them with such brutal force that one morning, in a flash of lunacy, they do it, they decide on it, they tell each other: They are going to find their way back to their families. It is a sign of madness, of youthfulness, of life. They are going to run away.

It goes on like this for three days. Talking and dreaming about their homes and their escape. They belong to a world that has not disappeared, given that they remember it, and they will go home to it, retrace their steps, return to the starting point. Bakhita pictures herself in her mother's arms, held close to her with her eyes closed, she will breathe her smell of milk, her sweet sweat, her twin will be there, that other self who has waited for her and thanks to whom she has not entirely left the village, one part of her is *abda* and the other has remained free and takes refuge on her father's lap every evening. Emotion is a driving force and a form of paralysis, Bakhita is caught in the countercurrents of the dream and her fears, she wonders whether Olgossa still exists, whether her capture saw the village set on fire, whether the inhabitants have fled this now dangerous place, do places still exist when they have been abandoned?

In their innocence and their hope, in their rambling discussions, she and Binah imagine their villages are near to each other, their families together, finding one would mean finding the other. By day they work on one of the zareba's farms, among other slaves, world-weary taciturn old women, they are watched by a guard and still chained. And yet they will find a way, they know they will, escape starts in the mind. In the evenings, Bakhita sings her funny song, she teaches it to Binah deep inside that hut full of images, songs, and anecdotes about her family, stories too, they tell each other stories, the one about the magician who mends little girls, the one about the wild mother, it all comes back to them, and the game with pebbles, the game involving the moon, it all blossoms again, feels so close at hand, their world is about to change, is already changing.

It happens one evening. The guard comes in from the fields with his cart full of corncobs. He is irritable and in a hurry. He hauls them out of the hut and tells them to sort through the corn, he needs to sell it before nightfall, they'd better be quick about it. He removes their chains so they can work more quickly. They hear the chains fall. Feel their feet glide freely over the ground, their ankles dance back and forth, they can stand up, turn around, move without hurting someone else, their legs feel like feathers, they could fly. It makes them shake all over. Almost frightens them. Because they know. Now is the time. They must do it now. It needs no discussion. They must do as they are told and sort the corn to avoid being beaten, but they must also not sort the corn and run away. Their hands shake, they grade the corn and glance around, quickly, like birds, turning their heads, the corn, the village, the corn, the paths leading out of the village, the noises, the smells, the world breathing, the corn, the world opening up and closing in again, the corn, and then the guard goes into his hut. He leaves them. Quite alone. The two of them. Unchained. They hear the call to prayer and the voice does not frighten them, it is a voice on the wind, in the sky, somewhere else.

Bakhita's heart starts its tom-tom beat again, as it did when the men snatched her behind the banana palm, the same call beating in her ears and gently leading her body away, thumping, insisting, never stopping, thumping, insisting, until her head spins… They can no longer concentrate on sorting the corn into cobs worth selling and those to be fed to the livestock, they toss them at random, wherever they fall, they look toward the guard's door, still closed, they watch, hopeful, waiting for the moment when they will start to run. Children are playing on the hillside, their shouts and laughter carried in the fading evening light, the braying of donkeys waiting for food, dogs hovering around men who are about to feed them, and it is very lucky for the two girls that the dogs are hungry. There is that woman, beside the well. She has filled her urn, drawn it up, settled it on her head, and is now standing there. Binah starts to cry because the woman has stayed by the well for no reason, all alone, with her tiredness and laziness. The guard's door is still closed. A man walks past the hut, hesitates for a moment, and then decides not to knock, heads off again, he has prayer beads in his hand, shunts them very quickly through his fingers, looks down at the beads, then walks off, his great tall twisted body rolling, and the woman leaves the well. It is dark. There is no one around now. In the silence they can still hear the donkeys' braying. It sounds like cow horns blown into by musicians. Sounds like distress. Sounds like a signal. Without a word, without a look, they lob the last corncob and take each other's hand. And run.

———

Aimlessly. As fast as they can. They run. Night is closing in, and they run over a land with no sky and no light, the moon has hidden behind clouds, the darkness protects them. Their hands are clenched, clutched together, and their breath whistles like flute music, they run, without thinking where they are going, no longer feeling tired or afraid, straight ahead they flee. *I won't let go your hand.*

They come to a forest. Impossible to run fast through the trees and roots, they slow down. The trees are full of birds calling to one another for the night. From among the branches comes the sound of their wings, quick erratic flapping. There are monkeys, with their shrill cries. The tall, tightly packed trees, so close together, their branches reaching toward the sky, drawn by the open air. They walk quickly for a long time. And then stop. It hurts to breathe. Their sweat streams like rain. Their mouths are hot and dry. They don't know where they are. Don't know which way they should head. They must keep going.

And they walk through the darkness, which is a new world, gathered weightily around them, but at the end of this world their mothers wait for them. They can no longer feel their legs, they are beyond exhaustion and pain, beyond all thought. All at once there is a light, a glow coming from the depths of the forest, a flame passing between the trees without burning them, held high and steady, the girls set off again, running once more, their feet catching on roots, and the whole forest suddenly lights up. There are flames everywhere, as if the one following them has lit others, fed them with its fire, both in the forest and in the sky, these quivering yellows and reds, they are surrounded by war. Still they run. They fall, hurt themselves, get back up, and just before they are caught among the flames, they give up altogether, the fire has won, they stop. Bakhita's bleeding legs shake as if pursued by whips.

She catches her breath. Looks around. The forest is filled with darkness. There are no more torches. There can never have been any. They were threatened only by their own imagination, hunted down by their incoherent thoughts. They hear the last few birds call to one another, the last leaves rustle together, the monkeys howl, and then everything, absolutely everything, falls silent.

Bakhita and Binah are two lost children, they have run in circles, invented a forest fire, and in this imaginary chase, come back to where they were. They stand silent and helpless in the still of the forest, holding each other's hand. They are alive. They are not startled when they hear the slow calm footfalls approach. Think they are imagining again, but soon a deep, listless roar sounds in time with the pacing. It is a big cat. Patient. Infallible. Bakhita pushes Binah against a tree and she climbs up, spurred on by fear, climbs easily. Bakhita follows her. She will remember this night her whole life. It is like a fable, a myth. It will afford her a sense of pride that will slightly embarrass her but will remind her of the true savagery of a Sudan that was her country and that she confronted. Children will always love to hear her tell it. The wild beast coming to eat the escaped little girls. They will enjoy picturing Bakhita as a child, sleeping in a tree, like the monkeys and the birds.

What she will not describe to the children is little Binah's sobs, their terror. What she will not say is that in winter, when the wolves of Veneto howl in the surrounding hills, it is Binah that she hears. Binah who calls to her and whom she does not save.

In the morning the forest wakes them, the clamor of birdsong, as if the trees were exploding, the calls and famished cries of animals, incessant, discordant, furtive cries in the encroaching daylight. The light barely passes through the densely packed tree trunks, and way up high the leaves are the transparent color of water. The spirit of the night has been appeased and is giving them another chance. It is the first morning without chains or guards, it is the first day.

They pick fruit, unsure how to open it, unsure even of its name, the world welcomes them and feeds them, that is something they remember, a time without threats. Their impatience to see their mothers drives them on, and after walking for two hours, they emerge from the forest onto a large plain. It is a wide new landscape, they want to run across it, but it is covered in small hillocks, as if the earth has boiled and bears the scars of its burns, thousands of blisters, walking is difficult and very soon painful. There are also bushes full of thorns gusted toward them by the wind, drifting against their legs and scratching them. They can do nothing to defend themselves and walk on in spite of everything, on they walk and the sun is high, the blazing sky comes all the way down to touch them. This is the way home to their mothers, they must take this route, and they talk to their mothers all the time, to soothe their anxieties, Bakhita tells her mother what she has seen, and what has been done to her, and her mother forgives her. This forgiveness sustains her, and for her mother's sake she keeps going through this day of thorns and heat.

The day fades to gray, evening will be here soon, and with it, nostalgia and apprehension. They have stopped talking. On they walk, disappointed without admitting as much, disoriented and hesitant. And then they both hear it at once. A human voice. It roots them to the spot. They freeze, try to locate it. The plain is deserted. They are two tiny black spots held in the hand of twilight. The voice is drawing closer. They crouch behind a thornbush and wait. The voice is right there. With words full of anger and threats. The guard has found them. His voice is carried on the wind. They take each other's hand. Binah starts to cry, her hand shaking furiously in Bakhita's, as if someone were trying to separate them. The voice is very near now, and it is the voice of a whip. A voice that frightens even when it says nothing. It has come looking for Bakhita many, many times. It used to come while she slept. Told her she had no right to rest. Came when she was praying. Told her she had no right to hope. This same voice is here, in the plain they thought was deserted. Crouching behind the thorns, they know the guard will see them, but they do not have it in them to stand up and face him, do not have it in them to let go of each other's hand. Heads lowered, huddled in on themselves, they wait for him and wet themselves, dirtier and more ashamed than ever. The guard may be standing right over them now, patient, reveling in his own anger. They shut their eyes so tightly that their eyelids quiver, they chew the insides of their cheeks, inside their firmly sealed mouths, and they wait. The whimpering. The moans. The whistling coughs. Bakhita recognizes the watery gurgle from the women's throats. It is slaves. Slaves are filing past them. Slaves coming back.

The slaves trudge past with the heavy clank of their chains. They drag themselves, pounding the ground with their misery. The sound of iron clanging and creaking on the wind. The long line of exhausted and dying figures. Their grimaces of pain and their burned lips. Their blinded eyes. Their torn skin. And it does not seem to be a caravan passing but a single person, a single agony planting its footsteps on the plain and crushing it.

They watch the slaves walk past. Then watch them disappear. The guard's voice has faded to nothing. Misery walked right in front of them this evening and spared them.

Staying on the plain is like making an offering of themselves, they are too visible and need to get away from the route taken by the caravans. The only other landmark they have is the forest so that is where they go, despondent and terrified by the darkness, they retrace their steps in the hopes these steps will lead somewhere, but they cannot read the sky or the earth, and their shadows follow them haphazardly.

Binah has a toothache, and she moans and holds her cheek. Bakhita can no longer feel anything, no pain, her body is beyond suffering, all of it. They walk until deep into the night and when at last they reach the forest, tall and upright as a giant queen, they feel no relief but horrible bewilderment. Bakhita cannot identify kindly spirits. She peers into the dark and tries to remember what her mother told her of the world, she is afraid the night will slink away and make her disappear. Anything could happen. Everything already has happened. This time they don't have the courage to sleep in a tree with the fear of falling, so they succumb to a fatalistic faith and lie down on the ground. Binah still has a toothache. The sand has gouged wounds on Bakhita's feet, the pain throbs all the way to her heart. This is the tiny part of her that is still alive. She lies on the hard dry leaves, not moving, not afraid, not sad. She drifts. And suddenly it happens. A thread of light, a hand resting deep inside her, taking her pain, the pain in her soul and in her body, the hand envelops her without disturbing her, like a veil coming to rest. She breathes without it hurting. She is alive without being terrified. Surprised, she waits for a while, wonders whether it will last. It does last, so she sits up and looks at the night sky. It is clear, shimmering with a warmth that washes over her, and she surrenders to this warmth.

She has described that night. The serialization of her *Storia Meravigliosa* describes "her meeting with her guardian angel." She herself did not give this name to her night of consolation. It was a mystery and a hope, but mostly it was an urge to keep living, with a dazzling, searing conviction that she would not be entirely alone.

The following day, less sure of themselves and less innocent, they walk for a long time and come out of the forest, not onto the plain crossed by the caravans but onto the savanna. It looks vast to them. Stretching as far as the eye can see. Bakhita will always remember this savanna as like an ocean, never-ending low waves, the savanna kept rolling out before them, as they walked they forged more of it, making them lose all sense of direction. It seemed to those two little girls a vertiginous expanse.

They stumble on the grass, uncomplaining. The wind buffets them, drops away, then comes back with a scornful slap. The grass cuts their feet and legs, still they keep going under the huge sky that tells them nothing. The scenery never changes, the same hours under the same empty sky, on they walk, their eyes burning, their lips bleeding, and Bakhita can feel her body shriveling with thirst and hunger. She can feel her thirst inside her muscles and under her skin. Can feel that soon she will no longer feel anything.

And then all at once there are fields. At first they don't believe it, everything is hazy and surreal, suddenly these fields, like an illusion. Binah hears the stream before seeing it, a sound battling against the wind, a tiny little sound mingling with that howling blast. Bakhita, though, does not hear it. Without Binah she would be dead. Without Binah she would not have had the strength to believe it: Within the sound of the wind, there was also the sound of water. They drink for a long time, and when they are no longer thirsty, still they drink, they drink until they retch, reckless as horses. They drink and they wash, feeling the warm glide of water, tears of gratitude melting into the river water. This is another moment that tells them their childhood is not far away, oh, how they will surprise their families, the happiness of it is dizzying, almost painful.

They start walking again and now have an urge to talk once more, they tell each other, once again, about the loved ones they will go home to, the living and the dead. Parents and ancestors. Bakhita knows Binah's stories, she believes she understands some of them fully, the younger sister whom Binah taught to walk and whose name is Mende, the little cat her father gave her whose name is Cat, meanwhile Binah always wants Bakhita to sing her funny song, "When children were born to the lioness," and their recollections, whether understood or misunderstood, become intertwined, as if they were gifting them to each other to have more of them. But the image of their mothers. Their mothers' voices. These they keep for themselves, with such hope, so much hope, that it is held within a sob. They must not be reduced to two little girls too soon. They must hold out. Be brave. And have strength enough for two.

The next day is a happy one. It is the third day, they are so close now. No more forest, no more plain of slaves, no more swaying grass on the savanna, now there are fields and herds, men's handiwork. There is life and signs of life. They instinctively stay away from villages. They watch out for peddlers on their heavily laden donkeys or boney oxen, can hear them coming a long way off, selling fabric, onions, glassware, iron and copper rings, and sometimes humans, mostly the old and the sick, the weak ones whom slave traders do not want slowing them down, having a slave to sell boosts a peddler's trade slightly, anyone who fails to sell this commodity truly is the poorest of the poor. The girls are starting to understand this. They also watch out for chained slaves and solitary men, they have acquired an animal's self-restraint and apprehension, they continue on their way with their eyes trained far ahead, walking on and on through this world, a world that attracts and intrigues them, and they wonder which of them will be first to see her village tree loom on the horizon. Binah suddenly nudges Bakhita.

"Is that your mama, over there?" she asks. "Your mama? Over there?"

Bakhita does not know where to look, Binah points out a woman carrying a happily singing child on her hip and another asleep against her back.

"It's her! Isn't it? Is it your mama? Your mama?"

Nothing about the woman looks like Bakhita's mama, not her height, not her face, not the color of her skin, and what would she be doing here, in this village that isn't hers? Bakhita points at a herd of cows.

"Are those the cows from your village?" she asks Binah. "Are they? Your cows? There! Look!"

They fall silent and start to cry, discouraged and disappointed, as if each feeling the other were making no effort to recognize her home, as if the other were being willfully difficult. They would like to ask someone the way but dare not talk to strangers, would like to ask for help but the moment they open their mouths it will be obvious they are not locals, oh why in some hill, some goat pen, some field, some passerby isn't there just the tiniest sign of their families? So many people and nothing relevant to the two of them, after three days of trudging and bravery, nothing familiar. Still they walk, and soon darkness creeps alongside them, leading them gently toward another long night in the open. Then out of nowhere it appears. Their amazement stops them in their tracks.

"There it is!" says Binah.

Bakhita looks at it. Terror clutches at her throat.

Binah is happy.

"There it is!" she keeps saying. "It's there! We're there!"

The glow burning in the distance is the fires in Binah's village, the fires that stand vigil through the night. To Bakhita it means something else. Ever since the raid when her village went up in flames, fire has meant something else. Binah takes her hand, laughter rising in her throat, anxious, stifled laughter, and she starts to run, dragging Bakhita with her. Bakhita thinks they shouldn't go but gives in to Binah's enthusiasm, following her against her own will, because she too wants to cry, "Mama!" Wants that to be possible. To holler it as a last resort, a victory cry, Mama in every modulation, a call, an order! And so they run and the fire pierces the darkness, and when they stop briefly to catch their breath, a man approaches. Instinctively, they back away. They eye him with all the suspicion and defiance they can muster.

A brown dog joins the man.

"Drink? Just a bit?" the man says, handing them a gourd.

They hesitate, reluctantly refuse it, he insists. They reach as far as their arms will allow, one of them snatches it. They take turns to drink and it is almost as wonderful as bathing in the river. It calms them. Soothes them. They are overwhelmingly tired all at once, in this moment of respite. They hand the gourd back to the man, mumble *Shukran,* and move on, holding hands and walking slowly, as if dazed and sickened, slowly toward the fire. The cold closes in with the darkness, and the stars come out, flung up there as a welcome sign, and yet far away and chaotic. The orange moon is big as a sun. Soon the small dog comes and trots beside them, they huddle together and it accompanies them, the man whistles to it, calls it, it is a disobedient dog. The man has to come and get it. He disciplines it with a kick and asks the girls something in a dialect they do not really understand. His hands, his eyes, the intonation of his voice: He's asking a question. But what is it? Bakhita doesn't like his voice. Binah understands, though, and replies by pointing to the fire burning in the distance.

"Over there."

The man looks surprised.

"Now?"

Bakhita tugs at Binah's arm.

"Yes, over there."

The man mimes that the fire is a long way away. They don't care. He mimes the cold. The dark. They don't care. He points to the wounds on their legs. They don't care. He points at the night sky and growls like a wild animal. How does he know? How did he guess that they know about wild animals? That this happened to them?

"We're not frightened," says Bakhita.

"Very good!" the man replies with a smile. Then he brings his hands together against his cheek to mime sleep and gestures toward his hut.

"You sleep here and tomorrow you go there."

They say no and set off again, the fire really is far away, they keep their eyes pinned on it, forming a small procession, their childish stubbornness starting to lose its conviction, and then suddenly Bakhita screams in terror, recoiling and bent double, contorted with fear. Binah is confused. The dog runs ahead of them and comes back with the snake in its mouth. Bakhita is still screaming, the man beats the dog, opens its jaws, and hurls the half-eaten snake a long way off. Bakhita is crying. The man puts his hand on her shoulder.

In his hut he gives them food and drink. Next to this shack is a sheep pen. They can hear the scuffling of ewes and rams shut in for the night. The dog sits on the doorstep, protecting them from big cats and snakes, the girls assume he is watching over the herd, he's a good dog. The man, the shepherd, tells them to get some rest in his hut. Tomorrow, as soon as the sun comes up, he will take them all the way to the village, where the fire burns tonight. Okay? Tomorrow? Their mamas? Do they understand? Is that all right? Their mamas? He doesn't want to force them. They can leave if they want to. They no longer have the strength to say they don't want to. They fall asleep instantly, nestled against each other. They have reached the limits of what they could achieve, of what they could possibly endure.

When the man wakes them in the middle of the night, they do not realize it is the middle of the night. They think it is daytime and the man is waking them to take them to Binah's village. It is cold. The girls emerge from their sleep and are still in the land of dreams, then they see the dog, recognize it, but it is growling now and baring its teeth. They snap awake as if a pail of freezing water has been thrown in their faces. Bakhita hears Binah scream. Then she feels it. The chain around her ankle. Binah tries to run away, but succeeds only in tripping Bakhita. They are both on the ground. Binah shrieks, tries to crawl, her hands clutching at the icy ground, Bakhita catches hold of her hand, draws her close, and holds her tight. Binah sobs in her arms.

Bakhita makes no sound. She feels no surprise or anguish. She is no longer afraid. She is as high up and cold as the stars paled by the moon. She lives far, far away, beyond this night, with her little Binah in her arms. Chained to her. Again.

The memory of what she and Binah experienced in that sheepfold is one of her greatest traumas. An alarm woke inside her, a memory that lurked in all her fears and many of her nights. Like a visitation. The fire in Olgossa, then the cell in which her captors locked her, and now this sheepfold, these are three abyssal depths. The steps to hell. After the shepherd has chained them, they are shut in the sheep pen, trampled, butted, bitten by the whole flock, the animals walk over them, smother them, ram them, and soil on them, and still the chain around their ankles, digging into their calves, and Binah moving only when she sobs. Bakhita has no words to comfort her. They do not speak. But touch each other's hand. Sleep a little during the day when the sheep are let out, sleep on the filthy ground, in the stench of droppings that makes them nauseous, sleep in brief snatches, tormented by thirst and hunger, and when the sun goes down, they hear the flock return, the fear of that bleating coming nearer is as long and sharp as a needle, and when the rams fight they are butted by their horns, and they cry at the injustice of it all. And yet, treated like animals, mistreated by animals, shut away, trampled, chained, still their personalities, their dreams, and even a part of their innocence, of who they are, live on.

The shepherd comes for them one morning, drags them outside. How many days, how many nights had they spent in the sheepfold, they do not know. Three days? Ten days? Thirty? It was a nightmare in which time had no business. They lived in a time distorted by violence, at the mercy of a cruel, sadistic, backward man. When they come out of the sheep pen they look more like two old women than two little girls. Their skin is blighted, scabbed, and dirty, two stooped figures holding hands, their nails broken, they emerge into the daylight, half human and half animal, with the same obedience and the same mute passivity. They are hauled outside, offer no resistance, do not think or anticipate anything but simply obey. Slavery has caught up with them once more, as if every other form of life has disappeared. The only truth is slavery.

The shepherd wants to sell them to a dealer who grimaces as he prods them, Bakhita understands that they are worth very little. But they are young, *That's what sells best.* Children. They are easier to mold. *To make just the way we want them.* The girls are asked to squat, stand up, squat again, they are touched in intimate places, and Bakhita feels ashamed to be so dirty, this shame is the first sign that she is still alive. When the men remove the chains to watch the girls walk, Binah falls, Bakhita cries her name in a voice that grates like rough stones because that is what she is now, full of earth and stones. She is frightened of being bought without her friend. Sprawled on the ground, Binah looks at Bakhita as if seeing her from far away, as if trying to remember who she is. The daylight is blinding, Bakhita reaches her hand out to her friend. Binah looks at her but does not move. The shepherd kicks her in the back to get her up. This makes her curl into a ball, she turns her head slightly toward the sky and simply stays there. Bakhita is still reaching out her hand. She wants to hear that story again, the one about little Mende and Binah teaching her to walk. Wants to sing her funny song to her again. Because she knows, knows that if Binah has the strength to get up, they will start living again. But if one is chosen and not the other, then the other will be sent back among the rams and ewes. Alone with them. And that, that would not be possible. Alone with the shepherd. That would not be possible. The dealer grows impatient. His slaves wait behind him. Shaking with exhaustion and anger. The ones crying must have been caught only recently. And these newcomers are constantly whipped, even when standing, even when waiting, they are whipped, Bakhita can hear the guards grunting with each lash, the whistle of the whip before it strikes their skin with a wet sound, the groans from the men and the whimpers from the women. She tries to forget them, leans closer to Binah and whispers "Awadir," the name she had as a beloved child. Binah opens her eyes. She wants Bakhita to forgive her, but she can't do it, she can't take any more. There. It's over. This is where she stops. Her eyes ask for forgiveness, and then they close of their own accord, such a gentle relinquishment. Now Bakhita forgets the dealer, the shepherd, the guards, and the whip, couldn't care less about them in fact, she is determined to save her friend, touches her shoulder and reaches out her hand firmly, this hand that Binah has so often held, this strength.

"Don't leave me," says Bakhita.

Binah smiles slightly, a desolate smile.

"Don't leave me all on my own."

Binah hesitates, would like to smile at her but can't manage it.

"Come, please..."

The dealer strikes Bakhita and she backs away. He says something angry and strikes her again. Bakhita puts her arm in front of her face until he stops beating her, and then she slowly lowers her arm, and sees, standing before her, Binah. She has picked herself up and is waiting to be inspected. The dealer turns to her, spits on the ground, and screws up his face as he feels her bones and her stomach, then he slaps her legs, lifts her eyelids, and when he holds her chin to look inside her mouth, Binah steps back, her teeth hurt so terribly, her cheek and throat are burning. The dealer opens her mouth wide, as if trying to split Binah open in two, open her up by the mouth, and he delves his fingers inside. He pulls. Binah looks like a little horse. Her eyes wild like a frightened horse. She moans and backs away but the dealer has her firmly by the jaw. He pulls out two back teeth, two molars, and throws them on the ground, then resumes his deliberations with the shepherd. Binah spits trickles of blood, Bakhita puts her hand around her back, wants to tell her she will be better off without her damaged teeth but says nothing. She is crying. Because it is over. They will not see their mothers. She looks off into the distance all around, but of course in such dazzling daylight, there is no reason for a fire to wait for them anywhere. There will be no more reunions or hope of reunions. The world is too big, too poor, too grasping. And it is now, in the middle of this haggling between the dealer and the shepherd, their arrangements and arguments, in the middle of the sobbing of slave men and women, the sheep bleating, the cock crowing, in the middle of all these scrambled sounds, it is now that, somewhere among the slaves, Bakhita hears a baby cry. She immediately thinks her mother is with the slaves. Spins around to look at them. Scans them to find her mother, it is a small caravan, she has very soon looked at them all, and just as soon realizes she was wrong. Her mother is not there. But still. She will never be rid of this. All her life, till the very end of her life, when she hears a baby cry, she will think it is in her mother's arms. Even when her mother would be too old to be a mother. And too old to be alive. Every child crying will be in her mother's arms and waiting to be consoled by her.

Binah hears it too. The cry of someone younger than she is. Both girls are old enough to be big sisters, old enough to be little mother figures in their villages. This baby is more fragile than they are. And Binah blows her nose with her fingers and takes it upon herself to stop crying. The baby keeps screaming, and Binah shows that she can stand upright, like a big girl. She finds it difficult to breathe, the pain in her mouth radiates over her whole face, but the baby reminds her how it goes. This tiny child, this latest addition is part of the caravan, so, at seven years old, the two of them must go too.

They are bought together, Bakhita and Binah together. Once again. And once again they walk between the guards, unchained. They set off. Keep going. *I won't let go your hand.*

With this small caravan they tread the soil of a Sudan laid open to the vast sky and sullied by bartering and trafficking. They walk and Bakhita realizes that the time spent running away was wasted, the world of slavery is her world, but there are always hopes to keep her alive. Perhaps they will pass her village. Perhaps they will find Kishmet. They will not spend their whole lives on these paths, one day the walking will be over, one day there will be something else, and whatever it is, it cannot be worse, they have already been through the worst. Bakhita follows the long, sinuous, dangerous path, like the snake shapes her brother used to draw to frighten her, and she decides she will never be afraid of snakes again. The snake that made her scream on the night the shepherd caught them will be the last. No longer being afraid of snakes feels like conquering them. And she finds this resolution strangely reassuring. Is amazed by it, would like to share it with Binah, but talking is forbidden and anyway, they do not have the strength for it. Everything is concentrated into walking and the energy it requires. But the appetite for life that comes over her now, in this captive state where she is ranked lower than a donkey, is like a promise she makes to herself: She wants to live. This thought belongs to her. No one can take it from her. She has seen slaves abandoned to the vultures and hyenas. Has seen unsalable slaves and those sold off to the destitute. Does not know whether she is worth money, a goat, four hens, some salt, a few copper bowls, necklaces, pagnes, a debt, a tax, does not know what would be given in exchange for her, but she does know one thing: She does not want to die abandoned by the roadside. So she obeys. Keeps walking. Concentrates on the effort of it. She is with Binah, saved from the sheepfold and the shepherd. She walks. And she has a friend. A life other than her own that she holds as dear as her own.

But there is the baby, still. The crying baby. The mother is not chained. She is very young and this is her first child. She was so frightened when her hut caught fire that her milk has dried up. This is what Bakhita gathers from hearsay within the caravan. The slave drivers set fire to her village. As they did to Bakhita's. And the story is the same everywhere, violence endlessly repeated, rifle fire and torch fire, fire that engulfs huts and the people inside those huts, fire that consumes animals, trees, fields, fire that runs faster than life itself.

After a while this crying baby makes it difficult for Bakhita to breathe. She finds it hard to walk without losing her balance. And she is not alone in this. In among all the chains, the sighs, and the blows, all the turmoil, this baby is the only thing anyone can hear. His mother holds him to her. Tries to rock him but she is shaking so much her arms twitch and jerk, and while trying to cradle him, she squeezes her breasts and attempts to milk them, the baby latches on to a nipple, releases it with a wail and then tries again, his mouth twisted, he knocks his head against his mother's chest, mouths her nipple, and immediately starts to cry again. The nearest guard, a short man, compact as a block of stone, whips the mother to bring an end to the wailing. "Shut him up! Shut him up!" he yells. He is young, but old enough to have children, perhaps he has some. And is genuinely troubled by the baby's cries. Or perhaps, Bakhita thinks, perhaps he is afraid. She thinks she can see this in the man's cruelty, thinks she can see fear.

———

Hands reach out to the mother and then fall away. Women look at the baby and then look away with a grimace of pain. Others are irritated, like the guard, and anguished too, they are familiar with the dreaded, much repeated story, the story written in advance. And then there is this young boy who is so angry that if the guard met his eye, he would burn on the spot. His head is shaved, his features already strong, both stubborn and kind, the face of an older brother ready to fight, but who still carries within him a fragile gentleness that hinders him.

After walking for one long hour, perhaps two, the caravan comes to cultivated fields. There must be villages nearby. The mother barks a brief laugh, like a sob. She is still shaking the baby in the hope of lulling him and her face spins in every direction, she wets herself in panic, does not feel the stream of urine down her leg, looks around wildly and suddenly throws herself at the guard. She has seen a goat. She says she will be very quick, she won't delay the caravan, will run straight back. The guard shoves her aside with an elbow in her temple. She almost smiles, is not discouraged. It is as if she cannot see what is going on, as if she has lost her mind. She is with them and yet far away already, so far away. She comes back at the guard, with her crying baby, and tells him that if her son grows up he will fetch a high price. She turns to the slaves, wants them to agree with her, yes, it's a good idea, if the baby has the goat's milk, if he doesn't die, he'll be valuable. But no one believes they will stop for the baby to suckle at the goat's udder. The angry young man shouts some words no one understands, his voice shakes with rebellion, bounces off the stones, and dies away. The guard does not beat him. So the angry young man repeats himself, three times, repeats the words no one understands, three times, staring up at the sky, but the sky replies with nothing but the fierce sun. Bakhita and Binah take each other's hands, they are frightened now, accustomed to human danger. Their stomachs churn in dread. Something evil hangs in the air, curdling it. A young woman, but one old enough to be the baby's grandmother, looks at the mother and says very quietly, *Asfa*. Sorry. And she shakes her head helplessly, because the young mother, who is the same age as Bakhita's older sister, fourteen at the very most, does not understand what is happening.

The caravan walks past the goat, past the fields, past the stream, and now the land is empty again. And still the baby's cries can be heard like an ancient song, modulated with his mother's sobs. This music wraps itself around the slaves, weighs them down, shrouding them in its distress. Some cry, very quietly, with all the impotence of pointless tears. The angry young man walks more upright than the others, as if this will help contain his fury, his eyes focused dead ahead, his jaw clamped like a trap closed over its prey. He seems tireless. Bakhita thinks he must be a good brother and a good son. But looking at him hurts her almost as much as hearing the mother and her baby. Perhaps they have nearly arrived, someone kind will buy her, someone who will give him some milk, Bakhita thinks. This won't go on much longer. And then she sees the hill. Is reassured by it. The landscape is changing, which is a good sign, they will arrive somewhere else, in a village perhaps. But the hill becomes a wall. They are at the foot of this hill, and the whole landscape has become the hill, become the hill alone. Bakhita looks up to see it in its entirety, and she almost collapses. It is very high and covered in rocks, like a giant stone that has broken open. They walk barefoot over this smashed stone. Bakhita looks at the mother, she is watching her baby as she walks, and he is crying more quietly, moaning, his head tipped back, taking the full scorching heat of the sun like a torch trained on him. Bakhita and Binah help each other, hold each other by the elbow, the hand, the wrist, heads lowered. Even the guards are having trouble walking, they whip without shouting now, but grind their teeth, and when they stop to drink, there is something plain to see in many of the slaves' eyes, the urge to kill them. Thirst hurts Bakhita even in parts of her body she did not know. Places inside her contort, and her legs ache so much they feel as if they are not hers. The angry young man looks at the baby and mutters quietly, his eyes like two dark flames.

On the hillside the baby starts to cry again. The caravan leader brings them to an abrupt halt. The chained slaves jostle and bump into one another, their breathing like the hot roar of a forge. "Get that idiot to shut up!" the leader yells at the mother. She looks at him with a distant sort of astonishment and puts a nipple into the baby's mouth, her hands shaking. "I can't take any more! I can't take any more!" howls the leader.

The baby's cries grow louder, Bakhita tries to talk to him, inside her head, sends him solace, kind desperate words, the sun beats down so hard the air quivers, everything is hazy, as if already out of sight. The leader comes over. Says he will make the baby shut up. Make this idiot, this half-wit shut up. But the mother does not cry out. When he takes him from her.

She does not cry out, simply opens her mouth and her grimace engulfs her whole face, like a war mask. Where does she find the strength to throw herself at the leader to reclaim her son? She is so young and so thin, no one would ever think she had such strength, her scream is more powerful than she is, and her fists so violent on the caravan leader's face. But powerful, of course, she is not. And she does not succeed in taking back her child. She tries to grab him, jumping up, launching herself, and the leader steps back, laughing. He holds the baby by one foot and swings him around in the air, like a rope to lasso an animal. The baby vomits and the man slams him against a rock. The baby convulses. His eyes bleed and he twitches like a fish hauled out of the river. A slave woman falls to her knees and prays, sobbing. Others look skyward and wail.

Bakhita does not understand what they are saying. She finds it hard to stay standing, can feel Binah holding her hand. Can feel only this. That is all. When the mother asks the leader to kill her, Bakhita does not understand this either. The girl is kneeling, imploring, "Kill me! Kill me!" Bakhita has forgotten what it means. Life. Death. Must they really stay *here*? She does not understand the things she sees. They happen, and she does not understand them. Stupefying.

A slave bellows furious words at the leader, others join him, and there is a buzz of rage, dialects, prayers, and revolt. Then the leader raises his whip and strikes the mother, whips her until she falls to her knees, until there is nothing left of her but an expanse of torn skin. Now all the slaves fall silent. The only sounds are the blows and the leader's grunts, as he sweats and slavers with rage. The mother's body jolts and then peels open to the blows, and the stones turn red. The sound of the vultures' flight resonates against the stones, a slow heavy flap beating the hot air. The angry young man folds in two and vomits. The men chained to him have to lower themselves too, as if prostrating themselves. The angry young man has lost, his rebellion has achieved nothing, and he knows he will never be proud of himself again, knows he is the man no one will ever turn to for help. *Ila al'amam!* The leader orders them to walk on. Bakhita is crying in Binah's arms, she cannot obey. She looks at the sky. Wants to read a sign somewhere. Wishes the guards would order them to dig up the earth so they can lay the mother and her child in its embrace. Wishes they would order them to sing. Wishes that something here, among these stones, represented humanity. *Ila al'amam!* She starts to walk again. Like the others. She obeys. She no longer knows who are the living, and who the dead. On which side life lies.

After walking 190 miles, the caravan comes to the heart of Sudan, to the great caravanseray center of El Obeid, the capital of Kordofan. The town lives off trading gum arabic harvested from acacia trees and slaves who are sent on to Egypt and the Red Sea. Of this town that she reaches in a state of exhaustion, Bakhita's first memory will be the noise. After several months of walking, the souks, the calls to prayer, the crowds, and the animals are a violent contrast. She will remember the great depths of this noise, a clash of ironwork and voices, as if everything were breaking. A chaos in which she understands nothing. She is thirsty and in pain, her muscles knotted, rough and creaking, like the dry leaves of baobabs. She can no longer see the slaves with whom she has walked but can feel them around her, heavy shadows, breathing that walks when she walks, stops when she stops, they have become a single stooped, black creature. A single wounded animal. A quarter of the slaves have died along the way. Only Binah's presence feels real.

In El Obeid's souk the cries from animals and the cries of men sound the same. A fierce excitement. There is whistling, grunting, shouting across the clammy air, a swirl of smells, leather, tobacco, droppings, spices, grilled mutton, it clutches at the throat, is nauseating, there is dust everywhere, coming from the ground, whipped up by the animals and the wind, and men wait, squatting on this dusty ground beside the goods they are selling, time distorted around them into endless waiting. The town sprawls, lost between the gray earth and disconsolate clouds. This is a place of transience, of mistrust and hard bargaining.

Bakhita is projected into this rabble, relieved to have arrived but terrified to be a part of it. She is thirsty. They are all thirsty. They are exhausted and sick and unsure what will happen now. The guards chain them up, they wait for hours in the sun with no idea why they are waiting. Their guards have gone off to eat, to negotiate with the faroucs and introduce themselves to the faki, to organize their time here. After a few hours, the slaves are given water, and even though they know this is not a humane act but a precaution to avoid losing more merchandise, many of them say thank you. Lone men pass by and study them, appraising the new consignment. One of them, a portly wrinkled man with a huge potbelly under his djellaba, comes up to Bakhita, thoughtfully smoothing his mustache. She recoils slightly but he very soon turns away, drawn to two little boys sleeping nestled together, he looks at them briefly, silently, and then unceremoniously, steps backward, still smoothing his mustache, and moves on.

Like the other slaves, Bakhita is frightened. In every look, every person, there is some implication, something profane. To master her fear, she forces herself to look at all this life playing out before her. She wants to know where she really is, this world of organized slavery, with its armed men who walk past without even glancing at them, its heavily laden, veiled women who are never alone, its child soldiers who carry rifles taller than they are, and she sees other children too, younger still, bringing the flocks back to their pens, as the children did in Olgossa. She does not want to think of her village, of her failed escape, she concentrates as best she can on the present, chained to Binah, piled together with other slaves forgotten in the glare of the sun. Thinking of her family gave her the strength to run away, but for now that thought is too heavy a sorrow to bear.

From her experiences in Taweisha, she knows there will be nothing peaceful about El Obeid. Here everyone is a slave trader or a slave driver, a slave or the wife or child of a slave, even the slave of a slave, a life with a strict hierarchy under the high command of the cleric who himself is under orders to the main traders. Any respect is paid to them, the wealthy and the religious leaders. Here men are laden not only with what they have looted from raided villages but also with what they have ripped from elephants and other wild animals. Their mules and yellow-toothed camels carry treasures of gemstones and gold, they have scraped away at the earth and the trees, disemboweled the natural world. They sell people and horns and hides, salt, gum arabic, and copper, in their view the world is here to be plundered, and Bakhita hears the racket of countless workers hammering wood to form enclosures, the cries of animals and of people, equally captive and innocent.

After an endless stretch of time, the guards come for them. Night is falling and a chill is gathering with the dusk, features that invariably go hand in hand, as if the stifling heat of each day could only possibly be followed by biting cold, there is violence in everything, a violence that never capitulates. The traders, guards, and faroucs start their sorting process. Women on one side. Men on another. The healthy to one side. The sickly to another. The slaves dread this dispersal, their whole lives are at stake, yet again. The guards have been drinking and smoking, their orders are brutal, unintelligible, and contradictory. They are in a hurry, cannot bear the fact they still have to deal with these slaves, almost resenting them for all the miles they have endured, hating them for this work that goes on and on, a stench of anger and frustration hangs in the air.

A few gawkers watch the selection, the turmoil and racket of it, and among them Bakhita recognizes the man with the thin mustache and huge stomach. He comes closer, talks briefly to the farouc, who appears to be the agent in charge and who soon issues an order, his voice deep, his words clipped, he is swiftly obeyed, and the two little boys who were sleeping side by side earlier are brought over. They are immediately frightened. Being picked out always means being under threat. There is the instinctive fear of a violent beating, the fear of being separated from the group, as if being together constituted security. The man, a minor subcontractor, wants them both. He takes out his money. The farouc brushes it aside angrily. The man comes back at him. The arguing begins, a customary game, a ritual. The two little boys whimper, turning around to look at the other slaves, none of whom is family to them but from whom they do not want to be separated. They scratch their legs, their arms, sniffle, succumbing to panic. Eventually, when it is completely dark, the farouc pockets his fee and hands the man one child, not two. A standard little scam, he will strike the boy from his list, the trading boss will never know. Bakhita has watched the scene and grasped that the boys are brothers. She expects wailing, sobbing, some sort of resistance, but the little boy who has not been sold says nothing, hides his face with one forearm while his body very slowly folds, lets himself drop to the ground, and, curled into a tight ball, shudders soundlessly on the thin soil, with his arm still covering his face, his whole body shakes and stirs the dust. The guard picks him up with one swipe of his arm, the child weighs very little, he stands him on his feet and thrusts him toward the group of healthy men. One of the men is struck by the boy, as if by a ball thrown at random, and he opens his hands and gathers the child to him. The cry that Bakhita then hears does not sound like the cry of an animal, nor that of a man, nor that of the other brother, but the cry of pure pain, calling out, above and beyond all that is human. It is the cry of loved ones separated, but what she wants to remember of this scene is the child gathered in by the slave's open hands.

She is disoriented, she has Binah's hand and Binah is dragging her to join the group of healthy women. They are to be washed with great pails of water, fed, allowed to recover. The other group, the sick, will be treated and then sold off to Bedouins. The third group, those who are too old and too weak, are thrown into a ditch. In this last group is the angry young man, the boy with the blazing eyes.

When they left that hill, after abandoning the mother and her baby, the young boy had vomited and then started to cry like a little child. He had lost all his anger, all his pride, all his maturity. His was in terrible distress, and it shamed the men chained to him. They told him to pull himself together. He was tall, he must have been initiated into manhood already and surely had not slept in his mother's hut for a long time now. But he did not hear them. He wept and his teeth chattered, perhaps he had a fever, a terrible fever freezing him inside. The guards took turns whipping him until it became a habit, he and he alone was the one to be whipped, one blow after another, all along the way. He walked hunched, his knees bent, his arms dangling the length of his mangled body. And after miles of walking, when the caravan was trudging down the other side of the hill, when the whip had laid bare his shoulder blade and ripped the skin from his back, it took out the angry young man's eyes, the eyes of this boy who no longer had any anger left in him.

Over the course of several days in El Obeid, they are given food and water, they are washed, their hair is shaved or braided, their nits killed, their nails trimmed. They are dressed in pagnes, ointments are applied to their wounds and palm oil to the soles of their feet, they are given bitter herbal infusions to drink and muddy roots to chew, they are allowed to sleep. Now they can be sold.

And one morning they are exhibited on the open market. A day they have anticipated and dreaded. Being put up for sale. They are crammed into a large shed on a stretch of wasteland, and they wait, chained and silent, outwardly resigned, terrified deep down. Binah is next to Bakhita, they are not the only little girls, but they stand very close together, and no one has anything to say against this, they are together, one lot. The clamor of animal cries and men shouting in the rancid air, the drums, the calls to prayer, all this has fallen silent to Bakhita's ears. The smell of tanned hides and coffee, of mint and burned iron have disappeared. She is standing, half naked and for sale, and she hears and feels nothing of this particular reality. At dawn her mind flew high into the sky, free, like a bird, a bird that knows nothing of El Obeid. She took it and cradled it in her hands, then set it free over the marketplace, and she can see it flitting across the sky like a veil in the wind. She watches it inquisitively, has this ability to imagine herself somewhere else, to escape a body that belongs to everyone and live her own secret life. She is inside the shed, and she is with this bird. Occasionally, of course, she does hear the men. *Djamila*. Someone points to her, she is unchained, steps forward, and does what she is asked to do. As usual. From the front. From behind. Quickly. Slowly.

Eyes lowered. Head tipped back. Calm and expressionless. Patient and obedient. Sometimes the hands are fat and clammy. Sometimes it is just a finger, prodding and studying one body part after another, like a bird's beak. Bakhita thinks about the clear skies, she adds some white clouds, for her bird, draws shapes, throws outlines onto the sky. She is asked to speak. She speaks. It makes people laugh. She smiles. Flies settle on her lips. She closes her mouth. A stick splays open her intimate parts. She adds another bird in the sky, to come and meet her bird, and wonders what will come of this. *This is what sells best. Bad luck for you.* She goes back to her place. Is chained again. Cannot focus properly on the second bird, and it vanishes all too soon.

After she has been exhibited, her concentration founders and she hears what is being said around her.

"How much for that Negro girl?"

A man in the crowd is pointing to a beautiful girl with generous curves and muscled thighs. The man asking her price is a slave himself, a soldier, privileged. He has come to buy himself a wife this morning. She will go on campaigns with him, be his servant, and bear his children. He has eleven children already, from his two other wives, he is respected. The chosen slave girl walks up and down for the soldier, while the dealer points out how strong and submissive she is. She knows that if she becomes the soldier's wife, she will have children to serve in his army, children who will not be taken from her, few slaves have such luck. The soldier is an aging man, he looks at her through half-closed eyes, his mouth twisted, he steps closer and she can smell the beer and cold tobacco on his breath, he hesitates, clicks his tongue against his teeth, touches her halfheartedly, and suddenly asks to see another girl, a younger one, barely twelve years old, almost fully formed.

"This one's Abyssinian," the dealer says, "and that's always more expensive."

The first girl has gone back to join the others. She is not as pretty as Abyssinian women who are the most sought after and renowned.

She is not young enough to be trained for the harems. Too beautiful to be a simple servant, working in kitchens or doing housework. Not tough enough to work in the mines. She is still one of the valuable slaves, perhaps another soldier will come and buy her, perhaps she will have children, her own children by her side her whole life, that is all she can think about, this hope she has invented for herself, because everyone needs some kind of hope, must tell themselves the story of a possible life. But the soldier has already struck a deal, the business quickly concluded, he hardly asked the Abyssinian to walk and bow down before he paid for her, she is not only beautiful but healthy too, he is pleased with his acquisition, will have her in his bed this very evening. Twelve years old... He smiles in spite of himself. A young landowner comes over, eyes the soldier's acquisition, he has recognized the girl's race, is slightly sickened and frustrated, even though prices have dropped, he cannot afford much, if only he weren't throttled by taxes he'd buy himself a little girl too, but everything goes into the fields, all his savings, the moment he has so much as a piastre put aside he buys new equipment or older slaves who'll die after barely a couple of years. It's all down to the British governor, Gordon Pasha. Even though he works for Egypt, he's been trying to wipe out the slave trade, it is at its height, a huge industry, no one flocks to the Nile with its steamboats anymore to buy slaves and ivory along the riverbanks, they seek out merchandise farther afield, in Uganda, southern Sudan, and southern Darfur, Darfur is a good breeding ground, but you have to get there, cross deserts and impassible rivers, many die on the way there or the way back. Still, the country's crammed with people for sale, and he doesn't even have a scrap of a girl in his bed. He leaves in the same state as he arrived, tired and jealous. The dealer has unchained Binah, a wealthy negotiator is organizing a celebration and has come to find gifts for his guests. Binah looks at Bakhita, how can they stay together? Bakhita asks her imaginary bird to protect her friend, speaks to it, using simple words that the bird will understand, she is sure it will, wants it to, and the bird hovers over them both, its wings open like a caress, drifting from one to the other. The negotiator looks at Binah, feels her perfunctorily, he is tired before he even starts, she's beautiful, yes, but a tad too young, bound to have no idea how to, wouldn't be effective...It's not that his friends don't like children, but he wants his next party to be wild, intoxicating, with dancing, singing, erotic youngsters, this little thing's almost in tears already. He gives an exasperated wave and the guard takes the child back. Bakhita totters, and there is a furtive movement as Binah's hand slips into hers, she confuses it with her bird's beak, its soft, soft head, and so she thanks it, bows her head in turn. Binah sobs quietly, relieved and tired. *I won't let go your hand.*

And the selling goes on, countless hours in the unrelenting heat, felled by exhaustion. The air is fraught with dread, El Obeid's true name is dread. The burden of human suffering weighs down on the town, the place is cursed. The selling goes on, all day long, with slaves bought, slaves sold off cheap, slaves separated and pleading, pointlessly wailing. It never made any difference, Bakhita would say later. The screaming and weeping never made any difference. It was like a song no one even noticed, "the song of the separated." The slaves were never free of their self-disgust. The longing to have a different body, different skin, a different life, and a modicum of hope. But hope in what?

Evening is falling over El Obeid's market, the white bird is now just a dot in a deadened sky, Bakhita is losing it, if she wants to survive she must find it, return to that in-between world, but her concentration is wearing thin, she is gagging with thirst, sweat streams down her chest and stomach, the buyers' voices loom close, like their fingers, the bidding goes up, piastres change hands, there is shouting and laughter too, people call out to each other and taunt each other, brag and flatter,

Bakhita keeps hearing the word *djamila,* she's beautiful, but what point there might be in a little girl's beauty, other than her own parents' pride, Bakhita cannot think. And fear cranks up along with exhaustion, they all stand motionless and servile, as if facing cocked rifles.

Bakhita suddenly hears Binah's laugh. There is demented joy, almost panic in this laugh. She does not understand straightaway. Their chains are being removed. A man has just bought them. With no fuss or show, he bought them. He is a civilian, Arab, tall and broad, almost square, his eyes gleam as he studies the two of them, as if he has just made an amusing discovery. She feels Binah's surreptitious hand in hers, hears her idiotic nervous laugh. She keeps saying, "Together! We're together!" It is the end of the day. Those who have not been sold head back to the camp with the guards. Bakhita and Binah do not go with them.

Bakhita does not immediately grasp what this means. What will they do for this man? Why did he buy both of them? Where's he taking them? There are no answers, this is an unknown situation, and she convinces herself that Binah is right: They are together and must think of nothing else. She now surreptitiously puts a hand on her friend's back. Binah's little back arches in surprise, and she smiles. And then she sobs, briefly, loudly. Bakhita looks at her, and she loves her. She knows this is a danger. But she truly loves her. She looks at the sky and thanks the bird, who is now gliding so high, swallowed by the darkness of evening.

Held by a guard, they come out of the market, leave the souks behind. How long is it since they have walked without being in a caravan? Space feels different, they almost seem to hover in its lack of density. A whole other life is starting, and Bakhita wonders whether her sister is waiting for her in this other life. Trembles with this newfound hope.

They walk along a small beaten-earth path lined with puny eucalyptus and palm trees swaying in the evening wind. Spot the high red walls of a house, with unglazed windows from which the first candlelight glows. See the deserted terraces, and as they come closer the house looks like a mountain to them, towering and mysterious. They grasp that this is where they are heading. Not a hut. Not a sheepfold. This house in front of them. What will they be doing in all its enormity?

The garden smells of stables, henhouses, and the clove fragrance of carnations. A skeletal cat runs over the roof of a building at the far end of the garden. There are two small houses there, at the end of the garden. It's almost a village, then? Men and women sidle by, black in the evening light, like deep shadows. Will they be living with these people?

At the front door a black man rushes to greet the man who bought them, bows deeply, *Ia sidi,* my master, his voice is hideous, high-pitched and childlike, he opens the front door wide, and following their new master, the girls enter. Enter this towering mountain.

They follow him to the second floor, the preserve of the womenfolk. When their bare feet step onto that cool, flat, level floor, they take each other's hand. It is difficult walking on this featureless surface, and when they have to climb the stairs, their heads spin, it is like walking upstream through a torrent, they think they will fall, and look up to avoid seeing their own reflections in the floor. On the upstairs landing a veiled woman hurries toward the master, kisses his hands, and disappears. He keeps walking, without a look, without a word, on he walks, he is master here, owner of this house. Bakhita and Binah follow him on and on through endless corridors. Bakhita thinks of snakes. "The snake house." This is how she will always remember it, will always be afraid of it. They walk along corridors strewn with braided mats, past rooms with open doorways that have silk slippers left beside them. Here and there women stand waiting outside rooms, others walk past carrying trays, candelabras, those who are bare-breasted hastily snatch up their skirts before the master and cover their faces as he passes. Those who are veiled lower their eyes. The terrified world opens up before the master. Bakhita and Binah see huge unfamiliar objects in the half-light—divans, armchairs, stools, tapestries, mirrors—and Binah cries out when she has to walk past a desert fox baring its teeth. Its eyes are red, its jaws open wide, with teeth as sharp as small daggers. She will never pass this stuffed fox without worrying that it will come to life and tear her to pieces. The day she stops being afraid of him, he will wake, as offended spirits do.

And then they go into a bedroom, the room of the master's daughters, Sorahia and Radia. Scarcely older than themselves. The sisters lie on an ottoman, languidly eating fruit, the room has large windows with no glazing or shutters, one looks out over the hill, the other over the marketplace where the last camel calls and horse whinnies can be heard. It is already a different world, that world below, that faraway hub with all its trafficking, here the candlelight is gentle, it flickers, and mosquitoes hover around it, there is a smell of lemons, slightly acidic, familiar. Through the other window come the last rosy beams of the sun, Bakhita thinks briefly of all those who are still chained while she, she is saved, but from what she cannot say.

Seeing their father, Sorahia and Radia have gotten to their feet in a ripple of giggles and clinking bracelets, they come up to him and he seems to relax at last, his voice gentle, his voice happy.

"Look what I brought you back from the market!" he says pointing to Bakhita and Binah.

It always strikes a little blow to the heart. An assault that surprises every time. This way of talking about them, the tone that speaks louder than words, the disdain and relish, as if they were deaf. Completely brainless. Will they say *djamila* again, the word that always goes hand in hand with money?

"*Shukran, Baba!*"

Bakhita understands this word, she knows it and thinks it beautiful. *Baba.* A word you want to say. Over and over. A word so suited to evening. She looks up slightly, and through the window she sees the dark mountainside, a pale quarter moon has alighted just above it. A very peaceful sight, a contrast to the excitement in the room. The two girls are talking loudly, jumping up and down, clapping their hands.

"They're black! They're so black!"

They make Bakhita and Binah walk, turn around, they run a finger over their skin, scratch it, touch their frizzy hair, give little shrieks of terror, they want to have them right away. Their father curbs their impatience.

"They need preparing. They've come straight from the market."

Bakhita will never forget that it is just as the sisters start their cajoling—"Baba, can't we play for a bit! Babaaaa . . . please . . ."—it is at this moment that he comes in. He comes in and everything freezes, the air stops circulating, as if the windows have been blocked up. When the master sees his son, Samir, he stops laughing. His eyes darken and a scornful smirk twists his lips. Samir is fourteen. He is no longer allowed to be in the women's quarters, but he sometimes sleeps in his sisters' bed, or his mother's, his girl cousins'. He is almost a man. Soon he will leave the harem and go downstairs to the mandara. His eyes are round, too big for him, bulging from his eyelids, his face is smattered with brown blotches and chicken-pox scars, a battlefield. In all the years he never vanished from Bakhita's memories, nor did the smell of him, which could still terrify her, even in her old age, even in a different place, on another continent. A smell as if a dead animal and a bitter fruit had been burned together. The smell comes from his skin but seems to emanate from inside his stomach, like something stale and forgotten. They all stop talking, and this silence is telling. Sorahia is the eldest. She gives her father a meaningful look. Bakhita and Binah instinctively back away and keep their heads down. Samir comes over, circles them without a word, with an exasperated sigh. It is like being up for sale again. The terror of being appraised. Sorahia says surely her brother has a gift too.

"Doesn't he, Baba, Samir has a gift?"

Bakhita cannot understand such boldness. That is not how you address your father. You don't tell him what to do. She thinks a fight will erupt and is frightened. Is ashamed to be half naked, covered in sweat and dust from the market, ashamed that this family is airing its rivalries in front of two strangers. The silence is brutal. In a flash Sorahia grabs hold of her arm and shoves her toward Samir, she knocks against his flabby stomach, his cloying smell.

"This one's the prettiest," she says.

And she makes Bakhita twirl around on the spot, spouting long, hurried sentences that Bakhita does not fully understand. Bakhita circles like a mosquito in candlelight, sees the night closing in around the windows, all that darkness dancing about her, and this headache keeps on at her, making her want to throw up, and when Sorahia stops making her twirl, she is as dizzy as if she had danced for hours, danced a dance that never releases you, summons nothing and no one, the forced dance performed for masters. The smell of dead flesh and bitter fruit seeps from Samir's forehead. Bakhita sees a trickle of sweat on that damaged face and looks away again. Sorahia will train her. This much she understands. Without really knowing what it means. Then she will give her to Samir, for his nights, before he is married. This too she understands. And what this means, she knows.

This is how life in service began. And this was the first master. He was an Arab chief, a wealthy man who liked to buy and barter, knew everyone and every trick of the trade, had for many years had dealings with the Egyptian government in the days when slave raids helped him pay his duties and taxes, and now traded with corrupt governors, the very men involved in stopping the slave trade. He had first grown rich on ivory trading, proud to have trained boys stolen from their villages who went on to be the most barbaric of poachers. He never took part in any carnage, he had underlings for that, impassioned men who ordered his slaves to seize ivory, but also children, livestock, foodstuffs, anything they could steal they stole, backed up by rifles. The master knew the price of a billiard ball, a dagger handle, a necklace. Was acquainted with large-scale murder. He could convert a hut, a hamlet, a village, or a whole district into pounds of ivory, and would do this sometimes when his guests asked him to, but with details, all the details, time enough to establish the splendor and adventure of it.

Bakhita and Binah lived in the slave-women's building at the end of the garden. Behind it was a tiny building in which married slaves lived. Bakhita never forgot the couple whose third son she watched come into the world, the child of Idris the slave and Mina the slave woman. In keeping with Islamic law, the master had authorized this marriage, and the children belonged to him. Mina was an ugly woman and worked in the kitchens. Idris's choice of her as a wife was the subject of ribbing, and he often muttered that he would soon have another. But Idris never did have a second wife, and what bound them together remained a mystery and a source of amusement. Bakhita watched them live their lives as if they were out for a stroll in a place where life was worthy of humans, even if there was the constant fear that the master would come someday for one of their children and they would never see him again. They would sometimes be alone together in the evenings, would eat together, feed their boys, and Mina must have sung lullabies to send her children to sleep. This life existed. And Bakhita remembered knowing a life like this. The third building, next to the women's quarters, was for the slave men, and Bakhita never set foot near it. She sometimes heard fights, violent arguments, there would be altercations, scores to settle on several consecutive evenings and then nothing for weeks. The fights often took place during Ramadan, which was so hard. Bakhita remembers hearing a man's cry, once or twice every night, he cried out, perhaps in his sleep, a cry of despair coming from far away, calling to her. No one replied to him or reprimanded him. He cried out and then came the stillness of the night once more.

When they enter the slave quarters on the first evening, into its gloom and its damp smell of filth, boiled vegetables, and tobacco, Bakhita immediately looks for Kishmet. Penetrating this cavernous silence filled with women is like swimming in the depths of a river. A secret tight-lipped world, populated by different species. Even before they see the two girls, the other women all know that the master has brought them home from the market for his daughters. They have few illusions but always the same persistent hope, curious to see the newcomers. These girls might be their sisters, daughters, or granddaughters. And if they are not, they may have known them, may have heard talk of them. The women come up to the newcomers, touch them, try to recognize them, understand their dialect, decipher markings on their skin, they ask where they are from, which villages they have traveled through, which masters they have served, in which zarebas, and have they seen Awut, with the eagle marks on her cheeks, or Amel, a tiny little girl with her sister who sings like a trilling skylark, or Kuol, the baby from the Zande region, who must have been taken with his mother, who was very young; and old Aneh, from Maba, a wise man with long arms and gnarled hands, have they seen him? Words in different dialects, words in Arabic, unfamiliar names, the women's eagerness, enough to make nonsense of it all, make them confuse everything. Perhaps they *have* seen Awut, Amel, the babies, and the old man, but they do not remember and, even though they have never fully understood these questions, they have heard them all before while they walked with caravans, and in the camp at Taweisha, and in every village through which they walked, these are not questions, they are a litany of hope and despair, of lives stolen, lives flown away, children who have no trace of childhood left, a collapse of any chronology or normality, so how can anyone recognize anyone else, given that they are all lost the moment they belong to masters? Bakhita has no answers for the women, but she keeps saying her sister's name and tries, in a dialect the women do not understand, to say that her sister is sixteen, she is from Olgossa in Darfur, she is a Daju and her name is, or at least was, Kishmet. The women shrug and drift away. This girl has traveled a great distance and has nothing but her own ignorance to offer. Bakhita remembers the mother and her baby boy crushed against the rocks. Was his name Kuol? Where was he from? She will never tell this story to anyone. And that angry young man who had no anger left, she will never let any woman believe he may have been her son.

Binah is so frightened that she has retreated to a corner of the room and sits with her head down. She wants to see no one and desperately wants no one to touch her in the hopes of finding a beloved child. Bakhita joins her, Binah rests her head on her lap, and Bakhita gently strokes her hair and allows her own thoughts to wander. She believes Kishmet is here in this town. Knows it, feels it right down to the depths of her stomach, there are no questions to ask, no doubts at all, it is self-evident. Her older sister's presence gives meaning to her being here, in the first master's house. That whole journey was to bring her closer to Kishmet. Nothing was pointless or haphazard. She walked well, obeyed well, and has come to the right place. She will find her sister and return to Olgossa with her. Binah has fallen asleep against her, she lifts her gently and lies her down on a mat that one of the women has brought them. She settles on her own mat, closes her eyes, and sings "When children were born to the lioness" deep inside herself, in the words and rhythms of her mother tongue, so as not to forget them and to keep herself as far removed as possible from what she has seen this evening, and what she has understood, Samir, his furious face, Samir against whom she was shoved by Sorahia. *Djamila.* Her beauty, the curse of it.

Bakhita stayed in service to her young mistresses for three years. After physical violence, the endless walking, imprisonment, thirst, and hunger, she would almost give thanks for living in a harem. It was a closed world, peopled with mistresses and slave women, all living together and all captive. No mistress could be seen by a man, no mistress could go out alone and never after sundown. The wives accepted polygamy, accepted the concubines, the other children, and the *umm walad*, slave women married to and impregnated by their husbands and therefore mothers to his children, granting them half-free, half-slave status. Life was a carnival of deceptive masks and false happiness, a party that could so quickly fall apart.

Bakhita did her best. She wanted to be kept. To be kept because they were pleased with her. Because they liked having her. But she never mistook this for love. She knew what love was, had experienced it from her parents, it was a form of gratitude, a form of sharing, a force. The mistresses' love for her was a whim. She lived in a state of apprehension and submission. The plan to find and escape with Kishmet was an antidote to despair, a secret goal. Something deep inside her that made her unique.

It was Zenab who prepared Bakhita and Binah for the young mistresses every morning. She tended to their hair, perfumed them, and dressed them. Zenab had been in the master's service for forty years before being freed. She still thought of the master as her boss and had suggested that she prepare the two girls. She never mixed with free families, who were higher ranking than she was, she never left the house, spoke to no one, and spent all day in a corner of the garden, sucking on a long pipe, her tiny eyes half closed. She smelled of cold tobacco, the mint that she chewed between smoking sessions, and cat pee. When she put pearls in the little slave girls' hair, copper bracelets on their wrists and ankles, her every movement released a dark hostile smell. Her face was expressionless. Her gestures abrupt. Bakhita and Binah never heard her speak. She was as wrinkled as Bakhita's grandmother, and Bakhita would have liked her to tell the story of her wrinkles, as her grandmother used to, with a significant event for every one of them, a birth, a bereavement, a fight, her grandmother knew her whole family's history, the stories of "those we see now, ancestors in the past, and those yet to come into the world," as she used to say. Bakhita's past was fading now, and the future belonged to other people. Every day was a day of suffering and toil. She had to please the young mistresses. Do everything they wanted. Everything their imaginations contrived. Their orders and counterorders, their impulses and fantasies. Living to obey and please. And getting up every morning with only one aim: to survive the day.

When Bakhita comes to live alongside the young mistresses, in this large room with its deep divans, its countless carpets and cushions, its silk *chilla* mattresses on the floor, its gilded side tables and trays in earthenware and silver, the room in which Sorahia and Radia sleep, eat, play, entertain their friends, when she starts living in the harem, she thinks her new name suits her well. *Bakhita the lucky one.* Bakhita who no longer walks over rocks. Is no longer shut away with ewes. No longer sleeps in trees. And, as Binah keeps saying with such astonishment, is no longer truly hungry or thirsty. She tries to be "gentle and good," as her mother taught her, gentle and good, thanks to this, this distinguishing trait, she stands out and is alive in the first place. She wants to put joy into everything she does to show her young mistresses that she is happy to do it, to obey them, and that they are right to keep her. Most of the time they lie on mattresses, and she fans them. She thinks they invented this. Thinks they came up with the idea of this game: giving her the big fan to waft slowly over them. She thinks it a good idea, because it is very hot and she sweats a great deal, but she is never thirsty now, or not for long, and you couldn't really call it thirst, just a slight discomfort. She fans them and does her best not to move, not to shake, and not to breathe too loudly. "Don't puff like an elephant!" they say, laughing, and even though Zenab perfumes her every morning, she knows she smells bad because of all this sweat, but Sorahia says it's because she's very black, adding "and very pretty too." *Djamila!* They are proud of her. When their friends come to visit, they show off everything their slave girls can do. Their favorite is playing the monkey. Bakhita gives loud shrill cries, scratches her armpits, and throws food in the air to catch in her mouth. Sometimes she plays the horse too, rearing and galloping, and their friends take turns riding on her back. She does everything asked of her. Everything they want. When she has not been a good girl, they stand her in the corner. When they want to impress their friends, they ask her to sing and dance as people do in her tribe, to do it very loudly and with all her heart. She does it, and does it with all her heart, but never sings her funny song "When children were born to the lioness." That song is her secret, and she wants no one laughing at it, slapping their thighs and whooping. When they are very pleased with her, the young mistresses allow her to sit at their feet and sometimes they surreptitiously stroke her head, pleasing little pats. Bakhita dreads these moments, always afraid the girls' pats will grow more insistent, as if on the taut skin of a drum, she pictures herself being driven into the ground by these repeated blows, falling into the hands of the mandara, into the world of men, the terrible stories that circulate about what happens to slaves on feast days. And what happens to them when the feast days are over. The torture. The murders. The sacks full of women stitched inside and thrown into the river. These pats on her head are caresses but full of threat.

On the women's floor there are also very young boys, and Samir. At first he makes no demands, simply prowls silently, barely looks at her, apparently more drawn to Binah whom he enjoys reducing to tears every day. It is a ritual challenge that amuses him. She must cry in front of him every day. Waiting for this performance is a constant strain, Bakhita's nerves are raw, she wishes she could take Binah's place when Samir beats her or humiliates her, shows everyone her missing teeth, her faltering voice, and her fear of stuffed animals. He pecks at her with a stuffed eagle, forces her to sit astride a stuffed crocodile, she pleads with him and sometimes wets herself. And then she cries. How did Samir discover this fear of Binah's? Did Zenab tell him she was afraid of passing the desert fox every morning? Through her or one of the others, everything gets out. Everything is passed on. Everyone listens and everyone spies. It passes the time. Slaves, be they women or eunuchs, servants, freed slaves, mistresses, they all live in a closed world, a prison without bars. There are so many slave women in the young mistresses' room, serving meals, circulating with jugs of drinks, lighting candles, and singing and dancing for the mistresses out on the terrace in the evenings, those long nights when everyone is bored, when the master's wives, his children and concubines tell stories and drink coffee. The days and nights go on forever. Many slaves sleep right outside their mistresses' bedrooms, which are never locked, they sleep in corridors, on the bare floor, ready to serve at all times. When Bakhita and Binah are finally allowed to go to bed, in the building at the end of the garden, they enter another hostile world. The women who work in the kitchens or in the master's fields do not like the two girls. The girls are in a comparatively privileged position and the women are poised, waiting for this to end. Because end it will. And then the girls will understand what it really means to be a slave: They are whipped every day, their bodies are nothing but open wounds, permanently giving off the heat of their searing injuries. Pain crackles beneath their skin day and night. Madness lies in wait for them. Bakhita is frightened of one called Mariam who constantly calls for her children, chases after them and scolds them tenderly, wants to feed them the whole time and give them drinks, and never realizes that all she is talking to and chasing is a couple of ducks. Her children were sold, both of them together, a single lot for the master when he lost a bet. Bakhita thinks of Kishmet. Does she miss her child? He would be more than two now. Has she had others? Has she been allowed to keep them? Did she beg, did she sing the lament of the separated, which never does any good? When Bakhita's fears are too unbearable, she thinks of the warm hand that rested deep inside her that night when they escaped into the forest. She does not know whether it was an ancestor, a spirit, or a ghost, she does not know how to describe it, it would be impossible to explain. But she begs for this hand to return. Occasionally it does. It carries her away at night, lifts her above her fears. Above life in the harem, above El Obeid, perhaps even above Sudan and the whole of Africa. To a place of clemency and rest. There she feels gentle and good once more. As her mother saw her.

A couple of years after Bakhita came to the young mistresses, two major events take place at a time that she will come to call "the time of great sorrow," two comparable nightmares. The first of these events is a long-anticipated outing to the slave market with the young mistresses. The second, the preparations for Samir's wedding.

Bakhita is nine years old and she is terrified. The market and the wedding fill the masters with the same violent excitement and they all seem to be in a permanently frenzied state. Samir has grown. He is to leave the harem. And to marry Aïcha, who was betrothed to him six years ago and whom he has never seen. His mother bemoans her fate, clutching her son to her with shamelessly loud wails. He meanwhile is proud, disappointed, and impatient in equal measure. One minute he whines like a baby, the next he is as cruel as an aging king.

Bakhita remembers the annual fights held in her village to celebrate the harvest. Boys reaching the age of manhood wrestled with adolescents from other villages, brotherly wrestling, like a dance. The whole village stood behind them, filled with pride, and then her brother became more than just himself, he was, in her grandmother's words, "our ancestors, those we see before us, and those yet to come into the world." The women put on their finery and dressed up their children, it was as if a single powerful and venerable person had been multiplied into hundreds of others, with the same intense indefatigable intentions. But in the snake house, celebrations and preparations for the wedding are like the preparations for the great market. There is the same fierce joy, the same anxious organization, orders and accusations from morning till night. Everything is tense, as if the household were waiting for some vengeance, and everyone lives in a state of panic and fear. The master wants to buy, sell, and make profits in the great market, he goes looking for merchandise, for men and animals, ivory and gold, he is gone all day, returns and shuts himself away to do his accounts, flits from the most vociferous excitement to the most abject despondency. Punishes and chastises his slaves, ascends to the harem and pesters his wives. He wants unsurpassable sweetmeats for his son's wedding, and glorious riches as magnetic as the flames of a fire. And again he does his accounts and again his mood soars and plummets, uncontrollable and volatile, he is absolute master, but in the end he has no notion of what it is he masters. Marrying off his son amid great splendor or coming home from the market richer than ever is the same victory in his eyes. But before being victorious he must fight, and so he no longer knows any rest.

In Bakhita's memory the two events are confused but what came first was the great market. From the slave quarters and the young mistresses' room they can hear the sound of travelers gathering day and night, travelers passing through El Obeid before going on to Khartoum, hundreds of ethnic groups, men with their flocks who have walked for days and nights, months on end, to exchange, sell, and buy. Bakhita knows that these men come weighed down with goods, she knows some will have "ebony" and among them, the most precious of the precious, will be her sister. She knows it, quite simply. A certainty that makes her want to scream. The waiting becomes physical, overwhelming. In the evening, when she lies down to sleep, she imagines their reunion, she tells herself the story of seeing Kishmet again, this rediscovered love to give life meaning.

Of course, she has been out in El Obeid before the great market, to accompany the young mistresses and the eunuchs. Going out with a few slaves is a sign of wealth, the prettiest are chosen, and Bakhita is a beautiful ornament. Of course, she has already looked for her sister in the crowd, outside houses, in the backstreets, the bazaar, at the corner of high walls, on the way to the cypress-lined cemetery, she has already hoped but never with this certainty. What she discovered was the life of a small town that once seemed huge to her. The world took shape, and she did not always have the words to understand what she saw, destitution right next to swaggering displays of wealth, she sensed the peculiar fatality of it, beggars and slaves showing no signs of rebellion, girls waiting on the doorsteps of seedy cafés, water bearers, and countless pitiful little shops. She walked by with her veiled mistresses and their eunuchs, like colorful birds, chirping and whisking away, like butterflies in all that filth. She saw sick, disabled, and abandoned children who would soon die, and no one would remember them. Except her. She does not yet know it, but she will not forget these children in the streets of El Obeid, and she will find them again in other places, living other childhoods, in other streets, in universal destitution.

Sorahia and Radia have been planning to take her with them to the great market. They will go with their mother, three eunuchs, and few servants. Bakhita has been waiting for this morning as if for a planned reunion with Kishmet, a reunion she announces to Zenab, murmuring one morning, "My sister will be at the market." She says it in Arabic, goes to this effort, and announcing it in Arabic makes it official. *Okhti.* My sister. My older sister. My sister, Kishmet. She will be there. Does Zenab understand? Bakhita has a family of her own too. Someone who loves her and is not far away. That is a fact, certified by the use of Arabic. She has an older sister, who has a two-year-old child, yes, and she has a twin too, and her father is brother to the village chief, it is a big family and her grandmother knows its entire history and, oh, if she only knew enough of Zenab's language, the things she could tell her, while Zenab adorns her and perfumes her, she would tell her everything, because as the great market draws near, she has lost all caution and all sorrow, and the hope she carries within her is so powerful that it radiates in spite of her, even if she wanted to hide it she could not.

Her inclusion in the outing to the market is canceled at the last minute. Without any explanation, of course, perhaps there is no reason, a careless mistake or a trick, she will never know. The young mistresses leave, and Bakhita stays in the harem all day, standing at the window of their room, she waits on the terrace in the crushing heat and looks down into the town, and she is not in that town nor in the great market where her sister will appear and will not be reunited with her.

She waits. From when the sun is brutal to when it declines, in fierce heat and in darkening air, she waits. She watches the vast crowds, people meeting, swathed in so many colors, amid shouts and dust, she scours the faces, watching and singling out Kishmet from those who are not Kishmet, she stands ready and attentive all day, with the heat and her thirst and her spinning head, and after hours of patience and hope, she sees her. In that crowd of teeming miniature figures is Kishmet. A few seconds of disbelief, a savage realization, an explosion of light. She is there, down there, outside the house or nearly, in that group of slaves heading to market. Bakhita cries out her name, and in that cry she recognizes the cries of the womenfolk of Olgossa in flames, she hears her voice as she has never heard it before, this cry is her voice that has been asleep and is now waking and taking hold of her, as if in a trance. Kishmet turns around. And Bakhita sees everything she thought she had forgotten. Her figure, her eyes, her mouth, the way she turned around, lively, alert, it's her, Kishmet bringing to life her childhood, her tribe, her former existence. Kishmet has turned around and has now been beaten by a guard. She falls to her knees, gets up, turns around toward the voice again, but chained to the others, trapped and dragged along by the others, she moves away, is swallowed up, no longer exists. Bakhita wants to call to someone in the crowd, signal to someone, ask for help. She watches Kishmet disappear and stays there, frozen in terror, and then she comes to the very edge of the terrace, opens her arms, stripped of all fear and caution, and throws herself toward the great market like a powerful bird. A hand grabs her, slaps her violently, and she faints into this hand. The slave woman who saves her does not want to be accused of negligence or laziness by the mistresses, so she simply snatches her back from death then leaves her there on the bedroom floor, unconscious.

She is absent from herself, not there, for a long time. Samir senses it immediately. The young slave girl has lost some of her vitality. He wants to get a reaction from her, to test his virile powers on this lifeless little girl. Before taking a wife, he wants to try out his strength, the strength that will be his weapon as a man and the law by which he lives.

Bakhita is almost ten years old. Her life in the harem is to come to an end, but she does not know this yet. Samir calls her one evening and the young mistresses allow her to go to him, she puts down the big fan and goes into the room where he is waiting for her.

He tells her to come closer. From his tone of voice, she thinks he is about to beat her for some blunder she has made, she cannot think what it is but there's bound to be something, there always is. She throws herself at his feet, prostrating herself and saying, *Asfa*. Sorry. Please don't beat me. *Asfa*. It makes him laugh. He kicks her away, and she falls again. He orders her to stand up, she stands up and can smell his smell, like sour fruit and dead animals. She starts to cry softly. He slaps her to stop her crying or to make her cry more, she doesn't know. He slaps her to knock some sense into her or knock the sense out of her. He slaps her out of habit. Her teeth smack together, her temples hurt, she keeps her head lowered, as is expected, and sees the design on the carpet, reds and yellows, birds and moons, she thinks it strange that there should be moons rather than suns, she takes the slaps and tries to think about this, why moons and not suns, Samir's breath comes closer, she steps back, then his slap is so powerful she falls onto the carpet, onto those birds and moons. He roars that she is an idiot, then throws himself on her. He takes her head in his hand and knocks it against the floor, as if wanting to shatter it, break it in two, he is on top of her, like a mountain, full of stones and with snakes under the stones, brimming with loathing, he wants to kill her.

What happens next, the sacking, being beaten outside and in, this she knows already, it is the endless abyss, the abyss in which there is no form of help, it is her body and soul held together and crushed together. The crime from which you do not die.

When the young master has finished he gets back to his feet. He orders her to stand up too. She cannot. Her legs are shaking, she cannot. He snatches her by the arm and hauls her up so she can stand, but she is still shaking, as if performing a strange crouched dance, she cannot obey, cannot catch her breath, she is wracked with tremors, as if under an evil spell. The young master is still yelling, words she does not understand and others she does, saying she is impure, *najas*, and he starts to beat her again.

And it occurs to her that she is dirtying the carpet, because she has fallen again and is bleeding in several places. She thinks the young master will break his whip, break his own hands and his feet, he batters her so. Thinks the house will collapse with the fury of his shouts. Thinks her body will open in two. Thinks it is over. Also thinks she wants to live. She crawls to get out of the room. The master follows her, kicking her violently as if pushing her on her way. She takes refuge in the young mistresses' room, Sorahia and Radia are lying on their mattresses on the ground, eating, they eat out of boredom every day, spitting out grape skins, date pips, Bakhita takes refuge behind them, asks for their help. *Ainajda*... *Ainajda*... Samir keeps kicking her. His sisters keep eating.

Bakhita is now a broken toy. And impure. So she will be driven out. Later, when she is asked why, asked exactly what happened, she will say, "I broke a vase." To one person, and one person alone, she will tell the truth. One person alone, who will keep to herself the story of the offense.

After the beating from Samir she is carried to the slave quarters where she stays for a whole month lying on a mat, trying to survive. No one tends to her or talks to her. Someone leaves food and water beside her without a word, not concerned whether she touches it or not. She calls Binah, who does not come. When she opens her eyes, she cannot see her. She never feels Binah's hand in hers. No longer hears her voice. When she regains consciousness, she is told the master had a gambling debt.

She will never remember when she saw her for the last time. Binah's disappearance is like the disappearance of her own name, like her heart stopping. Binah was her chance of survival. Her humanity. Even freed, faraway and elderly, Bakhita will keep her with her. All the time and until the last day. With Binah, she realized every slave's dream, they escaped, they disobeyed, they had that special value, that strength.

The day she can get up unaided she is deemed ready to work again, no question of her showing her face in the harem, she works in the kitchens at the far end of the yard. It is an unimaginably dirty place that the mistresses never see, a place it would never occur to them to go. The walls are black with filth and smoke wafting from the oven, there is no chimney, cats wander among cockroaches and rats, dogs eat straight from cooking pots. Bakhita gets up every day before the first call to prayer to light the oven and boil water. She fetches wood from the store, and sometimes looks up toward the young mistresses' windows, the deserted terrace. It is already a distant world and may never even have existed. She prefers looking at the sky, the day about to break, wonders whether, at this very moment, her mother is sitting on the baobab trunk on the ground, whether she is watching this daybreak, as she once liked to. But she dare not speak to her. Has no promises left to make her. Will secure neither her mother's forgiveness nor an end to her own suffering, and is quite alone as she makes her way through a world that buffets her like a ravenous wind every day. She is lost in this world. Binah's absence is a separation that rekindles others. To avoid this suffering, some slaves choose never to love, choose to forget a heart that can only ever suffer. Bakhita talks to the hens, the dogs, the blackbirds, the last stars fading in the newness of the day, talks to the wood she fetches, the water, the wind, wonders whether the moon could possibly remember her name, and feels that the last peaceful place, the only shelter is to be found here, in this moment when the night vanishes to give way to day. And then she goes back to work, a stubborn little donkey with its head lowered, always working, always obeying, and being beaten without trying to understand why or who it is that orders the beatings, who deserves them, who decides it should stop or start again, and she thinks of Binah's hand in hers, the strength it gave her. *I won't let go your hand.* It may be true, still. She decides it is.

Months go by like this, in the snake house where everyone gets through his or her day behind a shield of indifference, in the turmoil of instructions and beatings, the fear-filled confusion of it. And one day the master sends someone to fetch her. A eunuch takes her to his study on the men's floor, she walks past the stuffed fox that so frightened Binah, and understands that there in the master's study, misfortune sits waiting for her casually. Ever since Samir roared that she was impure, the master has wanted to sell her, she knows this.

Today he is with a man in military uniform who examines her. They go outside so the officer can see her in daylight, watch her run.

Tired to the bone, she runs, runs to go nowhere, runs in that glorious impassive garden, and when she stops, she looks down and waits. Money changes hands. And so she walks behind her new master, her hands chained together, held by a guard, off she goes. She tries to take Binah with her, to keep her birdlike heart next to her own and to leave behind their days of suffering, their days of shame. She remembers Binah's smile as she said, "We're no longer truly hungry or thirsty." And takes with her this childish gratitude.

She leaves the snake house with nothing, not one item, not even a stone, a handful of dirt, a word, a goodbye, a glance. Nothing. Only fear of the unknown, and this impurity that everyone, she is sure of it, can detect in her downcast eyes, her featherlight breathing, and her voice that has changed, become so deep, and now sings out of tune, wavering and rambling. She talks less, is cautious, unsure of herself, and it is not her words that are a *jumble* but herself. She is ten years old and does not know how to grow up. Grow up well. Grow up gentle and good, she the impure, damaged girl robbed of innocence. Her life is like a dance performed backward, a whirlpool of dirty water. She casts about for some point of reference, thirsts for something she cannot find. A piece of advice. A wise word. She does not know which way to turn.

The man who has bought her is a Turkish general. He oversees armies of slaves serving the Turkish-Egyptian government whose laws preside over Sudan. His militias of slave-soldiers instill order, collect taxes, arrange livestock raids and slave raids.

The general's house is expensive but austere, a huge square red building with grilles at the windows, the yard is bare with no flowers or trees, the fountain has run dry, and in the dovecote the doves' cooing is as weary as a lament. The central courtyard is dark, never reached by the sun. On the first day, Bakhita does not notice the gong standing here. She will very soon dread hearing it sound because it broadcasts the masters' anger, anger that always demands the same appeasement: A slave must be brought down into this yard and beaten.

———

The house is ruled over by two women, the general's mother and his wife. They despise each other. Their mutual loathing is like a sweetmeat they feed off of constantly, seeking it out, stirring it up like old embers that can always be rekindled. This loathing exhausts them and yet fires them up, they sometimes revel in it, their disgust for each other so powerful it unites them, hatred as a shared asset, a common illness. It is to these two women that the general gives Bakhita, she is to serve his wife, to learn how to style her hair, dress her, *without ever touching her,* she will learn to predict her orders, her every wish, to anticipate her blows and accept them. Her mistresses speak Turkish, the slaves Arabic, and once again Bakhita understands things "by ear," from intonations, gestures, expressions. She is mostly very happy not to understand what the two women say, words that sound so coarse that more than once she is surprised their tongues don't burn under the weight of their vulgarity.

It is Hawa, a Dinka slave girl a little older than Bakhita, just twelve, who trains her, teaches her how to take care of the mistress *without ever touching her,* how to remove her robes, nightshirt, and long pants in the morning, to untie the cord, knot the golden belt, slip on the percale djellaba, ensure it falls perfectly, remove the night veil to brush and braid her long hair before hiding it under a gauze veil, and, *still without touching her,* put on her earrings and diamonds, her huge rings and pearl necklace. Repeat the process in the evening, in reverse, help her remove her dress, slip a long white simar over her linen pants, and, without touching her hips, secure them with a hemp tie, and when her mistress asks her to tie it tighter Bakhita knows she is prolonging the ordeal, boosting it with the occasional rather repetitive and predictable variation, then, standing on tiptoe, Bakhita puts on her nightshirt and two or three robes over the top. She puts the night veil over her head and lets her hair fall to her waist. *Without ever touching her.*

The whole exercise is a terrible ordeal. The ceremony is impossible to carry out without coming into contact with her mistress's body, her skin, it is a refined form of torture, a game in which her mistress delights and which invariably ends with the gong being sounded, and the arrival of a eunuch who leads Bakhita into the courtyard where a slave-soldier beats her conscientiously. Her mistress calls this "handing Bakhita over to the crows," black against black, tone on tone. A slave beating a slave. Slaves obey orders, Bakhita hears them swearing about these *jengas*, these "Negresses," all part of the hierarchy of captivity, there are higher slaves and lower slaves, and because of—or perhaps thanks to—her beauty, Bakhita is not the lowliest of the low.

The household and farm slaves sleep in two separate buildings—one for men, the other for women—two dilapidated buildings that reek of damp straw and urine, that swarm with rats and are rife with sickness, but most of all that are governed by fear. The slaves are frightened the whole time. Frightened of sleeping when it might be time to get up. Frightened of not sleeping and being too tired to work the next day. Frightened of the beating that will wake them and the beatings of the previous day. Frightened of the beatings that do not materialize but will later catch them by surprise. Frightened of the old slaves and newly arrived slaves, those who know too much and those who arrive full of dangerous innocence. Frightened by day and frightened by night, because the general's wife comes to beat them every morning before the rooster crows. And those who have worked through the night and have barely settled on their mats are beaten all the same. And the women who are with child, and those just surfacing from a dream, and those whose minds are still lost in the night, and those who are sick with fever, and those who are so old they will soon be thrown on the dung heap, and little children still at their mother's breasts, all of them, still lying on the ground, are beaten just the same. Every morning before the rooster crows, the general's wife shrieks with furious relish, "*Abid!* Slaves! You animals!" And then she seems better.

It is in this house that Bakhita grows up. She does not speak much to the others, who never speak to anyone, and she is afraid of growing up like them, exhausted, starving, their eyes empty of all aspiration, with no wish to live nor even to die.

Although she still lives in El Obeid, Bakhita feels far removed from all humanity, Kishmet is nowhere, Binah is lost among the crowds of captives. She tries to remember her, her stories, her language, her daydreams, but they all belong to another girl, another girl who has no name. Tries to piece together her mother's face but it slips through her fingers, tries to hear the voices of people in her village but is losing the dialect. The effort she puts into surviving every day wears down her mind, and at night, no dreams bring back a taste of past happiness, the seven years of her life as a Daju, a twin, a gentle and good little girl who was afraid of snake tracks and who rested her head in the crook of her father's neck in the evening, while the sun disappeared behind the hillside. One day she closes her eyes and sees her heart. It is a bird with its wings folded back, sleeping softly. This image soothes her, it is as pretty as a present, but most significantly it means she is not dead. Just asleep. She is asleep. And one day she will awake.

Bakhita will spend four years in the Turkish general's house, until she is *thirteen or thereabouts,* in 1882. Her body is starting to grow tall, like the people of her tribe, it is supple and a deep black, her slightly almond-shaped eyes still have a remarkable innocence, like a diffident interrogation, her face has a beauty she herself cannot see and it is a burden to her, a perfect oval, high cheekbones, and most strikingly a nobility derived from her natural grace. This face maturing and this body growing in a house full of furious souls are a source of misery, like a tree in the wrong field.

She is almost twelve and her breasts are beginning to show. Her masters and mistresses are clothed. Slaves wear only a wrap at the waist. Bakhita would like to be hidden, invisible as a spirit, covered up like a mistress. In Olgossa being naked was as natural as the grass in the wind, wearing nothing but a wrap in the master's house is a permanent source of shame.

The Turkish general called it *the rag game.* It was quick and always made him laugh, like a magic trick that startles every time. She cannot remember the first occasion. The master calls for her, she runs to him, prostrates herself, begs forgiveness, he tells her to stand up, she gets to her feet, in a flash he snatches her budding breasts with both hands and twists them as if "wringing out a rag," as if trying to detach them from her body, tear them from her flesh, melt them away, that is what he says, he wants to make them melt away, to be relieved of seeing. She cries out in pain and terror, it is brutally painful, dumbfounding. She thinks the master has invented this torture for her because of what she has done, what she represents, she does not realize the master never invents anything. This rag torture has been inflicted on women for centuries, and if only she had been told she was not alone, perhaps she would have resented the master and not herself.

Occasionally the slaves talk among themselves. A little. Brief stories, in snatched moments, lightning flashes. Because the rations were slightly more generous that evening, because they had time to watch the sunset, because they saw a foal being born, because they remembered a song from home. Because life cannot be cut off from life all the time. And so, just for a moment, they risk a sense of beauty, which reminds them that they are a part of this life. They talk using the words of the poor, scant concrete words, a brief interlude stolen from the anonymity of exploitation. It dies as swiftly as it arrives, a letup amid the struggle, and then they head off alone again, each in his or her own silence, his or her own past, they stop talking, to get on with the business of enduring.

One autumn evening when Bakhita is cuddling a kitten only a few weeks old, she feels happy. She is astonished to rediscover the feeling. It is a disturbing kind of joy, almost a sadness, because it is such a powerful reminder of what once was. The days when she was a part of life. Hawa is sitting on the ground beside her, they should be heading back into the house, but they appropriate this moment, allow themselves a taste of the evening, of the sky and the softening air, they are accomplices, these two girls who share the daily ordeal of serving their mistresses, the sadistic *without ever touching her* exercise, they sometimes laugh about it together, the absurdity of it. On this autumn evening, with this kitten in her hands, as warm as a loved one's neck, Bakhita confides in Hawa in a proud whisper, "I escaped once. Do you understand? *Firar.* Do you understand? I ran away. With Binah, my friend, we ran away." Hawa understands and Bakhita describes it. She strokes the cat and rediscovers the pleasure of storytelling, of another person listening, the simplicity of sharing: "In the tree, yes, we slept in that tree! The big cat walked right by! Under the tree!" Hawa laughs in places, sighs, and listens to the story, Bakhita carries her along with her, whispering about her foolhardy escape, and whispering she may be, but she is heard. The general's mother, who always announces proudly that she speaks and understands no Arabic, hears and understands every word.

The gong sounds. The punishment is meted out.

For a whole year Bakhita was chained, with a chain around her ankle like a rabid dog. Day and night her leg was a deadweight of pain, an inflamed rod of iron that dragged at her hip, her back, her arm, clung to the nape of her neck, where it throbbed constantly. It was not only difficult for her to walk, climb stairs, crouch down, or stand up, it was also difficult for her to do anything sudden. And that is what the chain intended. For any sort of impulse to be impossible, not only physical impulses but those in her mind too: the caution and instinct without which a slave is reduced to a prey animal.

With this ball around her ankle, the twelve-year-old Bakhita tottered and puffed like an old woman. She could be seen and heard coming from far off, and although some slaves looked away as she came near, others asked her to make less noise. When the chain was removed for a few days' indulgence to mark an Islamic holiday, she limped as if her balance was thrown, part of her body needed this weight to stop her from falling. When the celebrations were over and the chain was put back on, it felt as if she were being locked away inside herself. She was her own prison, cut off from everything, burdened and a burden, and her presence disturbed the others, reminding them of the martyrdom they would rather forget, the long journeys walking in chains that had brought them to this hell. Her ankle was swollen, scabbed, and inflamed. And she took to talking to it in the evening, on her mat, she stroked it like a small pet, consoling the punished, tortured part of herself, because this could not go on, she did not want to limp, to be useless. A useless slave is a slave who is fed for no benefit. A slave who is soon discarded. Hawa sometimes managed to steal ginger roots that Bakhita chewed, spat out, and smoothed over her ankle. The inflammation abated slightly. Bakhita could picture her grandmother grinding herbs and healing people, she tried to remember but could not, what were those herbs, which herbs grew in her village, what were the names of the flowers, the plants? What was left of a Daju from Darfur in her now? How many years had she been a slave? Time went by with no points of reference, she tried to count the Islamic holidays, the rainy seasons, but it was mostly muddled and discouraging. She did not want to be discouraged. Did not want to stay chained. Did not want to grow up in the Turkish general's house. To bear the general's children someday, as the others did. And then for the master to take them. She could not find her bearings in the passage of time, and yet time was passing and carrying her along with it. Her fears were bottomless chasms. To forget them, she leaned closer to her old-lady ankle, talking to it, tending it, and in this thoughtful attention, without realizing it, she found a way to survive.

Bakhita is thirteen *or thereabouts,* a young girl with mutilated breasts and terrifying signs that motherhood is possible, she is afraid that this too is clear to see, that the master, who never misses a thing, knows, everything about her seems to be blameworthy in his eyes, who she is, what she does, even what she sees and hears. She is never in the right place, and everything condemns her.

She and Hawa witness an argument between the general and his wife one morning. They are in the mistress's bedroom and Bakhita, *without touching her,* has dressed her and arranged her hair just as she likes it, opulently with an abundance of veils and colors. Heads lowered, hands behind their backs, as silent and motionless as the carpets and cushions around them, they wait for the next order. On this particular morning, the light in El Obeid is cold, it is nearly winter and everything is pale, a slow-moving sadness. For once the general's wife does not shout. She threatens the master with a loathing as icy as well water in winter. Such spiteful words that the general who commands armies, the general who gives the order for attacks and collects medals, the general, beaten down by her words, bows his head. Like a slave. But then he looks up. Steps closer to his wife, and when he is right in front of her, raises his arm above her face for a long, endless moment, his arm shaking with rage. There is silence and the tense buzz of silence. There is breathing, almost choking, the slamming rhythm of it. And then the general lowers his arm, and looks at them, at Hawa and Bakhita. It is not long before they hear the gong.

Two soldiers throw them to the ground in the courtyard and beat them. It goes on so long that it will go on a whole lifetime. Her thigh will always have this hollow, this missing flesh, gouged out by the canes. The master watches the torture, and when he feels fully appeased, he gestures for the soldiers to stop. They stop.

Bakhita and Hawa, both unconscious and bleeding, are carried to their mats, and they stay there for more than a month. It is impossible for them to live anywhere but in this pain. They are overrun with suffering, teetering on the brink of consciousness, with no thoughts left in their minds, only pain. There is neither clemency nor help. No one to lean attentively over their mortified bodies. Firstly because it is forbidden but also because pity could make even the most resilient slave weaken, and weakening is dangerous, weakening can be fatal. Every one of them is here at the expense of a tremendous effort of will, colossal strength, and endurance. They have survived. They will not lose this fight out of compassion for two beaten slave girls. Being beaten is an everyday occurrence, standard. Many of them are like Bakhita, young, frightened, unsure where they belong and with no idea how to behave. They should not ask these questions. Every one of them belongs in some way, no slave is ever bought by chance, lives or dies by chance, is beaten or assaulted by chance. They are wrong to believe they are at the mercy of unpredictable violence. Masters take great care of their households and know exactly how to run them. And yet now, in the 1880s, these masters are still deaf to an advancing threat. A man, the Mahdi, the savior of Islam, a Sudanese cleric, is standing up to Egyptian occupation. He promises the enslaved, exploited population that Sudan will be liberated and Islam reintroduced. The Turkish-Egyptian government is unaware of the Sudanese people's anger and strength, because that strength has always been on their side, has belonged to them, as do the Sudanese themselves. This government rules and oppresses as if the world will stay in its clenched fist forever, but this world is developing cracks, this world will shatter, soon it will fall apart.

During this month of suffering, lying on her mat, Bakhita is also alive and, in her own way, not part of the world. Locked away in pain, her body works at surviving, healing, and very gradually her mind wakes and hears. She hears the earth shudder beneath her, shaken by the bodies of slaves who were here before her, who slept in the same place, on the very same mat. The earth has kept traces of these bodies, their breathing and their warmth, the water of their tears and the thickness of their blood, and it remembers everything, how different they all were, how their minds could never be mistaken for one another, and each of them would have so much to tell, the landscapes they saw, the animals they loved, their favorite time of day, the food their mothers made, the person they secretly loved, their personal talents, the earth remembers everything. And this earth tells Bakhita that this is not right. A slave's place in life is not right. There is no other girl on earth like her, she is irreplaceable. She may not truly remember her mother's face, may not be able to draw it in the sand, but her mother sitting on the baobab trunk on the ground, as she waited for the sun to set, this she has not forgotten, and this is all that matters. Her mother's face has changed and will change again, but her love for the next day will go on forever. For days and nights, Bakhita listens to the earth, and one morning she gets up. She sways and clings to the walls to help her take a few steps, looks straight ahead, gives her painful leg a chance to familiarize itself, to relearn, you cannot stay among the sick for too long, you must not be one of the useless slaves, you must not die. The earth has spoken to her, the sacred earth that honors the people of her tribe has singled her out. And so she gets up.

She steps, staggering but resolute, into a world on the edge of a precipice. Mahdi's armies are growing larger and larger. The masters' slave-soldiers are joining his armies, men who will now fight for their own country. Their battles are bloody, their offensives increasingly frequent, the belly of their rebellion swelling. In the general's house in El Obeid, the masters throw parties and buy a pair of Circassian slave girls and a eunuch, in the Turkish general's house they live a life of decadence and pride.

It is in this atmosphere that the general's wife wakes one morning with a new idea. She is pleased with her idea. An idea that cannot wait a moment longer. "So beautiful! They're so beautiful!" *Djamila! Güzel!* She gazes at three of her slave girls and points at them, shrieking as if she has forgotten something that is in fact right in front of her. *Güzel!* she cries to her mother-in-law and points to her three Negresses, Bakhita, Hawa, and another girl, such a young girl, six at the very most, who has arrived so recently that the master has not yet given her a name and she is known as Yebit, "she who deserves no name." This child never seems to understand what is going on, what she is doing here, in the women's quarters, where she clumsily hands around the tray with the washbasin and jug, where she drapes mosquito nets over the beds, brings in the night lamp, cigarettes, an ashtray, always with those great astonished eyes of hers that she forgets to lower as she hopes for approval but finds nothing. The master brought her home from the market one evening with three other little girls, who played a role in the men's feasting and celebrations. Little Yebit speaks no Arabic or Turkish, Bakhita does not know where she is from, nothing about her gives any clue as to her story. She does not complain, keeps her big black eyes open like two perpetual questions, and seems to be waiting for something that never comes.

Djamila! Güzel! The general's wife points at them with an eager impatience that her mother-in-law shares, yes, the two are in agreement for once. They come up to the three slave girls, fingering them with their cold hands, their nails, they assess them, stroke them, scratch them, and clap their hands. "Why did we never think of it before!" They step back to look at the girls, evaluate them more fully, Bakhita thinks they plan to sell them. The three of them. As a lot. They will leave, go somewhere else, serve another purpose. She is wrong. They are not for sale. They are to be adorned.

The wife and mother want to be proud of them. They want to show their friends that their slave girls are beautiful and belong to them, like symbols proclaiming the fact, like drawings, markings, like a flag or a coat of arms. Some people have taken to dressing their slaves, and they do not like this new fashion. They think a clothed slave is as ridiculous as a monkey in slippers. No. *Their* slaves will be admired naked. And it is their skin that will be adorned. Their Negro skin that will display their masters' wealth for all to see.

First they are taken to a room. A room they have not seen before. Dark, with heavy drapes at the windows, cutting out the daylight and thick with dust, like powder. Bakhita looks at this dust for as long as this takes. And it takes a long time. The tattoo artist they have summoned, who is *the best,* brought pages with designs on them, and she shows these to the mistresses. Before Bakhita's lowered eyes, the dust is like stagnant sand, gray and weighty. The mistresses study the designs to choose which ones the tattooist should use, and they cannot decide. There are so many choices. And they are very beautiful. *Güzel. Djamila.* Really very beautiful. Bakhita does not yet understand what form the danger will take, but the tom-tom is back hammering all over her body, and the sound of this tom-tom is as powerful as the dust is inert. Little Yebit, who is usually so gentle and passive, so trustingly submissive, moans softly. Bakhita brushes the child's fingers with her own, Yebit clutches hold of them as hard as she can, her nails as pliable as a baby bird's beak, her fingers slick with fear, Bakhita knows the child is calling to her mother, so she squeezes her little fingers tightly, these fingers that have not yet been disfigured by slavery, these very young fingers that know so little. And then Bakhita understands. What is to be done to them.

The two women eventually agree on the designs that the tattooist should draw on them. *That will look perfect!* And then suddenly they disagree. Their voices grow louder, the insults fly. Bakhita and Hawa dread hearing the gong, and obscurely, in spite of themselves, they feel this is their fault, this arguing, this indecision. It is to do with them. It is their fault. The younger girl is crying now, and her tear-stained face looks up to Bakhita who smiles at her and, still holding the child's hand, swings her arm back and forth gently, like a game. She wishes she could cradle her, all of her, carry her in her arms and rest her face against her neck, so she would stop seeing and hearing any of this, would simply inhale the smell of her skin…Fear creeps back again. Bakhita wonders where, on which part of their bodies the tattooist will be working. That is precisely the subject of this quarrel that cannot be resolved. The two women call for the general. Whose side will he take? His wife's or his mother's? Which of the two will win? Soon they hear the sound of boots, his furious virile stride.

Bakhita wishes she were the dust. Wishes she were the drapes over the windows. She *truly* wishes she were an object. Not a slave. A real object. When the general comes into the room, fear arrives along with him. Please don't let him touch them, don't let him stay long, let him pacify his mother and wife. His mother speaks first, explaining: She wants the slave girls' faces to be cut *as well*, she's right, isn't she? Bakhita and Hawa glance at each other. The little girl does not understand their Turkish words. Their faces to be cut *as well*. Now Bakhita wishes the general would stay. A long time. Wishes he would cancel what is about to happen, given the situation, given there is no common ground, wishes the tattooist would leave and they could get on with something else, another entertainment, singing, dancing, games, an outing to the bazaar. The general turns to his wife, who shrieks, "It's out of the question! Not their faces!" His mother sniggers and says her friends have their slave girls' faces scarified *as well*, that's how it's done these days. "That would ruin everything!" says the wife. She has her arms crossed resolutely across her chest and gives her husband a defiant stare full of familiar threat. In Bakhita's hand little Yebit's fingers shake like tiny animals wanting to flee. Oh, little sister, Bakhita thinks, you won't get away! And she realizes that what is about to happen to them will be terrible, she has already seen it, on other people, and it always makes her shudder. The swollen ridges all over their bodies, like plowed land, like a lion's lacerating scratches, their skin burned, prominent, deformed. "I agree with you." The general says this to his wife. He is rallying behind her. Not their faces *as well*.

The gong sounds. They are taken down to the courtyard. Bakhita releases the young slave girl's hand, and the child turns to her with eyes full of desperate questions, so she blinks at her subtly to mean *I won't let go your hand*. She knows the child understands. She also knows she is accompanying her to appalling suffering and wishes she could apologize to her, apologize for this life.

Two slave-soldiers are waiting in the yard. Two strong men. And the general's wife asks them to do it. To put little Yebit on the ground, on her back, and hold her down, while two bowls are brought for the tattooist: one full of flour, the other of salt.

Bakhita has not protected little Yebit, has not consoled her, she watches her. The child is shaking so much that the tattooist has to start the designs in flour on her body all over again three times. She looks up at the mistress resentfully. The mistress gestures to a slave to calm little Yebit, he slaps her, and this knocks her out for a few minutes. Then the tattooist starts her designs again, working carefully, her wrists dancing, it is almost pretty, these arabesques, her skill, a form of craftsmanship, white against black, luminous and so aesthetic. And then she takes a razor from her apron and follows the flour patterns, slicing into the skin twenty-three times, very deeply, starting with Yebit's stomach, where the blood springs up, as if the old woman were releasing red rivers, her stomach, then her arms, her thin legs, such short little legs, the child howls like a wild animal, the tattooist's hands and arms are bathed in blood, but she pays no attention to this, sees her work through to the very end, and once the cutting is done, she assiduously opens each wound to fill it with salt, then presses down on it very hard, so the salt penetrates deeply. The child's furious screams die down, grating in her throat, then she groans and falls silent, her body like an angry ravaged land convulses before freezing like an animal brought to ground. The soldier slackens his hold. It is over. With a nod, the mistress indicates for the little corpse to be removed. The tattooist is back on her feet, a pitcher is brought for her, she rinses her arms and hands, drinks some mint tea, breathing quite heavily. Bakhita falls at her mistress's feet, begs to be spared. Hawa sobs, begging along with her. Their mistress studies them with irritation and disgust, snaps a few sour words, and then instructs the slaves to beat them, a means of subduing them before they are tattooed. They receive the blows, wishing they could pass out, not be there for what is to come, forget what they have seen, what is about to happen, but they do not pass out, and when it is over the mistress comes up to Bakhita and, speaking very quietly this time, she calmly looks her directly in the eye and says, "You will watch to the bitter end!"

The tattooist starts with Hawa. Bakhita watches to the bitter end. Until it is her turn.

Bakhita did not protect that child. When she emerged from the slave quarters a month later she looked for her everywhere, wanted to know whether any part of her remained, something she could bury in the ground and offer to the spirits, but it was too late of course, and no one wanted to talk about little Yebit, who was not worthy of a name. Or a grave. So Bakhita looked up at the sky before a new day dawned and asked the stars to forgive her. But the stars remained cold. Bakhita lowered her eyes and asked the earth to forgive her. But the earth remained silent. Bakhita was thirteen *or thereabouts,* and had spent six years in slavery, and once again she was as powerless and terrified as in the first days, when Binah told her, "They are slaves," *abid,* and she had thought of her sister, before grasping that she was one herself. *Abda.* Like the others. No better or worse. Her body belongs exclusively to masters, her heart has petrified, her soul no longer knows where to live. She did not protect the child, she managed to find Kishmet but could not join her, she lost Binah, and she lives in a furious world that is eating itself up. Of the Madhist army's advances she knows nothing, and the day she steps out of that building, when she rediscovers the world of the living, it is as if she has been torn from her very self. Her wounds are swollen and, despite the salt, some still ooze and smell bad. She has been decorated with one hundred fourteen cuts on her stomach, breasts, and right arm. The days of suffering, alongside Hawa, trying to survive, will be the last of her ordeal, but she does not know this. For thirty days, she battled with and overcame pain, infection, and the terrible thirst produced by the salt in her wounds. In her semicomatose sleep, she often thought she was on those long treks with the caravans, deprived of water, the hours under the sun spent not wanting to die. Dehydration made her head spin even when she did not move, her mind reeled, passing urine was unbearably painful, her mouth was dry, her tongue covered in scabs, she was feverish, delirious, her body hovering between life and death, and then it adapted to what it had become, this carved flesh, this searing tumescent skin, these scars for life, because there *was* life. Every day a bowl of water was set down beside her mat, and she did not always have the strength to take it. The tattooist was expensive, the mistresses did not want Bakhita and Hawa to die, they were storing up a surprise for their women friends and knew exactly how they would go about exhibiting the girls in town and which harems they would visit with them.

They will only just have time to do it. The mistresses may well be carrying on with life as if it were a reign, the general's wife may well beat her slaves every morning before the first call to prayer, the system eventually grinds to a halt... One day, it stops. One day, the general orders that they stop beating their slaves. Then he leaves El Obeid. He goes, no one knows where, but that particular order, the order to stop whipping the slaves, is chilling. It frightens the captives: Something is brewing, something is about to happen, and no change is ever in their favor, not ever. They are no longer beaten, but what will happen next? Their bodies are not used to being left unbeaten. They shudder in anticipation of blows. Their skin is ready, their minds wary, waiting to hear the sounds, the footsteps. In their quarters every evening they ask one another questions: Who heard the masters talking, who was in the market, who went into town with the mistresses, what are the masters' guests saying, the eunuchs, water bearers, servants, and soldiers? Who knows anything? If they are no longer beaten, it must be to drive up their price. The master needs money, but for what? They are to be sold, but to what end? They are to be separated, dispersed heartlessly. Pregnant slave women sob in their sleep, those who are married hold each other for hours on end without a word, mothers watch their children with terrified love, and at night they say the same words to them over and over, always the same words, words of love that will come to an end. The oldest among them hold their tongues, they have seen it all, they expect nothing and dread nothing, yet they are filled with disgust. The sick beg the cooks for herbs and powders to hasten their death, they know they will not leave the general's house, will be abandoned in their quarters, where they will die of starvation and thirst, they try to choose an easier death. Bakhita and Hawa talk occasionally in Arabic, their common language, but what binds them cannot be expressed in words. They have twin bodies, twin disfigurements, the same exhaustion and fear, the same daily ritual serving their mistresses with their whips and insults. And little Yebit. They have her in common too. Little Yebit. Dead like so many others under the tattooist's torture. Sacrificed with no god or ceremony.

One afternoon the mistress falls asleep and, just for a moment, Bakhita stops fanning her. She runs her hand over her own sweating brow. Looks at her hands, two black wings spanned open. She looks at them and all at once she sees Binah's hands again. And the hands of the young slave girl in Taweisha. And little Yebit's hands. She feels those childish fingers reaching for her hand again, very gently, like feathers, and then these fingers become more real, gripping hers, moving, almost dancing. She looks at her open palm. Her twin's hand, her friend's, the hands of the little girls in Olgossa to whom she told stories, they all come to rest in her palms, they all come, the hands of those she loved when she was free. Then she feels another hand rest in hers. Large. Slender. She recognizes it. Its deep warmth. Its reassuring pressure. It is her mother's hand settling in hers and closing it gently, with calm authority. Now she understands: Her mother forgives her. Bakhita softly squeezes her fist tighter. She does not know what will become of her in this toppling world, but now, and forever, it will be her mother's hand in hers telling her, *I won't let go your hand.*

They keep going. All of them. Given that they are not beaten, they could rebel, mutiny, avenge themselves, flee. But they do not know what is happening. There have always been wars between different militias, armies squaring off against each other, men taken captive, villages and zarebas attacked, they were born into this violence. And most of all they are hungry. And frightened. And have nowhere to go. They do not speak Arabic well. They are half naked and completely broken. They still cling to each other slightly, afraid of losing each other. They work less efficiently. Sometimes Bakhita touches her mistress when arranging her hair, and when she backs away, anticipating a beating, all she hears is things being thrown to the floor. Her mistress takes out her anger on everything around her except Bakhita. But the words she shrieks are for her. And these words are so full of rage, Bakhita thinks someone has cast a spell on the woman, because her anger at her slave girl is like a mountain she tries to climb but never succeeds. She has invisible chains, Bakhita can see them.

The slaves live like this for a few months, a life trapped in the cloying unwholesome mists of uncertainty. And then one night they hear the master's horse, its gallop more terrifying than the gong. He has them woken and brought into the courtyard, all of them. It is the first time they have been gathered in this way, men and women, all generations, countless tribes, there are those who were asleep in their quarters and those who never leave their masters' sides, at their service day and night, ordinary grooms, the Circassian girls and cooks, advisers and blacksmith, the slaves who are close to the master and the less-than-nothings, a whole society collapsing in a single night. Slave-soldiers help the master, as usual. The others wait, black in the black of night, thin in the slow chill, those that love each other and cling together praying, those that recognize this paralyzing fear, those standing in readiness, they all wait for the sacrifice. The master will sell them to private owners, dividing them into lots, drawing up lists and connections, they are herded, broken up, Bakhita is sent to the far end of the courtyard, on the right near the dovecote. Hawa does not join her. Bakhita tries to spot her but no one can recognize anyone, they simply hear the occasional cry in the darkness as someone says goodbye and a pitiful smattering of other words to a loved one, the whip cracks, swearing mingled with the supplications, children's shrill wails with the hoarse sobs of the old and the screams of mothers on the verge of madness. A glow appears at the mistress's window, Bakhita looks up. Now alone in her deserted harem, the general's wife watches everything she is losing teem beneath her and understands nothing of the injustice of it.

The general has decided to return to Turkey. He and his family will leave Sudan as soon as possible. The preparations are made in furious agitation, the masters must leave all their possessions in El Obeid, their wealth is slipping through their fingers and they are drowning in panic. They have so few slaves left, barely ten, and their daily routine is in chaos, they can feel they are falling, falling with nothing to help them, and suddenly everything disgusts them, everything appalls them, they realize they never liked this country, the constant wind, the soupy humidity, the freezing nights, and the desert all around. It is like waking from a long sleep. They look up, see where they are, and what they see is hostility and threats, a world that does not speak their language and mistreats their customs, they cannot wait to escape now, to go home and be back where they belong.

Bakhita stays with the masters. She is not chosen for her beauty this time but for her skill in serving the general's wife, who *made* her, what Bakhita wears on her person, forever, her scarified skin, her body was quashed and fashioned by her mistress, Bakhita is her creature. The general has granted that she may keep her, but Hawa is sold to a prominent landowner and farmer, and the general secured a good price for her, she was expecting his child, he made a double killing. Not one pregnant woman has been kept, they are to travel by camel all the way to Khartoum, nearly four hundred miles away. They need strong effectual slaves.

Leaving, in Bakhita's mind, always means hope. She does not realize that by leaving Kordofan, by heading north, to the shores of the Red Sea, she is traveling farther from Darfur. When she mounts the camel, when she is heaved onto this towering animal, she hides her fear, does her best to hold on, and sees the world from above. She is close to the wind as it dances through the trees, flutters flags, whips up sand and dust, close to the sky, and she looks out over fields, deserts, and mountains as far as the eye can see, El Obeid is smaller than she thought, which direction did she come from four years ago, where is Darfur, she is hardly even aware it is in the west, hardly knows which way is west, she remembers endless walking and changing landscapes wiping away the traces of her village; she has forgotten where she was born. And yet she is stirred as if it were possible, as if she were being given this opportunity, now, to be reunited with her loved ones. She is afraid of wasting time, screws up her eyes, looks in every direction, like a bird about to take flight. But what stretches as far as the eye can see during these days and days of traveling is the desert, with its vast dunes, its bare mountains, its invisible snakes, its elongated shadows, its sand dancing and clogging eyes, mouths, the tiniest patch of skin, and, rubbing against the saddle, Bakhita's permanently injured thigh opens and bleeds, she hides the wound as best she can, knowing she will be abandoned at the first sign of weakness. She is vigilant, obedient, but the whole time, through exhaustion, thirst, and pain, she looks out for Olgossa.

The heat is dangerous, weighing down on the caravan with its suffocating grip, so they travel mostly at night, navigating by the stars. The nights are freezing, they plow on, unsteady silhouettes on their swaying camels, and the masters' nervousness is matched only by their own anxieties. The masters' orders reverberate off the stones in the darkness, ancient echoes of the orders that came before them, from warlords to their slaves, every flight and withdrawal, the trafficking and bartering, the desert's pink-and-blue vastness greets this procession of figures who know no rest, these silhouettes swaying atop their elegant, foul-tempered camels, and bearing the downfall of a whole world on their shoulders.

Bakhita has looked out for her village but what she finds after these nights of traveling is a city, it is Khartoum that appears before dawn one morning, its pink hues dancing to the camel's queasy rhythm, through her sand-filled, sleep-thick eyes, she sees the city in the distance, its pinpricks of light in the expanse of night, and from the excitement taking hold of the masters, she knows that, once again, something is about to happen.

They do not go into the city but stop just short of it, the nearest outskirts, the first inn they come to will do. Bakhita follows the mistresses, she will sleep outside their door, on the bare floor, ready to obey their orders, their constant, uncalled-for, increasingly futile and pointless orders. The familiar feel of domination reassures them, keeps everyone in his or her rightful place, the general's wife uses any excuse to slap Bakhita, pull her hair, spit in her face, soothing her own rage and disorientation, she insults her in Arabic so that Bakhita understands better and everyone can hear, and realizes with sickening bitterness that she is fond of this stupid girl. She hates her and wants her. She weeps with anger in her bed with its holey mosquito nets, in this shabby hotel infested with mosquitoes and cockroaches, the moist air that drives you mad, and the shame of having only a handful of slaves to serve her. Is her life worth so little?

Bakhita is exhausted, her body a ragbag of pain, her soul searching for Kishmet. The city is so close, it looks so big, they say it is the huge crossroads of trade, where everything converges, everything lives, they say the Nile becomes a single river here, combining the Blue Nile and the White Nile, they say Egypt is close to the sea too, the so-called Red Sea, they say so many things, this is not just a stuffed desert fox opening its jaws but the Egyptian government. The master of masters. And she is *abda*. Trapped in her torment as if in a sandstorm, she sleeps on the doorstep and her tears scald and cleanse her sandy eyes. The general's wife cries out in her sleep. A mixture of Turkish and Arabic words. Bakhita clenches her fist to hold her mother's hand in hers, puts this fist into her mouth to avoid crying too loudly, and once again, in spite of herself, she hopes.

The next day is almost an ordinary day. Orders. Beatings. Hunger. Thirst and pain. Except. The master is losing his hold and his unyielding assurance. He is a nervous soldier now, as if stranded on too large a battlefield. He does his sums. Does them again. And the mistress sobs in bitter disappointment. Her husband is just a tiny scorpion, *Akrep!* she keeps saying, hounding him, *Akrep!* she says with her face veiled and with her face uncovered too, she is so beside herself, going so mad, *Akrep! Akrep!*, and Bakhita hears from another slave that they are to be sold, again. Will she not go to Turkey? The master has put the word about, *Slaves for sale*. Will he sell *all* of them? He needs money, more money still to get home to Ankara. The mistress is not wrong. The master is a scorpion stinging itself, he is losing the game, he was under pressure and he capitulated.

The mistress can no longer bear to have Bakhita tending to her, wants to kill her, bury her underground, wishes she could bury them all underground, along with her mother-in-law, who helps the general with barbed triumph. Bakhita puts down the hairbrushes, hair clips, and veils. Stays standing there, useless and petrified. Makes calculations. If the general does not keep her. If she is bought, that would be her fifth master. Is that right? She thinks it over. Remembers the two captors by the banana palm, remembers the endless walking, the sorting centers, her escape with Binah, remembers the shepherd and the snake in his dog's jaws, remembers Samir and the young mistresses, remembers the knives and whips and subjugation, she was so young when this started, and she now knows so much, and knows nothing. She has unlearned her customs and beliefs, would no longer know how to take a flock down to the river, beat sorghum, or sing in her dialect, and she wonders: If my mother said my name now, would I recognize it? As she asks herself this question, she hears someone call her.

"Bakhita! Bakhita, come here!"

That is how it happened, as simply as that. Just as it takes only one step to cross a frontier, and it takes only a signature to end a war, the thing you have hoped for over many years happens in a minute. Bakhita goes over. She is bought for the fifth time, bought by a man called Callisto Legnani, the Italian consul in Khartoum. And this man will change the course of her life.

When she comes before this master, Signore Legnani, on the first day, Bakhita prostrates herself, forehead to floor, arms outstretched, hands forward, and hears an order she does not understand. She kisses her master's feet, one after the other, three times, but the master repeats his order. In Arabic this time: *Taali!* Stand up. She stands up, eyes lowered, heart beating wildly, already unnerved by this new world in which, once again, she is doing the wrong thing. *Guardami.* She does not understand. She feels the master's hand on her, recoils instinctively when he takes her chin and forces her to look up, she knows she must not pull back, must obey everything, but she does not understand what he is saying. He speaks in Arabic again: *Shufi ilia!* Look at me! But she does not know how to do this. Look a man in the face. Least of all a master. She is filled with panic, looks into his eyes, cannot read what is in them, bites the inside of her lips to stop herself crying, avoid being sent away already, she looks at him but knows it is wrong to do this, he releases her chin and walks away. Nods several times, as if alone and terribly sad. Then he waves over a serving woman, utters more incomprehensible words, Bakhita apologizes several times, *Asfa, asfa,* but it is too late, the servant, a light-skinned woman, takes her away. Bakhita follows with her head lowered, she does not know where the slaves live in this house, in which courtyard they are beaten, she walks along corridors and comes to a dark, moist room filled with steam. The servant points to a large copper basin, a very long, empty tub, and explains that Bakhita must get into it. She is not familiar with this torture. She obeys.

Bakhita was washed that day. The servant, Aïcha, gave her a bath. When she felt the soft water on her skin, Bakhita rediscovered the purity of river water, childhood games, and her own mother. And yet she sat there frozen, astonished, and on guard. When the water sluiced over her tangled hair, the servant combed and arranged it, Bakhita thought she was being prepared for celebrations held by the men, but deep down sensed this might be something else. The servant looked at her scarified skin, her gouged thigh, the scars on her back, her deformed feet, she gave a brief sad smile and poured the water so gently over Bakhita's shoulders that once again the little slave girl thought that perhaps she was not being prepared for men.

Then Aïcha helped her out of the tub, handed her a sheet to dry herself, indicated that she should wait, and came back with a long white tunic embroidered with red threads and pearls. She stood squarely in front of Bakhita without a word, and as Bakhita did not move, they stayed like that for a moment, looking at each other, with the white tunic between them. Bakhita's hair dripped onto the sheet, she thought she had exhausted all her tears, she had never wept with gratitude, and even in this moment, this moment of silence between Aïcha and herself, she did not believe it possible. A moment of exchanged looks. With no threat. And so she reached out her hand to take the tunic, and Aïcha helped her. She put her head through, the sleeves covered her arms, and the fabric slipped over her shoulders, stomach, legs, her whole body. All that emerged from the white tunic was the black of her face, as if sculpted by light, and miraculously not scarified. All the marks of infamy were hidden, the tunic was like a veil, modestly hiding her, and for the first time since she had been captured she felt there was a part of herself that belonged to her alone. Her body, the object of profit and so much violence, had been returned to her, now hidden from others, it became a secret. Her secret. It was the first.

And it is with this body rendered back to her, this body that will not be beaten or lusted after again, that she is gradually reacquainted with the human world. She has something to herself, and it *is* herself. She belongs to the master, but a small part of her life is protected. She knows it might end any day, for a reason she will not understand, a decision that will not be explained to her, a goodbye to which she will have no right. She is dressed, her hair is arranged, with pearls in it, she wears bracelets. It is pleasant, and under threat.

She asks for news of Kishmet from the consul's slaves and servants, and the day that one of them asks by what distinguishing feature they might recognize Kishmet, she can think of no reply. Her preferences? Her voice? Her laugh? Her scars? Bakhita does not know. Her new name? Her children? Her former masters? Bakhita has no idea. She tries to count, to calculate the passage of time, tells herself Kishmet could be married to a soldier, living in one of Khartoum's countless garrisons, or in the house of a wealthy merchant, in a vast harem, as there are said to be here, dancing to divert her mistresses, or worse... She does not want to think about it. She tries to rekindle the intuition she had in El Obeid, when she *knew* Kishmet was there, in the same town, close by. But the intuition has gone, and she could not say whether her sister is alive in her heart or in the city around her.

One morning the consul summons her to his office. He is an affable man who talks in a soft voice that is not always easy to hear, his presence is almost an absence, his kindness, a form of self-effacement. He asks Bakhita for the name of her village. He asks in Arabic, so that she understands. It is a surprising question, out of nowhere, bound to be disguising a trap. Or bad news. Has she spoken of Kishmet too much? Has something terrible happened to her village? She looks outside, it is early but the sky is already white, the heat hazing the horizon. She asks very quietly if there was fire.

"Fire? What fire?"

Fire. After abductions, there is always fire, but she dares not say this to the consul and simply stands there, head lowered, her heart trapped, battling a grim sense of foreboding.

"What is the name of your tribe?" he insists. "Your family?"

"*La arif*..." she murmurs. "I don't know..."

"You don't know? Try to think...I want to help you. Do you understand? To help you."

She has heard that the master is a good man. That he has freed slaves. That he buys them in order to do that, set them free, and she wonders what they do, once they are free, in Khartoum.

"Tell me the name of your people. Your village. Your tribe."

She looks up at him in astonishment. Realizes that he wants to help her but, more important, realizes she does not know the name of her tribe. She has this realization here, in this office that smells of leather and tobacco, the air swirled around by the huge ceiling fan, the sound it makes of stagnant wind. She does not know the name of her tribe! She thought she knew it, had never considered it, simply looked for her family, they exist because she loves them, they are waiting for her somewhere because she misses them and will join them...the name of her village. Her family's name. Her head is full of Arab names, elusive questions...

"I don't know," she says again.

He does not seem surprised. He opens a drawer and spreads before her a piece of paper so large it covers the entire desk. He waves her closer. Tells her it is her country, Sudan. She grasps the enormity of this world she is seeing for the first time.

"You walked a long way. Where did you walk?"

She nods, yes, she walked a long way, for months, years, she walked a long way. Yes.

"But where did it start? Where were you before El Obeid? Where are you from? Which area?"

"Yes," she murmurs.

He starts again, faster now, firmer.

"Was it more in the yellow areas, the green, or the gray? Were there mountains? Hills? The Blue Nile? The White Nile? It was in the west, wasn't it?"

He prods the map with his finger as if about to produce sand or water from it, she does not understand how the great river can be so thin, or where the stars and moon are, does not understand what the map shows. Remembers the last image of her village, two men near the banana palm.

She looks at the map. "I don't know," she says again.

The consul does not lose heart.

"What animals did you have in your village?" he asks in his subdued, almost inaudible voice. "Oxen or buffalo? Asses or horses? Did you change villages often? Did you travel? On the move? Did you eat the animals? What gods did you pray to? What were your ancestors called?"

She bursts into tears. She wants to fall at her master's feet and for this to stop, she is walking on the edge of a precipice and he is nudging her over it with his questions, she is lost and has lost her loved ones. The consul gives her a handkerchief and some water. He folds away the map of Sudan with all the places and words she could not read. He folds away this land with no sky and puts it back in a drawer.

"I want to help you, there's no need to cry."

Bakhita looks at the drawer where the map is shut away with her family and all her dead hopes. Where are they? Where on earth are they all? She sobs, with her hands over her face, suffering more than when she was beaten and insulted, suffering at her own hands. The consul comes closer, smoothing his mustache thoughtfully.

"It's very simple. You're going to tell me just one thing, and then I'll know who to go to. A friend who knows your dialects…many of your dialects."

Bakhita has never spent so long in a master's office, has never been asked so many questions, she is exhausted, has lost all hope, is full of shame.

"Your name."

"Excuse me?"

"*Tuo nome? Ma smouki?* Name? Your name?"

Bakhita looks at the white handkerchief in her dark hands. She folds it in two. Folds it again. And again. Slowly. She has stopped crying. Can hear her breathing like an exhausted little donkey. The master is irritated now, a little disappointed too, of course.

"What's your name?"

She leans slowly toward him, and to show how willing she is to help, to show she is not *completely* ignorant, she says in her deep voice, enunciating each syllable clearly: "*Non lo so.*"

And backs out of the room.

This conversation marks the beginning of a long period of sorrow. She realizes she has forgotten her mother tongue. Her childhood is slipping away from her, as if it never existed. She cannot name it. Cannot describe it. And yet she can feel it within her, burning full of life, more than ever. She learned Arabic with a child's aptitude, but for seven years she has not heard a single word of her dialect. She remembers "Kishmet," this one talisman, one obsession, the name her sister most likely no longer has. She tells it to the consul, like a last hope, and from the weariness in his eyes, grasps that it means nothing, that it too might be a distortion, an illusion. She is back again with the long nights of despair, hoping for a dream, an intuition. But nothing and no one visits her. She is no longer beaten, is clothed like the masters, but has this sense of endlessly falling. She tries to sing her funny song, the one Binah loved so much, "When children were born to the lioness," she translated it into Arabic, in spite of herself, long ago. She knows she says *ami* for mama, and *baba* for daddy, but also *asfa, asfa, asfa,* forgive me for this abandonment. She thinks of the map of Sudan, would like to see it again, to learn to read the words on it, or at least to ask about them, she remembers so clearly the landscapes through which she traveled, and the sheepfold, the baby smashed against the stones, and Binah in the sorting centers, she carries so many lives within her, why are the images of her childhood lost? She tries desperately to claw them back. Remembers the things she loved, the fires around which they sat and talked for hours, her father's lap, her twin, her grandmother. She sees her village in her mind's eye, snatches of ceremonies, like far-off signs, the snake trails, her brother. "My little girl is gentle and good," her mother with so many children, her mother like a red flame, she repeats this exercise every night, memorizing her loved ones in the hope that their names will come back, but they stay locked away in this boundless anonymous love, and she reaches her arms toward people she can never hold.

Her day-to-day job is to help Anna, the housekeeper, and she discovers a whole new world to which, once again, she must adapt. First, there is Italian, this incomprehensible language with its words that dance, unlike those she knows, words that do not come from the back of the throat like Arabic but are plucked from elsewhere, somewhere in the chest, it will be a long time before she works out where. Outside the consul's house flies a flag she does not recognize, with no Islamic crescent, and inside it the men and women are all together. Italian women do not cover their faces and they walk openly among men, they all come together to eat in a room intended specifically for this, they call this a dining room, they wash their hands in a separate room and to eat use not their hands but forks and spoons, and they each have a glass to themselves, placed in front of their own plate. The kitchen is inspected every day, it is cleaned and cleaned again. They never pray to Allah, and the master has only one wife whom no one has ever seen, and he sleeps alone every night in an enormous bed, and his bedroom is locked shut, no slaves sleep in the master's bedroom or on his doorstep, no slaves sleep in the corridors. It is strange, at first, this absence of bodies that usually populate houses. Bakhita has so often heard masters cursing these slaves everywhere, spying on them, spreading rumors all over the house, masters loathe these subjugated bodies without which they cannot cope, despise them for being there, sharing in their daily existence, a sharing they actively seek out but also abhor.

The country is not unduly alarmed when the newspapers report on battles won by Mahdi's army, on the slave-soldiers joining him and the uprisings of Arab tribes, the country behaves as if this jihad were a minor revolt, while they remain complacently strong. Since the end of slave trading was announced by Gordon Pasha, the British army occasionally captures major traders and tries them in Khartoum, and then everything carries on as before. Corruption sets in. Egypt's infrastructures are abandoned to Western powers, and the debt it owes them grows so deep that the British take over its fiscal administration. European bankers and unscrupulous entrepreneurs hold the country at their mercy. All of Europe is here in Khartoum, men having discussions and taking maps from drawers, ambassadors of France, England, Germany, Austria, all of whom meet Bakhita's master, Callisto Legnani. All of Europe has its armies in Khartoum, and Egypt's army is mobilized. Mahdi continues his advances.

Bakhita adapts, to the new ways, the new language, lulled by Anna's accounts, telling her that Signore Legnani's wife writes to him begging him to come home, to this country where they speak Italian, a place called "Italy." She describes this country to Bakhita, it is so beautiful, so far away, so free, filled with sunshine, with no rainy season, and

Bakhita wonders what the map of a country looks like if there are no slaves, no deserts, no zarebas, and no violence, where all the men are like the consul, and his wife, his only wife, is she as kind as he is? Anna says she is, she is very kind, and happy, because in Italy women are not repudiated, even if they have no children, and they can go out alone, with no veil, and even after nightfall. This Bakhita cannot believe. But she forgives Anna because the woman loves her country and is good at describing it. She meanwhile carries within her only the ashes of a nameless tribe.

One evening, Bakhita sits on a bench in the garden at the end of her day's work. The last of the birds can be heard, it is always a surprise, this birdsong in the encroaching night. She listens to them and closes her eyes. The birds flit through the darkness, she senses the swallows' swift flight, the bats on their rounds, the wind in the palm trees, the occasional call of a toad. She opens her eyes again, the sky is closing in, dark and dense. The first stars are appearing, so small at first, like forgotten traces. She watches as they make the darkening sky grow bigger, and in that attentive evening, something in her wakes. This place is beautiful. This land of her ancestors, this Sudanese sky, is beautiful. And she wonders why the world is so beautiful. To whom we owe this. All the ugliness of mankind, she is familiar with that. The violence born of man's terrible anger. But the beauty, where does that derive from? This night hangs over the people of this world, free and immortal. And it speaks to her. As the earth did, remembering the suffering of slaves who came before her. Bakhita realizes that you can lose everything, your language, your village, your freedom. But not what you have given yourself. You do not lose your mother. Ever. It is a love as powerful as the beauty of the world, it *is* the beauty of the world. She brings her hand to her heart and weeps, weeps tears of consolation. She was so afraid she would lose her.

She is fourteen and is in her second year in service to the consul. She has seen freed slaves leave to go to a village, a Catholic mission, seen some leave and then return, thin and exhausted, she has recognized some sitting on street corners, crushed, she looked away to spare their shame, and she wonders whether another life may sometimes be possible. She listens to Anna describing this Italy with no slave-soldiers or child soldiers, no raided villages or fighting in the streets.

She is frightened of Khartoum. Can sense in it a violence she knows only too well, the violence of extreme poverty and the violence of profit, that unsparing combination. The city is dirty, overrun with cockroaches and locusts that fly into passersby, its cats are skinny and as fierce as desert dogs, people work and die in its streets, relieve themselves against its mud walls, slaves keep the great treadmill turning, the air quivers with panic, the Mahdi's name circulates like a whip crack, the *padrone* speaks English with the other ambassadors, late-night smoke-filled meetings, Bakhita hears these men's voices, hoarse with weariness and anger, something is slipping through their fingers and they do not want to let it go. The British have taken control of the country and administer it with the arrogance of those who have never lost. Neither their victories nor their pride. The *padrone* is not so gentle now, has become persnickety and obsessive as if losing confidence. His wife's letters are more frequent, "imploring," Anna says, she can read and does not deny herself this privilege when she cleans the master's office.

"Come home soon, she writes him. *Subito!*"

"She speaks to her husband like that?" Bakhita asks.

"Of course. She's Italian."

"The Turks are like that too."

"In any case, I think the *padrone* will go home. He'll go back. I can tell."

"Back? To El Obeid?"

"To Italy!"

Of course, at first she thinks it is not for her, Italy is not for her. It is a word used by other people, those with skin as white as a plucked chicken, those who have dreams and brag about their good fortune. She is used to seeing masters on edge and impatient, and knows that Anna is right, the *padrone* will leave. He anticipated this, wanted her to go home to her village, not end up begging in Khartoum's insalubrious streets. But given her ignorance, her inability to name her family, she knows what will become of her when the consul leaves. In a backstreet or a palace, she knows what will be wanted of her. She will go back to where she came from, to violence and shame. And with no premeditation, she reaches the decision one day: No one will ever take her white tunic from her now. Ever. She is in the washhouse, washing sheets and tablecloths, the heavy cotton fabrics the Italians so like, the water is icy, and she is watching her hands rubbing, rubbing, rubbing. She is carried away by the movement, it is like a chant, in time with her thoughts. All of a sudden, she springs to her feet, knocks over the basin of warm embers, wipes her hands on her apron, and runs to the *padrone*'s office. She prostrates herself at his feet, he does not like her doing this but she does it because she would not have the audacity to beg him on her feet, face-to-face with him.

"Take me with you... *Padrone*..."

He does not even understand, thinks she wants to go home, thinks her a little stupid because she does not speak his language well and because, despite his goodness, he views these Negroes as simple submissive animals. And he likes animals. He is a nonviolent man. Cannot bear to have people prostrating themselves at his feet, it is physical, visceral, he cannot abide it, he makes her stand up and tells her that he has run out of time to look for her village, he is preparing to leave, to return to Italy. She is standing facing him now.

"Take me with you, *padrone*," she says again, still not looking at him.

He likes her very much but apart from a little boy whom he has promised as a gift to some dear friends, he will not be burdening himself with any slaves, even Anna will have to wait until he sends the money for her journey home. He has already started selling the last of his slaves to private owners, or freeing them, and on top of these dealings, he divides his time between the telegraph office, the newspapers, meetings, and packing cases. With the peculiar bitterness of leaving defeated. He asks Bakhita to bring him some coffee.

She is overcome by her longing to leave Sudan. Tries to work even harder, thinks the *padrone* will notice, the way she washes the floors, polishes his shoes, irons the tablecloths, but very soon realizes he has noticed nothing. He is busy. She knows what he is feeling. He no longer sees what is going on around him, he is preparing to leave and can think of nothing else. He will set off for Suakin by camel, travel through the desert for several days, then will cross the sea on a huge steamboat, that precious ally of those who trade in the insignificant creatures called slaves. Bakhita thinks she *is* significant, though. The earth and sky told her so. One night she is in the slave quarters lying on her mat, and the moon is so full and bright it lights up her mat. She reaches her hands into this shaft of light, a brightness with all the beauty of surprise, of something exceptional, while everyone around her sleeps. She is alone with this moonlight that has woken her, and when morning comes, laden with clouds, she notices that the day is strangely darker than that moonlit night. She considers this during her day's work, what she saw that the others did not see, she helps carry trunks, pack bags, hears the hoarse calls of the camels the *padrone* has just bought. She hears him talking to the camel driver, does not understand what he is saying, he is speaking an unfamiliar Arabic...She comes out of the house and into the yard. Does not prostrate herself. Does not apologize. Hardly even lowers her eyes. Dares to be a slave girl standing between two men: the camel driver and her master. In her clumsy Italian she explains to the master that he will have to hobble the camels every night, animals must never be allowed to roam free at night.

"I have already traveled by camel," she says. "I can help. Take me with you, *padrone*."

"So you think you're indispensable now?"

"Camels can die, you know, *padrone*. They fall down and die. You think they don't need water but they fall down and die."

"I'll take care of the camels, don't you worry."

She can feel her face blazing with emotion, her body shaking with restrained energy.

"Take me with you, *padrone*."

"But, my poor Bakhita, what on earth would you do in Suakin? Do you know what Suakin is?"

"Take me home with you, *padrone*, to Italy."

He roars with laughter, waves her away, and turns back to the camel driver with a skyward glance to prove his clemency. He could have been outraged by this audacity but was not. He is a good man.

Bakhita will make her plea three times. She feels within her the same warm luminous hand that saved her on the night she escaped with Binah, and she understands that this is exactly the same, she must flee, she must run and not look back. This is a different walk, a different crossing, imploring the master and persuading him. She wants to live.

Feels such strength within her, she, Bakhita, tidy and clothed like a free young woman, and she emancipates herself, grants herself this, this dignity. The *padrone* will leave the next day, at nightfall, to avoid the heat. She has seen the little boy, promised as a present, his name is Indir, and he is as frightened as a young caged animal. He asks for nothing, simply watches, sucks his thumb when he thinks no one is looking, and cries sometimes when he hears men shouting. He is slender and graceful, will make a handsome gift, the *padrone* must owe a great deal to the friend he has in mind.

She is already losing some of her assurance as she walks the corridors toward the *padrone*'s office. Her heart beats hard, even in her ears, her blood thumps, the world around her muffled by it, she shakes as she makes her way closer to him, her right leg slightly lame, as it always is in tense moments, the pain in her thigh stirs and she is short of breath, beautiful and gracile as she is, she sometimes has the slow halting gait she will have in old age, as if invisible chains are resurfacing. She is out of breath when she comes into the room.

"I know about looking after children," she says with no preamble. "Little children."

He looks up, astonished, and studies her for a moment, she really is pretty, very pretty, the poor girl.

"I know, Bakhita, I know."

He says this and goes back to his work, stowing tiny flags in a box of ebony and mother-of-pearl. Like a nostalgic child who regrets growing up.

"He is a fine gift."

He turns to her again. Is she still here! That deep voice of hers, he can never get used to it, it sometimes startles him and he has to smother his laughter.

"Indir will make a fine gift. Fragile to cross the desert."

This time he bursts out laughing, she's cunning as a fox.

"No, Bakhita, I won't take you with me! You know about the desert and camels and little boys, yes, you know a lot of things. But not the cost of a crossing on a steamboat. It's very, very expensive. More expensive than a slave. Do you understand?"

He says this too quickly, she does not catch it all. Except the laugh. And the look in his eyes. That says no. And she does not prostrate herself but crumbles. Collapses at his feet and sobs, incapable of restraining herself, her sobs wrack her body as if she were being beaten, tears derived from so many years of suffering endured that she cannot hold them back, does not even think to but simply sobs, loses all hope, all her resolutions, she is good for nothing, no good to anyone, she exhausts herself sobbing, wishes she could die of it.

The consul hates women crying, so a slave girl crying! He backs away. Goes over to the window and watches her. Her body is shaking, and the neck of her tunic reveals a shoulder. He sees the long scar shuddering as she sobs. A sinuous, beautifully executed design. And he is suddenly devastated by this aesthetic torture.

"All right," he says.

She does not hear him, she weeps and chokes on her own tears. He comes over to her. He shyly covers her shoulder, makes her look up, looks her in the eye, and says, "All right, yes to Italy."

Like any upheaval, it is a deliverance and a source of suffering. A life change that happens in a few seconds. She is to leave. She is to live in the country of white dreams and soft sunshine. In a place where villages are not set on fire. And children grow up where they were born. It takes her breath away. It is almost unfair such a place exists. It is unfair but so good. She will never save Kishmet. It is too late now. Will never console her mother. Must accept this betrayal. She is saving herself, and herself alone. She is trapped between warring emotions but carries within her the certainty that she is right. She is leaving. Tearing herself away from everything she knows, everything she hopes to see again, tearing herself away from the possibility of ever remembering the name her father offered up to the moon. She talks to her twin, asks her to protect their birth, to carry that part of her, the part that is free and connected to their ancestors. Through her twin, she is not betraying herself. She is leaving Sudan. And staying here. Still integral to their land. Their traditions. Their language. She will always live here. She asks her twin to speak her name as often as she can. Let it ring out everywhere. In the wind and the water, let it fly and come to rest on stones, fields, peaceable animals. She gathers up some red soil and puts it in a handkerchief. For the first time in her life she packs her things. And she knows the *padrone* will not leave her to die in the desert. Will not abandon her to the vultures if she is sick, and she feels borne on the shoulders of invincibility.

And she is responsible for Indir. Indir who does not know she has him to thank for this journey. Indir who knows nothing. Who understands no Italian or Arabic or Turkish, who follows Bakhita around like a miserable little dog. She wonders where he is from. There are so many motherless children. Where are the childless mothers, she never sees them. They have sung the song of separation which never does any good, and they are heard no more, they go mad in silence. Indir has big gentle eyes with very long lashes, and he is trusting, with all the sorrow of knowing he will not rebel. Bakhita can see this. This little boy will never grow nasty or mad. He harbors within him the secret of violence, and expects nothing. He does not look like a master's child, his skin is a dark black, his lips full, Bakhita smooths her hand over his head, feels small bumps, and he blinks quickly when she touches him, stiffening slightly and smiling apologetically. Bakhita decides that he must be worth a great deal to have been chosen to leave with the master. Khartoum is one of the major castration centers. And the child has about him the strange gentleness and suffering that, she knows, will always be invisible to others. He will grow into a man with childhood memories that can never be shared. A man with no descendants.

Callisto Legnani was the last European to cross the desert before the fall of Khartoum on January 26, 1885. Four of them set out: Legnani, Bakhita, Indir, and Augusto Michieli, a friend of the consul's who knew Sudan well having traded there for many years. His wife was meant to have joined him, but never did. She is fragile, and sad, weighed down by a hidden, buried sadness. Deep inside Augusto Michieli is a form of defeat that does not dent his lust for life or his enterprise. Away from his wife, he feels like a young man. By her side, he is afraid of sorrow and anxious about everything, he is a hundred years old.

The consul is pleased with himself for taking Bakhita, sure his wife will be delighted to have an extra servant in her service, and Bakhita is remarkably practical for her age. Perched on her camel, with little Indir huddled against her, she has the assurance of a mother. She comforts him, protects him from mosquitoes, horseflies, the sand, thirst, and the sun; in the evenings she throws a handful of millet flour into boiling water and stirs it with a stick, feeding them off a smattering of nothing. The two donkeys they have with them are laden with bags, provisions, and gifts. They plod through the heat, maddened by horseflies, at nightfall Bakhita covers their bleeding necks with ashes. They bray so loudly in the night the consul is afraid they will alert jackals. Bakhita pats their foreheads, twists their ears. They immediately stop. She gestures to little Indir to do the same. The child twists the donkeys' ears, and throws his head back to laugh, surprising himself with the pleasure of it. The camels bite each other at night and pick fights. Their jaws can be heard grinding, chewing the cud, as if the darkness itself were grinding at something. The *padrone* asks Bakhita to help him hobble them so they don't stray in search of food. She shakes as she runs the leather strap between one hind leg and one front leg, the constant clinking of the hobbles stops her sleeping at night. And yet she likes these desert nights full of threats. Likes the violence of nature that drives men and animals closer together. Likes this dangerous connection, the fragility of their lives. The country is walking. Fleeing. And yet slowness is the rhythm of survival. An implacable country, a plundered land. In the oases through which they travel, she sees slaves cultivating palm trees, picking dates, shoring up irrigation channels. They are stooped figures. Whether they are here or somewhere else, in fields, salt mines, gold mines, or gem mines, they are all stooped. Men broken in two. Their chests down near their knees. Their bare feet as tough as old leather. Their souls trapped. Their hearts bled dry. They are taunted. Accused of having no will to rebel, no dignity. They are said to be lazy, they have to be beaten if they are to work, otherwise they would make the most of having bed and board without even thanking their masters. In those desert nights, with little Indir asleep against her, Bakhita listens to the two Italians snoring like their donkeys. Is not sure whether to laugh or cry. It could be so straightforward living together. And it always feels like a revenge. She wants to say *asfa*, but has no idea to whom she would say it.

They covered more than five hundred miles between Khartoum and Suakin. Everything she saw, she saw for the first time. She crossed the Nile and loved its impassive power, the red water in the setting sun, moonbeams striping the night sky, the endless play of passing hours, all those hours on that life-giving water. She realized that no man, no king, pasha, sultan, governor, military or religious leader, no man held Sudan in his power. This was the master. She would have liked the consul to gather the four of them on the banks of the river and say a few words, but he would surely have refused to approach the water's edge because of the crocodiles and the hippopotamuses whose blood-curdling cries terrified him. So she asked him to trace in the sand the journey from Taweisha to El Obeid, El Obeid to Khartoum, and Khartoum to the shores of the Red Sea, including a depiction of the great river. She often thought of the map in his desk drawer, and wished she understood. The consul drew long lines in the sand, they went on and on, such thin lines that meant nothing, and those days of walking felt abstract and diminished.

"Do you understand, Bakhita?"

"Yes."

"What do you understand?"

"I was very young."

He thinks the girl doesn't understand a thing, for sure, and wonders whether he's doing her a disservice taking her to Italy. He looks at her, she has taken Indir in her arms and is rocking him gently, she's spoiling the child, loving him like that is no way to prepare him for the life he'll have. The consul struggles to understand her, she is both docile and thoughtful, with an infallible yet somehow elusive presence.

If she were not so obliging and hardworking, he would criticize her dreaminess. His wife will train her better than he can.

And then one day the Red Sea, like an invasion, a sudden definitive relief, opening up to everything unknown. Bakhita discovers the sea with Indir's hand in hers and feels the same age as him. The age at which to stand facing the ocean for the first time.

"That's where we will go," the consul tells her with a sweep of his arm, as if offering her the sea with this journey.

"*Si, padrone,*" she murmurs in Italian, out of courtesy.

"Please tell me you won't be frightened."

He wants to laugh, she stands there, frozen to the spot, her eyes, as usual, hovering between keen attention and gentle contemplation. "A desert gazelle," Augusto said one evening. Legnani had laughed awkwardly.

"You won't, will you? Be frightened, I mean."

She does not reply. Apart from snakes, she has always feared people more than the natural world or animals. She would like to tell him she has slept in a tree with monkeys and birds, has slept in a sheepfold with ewes and rams, that without her, he would have had a difficult time with the camels and donkeys, and the nomads whose language he did not understand, and the wells he never spotted, and the sandstorms he did not tackle as well as she did, not knowing how to cover himself but still keep breathing.

"No, *padrone*. I'm not frightened."

She thinks she will put her trust in the sea. That with the sea there can surely be no other course of action than to hand yourself over. She will watch. And wait. Until Italy appears. With its happy women. Its happy children. Its husbands who arrive laden with gifts. And for the first time she wonders what she will do among so many lavishly contented people.

They stay in an inn on the Suakin peninsula for a month, waiting for the steamboat. They hear of the fall of Khartoum, Gordon Pasha's death, decapitated on the stairs of his palace, lootings by slaves, Egyptians dying along with many of the Sudanese inhabitants of Khartoum, the city burning and in ruins. Bakhita is sixteen, she knows if she had stayed there, she too would have been pillaged, like a city. She has nightmares of Khartoum in flames, hears the children in its streets, sees them reaching out toward mothers who do not come for them. She hugs little Indir closer, he does not know what he has escaped. With her, he is afraid of nothing. Not the shouting at the inn, not the sounds of Suakin, the steamboat sirens, barked orders, famished seagulls, the lowing of wild oxen in the furious stench of burning herbs and coal, of kelp and dead fish. The town is violent, like its inhabitants, all of whom are passing through, some on business, others fleeing. Bakhita senses all this without being told. She sees the sea as an enraged river and knows that this savagery inflames them all, it is a city of towering stones that quake despite their size. Boats are laden to the gunwales with treasures from Sudan, India, and Egypt. This is a world caught between two worlds. An independent city that stands outside time. Bakhita can smell the fear of failure here and the brutal drive of profit. She keeps Indir close, tries to teach him a few words of Italian. He must learn to say *Grazie, padrone,* and *Si, padrone,* and *Mi scusi, padrone.* But Indir does not want to learn. He just has that dreamy, absent look in his eyes and huddles up to her like a cat with no idea about the world in which it sleeps. She protects him from everything, including prying eyes. More than once she has heard negotiations between men who want him. This little castrated child is what they want. And they are astonished when the consul says, "No. He's not for sale. He is a gift, I have promised him to someone. No, I'm taking him to Italy, for a friend, I couldn't do that to a friend, no... I'm keeping him."

What of her...will he keep her too? She has faith, of course, the *padrone* is a good man, and if he keeps Indir he is bound to keep her, who would look after the child on the long crossing? He said 2,500 miles. Then added, "That's a lot. Do you understand? You could never travel that far on foot." She smiled and looked out to sea...not on foot, no...Sometimes the *padrone* has his head in the clouds.

And then one day it is time to leave. Leave for real. The yelling and jostling on the quay like in a marketplace. There are men and women in front of her and behind her, she is trapped between these people stamping and huffing, bumping into each other, she clutches Indir's hand tightly, he clings to her white tunic, crying. Now it is all over. She is leaving her country. It is over. And she wishes she would appear. The one person who might cry, *Don't go!* The one person who would find it unbearable. She hears people calling *Goodbye!* in every language but hears no one begging her *Don't go!* She turns around, looks over the bundles on people's backs, over their heads and shoulders, it is a heavy-laden world, a world of ropes and filth, orders and obedience, some people gesticulate to each other to say *Goodbye!* or *I'm here! Climb up here!*, there are those parting and those coming together. Some whistle, others yell. On the banks she can hear dogs barking themselves hoarse. Water slaps against the hull, and birds screech in the heavy wind. But the woman who might beg Bakhita not to leave, the woman who might open her arms wide to call her back, has never seen the sea, does not even know it exists. That Italy exists. Or that Bakhita is leaving. Bakhita closes her eyes to conjure them all, as far as her memory will allow, to take them all with her. With her eyes closed, she looks at images of her childhood, her long-distant childhood, when Kishmet was the big sister and watched over them, because that was the way of the world. Peaceful. And protected. She remembers that.

The journey needed to be long to give Bakhita time to absorb it. There needed to be that forty-day crossing, the slow progress through the Suez Canal, a corridor trapped in the desert between Africa and Asia, linking the Red Sea to the Mediterranean. There needed to be days and nights unlike anything else, skies that came down to the meet the sea, skies under which a human is reduced to nothing. And at every stage, witnessing the ceremonies of reunions and of goodbyes. Tiny people on the quayside, waiting. And being reunited. Watching as they hug and disappear together, still gazing at the shore but losing sight of them. Their faces gone. Lost in the crook of a shoulder. The moist warmth of a neck. Clasped to each other.

As the days go by she explains to Indir that soon they will be saying goodbye, he will be in one house and she in another, does he understand? They won't have the same master. Indir's face hardens stubbornly, he grinds his teeth, and she can tell he would thump her if he could, if he were not restraining himself he would hit her. He does not. But the closer they come to the Italian coast, the less he can tolerate this journey. He vomits, his forehead is clammy, he moans and refuses to eat. At first Bakhita is afraid, as if this now useless little slave boy might be thrown overboard. But Callisto Legnani merely criticizes her for failing to calm the child. She is amazed that such an intelligent, knowledgeable man should not understand a young boy's suffering. There is a remedy, of course. She knows it. But she cannot give it to him. She cannot tell him they will not be parted. At night he makes sudden, panicky movements, throwing his head against her chest in his sleep, winding her, she hears him cry, call out. Wishes she could console him. But she has never consoled anyone. And she remembers little Yebit who died at the tattooist's hands. It is an image that often comes back to her, and rather than feeling remorse or pain, she is aware of her powerlessness, her defeat in the face of evil. She strokes Indir's head, hugs his small body, grown so thin it is like a badly assembled collection of spindly lengths of ebony, he is clumsy and absentminded, she thinks the "operation" must have damaged his mind.

They sleep on the floor in the same cabin as the consul and his friend, who did not take the risk of trusting them to the deck reserved for slaves, servants, brigands, and every type of trafficker. During the day she stays on the upper deck, close to the cabin, not venturing into the boat's maze of corridors. Through the windows she glimpses lounges and dining rooms, and sometimes hears a piano. She looks at the sea and thinks of everything there is beneath it. The deep cold world where the sunlight stops. She knows they are sailing over long-dead souls. She has heard of slave crossings bound for whole new worlds, knows Africa is being robbed of Africa. Rifles are the great masters and yet…there are skies that console her, stars that flit across the darkness like showers of light, and moons so huge it seems the boat has drawn closer to the sky. She meanwhile is drawing closer to another continent. Another life. And for once she knows where she is going, she is going to the *padrone*'s house, she will be in service to his wife, Signora Legnani, in a city called Padua. She smiles at the consul when she thinks of this, unaware that soon he will vanish from her life, forever.

The boat comes into the harbor in Genoa. A slow sad entrance that bids a definitive farewell to Sudan, with the foghorn reverberating heartbreakingly around the hills. It is springtime, April 1885, the air is sweet, the sky as pale and clear as dawn. Bakhita pushes away Indir's hand clutching at her tunic, wishes he had already stopped loving her, also wishes she could hug him in her arms and tell him so many things there is no longer time to say. She does not know whether slaves are beaten to death here, in Italy. Indir takes her hand and cries, "*Si padrone grazie padrone mi scusi padrone!*" It is his surprise. His gift for their arrival. He remembered the words and learned them in secret. He says it again, "*Si padrone grazie padrone mi scusi padrone!*" She smiles at him, but her throat constricts with emotion, please let him be strong enough. She carries some bags, Callisto Legnani and Augusto Michieli, both also laden, walk ahead with the beaming faces of returning conquerors. The quay is as busy as in Suakin, bags of grain on the dock, cargoes in nets, dockworkers cursing, beggars and barefoot children. This is the first shock, the first inexplicable fact: barefoot children in an Italian port. Bakhita thinks they must be from another country, like herself, and are hoping to stay here, in the country Anna described to her, the country of sunshine and freedom. There is a woman on the quayside. She watches them and opens her arms wide. This is the first image Bakhita is to have of Maria Turina Michieli: a woman opening her arms like a mother. Augusto goes to his wife and hugs her discreetly, before planting a kiss on her forehead. Bakhita thinks Indir is for her, the gift is for her, can see it in her big happy eyes. But an argument breaks out and Bakhita more or less understands the gist of it, even though Maria and Augusto do not speak the same Italian she knows. Maria looks over at Indir and Bakhita, and waits for something that is not forthcoming. Augusto shrugs, as awkward as a child, and then his wife points to the two slaves, her eyes clouding with astonishment and rage. Her voice is curt, far too shrill.

"You have nothing for me, Augusto? *Nothing?*"

"The boy is for the consul's friends, Maria... And the girl is his own servant—"

"But what about me, Augusto, have you brought nothing for me? No Negro at all?"

"Maria... we left so quickly. Khartoum has fallen, you know, the news is terrible."

"What I know is that Callisto, *Callisto* thought to bring gifts. He thought of more than just saving his skin."

Callisto Legnani comes over, explains that the crossing with two slaves was dangerous and expensive, and it was a miracle they escaped Khartoum in time, a miracle they survived the journey through the desert. And then he adds very quietly that he promised a eunuch to some friends a long time ago, a Genoese couple who are waiting for them at the inn. In the morning he will leave for Padua with Bakhita, who is for his wife. Maria looks at the two men as if they have colluded in this, loathes them for disappointing her and loathes herself for behaving as they have always seen her: embittered and demanding. She was so happy she'd made this trip, had come to wait for them on the quayside in Genoa, she was expecting something different, and now it's all ruined. Bakhita follows them with the bags, walking with the rolling gait of the newly disembarked. The little streets climb up and up, they are narrow and smell of fish and sweet herbs like spicy flowers, these powerful dry smells are all new.

When they reach the inn, Bakhita knows from the look on their faces that these friends of the consul's, the Sicas, are Indir's new masters. It is a look she knows, appraising and thrilled. They have taken rooms for their friends, but they themselves are setting off immediately, they live higher up in the city. Signora Sica flutters around Indir, clapping and laughing. Once again, Bakhita does not properly understand the language, but Indir is for this woman. She says she adores him! What's his name? "Indir." She says, "No, Enrico," and she asks him to sing, she wants to teach him. "La-la-la!" she sings, gesturing for him to continue the arpeggio with his castrati's voice. But Indir simply says, "*Si padrone grazie padrone mi scusi padrone*" and looks at Bakhita. She nods, yes, well done, but still corrects him: "*Padrona.*" She thinks he is being more sensible than she is, he can tell that Signora Sica is kind, and happy to have him. The couples say their goodbyes, hand-kissing and friendly shoulder-slapping, Bakhita watches these strange codes, the woman adjusts her hat and takes the arm that her husband holds out to her. And off they go. Take a few steps, turn back. Look at Indir and wait. She gives a surprised little laugh. He whistles for the child to join them. Bakhita is aware of the air, air that every one of them is breathing, but it is different for each of them. She sees this familiar, perennial situation. A slave going to new masters. There is no violence. Only a shocking gentleness. The consul prods Indir in the back, with an embarrassed little laugh, his gift isn't absolutely spot-on. The child stumbles, freezes, and stays where he is. Bakhita crouches down to his level, holds him to her, and takes in the smell of his skin, whispers that he must go now, he must run over to his new masters. But all at once he starts howling, an unbearable screaming sound, high-pitched and heartrending, the friends eye one another in panic, make hushed plans with flushed cheeks. Not sure what to do. Maria Turina Michieli looks at Bakhita and sees what the others do not. Sees the little child being snatched away from this Negro girl, sees the love between them, she looks at the girl and wants her. It is no more complicated than that. She wants her. The consul grabs the child from Bakhita's arms, systematically opens his fingers gripping her tunic, the child growls and puffs breathlessly, carried aloft by the consul like a bag, and he turns back again, reaching his arms toward Bakhita and sobbing. The consul almost throws him at Signor Sica, whose wife backs away slightly, and then they leave. The child's exhausted cries can still be heard, the signora's shoes click-clicking on the ground, and then nothing, silence intercut with the song of indifferent birds. It is over. Maria Turina Michieli is still looking at Bakhita who, surely, must know a great many things. Carrying bags. Earning the love of children. And weeping in silence.

Bakhita watches from the bedroom window. There. This is Italy. Surely. She sees the sea swallowed up in the encroaching evening, as if backing away to disappear. Streetlamps come on in the small streets, and what Anna said is true, there are women out at this time and some walk alone, but they are all clothed and all white, try as she might, Bakhita sees not a single black or mixed-race face, not a single woman in a djellaba, not a single man in a turban, the voices she can hear inside the walls of houses are strident and full of astonishment, people call to each other in long tired words, words that seem to forget themselves halfway through, and Bakhita is surprised not to understand what they are saying. Are they speaking something other than Italian? And yet here she is. This is Italy. She has arrived. In this country where she has no sister, no one to search for, no one to recognize. She has left Indir, as planned. And her heart is broken. Why, at least once in her life, does she not help a child? The little slave boy thinks she betrayed him. He's right. She didn't beg the master to keep him.

It is now completely dark. There must still be men in the port, loading and unloading riches for the pleasure of gain. Her personal pleasure would be to be with her loved ones. To tell them about this journey, describe it to someone. Describe the land seen from the sea, which is always far away, even as you draw close. Describe the wind whipping up violently like a warrior. The men on deck playing cards and betting money as if deaf to the warring wind. And drinking. And fighting. The clamor or anger, all the time.

The only thing that soothes her when she goes to bed that night is knowing she will set off with the *padrone* the next day. She understands the language he speaks better and better, and knows how to serve him. He gave her the white tunic, he has never touched her, and he saved her from Khartoum, before Khartoum was consumed by flames, she owes him her life. There is a bed in her room at the inn. She smooths out the sheets, tucks them in more neatly, and then lies down on the ground. She longs for the heat of little Indir's body. Knows that at this very moment he is sucking his thumb and calling to her. She feels as if she is still rocking on the boat, and to overcome her land-sickness she breathes in time with this pitching, curls her body up tight and tries to follow the rhythm of the swell. It is the first time she has slept alone. Since she was locked up by her captors, she has never spent a night alone. And she suddenly misses Binah. Is surprised by this, has not felt it for a long time. The part of their life that they shared is so long ago now, did it really happen? Has she invented memories for herself with a little girl who made everything bearable for her? Did she invent herself a friend? A sister? A childhood? She no longer knows her origins. She listens to the sea, can hear it but not see it, its inhalations as long and slow as solitude.

When Callisto Legnani sees her the next morning, he comes over to her, smoothing his mustache, and from this mannerism she detects his embarrassment. Wonders what she has forgotten to do. What she has done wrong. But the consul's voice is as gentle as ever.

"Why did you want to come to Italy, Bakhita?"

"To see it."

"Ah, that's good... That's good."

"*Padrone*..."

"Yes?"

"Is this it? Italy?"

"Of course this is Italy! What did you think? This was just a stop-off?"

"I don't understand when people talk. Your friends. Are they Italian?"

"Well, naturally they're Italian. They're talking their dialect. Everyone in Italy speaks a dialect."

"Including you?"

"Well, I know both languages."

"Yes, of course, *padrone*..."

She understands that Italy is very large, as big as or perhaps even bigger than Sudan, there must be many tribes and many dialects, many warlords too. And is the *padrone*'s town far from here? Will they travel there on foot? She dare not ask any more questions. Afraid the master will laugh. But he is the one to probe further.

"So, tell me honestly, do you like Italy?"

"Yes, thank you, *padrone*."

"You shall like it here. No more slavery. Are you happy?"

"Yes, *padrone*."

He watches her, hesitates, smiles as if apologizing, and goes to join Augusto and Maria. All three of them look at her, and it is as if she were back in the slave market. As if she were not wearing her tunic. No protection. It should not feel like this, but her heart begins its tom-tom rhythm again, sensing danger. Maria looks at her, and there is something happy and victorious in her eyes. A glorious revenge. And then she turns away and laughs. Augusto laughs a little too, with relief. Bakhita does not understand what it is about her that these Italians find so amusing. She looks down and presses her hands together behind her back. Callisto comes up to her.

"You will go with my friends," he tells her. "To their house, in Zianigo. You belong to them now. Do you understand? You are to serve Signora Maria Michieli."

She does not prostrate herself at his feet. Does not implore him. Is dumbstruck. Would never have guessed he could lie to her. Because lie he did: The slavery is not over. Simply slower and not so noisy. Eyes lowered, she follows her new masters. Without even saying goodbye to the consul. Caught in all the commotion of their departure, the luggage, the things they say to one another, their gestures, and Bakhita, alone in her silence, follows them, not rebelling, follows them in her dumbstruck submission, a long slow sadness.

She does not understand a word Signora Michieli says. Augusto translates his wife's Venetian accent into the Italian that Bakhita understands a little. She learns that they did not buy her, but the consul gave her to the signora. She will be one of their servants, she will be happy. She is angry with herself, she has learned nothing: A master never loves his slaves. Why should the consul have kept her?

They climb into a black beast that spits the same coal smoke as the boat but cuts across fields, dives into tunnels, and whistles as loudly as it breathes. Bakhita does not show her fear. Does not ask what this thing is called. How long it will go on. The train stops frequently. Her masters do not move. Neither does she. At one point, they alight and change trains. She follows them. It goes on like this all day, watching Italy through windows. Fields as far as the eye can see, with stooped peasants, men, women, and tiny children. Are they free? Not one is black. And here again, they are all clothed. But they have no shoes. There must be plenty to eat here, as Anna said. Because there are so many fields.

At the end of the afternoon they arrive in Mirano. A horse-drawn carriage is waiting for them. The masters climb inside. She does not know whether she should walk alongside the horse or sit next to the coachman, but her masters gesture for her to sit with them. They leave the town behind and head deep into the country. She sees little donkeys ridden by old men, goats and sheep watched over by children, women sitting by the side of the road, groups of men in uniform, surely soldiers. So is there an army here too? She watches and feels as if she has been set down on the edge of the world, and the world is gliding slowly by. She catches her mistress's eye. The woman has a smile carved out of her face, like a cut made with a knife.

They go through Zianigo, a tiny village dominated by a massive church that is too big for the central square, and soon the horse sets off down an alley lined with cypress trees, with a huge house at the far end. There is a pink tree, a magnolia in bloom, almost hiding the front door to this comfortable home. Her new masters' house. Bakhita alights from the carriage and clasps the handkerchief in her pocket, the red Sudanese earth has dried, is not so soft now. There is a large garden and a courtyard, but she cannot see the slave quarters, so perhaps it is true and people are free here. The master says he is happy to be home, he looks at his wife, looks at his house, and then roars with laughter. He spoke in Arabic! He says the same thing again, differently, his wife inclines her head indulgently, and his smile instantly fades.

An old woman sits eating on the doorstep. Scraping her bowl to a slow rhythm. She looks up and shrieks. Her bowl falls to the ground, and she runs off making frantic signs on her forehead and chest, screeching something incomprehensible but surely dreadful. From the garden and the house itself women appear, and a few men, approaching gingerly to take the masters' luggage and eye Bakhita in mute terror. One woman spits, another brandishes crossed fingers in front of her, her arms outstretched toward Bakhita, muttering a hushed prayer. Bakhita is not familiar with this ceremony. True, the master is returning home after a very long voyage. So she smiles, if she could join in she would, but she does not know the ritual. Maria Michieli claps her hands and shouts three times. But they all stay where they are. Motionless and afraid, waiting for something. Augusto ushers Bakhita quickly into the house, and the servants no longer dare to join them but press their ashen faces up to the windows.

"They're more frightened than you are!"

"*Si, padrone...*"

"They'll get used to you, and they'll eventually realize you're not the devil."

She knows about the devil, he is feared by all Islamists.

"The devil, *padrone?*"

"Well, yes! The black devil! And please call me *paron*. Make an effort, learn their dialect."

There are finger marks and traces of breathy condensation on the windows from the frightened servants. She looks at these marks and thinks to herself that she will clean the windows. That is what she is here for. That is why she was given to the *padrona*...the *parona*...to make everything clean. And she wonders what is worse. Being *djamila* or *sheitan*.

For the first time in her life she has a room of her own. It has a bed. A nightstand. A gas lamp. A small dresser. And a window in a wall smothered with wisteria. The room is high up, over the stables. She does not light the lamp the first evening and hardly ever will. She understands better with outside light. When it is dark, it is time to sleep. Or watch the sky. When it is light, she gets up. Even if the whole house is still asleep. She gets used to sleeping in a bed, afraid of falling, sorry to lose contact with the ground and its reverberations. As the *paron* told her to, she makes an effort. Sleeping like the others. Talking like the others. Looking like the others. And in this permanent struggle, this life of adapting and terrible shame, this life devoid of love and tenderness, she will meet a man, the first man since her father who will truly love her. This man crosses her path like a star fallen at her feet.

His name is Signore Illuminato Checchini, but everyone calls him by his pseudonym as a local journalist, Paron Stefano Massarioto. He administers the Michielis' assets during the master's long absences, as he does for other estates. He is self-taught, a lover of the people, the peasants, whom he is quick to defend against landowners. He frequents every market in Veneto, knows the exact price of everything, the going rate for fruits, cereals, tobacco, and vegetables, he knows the day laborers and the sharecroppers, and they all trust him. He is also Zianigo's organist, he is an unclassifiable man, passionate, religious, warm, and amusing. What would be called a "somebody" if he were not first and foremost a humanist.

He comes to see the Michielis the day after the master's return. A professional meeting and yet not. Of course he will give an appraisal of agricultural progress on the estate, but like the others, he is also here out of curiosity. The previous day his two eldest sons, Giuseppe and Leone, told him there was a "black devil" in the Michielis' house. They saw her from the street! He questioned them, and then gently set them straight: It must be an African woman. The village can talk of nothing else. The woman is as black as burned wood, perhaps she is burned, will be reduced to ash any minute, she looks ill, as if she has been steeped in coal dust, has been swallowed up by the night. It's beyond comprehension. And terrifying. Stefano has seen African masks in the Michielis' house, and other exotic objects brought back from Sudan, but is this possible? A woman who looks like these masks? And when, as he talks to Augusto Michieli in the drawing room, he sees her walk past, he is shocked in spite of himself. He would like to hide his surprise but is deeply shaken. Michieli laughs at his discomfort.

"That's Bakhita. She's my wife's. She's sixteen, a slave from Sudan, she was caught when she was very young and has scars all over her body, if you only knew! She's a very good sort, a little slow but hardworking."

"Did you bring her back? Did you save her?"

Michieli stammers that... yes... she was serving a Paduan friend of his in Khartoum and he saved her, yes... Stefano says he is a blessed man for this, for what he has done, saved a human being, and Michieli launches immediately into cereals and tobacco. He does not like his manager's religious sentimentality and regrets all the fuss surrounding the arrival of this *moretta*, as everyone is already calling her, the "blackie," the "darkie." He is surprised when Stefano asks permission to invite her to lunch that very day.

She goes with him. Paron Michieli explained that she is to eat at his friend's house, she asked whether she would come back afterward. He explained that she was going only for a few hours, she thinks she is to serve in their house but has no idea what "a few hours" is. And does not understand a single word this man says to her. Eyes lowered, she follows him and asks no questions, simply going where she is told to go as usual. In the street, children come up to her, catch hold of her, and squeal, or follow her clicking their tongues, as if taunting an animal. One little boy licks his fingers and turns around and spits. Drawn by the children's cries, women appear, their hands in front of their mouths, some fall to their knees, others cross themselves, one dares to come close, tugs at Bakhita's tunic, apparently wanting to pull it off. Bakhita gives a hoarse cry. Everyone freezes, silent, and more people gather in this silence, a muttering of excitement and shameless terror, and then Stefano raises his voice, speaking deeply and firmly, chiding these adults as if they were little children, his authority calms them briefly. He comes up to Bakhita, bends an arm, and offers it to her. She recognizes the gesture that the consul's friends made, when they left the inn in Genoa. Wonders what she should do. She is a servant, and he a gentleman. Stifled laughter bubbles up again all around them, a few pebbles are thrown. Stefano is still waiting, his bent arm held out to her. And as she does not move, he brings his hand very gently to hers, she recoils a little, gives a shudder of fear. The man's hand is warm and rough. He puts her hand onto his arm and says something she does not understand. She is ashamed to be touching a man out in the street, but no one laughs at them, quite the opposite, she can feel the violence subsiding. On they walk, and others follow with careful footsteps and amazed whispers. They walk through the village like this, Stefano's face proud, while she keeps her eyes lowered. "Looks like he's taking her to the altar!" one woman murmurs as they pass.

In a way he is.

She comes and sits at the family table, in among Stefano and Clementina's five children. Three sons and two daughters, ranging from five to eleven. With Bakhita still holding his arm, their father announces in his powerful voice, "Here is the Moretta! I've invited her to lunch!" He can read fear and respect in his wife's eyes. "She has no one in the world. And has suffered a great deal." The children are silent, they want to please their father but cannot understand what they are seeing. She can see the fear in their expressions and reaches out her hand to lay it gently on the head of the youngest child, Melia, who starts to cry. She turns to Clementina, "*Asfa, padrona... Parona...*" Even Stefano is startled. Her voice is like a man's. "Well," he says, "let me introduce your little sister, *sorellina* Moretta!," and he laughs, and they all join him. Bakhita does not yet realize that she has been accepted into a family, and that they will now call her "little sister."

She is in service to Maria Michieli, but it is through Stefano that she will come to know the world in which she now lives. She is often invited to his house, and not one meal, one evening goes by without someone knocking at their door. Peasants come to beg him to intervene on their behalf with their masters. He invites them in, sits them down, and always offers them a drink, a little milk, and some bread for the children. He listens to them. Their pavano dialect is coarser, more abrupt than Venetian, and impenetrable to Bakhita. But she watches them and recognizes the exhaustion in them, the ugly, carved-out gauntness of the hungry. Their staring, almost stupid gaze. Their red skin that tears and eventually flakes off. She is amazed that this happens only on their hands, neck, arms, and legs. Pellagra bears its stigmata on the areas exposed to sunlight, and these slaves do not live naked. She recognizes the way they shake, too, the swollen bellies of their young children, the progressive paralysis, and just like in Sudan, the insanity of people who have no food and will die of it. They beg Paron Stefano, they weep, and sometimes even fall to their knees. She desperately wants to reach out to them. Tell them she knows them, yes, she is the Moretta, she has known them a long time. They are submissive and desperate. They work and they die, and their children are condemned. Having fled Khartoum, she knows that human beings can bear the unbearable until one day someone calls them and they follow. And then nothing can stop them again. But she says nothing and steps no closer. Zianigo's peasants are afraid of her, and she does not speak their language. She represses her impulses, and at night she tells the darkness what torments her. She finds it impossible to sleep until she has laid down her suffering, her inability to help these poor people. She talks to the sky, the sky that is the same the world over, and it makes her feel that the world is not all that vast. Not one morning dawns when she does not think of her mother, sitting on her baobab throne. Sometimes it feels imaginary, like someone else's life, but more often than not her presence is so palpable that Bakhita is sure her mother is thinking of her at the exact same moment and knows she is safe.

Parona Michieli behaves toward her with an irked sort of kindness, a forced indulgence, and this too Bakhita has seen before and recognizes: A woman who silences her unhappiness is a woman who carries a formidable enemy within her. This woman should dance and scream, on and on, exorcise the spirit that possesses her. But instead this woman talks softly, in her curt, gently questioning tone, she is always disappointed with herself over something, and others know she is around from her sighing. She is not jealous of the affection Stefano shows for the Moretta, he is a valuable ally on the estate, even when her husband is at home. Because even when he *is* there, her husband seems absent. Thinking of other things, planning his next departure, always. Running away from her. Running away from this house where no one is happy. Maria Michieli is herself a stranger to Zianigo and to Italy. She is from Petersburg where Augusto had dealings with fur traders and fell in love with her. She is not Italian and definitely not Roman Catholic. Naturally, she converted in order to marry, in a church in Paris, but she is Orthodox by tradition, although without conviction. She has one thing in common with her husband: irritation at Stefano's religious knickknacks. No, they do *not* have a crucifix in the house! And no, they do not go to mass! And who cares if people scorn her for this. Stefano, meanwhile, is great friends with the parish priest, he runs the choir, organizes pilgrimages, and helps with charity work. Yes, she would happily go to listen to the organ, she likes music, but set foot inside a church... In fact, she forbids him to talk of religion to Bakhita, he must not succumb to this Italian fashion for missionaries, must keep his notions of good and evil to himself, she can look after her servants perfectly well herself.

But Bakhita does not need to be told about good and evil. She knows this battle by heart and quickly comes to see that the world is a single world. The sea between Sudan and Italy is not a separation. It is a hyphen. Everything is the same. And men suffer. One morning when she accompanies Parona Michieli to the market she sees a handcuffed peasant walking between two carabinieri. She is horrified. Chains! Chains here too! Parona Michieli urges her on and explains, enunciating her words clearly, "He-stole-a-piece-of-fruit."

"Fruit, *parona*?"

"You understand Venetian!"

And she also understands that the peasant was bound to have planted the fruit tree in the first place. She does not know terms like "pilfering" or "penal code," but she watches and understands everything. She has no armor, it is immediate, life penetrates her, and she cannot protect herself from this compassion. What was it her mother used to say? *My little girl... My little girl is gentle and good. My little girl...* She looks at Parona Michieli and suddenly understands this woman, her spitefulness and her unhappiness.

She confides in Clementina, Stefano's wife, on the subject. They communicate as best they can with few words, a lot of gesticulating, and some explosive laughter. But Bakhita does not feel much like laughing on this occasion and is not sure how to broach the subject. She points to Clementina's youngest, little Melia, talks about the child and of Parona Michieli, establishing an association between them. Clementina listens attentively, puts on her hat, and indicates that Bakhita should go with her. They walk across Zianigo, come out of the village onto scrubby little paths, with the sound of invisible water between the stones, and on either side heavy low walls, extensive farm buildings the size of zarebas, and the huge patrician homes of the local nobility. Bakhita likes these walks, the smells of blackberries and vetch, the birds she sees for the first time and others she recognizes, blackbirds, skylarks, and eagles far off in the mountains. She is always afraid she will frighten someone, will be struck with a stone, but tells herself that if they see her often enough, the locals will grow accustomed to her and may one day allow her to approach them. Thanks to Parona Michieli, she is dressed like a European, has pretty clips in her tightly curled hair, and, for big family outings in a horse-drawn carriage with the Michielis, wears her scarlet dress, and even those who are afraid of her say so: She is beautiful. Astonishing though it is. Terrifying though she is. She is beautiful. And does not know it.

They climb a little way up the hillside, Bakhita hears the cows before she sees them and then all of a sudden . . . the little girl watching over the herd, near the river. A very young girl lost in her solitude, waggling her stick which is as flimsy as her own naked legs, and occasionally whistling and giving a short sharp cry. Bakhita points her out to Clementina and then pats her own chest. This little girl is who she was. She remembers this, and it is as if she is seeing herself, meeting herself. It was a long time ago and it is now. She would still know how to do it, take the herd to the river in the morning and bring them back to the village in the evening. Clementina understands and congratulates her, she will tell Stefano that same evening: "Bakhita knows how to look after cattle." They walk on, and Bakhita turns around, gazes at her past that has suddenly appeared in Italy, time turned upside down.

When Clementina opens the gate to the cemetery, Bakhita instinctively lowers her eyes. She knows where she is. She saw small cemeteries set up by Catholic missions in Khartoum. This is not for her and she feels uncomfortable, it is a forbidden place, like being in a garden where she has no right to venture. Clementina leads her to a tiny grave. Even before Clementina points them out, Bakhita understands the words she cannot read.

"Carlo Michieli. Giovanni Michieli."

Here lies Parona Michieli's unhappiness. She knew it.

That evening, Bakhita serves her master and mistress, they are dining in their large empty dining room, they make no eye contact, eat mutton, vegetables, rice, fruit, and bread, drink wine and coffee, all the things their peasants have cultivated and will never eat or drink. Bakhita watches the *parona*. Wishes she could tell her not to worry. Knows there is another child in her. No one should wait for a child in fear. She stands there solidly, watching her.

"She *is* slow, so slow!" Maria says to her husband. And, running out of patience, she explodes, "What?"

And the Moretta's deep voice risks a shy, "I'm here, *parona*."

Augusto smothers his laughter in his napkin. The *parona* flushes and looks away. So no one sees her tears.

This child is something they will wait for together. The mistress and her servant. Maria has not forgotten Genoa, little Indir's distress when he was separated from the Moretta. She knows he crossed deserts and seas with her, but also thanks to her, Maria is in little doubt that it was not her husband or his friend who took care of the child! The consul gave her Bakhita like a consolation prize, but this was in fact what she wanted, this Negress. And not merely on a whim.

Augusto has not guessed that for several weeks now Maria has been pregnant again. He thinks her pallor and sickness are part of her arsenal, his wife is hysterical, nothing to be done about it. She knows he would run away if she told him she was, once more, expecting a baby. As if it were not his, only hers, a child conceived by its mother and belonging only to her. He thinks the two dead children are her shame, hers alone. With her, children do not survive. That peasant children should die is customary and logical, they are fathered by drinkers of contraband brandy, by filthy, illiterate, immoral eaters of polenta. But Maria! She's *not equipped* to keep a child alive. The first time, granted, there is no defense against measles, but the second? She didn't even manage to keep him alive inside her, she gave birth to a dead baby. What came out of her was death. "God called him back into His fold, too," the archpriest said. And that was when Maria decided it was over, she did not want to hear another word about this God who needed her sons more than she did. Before the second child was given extreme unction, she had given him her father-in-law's name, Giovanni, and her breasts had been bound, it would not have been Maria who nursed him anyway, but those bound breasts hurt her appallingly, much more than when Carlo was born and she had watched him suckled by fat Alessia with her impassive eyes and immoderate bosom. She loathed them all, and their God along with them. God here and God there, like a linguistic twitch, an idol that inveigled its way into everything, meddled with everything, and to whom "she had to offer her sons," as if they were His.

This time, with this pregnancy that the Moretta alone has noticed, she will hide the evidence from them. So that no one—not Stefano, not his family, not the parish priest, nor their friends—can guess. She knows what people think of her, she is a foreigner and her husband would do better to leave her for a good strong Italian girl, a mother who would go to mass on Sundays, knit for the destitute, and follow processions in honor of the Virgin. Like other women. And like other women, she would bow her head under the weight of her sorrow, wear a black veil, and make offerings to the child-eating Lord.

This Moretta knows nothing of all this, she is silent and can peddle no gossip. Or even any truth. And so, one evening, Maria asks her to open the door to the wardrobe in her bedroom and indicates that she should take out the big blue box and set it down here, on the table, she has something to show her. And now, talking to this servant in Russian, she tells the story. Of the brief and beautiful life of little Carlo. She takes out the clothes, which she kept for the second child, because before she had even dried her tears, her mother-in-law had told her to "make another" straightaway, as if she had simply bungled a recipe. She did not want to make another, and that is surely why the second child was born dead. A tired little stand-in. Unable even to open his eyes. And when she took him in her arms, it felt as if it was his soul she held to her, a snuffed-out soul that wanted only to be forgotten. But Carlo! Carlito had grown and lived for four years! She describes in her own language the life as a mother that she had with him. Because she was his mother, whatever they say about her. She describes his first steps, his first words, the first little injuries and minor illnesses that she treated, yes, she could do all that! And she shows her his clothes by way of proof, asks Bakhita to touch them, see how beautiful they are, and, more important, how real. She has been forbidden to talk of this child, as if he reminded her of "bad memories," but she wants to talk of him, and to tell this Moretta, who listens to her speaking Russian and does not hide her tears, tell her what a good son he was and what a good mother she was. She likes to see Bakhita cry, because if even a foreigner suffers, well then, it's perfectly natural that she should be sad, isn't it? It's not an illness, is it? She's not mad, surely? She gets carried away, speaks more and more quickly, more and more loudly, mixing Venetian with Russian, and French, and English, which she also speaks, "*Guarda!* Touch them! Don't be frightened!," and she waves around his drawings, his teddy bears, his bonnets, his little socks, "So small!," with one hand over her mouth, she is laughing now, because these socks are so very small! She cannot stop laughing, her body rocking with laughter. "So small! *Mio cuore! Sertse maïyo! Amore mio!*," speaking in every language, and her heartbreak overflows.

Bakhita can hear, from all the way back in Taweisha, the screams of the mother whose baby she touched, his tiny, achingly pretty foot. She remembers she was beaten for it, and that the baby cried too. She comes up to the *parona* gently and takes her in her arms, it is an unexpected gesture, a forbidden gesture, which simply means: Rest. The *parona* takes refuge in the Moretta's arms and sobs. She has finally been given the right to grieve.

The child is born on February 3, 1886. The master had left Italy three months earlier, to return to Suakin, whence he writes his wife bleak notes anticipating her future unraveling, and tells her to look after herself.

When she goes into labor, Parona Michieli asks the Moretta to stay by her side, and for three days now Bakhita has slept on the divan, not daring to say she would so much rather be on the floor, her senses are on the alert, she gets up ten times a night, puts her hands onto the agonizing stomach, but knows that all is well. Parona Michieli can feel her stomach relaxing, at the Moretta's touch the solid rock of it turns to liquid, and her fears come down a notch, she even manages to go back to sleep briefly.

Bakhita is moved, as if seeing this, witnessing it for the first time. Even though she has seen so many births, whether celebrated or dreaded, to happy women or young girls torn apart by the pain, babies that were kept and babies that were handed over, mothers with empty hands and others like her own, a tree with its branches, she has seen so many children brought into the world, and so many worlds. She is seventeen, knows she will never have children, her slave's body told her so, withering under the blows. The *parona* will give birth lying down, and she is amazed to see her immobilized when she is to take this most intense of exercise, thinks of a gazelle being hobbled before being forced to run. But says nothing, and when the midwife arrives on the third day, the woman waves the Moretta out of the room. The serious business is about to start.

It is a little girl. The *parona* calls her Alice Allessandrina Augusta. Her birth is telegraphed to the father, and the whole village is in the know. Maria Michieli has finally succeeded! It is a girl, but she is happy all the same, and perhaps Augusto will be too, who knows, his wife will do better next time, they shall have a son. A few hours later, night is falling and the priest is summoned. The holy sacraments must be administered very quickly, before even a church baptism. The child will not survive. At Maria Michieli's bedside, the priest murmurs words in Latin and makes signs that Bakhita does not understand. His voice is gentle and desolate, he would like to have a few words with the mother, but Maria recites her prayers without conviction, staring ahead into a future that does not exist. She does not cry, is dull-witted and exhausted. She no longer wants to see the baby, or touch her, has already stopped loving her, loathes her. The midwife comes back and binds her breasts in resigned silence, vigorously tightening the white bandages, which are stained already, then leaves the house with obvious relief. The Moretta is allowed to stay. Waiting alongside the mother until the baby, now that she has been blessed, surrenders her purified soul to heaven.

The night grows heavier, grows deep and silent, there is condensation on the windows and flickering lamplight, there is the smell of blood and sweat, and this oppressive tiredness. The room is closed, cut off from the world, everyone has fled the sorrow, and time trickles by for these three individuals alone—the mother, the child, and the servant—with death drawing closer like the smear of inevitability.

The two women do not look at each other. The child who will die is alone in her cradle, and her suffering pervades the whole room. She is a tiny little creature, with a huge helpless presence. Bakhita comes over to the cradle that Parona Michieli asked to have placed far from her, at the other end of the room. Watches little Alice's bluish face, her shallow breathing, hoarse breaths, is reminded of a river hampered by a rock, can hear the current of this water held back, and can see life battling against the power of an already accepted death. And so she does something she has done only once, such a long time ago, when she escaped from Taweisha: *She does not ask permission.* She picks up the baby, takes off her clothes, sits down, and lies the little creature across her knees, spits on her hands, and massages the baby's chest, slowly, speaking soft incoherent words, her face so close to the little body that the *parona* can see only her mass of tightly curled hair and tilted neck. The baby grizzles weakly, hoarsely, Bakhita is caught up in the litany of her words and gestures, her dark voice mingling with the child's scant breathing, wood can be heard crackling in the fireplace, spitting and snapping, and the baby coughs harder and harder, and this is a language that Bakhita understands, a language of pain and revolt. She spits on her hands again, and massages, and talks, her face right up against the baby's face, receiving her coughing and crying as if they were a gift intended for her.

The parona *stays silent,* a dispossessed spectator, she feels hope bloom again, along with a refusal to acknowledge this hope. Bakhita lifts the child up, holding her under her arms, she is suffocating, choking on her mucus. Bakhita lies the baby down again, takes her little head in her hand, puts her mouth over her nose, sucks hard, and spits onto the floor. Several times, very quickly, almost without catching her breath, she sucks up the mucus and spits it out. A process as noisy and dirty as life itself. Repetitive, instinctive, authoritative.

And when at last the baby has stopped crying in pain but cries with hunger, Bakhita dresses her again and brings her to her mother. The *parona* shrinks away from her, her eyes ask the Moretta whether she would be mad to risk this, but in a slow steady movement, Bakhita removes the long white bandage and releases her mistress's breasts. She says the word she loves, says it in her deep voice: *Madre*. And shows her what to do. Because she, the *parona*, must do this. She must suckle her daughter.

She will be nicknamed "Mimmina." A nickname like a kiss, a delicious treat, an unbounded tenderness. And it is to Bakhita that Maria Michieli entrusts her. She has agreed to nurse her, but the Moretta must stay by her side, she is afraid the baby will get it wrong, will not "take" enough, or too much, and she does not know how to burp her, or change her, or wash her, hardly dares to touch her, this powerful and mysterious little thing. She has the baby's cradle moved into the servant's room, up there, over the stables, and day and night, Bakhita brings her down for her feedings. The roles are reversed, the Moretta is the mother and the mother becomes the wet nurse. What does it matter. Maria Michieli gave up caring what the good people of Zianigo think long ago, her husband is far away and her in-laws are stupid. She watches like an anxious enthralled spectator as her daughter grows, and her pride swells in tandem with her contempt for this world that has always rejected her.

Bakhita does not put the baby in her cradle to sleep. But cuddles her close, under the sheets. Her days and nights are now nothing but this, this constant appointment with the baby. One evening when the full moon is violent and red, as big as the sun, she holds the child up to it and speaks her name three times. This does not say what the world was like the day Mimmina was born, it says how the world changed the day she was born.

It is both a profound joy and a privation rekindled. With the baby resting against her, Bakhita weeps for her own mother, the need for her surfaces in good moments just as it surfaced in hell, an absence that can never be filled and that is conjured by everything. She wishes she could share this substitute motherhood with her, but also be returned to this state as a tiny powerful life in the arms of the woman she called "mama" in a forgotten language. Be the mother and the child. A love like this. But she feels broken in two and is astonished by the strength of this absence, will her whole life be hampered by this irreplaceable love? She rocks Mimmina, and thanks her for being alive. Within the love she gives the child are all the people she has loved and who have been ripped from her, lives known and lost, discreet searing wounds. With her eyes locked onto Bakhita's, Mimmina's unfocused gaze concentrates and replies, and no one would suspect what they say to each other in their invented language, what they give each other in their cuddles and shared sleep. Their two lives are connected, both saved and now inextricable.

Three months after Mimmina's birth, pressured by those around them, and influenced by Paron Stefano too, it has to be said, out of superstition, Maria Michieli agrees to have her baptized, a real baptism this time, in Zianigo's church. The Moretta stays at the door. Maria carries the baby, all in white lace, to the font where Mimmina's screams ring out against the cold stone. Maria cries too, all that emotion, people think, but it is only disappointment. She looks at the baby howling in her christening robe and cannot wait to hand her back to the Moretta, begrudges the girl for having powers she does not have, her gratitude tainted with resentment.

Bakhita enjoys Mimmina's infancy. At six months, the *parona* stops nursing her, and Bakhita now feeds her, cooking up little meals and gruels, it is she too who knits her bonnets and slippers, embroiders her layette, tends to her fevers, her diarrhea, her inflamed gums, she has learned everything, can do everything, "as clever as a monkey," the housekeeper says. She takes the baby for walks in the countryside around Zianigo every day, and their walk frequently pauses at Stefano's house. If he is not in, Clementina and the children welcome her, congratulate her on the baby's progress, her good health, her weight, her smiles; if Stefano is there, he always makes them a little snack, this man can never see anyone, be they famished or well-fed, without giving them something to eat. He always tries to talk to Bakhita of religion, cannot help himself. He points to Mimmina's locket, "Santa Maria, do you understand, little sister? Santa Maria!" Bakhita smiles her gentle disarming smile. He suppresses the urge to take her into the church to show her the statues, the crucifix and paintings. He could play the organ while she discovered the Virgin, the Christ figure, the saints and the Real Presence, Bakhita understands all this without words, he knows she does, but Maria Michieli has forbidden her servant from entering the church. This torments Stefano. Keeps him awake at night. He feels guilty, as if he were watching Bakhita drown and standing by with his arms crossed. Her soul will be lost, and he will have done nothing to stop it. And yet a tremendous power emanates from her, like a well-kept secret. He knows from his conversations about her with Zianigo's poor, and its wealthier inhabitants too, that it is not only the color of her skin that frightens them. It is not only out of ignorance, superstition, or stupidity that they avoid her. She is beautiful, she is gentle and resigned. But she is also indestructible. A survivor who carries within her an incommunicable world. And this is what frightens them, this power they cannot fathom.

How did this idea come to Stefano? How did he think it achievable? He decides to adopt Bakhita. Does she not call him *babbo,* as his own children do? He is already a little like a father to her, and if he adopts her, she will have a name, a family, an inheritance, and he could have her baptized, erase the original sin, and save her soul. He launches himself into a headlong crusade to find papers that do not exist, birth certificates and sales receipts, a forgotten village, a lost nationality, he writes, telegraphs, uses his connections, asks for help from the archpriest, the mayor of Zianigo, the doge of Venice, goes to Padua to see Consul Legnani, who left six months ago for Egypt, writes to Augusto Michieli, begs him, where he is in Suakin, to research Bakhita's origins, he has faith enough to move mountains, mountains in a country about which he knows nothing, and the more vain his attempts, the more determined he becomes, caught up in the panic of his generosity, but perhaps... perhaps he also knows intuitively that this needs to be done quickly, that soon this gentle life, this respite, will be only a distant memory for Bakhita.

Bakhita is running through the streets of Zianigo alone. Running as if fleeing. As she did, with little Binah's hand in hers, when they ran away. She runs and the children she passes flatten themselves against the yellow walls of Zianigo's leaning houses, the elderly sitting by their doors take off their hats and hold their tongues, the women think some disaster must have struck Mimmina, for disaster runs hand in hand with the Moretta, every local woman can see that.

She can feel the chain on her ankle, the chain she wore in the Turkish mistress's house, it weighs her down and makes her lame, she has her halting slave's gait once more, her slave's heart, and the fear that goes with it. Her tight shoes hurt, her dress clings to her sweating body, and under her hat, her hair is soaked. She trips in a rut on the small dirt path to Stefano's house and has mud spattered on her face like patches of crusty skin. Stefano already knows she is on her way, has told Clementina to fetch the doctor and send him to Maria Michieli, something has happened to Mimmina, he goes to Bakhita on the little dirt track, goes to take her in his arms, but she throws herself at his feet, like a poor peasant. He lifts her back up and does not recognize her face, it is both younger and appallingly old. Her eyes are the eyes of a very small child and yet something terrified and ancient emanates from them.

"Mimmina?"

"No."

"Maria?"

"No?"

"*El paron?*"

She shakes her head and points to herself, thumping her chest, her heart, showing that it is here, inside her that disaster has struck. He casts an instinctive eye over her, she has run here and does not look sick, he wonders briefly whether she has received the adoption papers, bad news of her family, her village, and immediately realizes that would not be possible, in all the efforts he has made, he has only ever given his own address. He sits her down on a stone bench. Facing the tall cypress trees that sway in their sad, sugary smell. It has rained all day and the air is saturated with heavy humidity, birds sing in the water-laden trees, the last grumble of thunder can be heard in the mountains in the distance. Something is coming to an end. And all at once Stefano understands. The shock of it takes his breath away. And yet it is so obvious. He is angry with himself for failing to anticipate this, for never mentioning it to his little Moretta sister, it is his fault, he should have warned her... But saying such things in a dialect she does not fully understand would have been worse still, more distressing and worrying... She is to leave for Suakin, with the Michielis. She will leave Italy. He puts his hand on hers, she is crying now, and it is the first time she has cried in front of him. And so he cries with her, he sobs, and they sit there on that bench, in the air damp with spent rain, filled with a pain against which they can do nothing, because there is no possible consolation for what is to happen. He would like to ask her forgiveness, if only he had thought of the adoption sooner, if only he had warned her this could happen. Augusto Michieli has left him to run the estate alone for a year now, he has not met his baby daughter, has never been away from Zianigo for so long... Stefano takes off his round spectacles and wipes his eyes.

"Suakin?" he asks.

"Yes, *babbo*, yes... *Aiuto*... Help..."

He looks at the sky. But the sky gives no reply.

He takes her back to Maria Michieli. The *parona* tells her to go change her clothes and relieve the housekeeper who is watching Mimmina. She adds that they will have words later about her escapade, one on one. Bakhita climbs up to the bedroom that gives her the illusion of freedom, the illusion of motherhood, of a life of her own.

Maria has invited Stefano to sit down in the drawing room, and she serves him a glass of grappa.

"I shall be needing you more than ever, Stefano."

"I know..."

"The estate will be entirely in your hands. Of course, there will be financial compensation."

He does not touch his glass. Looks out at the wet garden, the heavy magnolia and rain-battered flowers. Thinks how strange it is that the weather sometimes is in tune with our hearts. There will be more rain, the sky is colorless.

"Are you leaving for Suakin?" he asks, and hates the brevity of these little words.

"Mimmina is nine months old, and her father doesn't know her."

"Of course."

"He can't come home, I'm sure you understand, now's not the time to abandon the hotel."

"Ah...so he bought it, in the end..."

"In his letters he tells me the houses in Suakin are made of coral stone, can you imagine that, Stefano?"

"It must be very beautiful."

"He tells me Suakin is a peninsula and is almost perfectly round, do you see, I mean completely, like...like a pearl nestled in the Red Sea. Can you—"

"Imagine it, yes, yes I can, signora. It must be very beautiful."

"All of Europe is doing business there: the English, the Germans, the French, the Italians. Oh, the riches of the Sudanese coast, if you only knew..."

"I can imagine, signora."

"Africa, from the moment you reach the Suez Canal, Africa is...! Oh, Stefano, it's... a crossroads, a hive of activity, a—"

"Of course, of course, signora, but tell me, with the Moretta, aren't you afraid—"

"What? That when we arrive she will escape?"

"No, no, what I mean is—"

"Escape to go where, I ask you? She doesn't even know her own name!"

"What I mean to say is—"

"When the consul tried to help her find her family, she didn't even know the name of her village, she has no sense of family."

"I was thinking how difficult it will be for her to return to Sudan."

"Sudan or here, it's all the same, she'll be looking after the baby!"

"Signora, could I ask you something... I would never forgive myself if I didn't ask you... Tell me... Wouldn't you like to have her baptized? Have the Moretta baptized? Before you leave?"

"I'm very fond of you Stefano. You're stubborn and superstitious, but I'm very fond of you. You're the only person I'll miss in this country of scabious illiterates."

The rain thuds dully on the magnolia leaves and the drawing-room windows. The garden is very soon lost in a haze and there is no horizon. The thunder returns from the mountain like a lazy wildcat. It is suddenly almost dark. Stefano can hear Bakhita passing in the corridor with little Mimmina in her arms, their voices mingled, one so deep, the other delicate, like an intimate song. He feels like a dispossessed father. He feels he has been weak and has no rights. And so very sad. Maria has taken out her ledgers, Stefano's letters, blotting paper, ink, and a quill, he looks at the columns, the spidery scrawl, the dates and figures.

"Signora," he says wearily, "I should tell you that Giuseppe, my eldest son, is trying to teach the Moretta to read. Just a few letters. Nothing more. It's important."

"A few letters from the catechism?"

"No. From the alphabet."

"I'm teasing you!"

He would have liked to slip a pendant of the Virgin into the leather purse, but does not. Instead, he puts a little handful of this deep, dark Italian soil, this generous and accursed soil. He would have liked to write her a letter in which he told her that he loved her like his own daughter. Just those words, and perhaps a few of their memories too, in his home, around the family table, the dishes she tasted for the first time, those she cooked, her laughter that she brought to them, and the evening he sat down at the piano and she clapped in time to the music. Chiara had burst out laughing and *sorrellina* Moretta was ashamed and stopped immediately. He then started playing faster and glanced at Clementina, who quickly understood: She started clapping her hands and encouraged the children to do the same, and they all laughed at the incongruity of it, they had never clapped along to Mozart's "Turkish March" before. He would have written about the joy she brought into his house, and the respect he had for her, about everything he could see and the things he did not know: when she pulled down her sleeves to hide her scars, when she suddenly limped, when her slow serious eyes came to rest on pigheaded, snot-smeared street children, when she whispered incomprehensible words to Mimmina, when she picked up the stones people threw at her and looked at them sweetly before putting them back on the ground...He has so much to tell her, so much to write. But she understands neither writing nor Venetian. So he puts the leather purse in her hand, hugs her tightly in his brusque awkward way, and never mind about Parona Michieli, whispers in her ear, "I shall pray for you every day," and makes that furtive sign on her forehead, blessing her. And then he leaves, as miserable as a dog, he the exuberant local character goes home and, without even meaning to, limps like her, one foot here, the other over there, that vast Africa on whose threshold everyone is milling like children around a Christmas tree, more of them merchants than missionaries, true, and he will stay behind with the peasants who have no hope. And then out of nowhere he takes a turning, does not go home. With his halting stride he comes back into the village, goes all the way to the church. Climbs the narrow dusty wooden stairs, sits at the organ, and for her, for his little sister, almost his daughter, he plays "Ave Maria." Plays like this for a full hour, a slow solemn hour, so as not to hear the sound of the carriage taking her to the station. Not to think of the village watching her leave. This life coming to an end. He plays, and his mind is blank now, and then all of a sudden, he knows. People will say, not for the first time, that he's eccentric, harebrained. That doesn't matter. They will say, not for the first time, that he's a dreamer, an idealist. Maybe it's true. He will come into the church to play "Ave Maria" every day. Every day. And it will be his call to bring her back. Because he now knows, she will come back.

This is Sudan. Looking across at Sudan. A land. Detached from the land. Connecting the desert and the sea. The gateway to Africa. An island on which pilgrims stop on their way to Mecca, on the far side of the Red Sea, a sea whose coral is ripped out, whose shores are overrun with pitiful dhows and gigantic ships. People set sail for the Indies, the Americas, they speak Arabic and Turkish, Egyptian and English, they speak every language and, more than anything else, they speak of money. There are civilians and soldiers, governors and thieves, mosques and brothels, cafés, and all along the street, all through the day, markets. Because everyone is selling. And everything is for sale. Men, gum arabic, ostrich feathers, coal, elephant tusks, copal and incense, newly discovered riches, exportable riches. Some might think the world is opening up, making acquaintance with itself, expanding. It is in fact growing smaller, being broken up, hollowed out.

Bakhita arrives in Sudan in September 1886, eighteen months after leaving, and all her wounds reopen. This is the country of her ancestors, the country of her mother, the country of her color, her language, and her name. It is the country across which she traveled and that she does not recognize on any map. The country she survived but where she has no one to meet. From the hotel windows in Suakin, she watches. There it is, looking back at her, distant but also terribly close. By day the coastal strip is lost in mist, moisture hangs over it and the motionless sky leaves nothing to see. Her country is deep and isolated. Her country says nothing. By night the too-bright light of the city masks the stars, Suakin never sleeps, the island is always noisy and busy, intoxicated and dangerous, the shrieking of monkeys mingles with the cries of men, and it sounds as if the whole world is laughing. The stars are far away, only the moon is still here, shining above the city's brilliance, and Bakhita talks to it.

She is in this huge hotel as if in a lawless country and is aware of how vacuous this life of profit is, this life with no ties, no anchor other than the accounts books and the hotel's coffers. She does not know what to do with the tips men give her when she serves them their strong liquor and Turkish coffee. Has never known what to do with money. She left behind in Zianigo the tips that Parona Michieli's guests gave her when she served at receptions. She would thank them with lowered eyes and put the coins with the linen in her dresser, and then forget about them. She once heard a guest ask Augusto how much the Negress had cost him, and he, embarrassed, gave a reticent shrug, No, he would not discuss the rescue... And there in that drawing room was the knowing, admiring atmosphere that good society feels for discreetly wealthy men.

She does not leave the hotel, which is as Parona Michieli wants it. Sees nothing of the island. It is said to be as beautiful as it is dirty, as dangerous as it is powerful, still wild despite the rich traders' towering houses, it is said that the sun sets in the sea as if Allah's hand were diving into the waves, producing colors no one could ever name. Suakin is discussed like a living animal to be feared and tamed. There is talk of pilgrims in rags, contraband rifles, sharpened sabers, and big cats that prowl in people's houses at night. There is talk of the ghosts of the forty virgins, Abyssinian slaves pregnant by jinn, whose forty daughters founded the city, and who haunt its palaces. Talk of lost legends and a profitable future. The prevailing mood is of malice and misery.

She remembers the island. With little Indir nestled against her, in that stopgap inn, the smell of camels and leather, of urine and kelp, and the red soil she brought with her all the way to Genoa, after the days in the desert. Remembers the wild dogs and their fights on the port's muddy shores. Unveiled girls outside of inns, their eyes as empty as cloudless skies. Women selling old fish individually, and lepers sitting under palm trees, beside baskets of spices and dried coral. Remembers all the Sudanese people torn from their land.

When she is not serving in the bar, she takes Mimmina for walks in the garden, and it reminds her of the harems, those closed communities, the dovecotes, henhouses, the walls and terraces, and slave quarters. Here too the staff goes home to sleep at night in low-slung non-mixed houses, where the children have the eyes of old men and a longing to rest. She sees pregnant girls, and very young boys with that air of sad submission, who are told they are the lucky ones. To have masters. A roof over their heads. A bowl for food. And water. Who are told to be good and servile. And she knows, without looking at them, what each of them has lost, and the loneliness that will be theirs for all time. Because it is here, intact, eternal. Loneliness. Bakhita is not beaten now. She does not sleep in the slave quarters. But planted deep inside her like a stake is her need for something different. A different light. A little of the love she felt with Stefano and Clementina, a love that was so unlike her childhood but had the same music to it. She keeps her hands in the pockets of her apron, when she longs to reach out her arms, generously, with the full force of her youth. She is held back at night when she knows that there is a light, so close by but she cannot turn to it. She has never forgotten that consoling voice, the earth telling her this was not right. *Abda.* It was not right, and it was not her fault. So there must be something else for her.

Mimmina calls to her from over by the small fountain in the middle of the garden. She cries "Mama!" and Bakhita does not have time to scold her with a "You must say Bakhita, not Mama!" before the child is in her arms. They laugh together, happy and surprised. Mimmina just walked for the first time! She took her first steps toward her nanny. She breaks away from her arms, wants to do it again. Sets off, falls, picks herself up, crying and laughing, dirties her clothes, crushes flowers, and frightens the cats. She is afraid of nothing, studies the world now that she is standing. Bakhita smiles at her and knows. Today her little Mimmina learned to walk. Soon she will have to call her Alice. And Alice will never make the mistake of calling her "mama." The call of the muezzin rings out across the sky like a hoarse, lilting instruction, Bakhita looks at the child and knows she will not grow up here. Alice will go to school, like all white children. She will leave the garden. Leave Suakin. And what of her? Where will *she* live? To whom will she belong? She looks at this child, whom she saved from death and who is now splashing her hands in the fountain, proud and upright on her little legs. She has all the vigor and authority of someone discovering a new freedom.

Bakhita lives like this for nine months, in this mood of uncertainty, this travelers' hotel where, despite her eighteen-year-old's beauty, despite the color of her skin, the men she serves do not touch her. She does not lower her eyes so much. When she recognizes an insult in their voices, she eyes them fleetingly. Dares to, for a few seconds, and there is neither defiance nor anger in her eyes, but any man who makes inappropriate moves toward her gets a look that says, "I've seen all this before." And she remains an enigma. Submissiveness coupled with strength. This is what intrigues them, as if this slave girl, this Bakhita, were somehow out of place. Her master is a Christian, she will never be his wife or his concubine and does not appear to have any children by him. They see her looking after the master's daughter, sometimes even when she serves at the bar the child is in her arms, like a monkey on a tree. This slave girl has a status all her own. She speaks little, and her voice is as deep as a dark cave, she is a barmaid but dares to move with the slow confidence of those who are sure of themselves. She avoids men and takes an interest in children. She always has a scrap of bread or a piece of fruit in her pocket to give them, and she also makes some gesture, a hand on their head, a stroke of their cheek. Her mistress ought to reprimand her, these children are all contagious, hanging about outside the hotel gardens with their begging and their skin diseases, clustering around the gates like flies on sweat. The gardener chases them away, back they come. They are hungry, but she feeds them in vain, because they multiply as quickly as they die.

Bakhita lives in a time of uncertainty, but time keeps ticking by, the masters are busy doing their sums, and eventually these sums produce results. The results for which they have been working day and night. Success. No one tells her anything, but she knows, and because she understands some Venetian, she overhears conversations between Maria and Augusto. There is a buzz of panic and hope in the air, a life change starting with the nervous excitement of major decisions. Mimmina can feel it too, and however much the *parona* insists the child is teething, Bakhita knows that is not what makes her cry at night. But the nightmares. She knows, they have the same nightmares. Of steep sands, tall dunes circling them with wooden stakes all around, and there is no way out, no way of seeing the horizon, she and Mimmina are trapped there, within these walls, and they stay there. Motionless. Anxious and confused.

And then one day there are suitcases. Their open jaws filling with the mistress's and Mimmina's clothes. They are returning to Italy, they need to sell the estate and come back, because it has now been decided: The Michieli family will move to Suakin permanently. Bakhita has guessed as much, of course. The hotel is still just as busy and Parona Michieli reigns supreme, she is no longer the taunted foreigner in Zianigo, being foreign here means being African. Everyone else is at home. Bakhita's fears are reawakened. She is helpless and determined, there is a struggle between her fear and her survival, and just as she implored the consul, she asks Parona Michieli to take her to Italy with her.

"Too expensive, Bakhita."

She offers her tips. Maria throws her head back and laughs. She falls to her knees.

"Don't do that!" Maria explodes.

She stands up again, kisses the *parona*'s hands. Is slapped. For the first time by Parona Michieli. Only a few years ago she would hardly have felt this slap, an everyday forerunner to whippings and insults. Today, though, the violence of it rocks her life and reminds her that she is less than a servant, a slave. Straight after the slap, she and Maria have the same instinct, they look into the garden where Mimmina is. The child saw nothing, she is sitting with her back to them. But this is where everything is playing out. Around the child. Maria wants to make the journey alone with her daughter. She could leave the child with her nanny and spare her two exhausting crossings, but she wants to have this experience, wants to be alone with her daughter. She can picture herself returning triumphantly to Zianigo with her child in her arms or, better still, holding her hand and walking by her side. She is very fond of Bakhita but resents her, as the weak resent anyone to whom they owe a great deal. Bakhita watches Mimmina playing, beating her little drum. She lowers her eyes.

"You will do very well, *parona*," she says.

The steamboat for Genoa leaves on June 21, 1887. Maria asks Bakhita to carry the suitcases and come down to the port with them. When Bakhita steps out of the hotel she is struck again by the violence of Suakin, teeming with hidden lives and visible destitution, the threat and power of the place is in the air she breathes. Her eyes are burned by the clarity of the sky, and the sea draws her like a pool of silver warmed in the sun. Beyond the city's swarming streets and tall houses there are wastelands and arid fields, the wildness of uncultivated spaces, there are forgotten cemeteries and deserted hangars, boat carcasses, coal stores, and above all the memory of the thousands of slaves from the most intensive period of the slave trade, and Bakhita can feel it: The earth quivers with it, the life of stolen people. *Abid.* Unjust. Unjust. Unjust... She walks behind the *parona,* who holds her daughter close, dressed all in white as if for a ceremony, and it seems a shame because surely the *parona* knows that the coal will make quick work of dirtying these unsuitable clothes? She too has dressed in white, and she looks like a bride holding a child to be baptized. Mimmina looks over her mother's shoulder and talks to Bakhita, sends her words and dribbles, kisses and funny faces, Bakhita is annoyed with herself for not explaining again that they are to be parted, she can see the child has not realized it. She knows what it is like. Leaving the person you love. She spent the night watching her sleep and whispering to her quietly.

When they reach the port there is the usual air of panic and brutality, as if everyone were afraid of losing his or her place, not only on the boat but in the world too, as if their lives were being played out here. Perhaps because they are saying their goodbyes, for now or forever, there is a frisson of heartbreak on the quayside, the footbridge, and the decks. Bakhita does not know whether the *parona* will let her say goodbye to Mimmina, whether she will allow the slave to embrace her child in public. She hands the suitcases to the porter, and Maria turns to her. She wants to be kind. A great lady with nothing to be ashamed of.

"I'm relying on you to look after the bar, you know, Moretta?"

"Yes, *parona*."

From her mother's arms, Mimmina tries to grab Bakhita's hat, and Bakhita steps back slightly, when in fact she wants to move closer and take her in her arms.

"Say goodbye to Bakhita, Mimmina!"

Mimmina opens and closes her little hand.

"Blow her a kiss!"

The child blows a kiss. Her mother turns around and walks away. Bakhita did not have time to kiss her. She watches them move off in the crowd and stays there, upright and idiotic, jostled and insulted, can no longer make out anything or anyone in the heat of the crowd, is knocked, asked to move aside, totters under the harsh sun. And over and above the savagery and incoherence of it all she suddenly hears the cry of the child she knows as if she were her own daughter. It is Mimmina screaming, she knows it. She thinks of the song of separation that never made any difference, all those women watching their children leave, and she stays behind like them, silent and with no rights, but Mimmina's screams are growing louder, and soon she hears her coughing too, and then choking with rage, the juddering sobs of hysteria. Bakhita clutches her chest. This hurts her, too.

"A tantrum! She's having such a tantrum!"

Parona Michieli is standing right in front of her, and Mimmina throws herself into Bakhita's arms.

"Yes, *parona*, a tantrum."

And Bakhita hugs the child so tightly it seems she might turn and run away with her.

"It's incredible how willful she's become!"

There is a note of reproach in the *parona*'s voice, along with fear and a huge question: And what am I to do now?

"I don't have money for the fare."

"No, *parona*."

"I didn't buy you a ticket."

"No, *parona*."

"And you don't even have a suitcase."

"That doesn't matter... *Parona*... the suitcase..."

Exhausted and trusting, Mimmina falls asleep in Bakhita's arms. She has stopped coughing at last, the choking is over. She is sweating and her white dress is already stained. Bakhita can feel the *parona*'s terrible fear, does not look away, implores her with her eyes, and her sweat trickles from her hair down her neck, from her neck down her back. Maria looks at her daughter. And then, as if defeated, she murmurs, "It would be a shame to wake her."

And that is how Bakhita stepped onto the footbridge to the boat. She held in her arms a willful little girl who, without even realizing it, had just done what Bakhita did for her eighteen months earlier: She had saved her life.

Ave Maria, gratia plena . . . Dominus tecum benedictis . . . benedicta! Ave Maria, gratia plena . . .

Morning and evening, kneeling at the foot of her bed, Bakhita recites this prayer with Mimmina. The *parona* insisted on it. She taught them the Ave Maria, the Paternoster, and the Gloria. In Latin. Once the estate, the house, furniture, and livestock were put up for sale, Maria started wondering how her daughter would grow up in Africa. She consulted the doctor, and the priest while she was at it. The doctor recommended a dose of quinine in the morning and the priest the three essential prayers, twice a day. Paternoster, Ave Maria, Gloria. With constant repetition, and although she does not understand a single word, Bakhita doggedly learns the prayers, and it is not only morning and evening, she also recites them all through the day to remember them. People in Zianigo say the Moretta has grown pious, not baptized but pious, because when they come across her, she can be heard mumbling: "*Pater noster, qui es in caelis,*" "*Gloria in excelsis Deo,*" or "*Ave Maria, gratia plena.*" They no longer throw stones at her, they cross themselves slowly as she passes and whisper that it is a miracle, and even Maria Michieli is seen in a different light, they might almost like this foreigner now that she is to leave and they will no longer see her. Bakhita does not know why the *parona* asks her to say these words morning and evening, but despite her problems remembering them when she does not understand them, she likes this ritual that sits well with her contemplation of the day ahead and her secrets at night. And then there is Mimmina's little voice, Mimmina whom she is teaching something, their connection is growing stronger still, in the hard work of it and the forbidden explosive laughter, yes forbidden, because these words seem so serious, and in front of the *parona* they always have to recite them very seriously, while she listens with exasperated weariness.

Oddly enough, if there is one person who is unimpressed by this, it is Stefano. Bakhita's return was a double shock for him, the shock of surprise and of a revelation: Not in vain had he played the "Ave Maria" on the church organ every day he was in Zianigo. He prayed for her, intently, and they were bound together by unfailing filial love. But he is shocked to hear her recite the sacred words of these prayers without understanding them. So she can be made to say whatever you like, without any explanation, like a well-trained dog performing a trick? He thinks she deserves better and is frustrated that all she knows of Venetian are everyday words. It is Clementina who tries to calm him one evening and may have found a solution to his torment.

"You should be delighted, Stefano," she says.

"Be delighted? When I hear her reciting like a parrot? She says '*Sed libera nosam lo*' instead of '*nos a malo.*' *A malo,* Clementina! *Malo!* Evil! She knows what evil is, she really does, but she doesn't know how to pronounce the word."

"You shouldn't think of it like that."

"It hurts me to hear it! Yes, evil! *A malo! A malo!*"

"Calm down. You'd do better to make the most of the fact *la* Michieli has lowered her guard and talk to our little sister."

"And what am I supposed to do, then? Translate from Latin into Venetian? Are you making fun of me?"

Clementina goes over to her dresser, takes out something very small, and hands it to her husband.

"Give it to our little Moretta sister."

He looks at his wife in amazement and is suddenly calm. "You think so?"

"I'm sure of it."

"Won't you miss it?"

"No. It would make me happy."

"But it was your father's—"

"Stefano! Do as I say, won't you, just this once..."

He watches Bakhita as she sits in the garden, keeping an eye on Mimmina. The child is playing with Melia and Chiara at the foot of the big oak tree. Little Alice has grown so, she is thin, still fragile, but there is a life force in her, and she is such a happy child that she is recognized by her laugh, Mimmina's laughter is like another person's footsteps, it is what announces that she is there. She has the happiness of children who are never afraid, always protected.

On this particular afternoon, Bakhita is watching her, with her knitting in her hand because she never sits and does nothing, her hands are always occupied with something, and Stefano thinks she would look like any young nanny to Zianigo's wealthier families were it not for her color, and her calm, something young Italian girls do not have, and also, if he is entirely honest, her mystery. She has the slow sad expression of women who cannot be carefree, a deep smile with a distant goodness to it. Her beauty does not attract the young Italian men, her African culture is a natural barrier. She is not a foreigner among them, nor even a stranger. She is a strangeness. He sits down beside her, and she makes room for him and points to Mimmina.

"Happy!" she says.

"Yes. Your little Mimmina is happy. Very happy..."

She turns to look at him discreetly, questioningly, aware of his embarrassment, nothing can be hidden from her, she knows. From the way he sat down, the sound of his voice, she knows. He has something to say to her. She will wait. She has the patience of another era, which he, the ebullient Stefano, finds almost irritating. He hesitates. Waves a few times to his daughters, turns to the Moretta, and laughs a little, his hands spread, as if to say "They play nicely together, don't they?," and this Italian gesticulation is something the Moretta learned very early on. Stefano looks at the sky, clouds are coming in from behind the hills, a slight chill settles in the smell of cut grass and wild roses. Bakhita sets down her knitting and goes to put a cardigan on Mimmina. When she comes to sit back down, he is reaching one arm toward her, his fist closed. She stops and waits. Studies this outstretched fist, unsurprised. Then he opens his hand.

"There," he says. "Clementina gave it to me for you can you see it's a crucifix it's our Lord Jesus Christ who died on the cross for our sins he is the Son of the Father the Son of God and through him we will all be saved of course I know that Parona Michieli refuses to let me talk to you of religion which is why you need to keep this a secret but I can't hold my tongue any longer you see because if you are left in ignorance of faith I'm so afraid for you you're not even baptized what will become of you I mean I'm not saying this to worry you that's not my intention but here this is Clementina's crucifix it was given to her by her father who is now dead God rest his soul but she is happy I mean really really happy to give it to you."

He puts the small wooden and metal crucifix in her hand. Then jumps to his feet and bellows with completely uncalled-for vehemence, "Melia, I've told you a thousand times not to make your sister climb this tree, *mamma mia!*"

Bakhita watches this clearly emotional man who has just told her something incomprehensible but apparently very important. Something he could not keep to himself. And has given to her. A secret. She understands this much. He has given her a secret. She looks at the crucifix in her palm. He said "Clementina" several times. It is a gift from Clementina. She has seen this before, in Italian homes, at crossroads of country lanes, in the cemetery where Parona Michieli's babies are buried, seen this cross with this man on it. She once stopped beside a stone cross at whose feet a faded little bouquet provided a slightly mournful splash of color. She looked at that nailed man. Did not know they did this to slaves in Italy, too, and wondered why this particular man was depicted more than others. And she now wonders why this same man is nestled in her hand. Is it a warning? A protective talisman? She looks at it and then touches it with one finger, the small wooden cross and the metal body, such a thin man, with his head tipped skyward. She remembers the slaves who were nailed to trees as punishment or to stop anyone else profiting from them. This man is white. He is Italian. She is suddenly choked with sobs. She has abandoned everyone she loves. Kishmet will never be saved, and Binah could have died during a beating or been shut away in a harem. Tears spill down her face, her well-fed servant's face. She swears to herself that when she returns to Suakin, because they will go back there soon, she will help her people, she does not know how but she will do more than love Mimmina and be loved by her. More than serve men in the bar and hand out bread to street children at the hotel's gate. She is nineteen, she has been an adult for so many years! And she has done nothing in reciprocation for what she has been given, for her life that has been saved. Stefano sits back down beside her. He looks at her and cannot help kissing her, two kisses, resounding kisses of gratitude, one on each wet cheek of his little Moretta sister.

"She was illuminated!" he will tell Clementina that evening.

"Illuminated?"

"Indeed she was! There she was in tears, holding her breast with one hand and your crucifix with the other!"

"What on earth did you tell her?"

"Everything! I told her everything!"

"What about her, what did she say?"

"What did she say?"

"Yes, what did she say?"

"Well, she...she was crying, she didn't say anything, she just cried! She'd had the revelation!"

She had not had the revelation. An intuition, at the very most. The feeling, once again, that she was standing at a door and could not open it. She hides this object whose purpose she does not understand. It is the first time she has hidden anything, that she has a sense of possession. She is sure the *parona* would take it from her, cannot explain this, just knows it, and that is enough for her to hide the thing among her shawls and take it out only once Mimmina is asleep. She takes out the crucified slave and talks about him to the darkness, but the darkness does not reply, it is filled with the song of courting toads, the brawling of drunks outside, and the whickering of horses from the stables under her windows. The horses will soon be sold. Like the property and the land along with it. She will leave all this. This Italy of extreme poverty, whose peasants barely live beyond the age of thirty-five and whose young flee in their thousands for countries farther away even than Sudan. Giuseppe, Stefano's eldest son, explained this to her. Just as the consul once had, he spread out a large sheet of paper with lands and seas on it. That is how he is trying to teach her to read, with the letters for the countries. It is very difficult. And she has not managed to remember *A* for Australia, *B* for Brazil, or *C* for Canada, these places of exile for Italians without work. She is as black as ink. But cannot write. And everyone around her speaks new languages, their words like the countries on the map, shifting and far away, she cannot associate them with any of the feelings inside her, and shuts herself away in this uncertainty.

It is August, the *parona* is in a terrible mood, Stefano comes almost every day to conclude the sale of the estate with her. Negotiations with the buyer drag on and on, and the whole thing regularly goes back to the drawing board. Maria is tearing her hair out and telegraphs frantically to Augusto, who is growing impatient back in Suakin. The suitcases and trunks are ready. The furniture covered with white sheets. The paintings and better sets of porcelain sold. There are no curtains at the windows now. The floors are bare, the carpets rolled up at the far end of rooms. And the months go by. It is nearly fall. The buyer is always contesting some figure, some document, asks to speak to the master of the premises and not to his steward or his wife, this is a serious matter, involving substantial sums, the climate shifts, winter comes early, the carpets are unrolled, firewood is brought in, the negotiations have come to a standstill. Toward the end of the year, in November 1888, Maria Michieli decides, on Stefano's advice, to set off for Suakin and put the papers before Augusto so that he can sign the most important of them. The trip is expensive, she will leave alone with Mimmina, who is nearly three and coped well with the first crossing. She cannot decide whether to sell Bakhita to a wealthy family in Mirano, Zianigo's nearest small town. Bakhita is well-known there and widely admired, having been seen with Mimmina so frequently, serious and hardworking, a gem who needs no salary, never takes leave, even works at night and, as she speaks little Venetian, is as discreet as a stuffed squirrel, and tough with it, as these Negro girls always are. But it is precisely the instant enthusiasm of Mirano's bourgeoisie that persuades Maria not to sell the Moretta. Still, what is she to do with her during her absence?

She puts the question to Stefano, who cannot believe his ears. Providence has come knocking at his door! His prayers are being answered!

Bakhita will at last be delivered from *la* Michieli's clutches. He has a window of opportunity and feels like a little boy about to catch a rare butterfly, it takes a great deal of skill and speed, a great deal of calm and assurance. In the first instance, he suggests the Moretta comes to stay with him, Clementina and the children would be thrilled at the prospect, she will sleep with the youngest two, Melia and Chiara, who know her so well. He asks for no money for her keep, and when Maria returns to sell the estate once and for all, she can simply come to fetch her slave from him and take her with her. Maria has complete faith in Stefano. And says yes.

But Stefano lied. He does not intend to take Bakhita into his own home. He lied but does not feel he has committed a sin. An evil for the good. Because what this man wants, this man who is as pious as he is stubborn, what he wants is his little Moretta sister's salvation.

It is a serious matter. What Bakhita needs is specialists. People who know what they are doing. Giuseppe can keep on about *A* for Australia and *B* for Brazil, but she has never written a single letter nor read a single word. As for the crucifix, there is no knowing what influence it might have over her. When they recite the Benedicite before meals, she waits patiently, head bowed, for them to finish, and however many times he ends with a flamboyant sign of the cross, she never makes the connection with the crucifix he gave her. Worse than that, he is being taunted! His daughters burst out laughing when after his "Amen" last Sunday he made such an expansive emphatic sign of the cross that he jabbed Clementina in the eye with his elbow. Yes, specialists, that's what she needs. He immediately thinks of the Canossian Daughters of Charity who run the Institute of the Catechumens in Venice. Like other Italian congregations, these nuns teach adults and prepare them for baptism, and take in abandoned children. Sister Magdalene of Canossa, who founded the order, was born a marquessa at the turn of the nineteenth century, and opened the institute in Venice to its congregation in 1831. The institute is as old as La Serenissima itself, having been set up to pass on the Catholic Truth to tradesman and soldiers who reached its shores, and to baptize them.

It is here, then, in the Canossian institute in Venice, that Stefano would like Bakhita to live, for as long as it takes Maria Michieli to travel to Suakin and back. So when Bakhita herself returns to Sudan, she will be catechized and baptized, and he will be able to sleep in peace. Like his plan for adoption, he becomes obsessed with, tormented by this idea of baptism with the Canossians, particularly as he knows how averse Maria Michieli is to all things religious. He decides to lie once again.

"Something has occurred to me, signora... On the subject of the Moretta—"

"Won't you have her now?"

"Yes. Of course I will. But I was really thinking of you. You are such a worthy woman."

"Yes."

"An exemplary mother, and so brave—"

"What are you saying?"

"The Moretta... Is she useful to you at the hotel, over there in Africa?"

"I've already told you I won't burden myself with her on this journey, it's too expensive, I'm leaving her here."

"What I mean to say, signora, is when she returns to Africa, the Moretta will help you in the hotel again, won't she?"

"Very much so!"

"Mimmina will grow up. The Moretta will become more and more useful to you in the bar."

"Naturally."

"Well, believe me, a little education will be essential."

"Education? What education?"

"Um... Being able to read. Write. Count."

"Why does a waitress need to be able to read?"

"When you receive mail, orders, deliveries, if the Moretta could read, it would be more helpful than you can imagine."

"Listen, Stefano, I've known you ten years, so tell me what you're really thinking, because I have a lot to be getting on with. And much more important things to think about than whether Bakhita will ever be able to decipher an envelope or a case of whiskey."

Stefano then broaches the subject of the Institute of the Catechumens, a place where the Moretta would not only be instructed but also overseen, unlike in his household, where she would be coveted as a servant, well, he and Clementina would not be able to watch her night and day, she is nineteen, it really is a bit of a risk, Lord alone knows what might come into her head, thoughts of freedom, who knows? People are not as submissive as all that, and neither is the Moretta, she might be subject to all sorts of influences. He cannot quite forgive himself this last argument. Once again he allowed himself to get carried away. Well, if it struck home that's all that matters... But Maria Michieli is no fool. Stefano's arguments may be fair, but she knows that the sisters in this institute in Venice will talk to the Moretta of religion from morning till night. She also knows that, apart from the most elementary aspects of everyday life, the girl still does not understand Venetian, she can scarcely run an errand and recites her prayers like a list of vegetables for a recipe. Even so, it would be tempting to keep the girl shut away somewhere during her absence. She asks for a few days to consider the idea, she will telegraph Augusto. And give it some thought.

Against all expectations, she agrees. Stefano, for once, is at a loss for words. Asks her to repeat herself. She repeats herself. She agrees for the Moretta to be placed with the Canossian sisters in Venice for the duration of her trip to Suakin. But on one condition: that he himself takes responsibility for the process. And quite a process it is. Bakhita is an adult but, as a slave, has no status, no papers of any description, not even a purchase receipt because she was a gift to Maria Michieli. For administrative purposes, there is nothing to prove she exists. Stefano will have to go to the highest level, to his most influential connections to plead her case. He speaks of the need to convert the infidels, of how Africa can be saved by Africa, a slogan that is *en vogue.* He speaks of the prodigal son, the black Virgin, writes to wealthy ecclesiasts and high-ranking local government officers, reestablishes contact with a cousin whose sister took holy orders, and eventually secures the agreement of the institute's prior and meets Mother Superior, Madre Luigia Bottissela.

Nothing is explained to Bakhita. Melia and Chiara keep telling her they are going to take her to the *collegio,* to school, but this word means nothing to her. She knows she is not to be included in the trip to Suakin but will soon be living there, and for the rest of her life. She will go to join the Michielis. She also knows that Mimmina will grow up, and she is bound to change masters then. This period without violence is surely only a respite in her life as a slave. She obeys, without knowing where she is being taken, and even with the people she loves, she is always a little lost. She lives in the elastically expanded time of uncertainty, which is both very slow and very concentrated, time that lurches forward in successive leaps, like a rutted path, and then stretches out into uncharted monotony. She can see that Stefano is happy, happy for her. He loves her and is protecting her. But she does not know from what.

All six of them go to Venice: Maria Michieli, Stefano, Melia and Chiara, and Mimmina, in Bakhita's arms. Venice is not far from Zianigo, some twenty miles, they take a sluggish train that stops wherever a passenger requests it to and makes so much noise there is no point trying to talk, and they all keep up the restrained, slightly aloof behavior of major outings. They travel through the countryside like six peasants in their Sunday best who have never taken the train before. Mimmina has fallen asleep on Bakhita's lap, and Bakhita protects her head from the train's jolting, thinking she will soon say goodbye to the child when she leaves for Suakin with her mother. "A few days is very soon, there will be no more Sundays together," is how Stefano explained it to her, Sunday being the only point of reference on which he alighted. Mimmina is breathing against her chest, her deep inhalations, her abandon, these are the true rhythm of Bakhita's life. This symbiotic, trusting love. She has taught her everything a mother teaches her child, they have contemplated beauty together, watching the new day dawn and the old day finish, gazed at the sky as if it were some superior being, watched from the safety of their bedroom as the fury of storms transformed the landscape, then they opened the window when the sun came back out and the smells were as keen as a piece of fruit sliced open with a knife. Bakhita has taught Mimmina to call animals with brief noises and clicks of her tongue, and when horses and donkeys come over to her, she puts her hand on their submissive heads and says, "*Grazie*," just as Bakhita does, because we must always thank animals that work for men.

In the train on the way to Venice, neither of them has grasped that they are to be parted. This is an outing together, to Venice, where Bakhita came once long ago, when Mimmina was six months old, she remembers the train across the sea, the desperately poor streets, fishermen's boats, and women drawing water from wells on small squares where people sold herbs and bread. Poverty is the same everywhere. She soon recognizes it. It is a look in people's eyes that nothing can shift, a great weariness. Barefoot children. Women carrying too much and men who keep their anger locked away. And in Venice, as in Zianigo, people were afraid of her, and in the stinking backstreets that never saw the sunlight, she held little Mimmina tightly to her and breathed in her sweet baby smell.

Stefano rings the bell at the institute, a long yellowish two-story building with low windows, right at the far end of Venice, at 108 Dorsoduro, on the left bank of the Grand Canal. Bakhita is holding Mimmina's hand, the child woke the moment the train stopped, and together they crossed the wooden bridges of this city set down in the middle of the sea like Suakin, with its skies torn open by domes and the masts of ships.

The door to the institute opens, Stefano introduces himself to the *portinaia,* the doorkeeper sister who invites them in. Bakhita is not familiar with these sisters whose habits are not like those worn by the nuns she sees in the street, moving about in groups and veiled like women in the East, these sisters wear a shawl over their robes and a traditional headdress like the local women. The little party is shown into a long cold room whose walls and ceiling are covered in dark wood, the vast hearth is empty, there is a large table, a sofa, a few chairs along the wall, but they all stand in silence, Bakhita notices the crucifix on the wall, a pale Christ with blood all over his face. She does not know she is in the visiting room. Does not know that her life has just changed as radically as the day her two captors took her from her village.

In that visiting room Maria Michieli has a lengthy conversation with Luigia Bottissela, Mother Superior, who is soon joined by other sisters, all called "Madre," all attentive and disguising their shock at the sight of Bakhita, this young woman who is so astonishingly and entirely black. They talk quietly, earnestly, with brief nods of the head, full of diligent understanding. Stefano, hat in hand, hardly intervenes, leaves Signora Michieli to explain, lay out Bakhita's documents, her clothes. Everything goes as expected. Bakhita meanwhile, stands a little way away with the children, as befits a servant. He can tell she has no idea what is going on and has a fierce sense of betrayal. He would like to go over and talk to her, but knows he must not intervene, Clementina told him so the day before, "Leave *la* Michieli to manage the situation, exactly as if it were her decision. You hold your tongue for once, Stefano!" He stands, silent and anxious, how will Bakhita interpret this change? Will she think he doesn't want her in his house? If only he could tell her the battles he fought in order for her to be here at this institute today. Eventually, Maria comes over to Bakhita.

"You are to stay here. This is your home."

There is silence. Then Bakhita looks at Stefano, who did not think the information would be imparted like this, so bluntly. He can see she does not understand. That she feels singled out, isolated. Panic steals across her face. She clutches Mimmina a little more tightly. He comes closer, smiling, slowly weaving together the words "Suakin," "leaving," and "home." She needs to know that the options are leaving for Sudan or staying here. Now. With the *Madri* who have other young girls like her in their care. The word Bakhita picks out is "Madre."

"Madre?" she asks. "Mama?"

Mother Superior comes over to her, smiles at her, and welcomes her. Bakhita looks into this old woman's eyes and instantly sees who she is. She is good and knows many things. Bakhita smiles too, and inclines her head. But she has not set Mimmina down, and Stefano can see that *la* Michieli is pretending not to have noticed. With a sigh of relief, Maria Michieli thanks the nun, adjusts her hat, and asks the three little girls to say their goodbyes. Mimmina softly buries her face in Bakhita's neck. Maria comes over to them, looks her nanny in the eye. It is an order.

Bakhita knew she would be parted from Mimmina for the duration of her trip to Suakin, but she did not know it would be now. A feeling of falling once again, of being reacquainted with loneliness, like an ice-cold cloak. She takes her pain inside her like a dagger to her stomach and gently sets the child down. Nudges her slightly toward her mother, who is waiting. Mimmina comes to take refuge in her arms again. Maria yanks the child toward herself. She won't give in to a tantrum this time, not here, in front of all these nuns, she'll show them what a mother is. "You're coming!" she hisses between her teeth, and pulls the child by the hand. Mimmina wails that she is hurting her, so Maria picks her up brusquely, imperiously. "Now you be quiet!" The child howls and sobs. Bakhita steps back with her eyes pinned on her all the time. There is already nothing she can do for her. Not even console her.

Stefano is rooted to the spot, Melia and Chiara have also started to cry, while Mimmina is reaching out for Bakhita and wailing. Her cries echo around the visiting room, Maria teeters between anger and humiliation. The nuns watch, slightly horrified, and try to intervene, some fetch water and a little treat for the child, others pull up chairs, sit themselves down, but Maria cannot keep hold of Mimmina who arches her back and pummels her mother's knees with her furious feet, her whole body straining toward Bakhita, whose eyes glisten with tears, the nuns can see, they are confronted with genuine pain, and Signora Michieli can complain all she likes of tantrums and childish behavior, the nuns can see this is something quite else. An awkward tension settles over the room, like an unvoiced altercation. Mother Superior murmurs that, alas, she will not be able to keep the Moretta. She must go with her little mistress. Maria agrees reluctantly, this is yet another defeat but yes, she will have to take her daughter's nanny to Africa or the separation could threaten the child's health. This ever-present fear of death, the emotional blackmail, and at the end of the day, she's never alone with her daughter! Bakhita listens without understanding what has happened, but she can see the fear and pain on every face. Is it her fault? She said nothing. Did nothing. Is prepared to obey. But if only she could be allowed to console Mimmina... Stefano jumps to his feet, this time he *will* intervene, he cannot accept that their little Moretta sister will not be baptized, cannot accept that he has come so close to the goal and that it is all falling apart now, he will save her at all costs!

"That's impossible!"

Everyone turns to look at him, the only man among them, now almost forgotten.

"Stefano, surely you can see my daughter needs her nanny. It would be cruel to separate them."

"Yes, signora, it would be cruel to separate them, I agree, it would be cruel."

"Well then, let's go and let's have no more talk about it, I'm exhausted. All that work for nothing!"

Coats are adjusted, and hats, Maria Michieli gives Bakhita a nod which means "Off you go, then!" but Bakhita does not move. Inert, silent, she just stands there, unsure which order she should obey. And now Stefano enters the fray again.

"There's a solution!" he cries. "It's so obvious and so...practical. For everyone."

Maria Michieli sighs and looks over at the nuns, as if to say, "Don't mind him," and the door is opened for them. Stefano stands in her way.

"Little Alice can stay here while you make the trip to Suakin, signora," he says. "Leave her here. She will be taught too. When you come back she will know all sorts of things, children learn fast."

"Go to Africa without my daughter?"

"Don't subject her to such a tiring trip..."

Maria is at a loss for words. People always make a fool of her. Always imply her child can't possibly live with her. She is a mother with empty hands. All her best intentions are in vain. In this moment of astonishment, Mimmina takes refuge in Bakhita's arms. Silence again. No more sniffling sounds from the child whom Bakhita soothes with tender words, stroking her neck. Melia and Chiara come over to her and clutch their "little sister's" tunic, shaken by the scene, by the altercation between adults, but most of all by their father's emotion, he loses his usual authority when he talks to *la* Michieli.

Bakhita does not realize it but she looks like her own mother now. A tree with its branches. With these children clinging to her, she is beautiful, full of a generous beauty and a profound humanity. And Mother Superior sees this.

"How could the child stay here, Signor Checchini?" she asks. "She cannot live with the abandoned children nor with the unbaptized adults."

But when she asks this, she already has an answer. She knows it is not for her to supply it. Nor for Signor Checchini. The answer must come from Signora Michieli. The poor woman who understands none of this. The powerless mother.

And in her terrible, stealthy, guilty fear, Maria Michieli leaves her daughter with her nanny. She will land alone on the shores of a country that, without her child, already feels like an aborted dream.

On November 29, 1888, Bakhita and Mimmina both entered the Institute of the Catechumens in Venice. Stefano personally paid Alice Michieli's fees, the sum of one lira a day, and as he had done for his little Moretta sister, he handled the administrative issues and obtained the relevant papers, which was no mean feat, because this was certainly the very first time a baptized child would live among the catechumens with her black nanny.

On that November day, when the *portinaia* closed the door behind the Moretta and the child, not one of them could know that Bakhita had finally come home.

On the first day, Bakhita waits to be given orders. Imagining that here, as everywhere else, she will be serving masters. With Mimmina by her side, she will be doing housework, washing, cooking, gardening, sewing, and embroidery, whatever is asked of her. But nothing is asked of her on the first day. She wonders whether Parona Michieli explained properly. Slave. *Abda*. Do the nuns know what that means? She prostrates herself at Mother Superior's feet as Westerners do, upper body bent forward, forehead to the ground, hands absolutely flat. But Mother Superior pulls her to her feet with a smile. Baffling.

In the afternoon she simply sits in the cloisters where Mimmina plays fivestones and hopscotch, which Bakhita asks her to do quietly because there is a peculiar gentleness in this place, one she is trying to understand. The cloisters are unusually clean and calm. The little recesses in the walls are adorned with statues and ivy, rather straggly olive trees grow alongside oleanders with no blooms and lemon trees with no fruit at this time of year; red leaves caught in the Venice wind roll over the paving stones. Watering cans stand in line beside a pair of shears and a broom, everything apparently in its rightful place, everything neat and precise. The silence is broken only by a bell marking out the hours, a delicate sound compared to the city's heavy church bells that Bakhita can hear beyond the institute's walls. The city, which is so near and so far. This place is a shelter, she can sense it, a refuge. It takes her a while to realize there is not a single man's voice. Not a single shout. And apart from the languid cats on the roof, no animals either.

A stone balcony runs above the cloisters, and on one side of the quadrangle, over two floors there are rows of tiny, blue-shuttered windows, all identical and symmetrical. But the windows are silent. The afternoon is mild and deserted. Every now and then, a nun passes through the cloisters and tilts her head toward them, Bakhita can see they all do their best to hide their shock at the sight of her. She smiles shyly, spreads her hands, a gesture that implies a fatalistic, "Oh yes, I'm black. Very black. That's just the way it is. I'm sorry." And she can see their embarrassment, and the pink in their pallid cheeks. Only one risks a kindly little laugh at the sight of this Italian gesture coming from a Negro girl blacker than hell itself.

Toward the end of the afternoon, the air grows crisp, the sunlight fleeting, Bakhita is cold, sitting on this bench, but does not know where to go. She waits longer, submissively patient, and then all at once hears something. A procession. Murmuring. She recognizes these sounds and her heart freezes. She stands up to hear it more clearly, and when the rows of little girls walk past, led by two nuns, she snatches Mimmina to her, the child wails but Bakhita holds her tightly and hides her as best she can in her arms, her face pressed up against hers, forcing her to be quiet, almost suffocating her in her attempt to save her. The procession passes, fifteen or so little girls in gray pinafores, with clogs on their feet, no chains, and white like the most expensive slaves in Africa, the Circassians. Where are they being taken? Why have the nuns bought them? These children are not from here, she can see it in their eyes scouring the place for some reference, some form of help. They are here without their families. Did the nuns buy them to free them, as the consul used to? They have passed her now. The clunk of their clogs fades. Bakhita puts Mimmina back to the ground, the child hits her and says she's horrible and she doesn't like her anymore.

"You don't like me anymore?"

"No."

"Well, I still like you."

"I don't want you to."

"That's impossible. I still like you."

Mimmina gives her a sidelong glance, her eyes full of her childish anger and hunger for indulgence. And then, reassured, she goes back to her fivestones, her games full of imagination and daydreams, under the soft slow eyes of the woman she struggles not to call mama.

The day is over and they have done nothing but be together. They do not yet eat in the refectory with the other young girls preparing for baptism but in the kitchen, where Bakhita cannot swallow a thing. She is given a bowl of soup and is terribly ashamed, sitting there doing nothing, she is so embarrassed that she has tears in her eyes. Who can tell her why she's here? Do the nuns think she's worthless? That she doesn't know how to do anything and nothing can be asked of her? Where are the nuns she saw passing? And the little girls? This is a source of great concern, she wants to know why the cook is so gentle and why she herself feels so alone in this vacillating unpredictable world.

At night she sleeps with Mimmina in a room of their own on the third floor, their window looks out over the building opposite, on the far side of the canal, and the back of the basilica of Santa Maria della Salute. The fishermen who pass under their windows in their boats call out in Venetian, a different Venetian than that spoken by Zianigo's peasants, but in their gruff exchanges, she recognizes disagreements or greetings, men hailing each other. The November night is cold and comes early, seagulls are furtive shapes skimming across the dark sky, and foghorns remind them that the sea is nearby. With her forehead to the windowpane and little Mimmina in her arms, Bakhita feels protected. Together they watch the night close in, just as they normally do, the first to see the moon or a star appear has won. But unlike in Zianigo, here there is only a very small corner of sky. Bakhita hums and Mimmina rests her hand on her chest, she likes the way it reverberates under her palm, she laughs and Bakhita sings deeper and deeper notes, because what she wants, always and every day, is to hear this child laugh. Their life is full of rituals, and for several months now there has been the ritual of the three Latin prayers recited while they kneel at the foot of the bed with their hands steepled. They are sometimes halfhearted, sometimes suddenly diligent, Bakhita carries the child along with her because she rarely wants to keep going to the end, and says her *Amen* after the first phrase. "Amen no," Bakhita says. "Amen yes," the child replies. And Bakhita soldiers on, come what may. After their prayers on this particular evening, Mimmina joins Bakhita in her bed, it is their first evening away from home and she is sad, the sheets are rough, the pillow smells of mothballs, she huddles close to her nanny and lulls herself to sleep by gently tracing the tattooed marks on her arm, like a little path in the sand, while she sucks the thumb of her other hand. That is how she falls asleep, in this familiar landscape, her nanny's smell, with her hair tickling her neck, and no harm can come to her.

Bakhita is woken by a bell at dawn. It must be very early, the sun is not up, but she can already hear muffled sounds and surreptitious movements. She gets up softly so as not to wake the child, opens the door a fraction and sees them. Heads bowed, hands tucked inside their sleeves, the nuns walk along the corridor in the shadows, seeming to glide in the chill half-light, and now they disappear behind a black velvet drape. Bakhita goes back into her room and wonders what the nuns do behind the drape. She cannot help thinking of the little girls in gray pinafores and wooden clogs. Images of zarebas and markets, of caravans and harems spring up like knife blades, memories she thought she had lost, and the terror is back, perfectly intact, as if she were seven years old. Here she is in this bedroom in the middle of nowhere, and who would come if she called for help? She looks at Mimmina. A familiar face that reminds her who she is: She is nineteen years old, her name is Bakhita, she is nanny to this little girl whose name is Alice Michieli and who lives in Zianigo. She repeats this reality to herself over and over, but the memories lurk there, at the foot of her bed, the past is a loyal dog. A village on fire. A bundle behind a banana palm. Loneliness. And fear, fear growing by the day, like an empty landscape.

And then she hears it. It is quiet and mysterious. Slow and slightly sad. She comes out onto the landing again, barefoot. Strains her ears. The nuns are singing. A litany, high-pitched and almost shy. These women have gotten out of bed to sing at night. She listens to them, and her fears slowly dissolve in their song. Her body relaxes. Her breathing eases. The nuns' singing is clear and the velvet drape as light as a curtain of sand in the wind. Above the cloisters is the square of sky with the first glimmers of daylight, which belong to all those setting out to sea, herding animals to the fields, or working the land. Those who speak little and work so hard that they die of it and never even stop to wonder at this. She looks at this sky, is it morning in Olgossa? Is there an old woman sitting on a baobab trunk, waiting for daybreak like her, for the tasks to be done, and for everything that will never happen again?

The nuns very soon realize that the Moretta recites Latin without understanding it, that she knows neither the name of God nor the name of the crucified man, that she cannot read, write, or count, and that her language, made up of disparate, sturdy threads, asks first and foremost to be heard. "It's like sorting lentils or raking soil," says Madre Agostina, who is a simple, sensible woman. "It will take time and concentration," replies Mother Superior. Which amounts to the same thing.

It started the morning Madre Teresa approached the Moretta and Mimmina, both kneeling at the foot of their bed and reciting an incomprehensible Paternoster, interrupted by untimely *Amen yes*es from the child and *Amen no*s from her nanny. It was the strangest prayer ever heard, beyond offensive, a complete hotchpotch, ignorance to the point of blasphemy. Softly, the nun drew closer.

"*Pater*," she said to the Moretta. "Do you understand? *Pater*. You say it. Slowly."

"*Paternosterqui*."

"No. Just *Pater*. It means *Padre*. Father. Say it again."

"*Padre*."

"Very good. Father. You're talking to the Father."

"Me?"

"You. Every morning and every evening you talk to the Father, Bakhita."

"The Father?"

"Yes. The Father who is *in caelis*. *In cielo*. In heaven!"

"In heaven?"

"That's right! In heaven and on earth."

"On earth...yes..."

"Do you understand, Bakhita? Your Father is in heaven and on earth. And you too, Mimmina, your Father is in heaven and on earth."

"No, he's in Suakin!"

"No. He's in heaven and on earth. And mine is too. And your mother is too. And Bakhita's too. And Bakhita's mother's—"

"Amen yesssss!" Mimmina interrupts.

Then comes a crestfallen silence. And a profound feeling of helplessness. Madre Teresa goes to leave, terribly disappointed. She has failed. Then she spins around in the doorway, her robes fluttering like a bird flying away, and in a voice that she hopes sounds less desperate she cries, *"Dio! Dio!* God!"

She waits for a reaction that is not forthcoming. *Dio* is a word Bakhita knows. It crops up in every sentence in Italy, as *Allah* did in Africa. It must be the translation. And to comfort this nun who looks so disconsolate, she says in a deep and, she hopes, reassuring voice, *"Allahu akbar."*

Mother Superior asks Madre Marietta Fabretti to take personal responsibility for the Moretta. Madre Fabretti is fifty-four and one of the senior catechumen assistants, she has a naturally cheerful disposition and is blessed with great patience. The first thing she does is to ask no questions. To insist that nothing be recited or learned. She starts at the beginning. Behind the black drape. Behind the door. In the chapel attached to the institute.

It is a small Roman chapel with high walls of ocher-colored brick, a dark nave lit by candlesticks set into the walls; brass incense burners hang on long chains, pale flowers are arranged on the side altars, and behind the high altar is a painting depicting Christ on the Mount of Olives. At the far end of the aisle to the left, near the wooden door that leads out to a small square, a recess houses the baptismal fonts in all their austere simplicity. A smell of incense and wilted flowers fills the chill air, but that is not what is immediately noticeable, it is the silence. A true silence. One that eclipses everything around it, an enveloping silence, a welcome. Madre Fabretti sits down and invites Bakhita to do so too. Mimmina sits on Bakhita's lap. The pew faces the crucifix, and on this dark wooden cross the man whom Bakhita still calls "the slave" has his eyes closed, and blood trickles from his pierced heart.

"He's dead," Bakhita says.

Madre Fabretti says nothing. She lets her study that outstretched body, the nailed hands, and ravaged face.

"I know him."

"You know him?"

Bakhita takes from her pocket the crucifix she hid on her person when Parona Michieli was preparing her clothes.

"Yes, that's him," says Madre Fabretti. "His name is Jesus. Do you understand? Jesus Christ. That's him."

"It's a nice name."

"If you like... let's go outside now. Will Mimmina be warm enough?"

Madre Fabretti opens the wooden door and they are greeted by the delicate subdued light of late afternoon. Mimmina lets go of Bakhita's hand to run into the small square. They walk in silence to the Grand Canal, the sea air mingling with the wind carries an untamed quality, a restrained violence behind its initial beauty.

"Jesus died a very long time ago. A very, very long time," says Madre Fabretti, and she takes Bakhita's arm.

Bakhita pulls back momentarily and then accepts the gesture, uncomfortably, like the day Stefano offered her his arm to walk through Zianigo.

"Was he very far back?"

"Very far, yes. Jesus was very far back."

"An ancestor..."

"If you like. An ancestor. His father is the Father in the Paternoster. His name is God. Not Allah, not Allah at all."

"No."

"God."

"Yes."

It is the first time Bakhita has not noticed the frightened looks she attracts, the first time she has walked on a woman's arm, with this child running ahead of them to scatter pigeons and seagulls. There is something comfortingly familiar about this quay on the Grand Canal, a peaceful intimacy in keeping with the encroaching evening. Not yet nonchalance, but confidence.

"I'm a slave," Bakhita says.

"I know that."

"Are the little girls slaves?"

"No. The little girls are not slaves. The little girls are all alone in the world. Do you understand?"

"Oh yes."

The cold comes out of nowhere, with blue clouds massing on the horizon and merging with the canal. Mimmina, terrified by a dog, throws herself at Bakhita who takes her in her arms. The child is heavy, and Bakhita limps slightly now as she carries her. Ahead of them the whiteness of San Giorgio Maggiore on its island fades slowly in the darkness, and the fishermen's lights come on all across the lagoon. As one thing disappears, another comes to life.

"It's beautiful," Bakhita says.

Madre Fabretti is surprised. Did not realize beauty could touch this simple soul.

"The moon! The moon! I saw it first, Bakhita! I won!" cries Mimmina, pointing to a wavering moon, ensnared in cold mist. "But *you* can't see anything this evening."

"Do you think so?"

"I know so!" Mimmina insists, and she covers Bakhita's eyes, to play the blind game they invented. But Bakhita puts her back down again. Does not feel like playing. She has talked too much. Madre Fabretti takes Mimmina's hand and walks away with her. The Moretta's black face is swallowed up in the darkness, bringing out the bright gleam of her eyes.

Over the course of a year, Bakhita will learn a new language, new rituals, new stories, prayers, words, and songs, she will do her utmost to join the women with whom she lives, women who talk to God and Jesus as others address their parents, parents who are constantly by their side, eternally and everywhere. It is this "everywhere" that so affects her. Madre Fabretti tells her that God sees and hears her all the time. From her first day to her last, He is there. She is ashamed. Remembers the most violent scenes of her captivity. Did He see *that*? Was He *there*, that first night with her captors and the other nights locked away, nights of suffering, the days in the desert, the torture and humiliation, and with Samir, the masters and the masters' children, was He *there*?

"Yes, Bakhita. He was there."

"Shame... Madre... shame."

"He was there so you would never be alone."

The effect on her is violent. A struggle between her desire to live and a longing to give up altogether. She does not understand these words Madre Fabretti tells her again and again: "He loves you." And she thinks Madre Fabretti is wrong: He doesn't see everything, He's not there all the time, and He doesn't know. She's a slave, and no one, no master, even the best of them, no one ever loves their slave. And she believes that one day, somehow or other, Madre will understand what slavery is, and on that day she will punish Bakhita for hiding this monstrous existence of hers. A life as less than an animal. A life stolen, bought and traded, abandoned in the desert, a life without even knowing one's own name. She succumbs to terror at any moment, in any circumstances, in the kitchens where she learns to cook, in lessons where she learns the alphabet and her catechism, and she slips away without asking permission, without taking Mimmina. No one knows what goes on in her mind, there she is bent over her work and all of a sudden she vanishes. They know where she goes. It is always the same, she runs like a disoriented stray and looks for Madre Fabretti, who is always available to her, patient, calm, and anxious too about the turn events are taking. This simple soul is too sensitive, the shock of the revelation has profoundly shaken her, and more than once Madre Fabretti contemplates asking Mother Superior to summon the doctor. Stefano's visits with his family do the Moretta good, but this soothing influence never lasts long. She gets up at night, plagued by nightmares, and by day she has moments of exaltation and then weeps for no reason, she is sometimes found kneeling at the foot of the cross, begging forgiveness, prostrated Western-style, and it is impossible to break her of this habit or to stop her from calling God "el Paron." The master.

Bakhita really does understand, though: Jesus is the Son of God. Who created the night she looks out at every evening, with the stars and moon. Who created the earth, with all its bounty. Who created man and the animals. Rivers and streams. She has always known the universe is alive and must be thanked. Always has. Knows the living and the dead are together. And has always respected her ancestors. God is the master of the universe and of all men. She has grasped more than they realize. But is ashamed. Ashamed of herself. Ashamed of her hope. And ashamed of her sorrow. They talk to her of baptism. Tell her that when she is baptized she will be the *paron*'s daughter. The love she has been waiting to find for such a long time ("thirteen years," they tell her, "you were held captive for thirteen years," so thirteen years it is), that love is here now. Within reach. They tell her that if she agrees to be baptized she will be loved, and loved forever. Whatever she does and whatever is done to her. Is that possible? Sometimes she is overwhelmed with joy, wants to sing and give thanks. To stop being this Negro girl who comes ten times a day to disturb the woman she calls just "Madre," and who asks her to follow her one evening into the little chapel where she lights an altar candle, opens the book, and very slowly, almost breaking it into individual words, reads quietly: "Blessed are the poor in spirit, for theirs is the Kingdom of Heaven. Blessed are those who mourn, for they will be comforted. Blessed are the meek, for they will inherit the earth. Blessed are those who hunger and thirst for righteousness, for they will be filled. Blessed are the pure in heart, for they will see God."

And then she lets the silence breathe. She closes the book and waits. Bakhita is looking away, Madre Fabretti takes her chin with one hand and makes her look at her.

"I don't mind that you're crying, my darling. Look at me. Do you understand the beatitudes?"

"Yes, Madre. But is it true?"

Madre Fabretti would smack her over the head with the Gospel if the book weren't sacred. This Bakhita is so stubborn, her only prison is herself.

"But of course it's true," she says, spreading her arms. "And you know it is, don't you? Tell me you know it is."

"Yes, I know it is."

"Ecco!"

Her baptism is planned for the following January. But two days later, on November 15, a telegram from Suakin announces that Maria Turina Michieli will soon be home.

Mimmina is about to turn four, and she has not seen her mother for a year. She now calls Bakhita "mama" with no reservations, and together they learn to count with the abacus, to read with alphabet primers, and are taught about the lives of the saints. Saint Blandine, a Roman slave who was eaten by lions; Saint Mark, who died near Suakin in Egypt with his limbs broken and his body burned and was brought back to Venice; Saint Alice, the most beautiful of saints, wife to the king of Italy, an empress who loved the poor, whom Mimmina pretends to be, as other little girls play at being princesses. It is a woman's world, a protected, ritualized, reassuring world. She has a friend, young Giulia Della Fonte who lives opposite the institute, they play together in the square every afternoon, watched over by Bakhita. Her world is not Italy or Africa, her world is Bakhita. She lives in an eternal present where there is nothing to threaten her. She is told that her mother is to return, and this makes her happy, although she is not sure why, she is happy with a joy that hopes for nothing, anticipates nothing.

One evening when the rain is falling on the Virgin with her outspread arms at the very top of the Basilica's dome, Bakhita and Mimmina watch the darkness merge into the rain. Bakhita cradles the child to the rhythm of a monotonous tune. It will soon be over. This world in the institute. The Italy of Stefano and Madre Fabretti. The Italy of Mimmina's peaceful childhood and Bakhita's acquaintance with God, the father whose daughter she was to become, almost became, but deep down she knew very well. Knew this baptism would never take place. There is no justice in it, *abda,* there never has been, but that is what she is. And she has trouble acknowledging that at Mimmina's age she still lived in her village. Protected and happy in the same way, with a happiness that does not recognize its own existence. And she catches a very obscure glimpse of her father, a voice, an outline, his neck where she rests her head, and facing her is the other one of her, her twin. She will not be seeing them when she returns to Africa. They will always be on the other side of the island. She will be in the bar at the hotel, at the beck and call of men from every country and of every religion, brought together by alcohol and vice, and her days will be spent serving them and saying no to them. Trying to spare Mimmina... "It's impossible." She keeps saying this to herself. "It's impossible." She doesn't know why but it's impossible. She looks at the Virgin at the top of the dome, the Virgin who is said to have saved Venice from the plague. With her forehead against the windowpane she recites the Ave Maria quietly, her words clouding the glass, and it looks as if it is raining inside too.

Maria Michieli is at the institute the next day. She is reunited with Mimmina and Bakhita in the visitors' room, with Mother Superior and Madre Fabretti in attendance. Mimmina is happy to see her mother again, her mother who thinks this daughter has grown so beautiful, who's amazed at how much she's learned, she speaks so well now, and they hug, smother each other in kisses, they make a charming picture, to the delight of the nuns, it makes a change from the orphans and the young women who have gone adrift, this family scene is a blissful sort of break for them, and Maria, who left on a note of defeat, leaving the child with her nanny, now reclaims her rights. Bakhita hangs back slightly, ever the well-trained servant. Her mistress comes over and takes her hands.

"You've taken very good care of Mimmina. And you have too, my sisters. Your country is glorious, Moretta! It truly is. That perfectly round little island... can you imagine, sisters? A pearl set down in the sea... Well, enough of that. Moretta, there's something I must tell you, we've made great improvements at the hotel, the bar will be yours alone, and for the first time in your life, you will have a small salary. Oh, I don't have to do that, I know I don't, but I'd like to."

Bakhita backs away slightly. In that dark, dreary visiting room the only sound now is young Alice playing with her doll, as if she were in another world, a bright world all her own. And then out of nowhere, Bakhita's deep voice.

"No."

It is like an intrusion, something in the room that should not be there at all, unseemly. Madre Fabretti notices Bakhita's clenched fist and guesses that in this fist is her crucifix.

"I beg your pardon?"

"No."

There is a brief pause, a suspension of time, and Maria bats it away, waving her hand in front of her face.

"Well, yes or no, it makes no difference to me, I shall be back to collect you in five days."

She goes over to her daughter to say goodbye to her, explains she will return soon, but the word rings out again in the visiting room.

"No."

Sharper than a dagger in the back. A public affront. Without even turning around, Maria responds with an instruction issued in a slightly too-shrill voice.

"Go pack the bags!"

Mimmina bursts into tears. Bakhita does not move. Her lips quiver and her eyes look both frightened and alarmingly determined. Maria takes her daughter in her arms, holds her high, with the child's face against her own, rocking her to comfort her.

"You will do as you're told, Moretta, and on the double!"

"Impossible."

"What?"

"Impossible, *parona*."

"And why?"

A slight spasm constricts Bakhita's face, her cheek twitches, and she takes a deep breath.

"I'm not leaving," she says. "I'm staying."

Maria would almost be amazed, if she were not so violently, so profoundly angry.

"But are you mad, girl? Has the Venice air driven you crazy? You do remember that you're my slave and I'm your mistress, don't you? Does that ring any bells?"

Her vulgarity erupts in spite of herself, she would like to be different, more poised and authoritative, but does not know how. She feels like slapping this girl, and she understands why people beat their slaves, burn them, kill them.

"You belong to me. You were given to *me*. Has anyone ever heard a slave say no to a master? And this is what's going to happen: I'm leaving for Suakin and you're coming with me. We can't always do what we want in life, isn't that right, Madre Fabretti? Go on, get out! Go pack the bags."

"Impossible..."

Madre Fabretti comes over to Bakhita, takes her to sit on the sofa, tries to reason with her, she must obey her mistress and go with her, that's what was agreed, and you can't disobey your mistress.

"I'm not His daughter there," Bakhita murmurs.

"God's, you mean? God's daughter?"

"Yes."

"Don't worry about the baptism, don't worry about that, my darling, we'll bring the date forward. Of course you'll be God's daughter, I promise you that."

"No. Impossible. I'm not His daughter there. Impossible."

"We're God's daughters wherever we are, remember, I already explained that, He's everywhere. In Africa, Italy, everywhere."

"Madre... *Aiuto*... Help..."

Bakhita's sobs echo around the room and suddenly everything changes. This is not disobedience or capriciousness. This is something serious, that none of the nuns understands. Mimmina wails, calling

Bakhita "Mama! Mama!," and Mother Superior gestures to Signora Michieli to take the child out of the room for a moment. Madre Fabretti asks Bakhita to tell them everything she wants to say. She mustn't be afraid, must explain what's going on. The nuns wait, ready to discover a whole new world.

But they will never know what it is the Moretta confides to them. For she has never spoken so quickly or with so many Arabic and Turkish words, and African dialects, so many gestures, entreaties, and tears, it is like watching a rockslide tumble toward them with no means of defense, and they listen, stunned and illuminated, to the whole gamut of this young woman's strange words and deep-seated anguish. They do not know this is the first time she has told the story. The men in Suakin. The strangers she serves, and the other men, the ones she is terrified of seeing again, the tormentors, sometimes former slaves themselves, the ones who ask Augusto Michieli whether she's for sale, and to whom he replies, *Not yet.* Mimmina like a shield for her. And the children, boys or girls, summoned to these men's rooms. And her sister, Kishmet, whom she dreads recognizing in every prostitute she sees. She says that she is young and she is old, says she is twenty years old and everything has already happened to her. Says she has seen the devil and now wants to see God. But not in Suakin, you can't see God in Suakin, you can't be a child of God in Suakin. She talks about the man who cried out every night in the hotel, a single cry, just once, but every night, and she, she herself doesn't want to be afraid anymore. She is the stolen child, the child in the market, she's always obeyed everything, and she emphasizes this point, *everything,* and she thanks her masters every day for letting her live. She has obeyed monsters, and now she wants to obey God. *Abda,* it's not her fault and it's not fair. No. No, she says again. For the first time. No. It's the only word she has. No.

She talks in her *jumble,* more chaotic than ever, and when she stops, exhausted, ready to give up, to die, she hears someone speak.

"I shall support you."

And Bakhita knows it is true. For Mother Superior has never deceived her. Madre Fabretti takes her hand and they stay there like that, with this young woman who has experienced things they can never imagine and who, by some incomprehensible peregrination, has arrived here among them with her fear and her strength, her youth and her past. The Lord has never given them a more visible and poignant sign of His presence. They are deeply affected and secretly excited. Utterly unaware of how far supporting the Moretta will take them.

For three consecutive days, Maria Michieli comes to the institute and asks to see the Moretta in the visiting room. And, of course, her daughter, a key part of her strategy. She comes alone, and then accompanied by a Russian princess, and finally by a cousin of hers, an army officer. Her fight, she says, "has the backing of high-ranking people," who have advised her to confront the nuns who are overstepping their rights, which is why she has written to the president of the Charitable Congregation, denouncing them. She'll get her slave out of this institute or have the place shut down. As in any battle, those to whom she turns for support do not reason with her, far from it, they fan the flames and urge her on into a war she would never have waged without them. But in full view of so many friends enthused by the whole business and curious to see how it pans out for her, she feels forced to go on the offensive, it is not just her slave she wants back but her own lost dignity, and every tactic is permissible. And every tactic involves her daughter. She tells Mimmina that Bakhita is going to abandon her, and in front of the child, pleads with the Moretta, shedding tears of rage that pass for outright despair.

"Love her!" she shrieks, brandishing her daughter. "I beg of you! You know she'll die without you, why are you doing this?"

The child is plunged into the depths of terror, and Bakhita goes from slave to tormentor, from nanny to child killer. She wants to say that Mimmina has given her great strength, has given her tenderness and confidence, that Mimmina will live, even without her, she's grown up, won't be ill anymore. But she says nothing. She holds her tongue and clutches the crucifix so tightly that her palm bleeds. In the evening when she is alone with the child in their bedroom, they are drained, numbed by fear and bafflement. Mimmina tells her she doesn't want to die. Bakhita swears she won't die. "Ever?" Bakhita hesitates… "Never." The child says she'll be good the whole time from now on, she won't throw any more tantrums and she'll eat everything she doesn't like, she'll play with the poor children who frighten her, she'll help the nuns do the dishes, and she weeps as she asks for forgiveness.

"*Asfa*, Mama! *Asfa!*"

"You know that word?"

"*Asfa*. It's what you say. You say it at night."

Bakhita looks at this child who will forget her, will forget her nanny but not the furious wreckage of these few days.

"I want you to still love me," Mimmina says.

"I do still love you, Mimmina."

"You're black all over."

"Yes."

"Like the devil."

Bakhita did not think it would happen so quickly. How many days is it since Maria Michieli came home? Does a child-mistress always end up loving in the same way as a master? And they both cry, because there is nothing else to do but let it flow, this barbaric pain, this separation that marks the end of their life together, their games, their rituals, their songs, their private language, their wishes in the gathering darkness of evening, everything they are losing by losing each other. They gave each other the gift of life, the baby whom Bakhita massaged and whose mucus she sucked out, the slave whom Mimmina begged for on the boat, but they will never see each other again. The pain will not fade, will be sharpened by other pains, and by joys too, joys that will remind them of what they gave each other, joy, the scorching brightness of it, suddenly replaced by loneliness.

"*Asfa*... Mimmina... *Asfa*, my darling..."

It is the first time Bakhita has had a choice, and whatever price she must pay, she decides to stay in Italy. She wants to be baptized and become the daughter of a father who will never abandon her.

She has been told only that there will be quite a few people, a lot of people in the visiting room. Important men who will listen to her and listen to Signora Michieli before deciding whether she should stay at the institute or go with her mistress. The word "trial" has not been mentioned. But that is what it is. Madre Fabretti makes her rehearse a short, easily remembered sentence that expresses her wishes: "I love the signora, I love Mimmina, I love God: I choose God."

"Do you agree with that?" the nun asks. "The men who are coming—very kind men, you'll see, they're very kind—don't speak Arabic, or Sudanese dialects, my darling. Do you know that?"

"Yes. I must obey them."

"You understand, they are the ones you must obey. But Signora Michieli must too, she must obey them."

"These men, do I know them?"

"No."

"Oh... And you, you speak to the men?"

"No. I'll be praying. Praying very hard for you. But I'll be there, by your side."

"All the time?"

"The whole time the men are here."

"When?"

"Tomorrow. In the visiting room."

Madre Fabretti protects her from rumors spreading around Venice where this trial of a slave girl among the Canossian sisters fills every conversation, just as much in slums as in salons, in convents as in the streets, there are those who call for the immediate release of this African martyred by a tyrannical mistress, and those, fewer of them, who mutter about a subhuman nanny prepared remorselessly to let a little girl die. Madre Fabretti no longer allows Bakhita to leave the convent, no more evening walks along the lagoon, no more afternoons overseeing Mimmina and Giulia's games, no more errands in the market with the nun who cooks, she has even forbidden the other catechumen young women from having visitors since the *portinaia* told her that they mostly came only in the hopes of glimpsing the Moretta in order to talk about this sighting all over Venice. People are saying the child is on her deathbed, there is talk of witchcraft, of escape plans, one woman insists she has seen the Moretta abroad in Venice at night, her long black arms flapping in the air while she pronounces magic formulae to the statue of the Virgin. People laugh at her. But partly believe her.

Mother Superior keeps her promise and defends Bakhita. Turns to face the head of the charitable foundation, who refers the situation to the patriarch of Venice, Cardinal Agostini, who himself refers it to the Crown Prosecutor. The cardinal informs the Crown Prosecutor that Signora Michieli keeps the Moretta in a state of slavery and, according to African law, no one can force Signora Michieli to free her. The very next day the cardinal receives an answer: "Your Eminence, by the grace of God, the barbaric law of slavery does not exist in Italy. Any slave who sets foot on Italian soil breaks his or her chains." Mother Superior and Madre Fabretti meet the president of the Charitable Congregation, and their prior attends these meetings. Just like every humble parish priest and the bishop himself, like the lowly masses and the wealthy townsfolk, like men of law and their underlings, they too are passionate about this case.

———

The bells have not rung. This is what first intrigues the inhabitants of the Dorsoduro neighborhood that morning, when the patriarch cardinal's white gondola adorned with red and gold draws up to the banks of the Grand Canal. Something extraordinary is going on, but what exactly? The bells have not rung, so this is no celebration or official ceremony. The prelate crosses the Campo, followed by an ever increasing crowd, women from all walks of life bow down before him, trying to come close enough to kiss his gold ring, he blesses them in passing. His secretary, a feverishly excited fellow, hops and skips in his wake, but soon the crowds are confused about which way to go because now the Crown Prosecutor has arrived. A frisson of awed admiration ripples through the neighborhood, the Moretta's name is spoken in backstreets and on bridges, in squares and palaces, craftsman's shops and warehouses; a slave's name associated with the highest powers in Italy, the church and the king, is she really all that powerful, this poor Negress who has found God? Altar candles are lit in the basilica and also in more modest chapels, at the foot of statues, in oratories, and Venice comes alight in broad daylight and prays during working hours.

She is asked to stay in the chapel and not come out until Madre Fabretti comes to fetch her. Mimmina has been taken from her already. She does not know it is forever. Is shielding herself from this wrench. On the far side of the chapel door powerful men are taking their seats, men who will decide whether she stays or leaves. She knows that it is to them that she must say her piece: "I love the signora I love Mimmina I love God I choose God." Definitely no African words and no expansive gestures, and careful with that very deep voice, and calm, she must stay calm *the whole time,* Madre Fabretti has said this several times, stay calm *the whole time.* Don't look at Mimmina. Don't go to console her if she cries. Leave her with her mother *the whole time.*

The visiting room looks like a courtroom. His Excellency the patriarch cardinal is sitting on the sofa, above which the crucifix exhibits a nakedness in stark contrast with his red velvet robes, and next to him, his secretary has set up a desk and a large record book. The Crown Prosecutor, a number of magistrates, the president and members of the Charitable Congregation, lawyers, noblemen, Signora Michieli along with her allies, Mother Superior, Madre Fabretti, a few nuns. And on Maria Michieli's lap, Mimmina, who loathes this visiting room, Bakhita isn't here, her mother keeps asking her to stop fidgeting, but she scours the room the moment anyone comes in, she thinks it's her, she needs to go wee-wee. "I took you to the bathroom three times already. Stop it." Yes, she took her three times already, but they didn't see Bakhita, so where is she? Her mother kisses her and tells her to be quiet, and she'll have a present if she's a good girl, and look how pretty the big crosses are on all these nice men, but they'll be very angry men if she gets up again to go pee, *understood*?

It is only when the patriarch cardinal speaks that she starts to understand. She recognizes the words, the same ones used over and over since her mother returned: Moretta, slavery, Mimmina, die. Things about her. It goes on for a long time and she is bored, but her mother stiffens, holds her very tightly, and Mimmina grows anxious, wants to leave, she never normally stays with the grown-ups, not even for meals on feast days, little girls are never allowed to be with all these important people, and why isn't Bakhita here? She looks at the men in red, in purple, in gold, in hooded capes, coats, cloaks, cassocks, wearing regular hats, three-cornered hats, skullcaps, bright splashes of velvet and silk in the overheated visiting room, where the nuns were wrong to have lit a large fire, her mother says very loudly, with tears in her eyes, that the Moretta is her daughter, she loves her like a daughter, they are a family, she gave her a bedroom, clothes, hats, and gold earrings, and, most important, she entrusted her child to her. Mimmina doesn't want to keep hearing her mother telling everyone she's going to die and then weeping afterward, because even though Bakhita has promised that she won't die, it still makes her cry. This tragic story her mother tells devastates her all over again, she calls for Bakhita, and rather than going to fetch her nanny, her mother points to her for the benefit of all these men in their complicated clothes, all these people craning their necks for a better view, and she cries, "And look! This is the result! She's in tears already!" She sits down again, puts Mimmina back on her lap, and her friends have their say, the officer, the princess, using the same words—Moretta, slavery, Mimmina, die—and in the end the child confuses everything, is Bakhita sick, is *she* going to die, or is it herself, Mimmina? It all seems very serious. These people are making sweeping gestures. They're ugly and old. Where's her mama, the one she mustn't call mama? Where is she now? And her crying constitutes a reedy litany in the crowded room.

"Let us hear from the concerned party," says the patriarch.

It is as if no one was expecting this, as if all those speeches from different people have made them forget the "concerned party." People seat themselves more comfortably, jostle for space, clear their throats, like at the opera before the music starts. It is very hot. Stifling. It is about to begin. The Negress who cannot talk properly (they have been warned) is about to arrive. Word has it she is in the chapel, praying constantly to the Lord our God. Word has it she is extremely black, you have to disguise your surprise and be very patient.

Madre Fabretti comes into the small chapel where Bakhita is sitting with her face bent over her hand, holding the crucifix like someone else's hand in her palm. Bakhita sees the nun and understands. She has come for her. She will take her to the rich men before whom she must slowly pronounce her rehearsed sentence. From Madre Fabretti's solemn expression, from her apologetic but encouraging smile, she knows this will be as difficult as she anticipates. Her heart swells in her chest, her hands shake, and when she stands her right leg stiffens. With her halting step, her emotional disarray, and her determination, she walks into the visiting room that no longer looks like the visiting room she knows. There are so many people. It's a market. A public place under a fug of heat. She can hear Mimmina but not see her. "Bakhita!" This is the only thing she recognizes, the child calling her. Even the nuns are unrecognizable in this crowd. They are taller, there are more of them, frozen like statues. She can tell that these other people, all these other people are hot and thirsty. And frightened too. She immediately knows where the truly powerful ones are, recognizes them straightaway, they are sitting on the sofa. And all around them this brutishness, this curiosity about her. She hears whispering, sees the appraisal in their eyes. Madre Fabretti leads her to stand before the patriarch and the Crown Prosecutor, then backs away, leaving her alone. The cardinal smiles and, looking at the slave, addresses the gathering.

"Aha! Here is our Moretta!" he says with an air of satisfaction, then adds, "God has given us free will, whatever our race or religion."

This man will talk for a long time, she can tell. He doesn't look cruel. He looks happy, a little tired, he eats too much and doesn't sleep well. He is hot too, and his voice is an echo, talking to everyone and no one. Talking to himself. Bakhita waits for the right time to say her piece but the cardinal is making his plea. At length. Talking of absolute love and an uncertain future, what will become of her once she leaves the institute, is she aware of the dangers lying in wait for young girls in this Italy in which she is a foreigner, wouldn't it be better if, once baptized, she returned to her glorious Africa with Signora Michieli who promises always to watch over her, this defenseless easy prey, who is humble among the humble, poor among the poor…? Bakhita does not understand a word. When he has finished, she turns and tries to catch Madre Fabretti's eye, sees her elbowing through the crowd to reach her, whisper in her ear, tell her the time has come, she must say her piece, does she remember it?

"I love…"

Madre Fabretti points to her throat, not so deep, make your voice softer.

"I love…"

And all at once she cannot manage it. Everyone around her longs to hear. She can hardly breathe in this atmosphere of impatience, would like to run and hide but does not, she is gentle and kind, and they wait, patiently, powerfully. Well then? She must express her love. In just one sentence. Everything that is inside her. In just one sentence. Now.

"I love…" How can this be? She's going to hurt the only person she loves: "Mimmina…"

This is not enough, this truth is not enough. She must dig deeper. Keep going. A little further and it will all be over.

"And I want God."

She collapses, falls onto the dark wooden floor, curls up on herself, and hears the piercing inhuman cry, the animal cry that foreshadows death and never does any good: "Mama! Mama! *Aiuto!* Mama!" The visiting room erupts like wildfire, and she does not save Mimmina, leaves her alone in the flames and devastation, does not answer her call, never will. Never. This is the only truth. Never again. She beats her forehead on the floor, the room is emptying, the howling child is carried off, taken far away from this Negress to whom Maria Michieli screeches, "You ungrateful girl, you ingrate!," as if it were a curse. Bakhita cannot hear a thing now. Not the love or the hate. Not the final farewell or the decision, the words she has waited thirteen years to hear: "I pronounce the Moretta free." She does not hear it.

The Crown Prosecutor says this with more emotion than he was expecting. Is a little disappointed that she does not thank him, does not kiss his hands or prostrate herself at his feet. Thinks she is weeping for joy. She is devastated. Will never truly recover. She has abandoned her little girl. It is Friday, November 29, 1889. Bakhita is free.

TWO

From Freedom to Sainthood

The following morning, when Madre Fabretti comes for Bakhita in her bedroom, she finds her curled up asleep in Mimmina's bed. She looks at this black adult in the white child's bed and sees the burden of all the things she does not know, the past from before Bakhita's slavery, her childhood. And her loneliness. Like a constant ally. There is damage in her face, it expresses neither liberation nor exaltation, it expresses weariness and tears. She is a dispossessed mother. An exhausted, guilty child.

Stefano did not attend the trial, he let Signora Michieli fight for herself, stake her own claim, he was her steward and did not want to see her as all those people saw her, a cruel woman who thought herself the rightful owner of another human being. He truly knows her, he understands: Maria Michieli is a mother *afraid of being left alone with her child.* Afraid of letting her die. Afraid of having only that to her name, her children's deaths. After the trial, Mimmina fell ill, she slept restively and had no appetite, and surely she too would never entirely recover from this wound. Her abduction from the visiting room. She heard her mother's curse, "You ingrate!," and the whistling of the crowd waiting for them outside the institute, a crowd that followed them through Venice, insulting her mother, pitying Mimmina herself, heard what they shouted to one another through those streets striped with light and shade, "The Moretta is free! The Moretta is free! Oh, Lord! Oh, Jesus, Mary, and Joseph!," before falling to their knees, their hands clasped, their eyes to the heavens. Mimmina will remember the pure panic of that crowd, and her ambivalent feelings for her mother, a love tarnished with anxiety. Her mother's love like a death threat.

Two days after the trial, Stefano, Clementina, and their five children are at the institute. Seeing their little Moretta sister's dejected expression, they decide to take her out for a walk along the lagoon, but they have not turned the first corner out of the institute before they give up. Going out in Venice with Bakhita proves to be a nightmare they should have anticipated: Since the previous day, the inhabitants of Dorsoduro have been ringing at the institute's door to offer flowers and small gifts, wanting to show their love to this freed slave, wanting to see her and, if possible, touch her.

December has started very cold, and they cluster around the fire lit in the dark visiting room, where it is difficult to imagine so many celebrities gathered a couple of days ago. On their father's instructions, Chiara and Melia do not leave the Moretta for a moment, climbing on her lap, trying to fill the void left by Mimmina but succeeding only in emphasizing it, because they have not been molded to Bakhita's body since infancy, cannot know how naturally the two of them fitted together, without even thinking, without knowing it, forgetting they were in each other's arms just as others forget they are breathing or putting one foot in front of the other to walk. Stefano would so love for Bakhita to be happy again, he takes her hands in his.

"You're free now, my little sister."

"Yes, *babbo.*"

"You mustn't be sad."

"No."

"You're going to be God's daughter and you'll always, always be filled with boundless joy."

"Boundless, I know."

"And you're my daughter too. I'm not God, but still..."

"Our home will always be your home," Clementina says.

"Yes, and our children are your brothers and sisters, and when I die my inheritance will be shared between all of you, what's mine is yours. You will never want for anything, never be alone, don't be sad. What do you say? Do you understand what I'm saying?"

She understands and is frightened. Will she really become *God's daughter*? This "boundless" love, this love in the rising sun and the setting sun, this love in all living things, all things on earth, this love... is unbearable. Her chest has been cleaved open right down to her heart, her heart has been torn out and now she sees. Sees what filled her heart. What she was protecting, what she kept locked there so as not to die of it. Not the Madonna, no, her own mother, that woman who sat on the fallen baobab trunk in the mornings. She misses her. The simplicity of it could kill her. She does not know the words but knows that this particular absence has no name. She will become God's daughter, and she wonders whether within Him, He who encompasses everything, there will be a tiny fragment of her mother. And the feeling being rekindled now, the savagery of this raw emotion, nails her to the spot, and she knows they are right, she is earthbound, grounded, when she should be filled with joy. She will become the daughter of the one she calls "el Paron," the great giver of life but also the great *for*giver. He will grant her forgiveness. Forgiveness for her disobedience. Forgiveness for her mother. Forgiveness for Kishmet, for Binah, for all slaves. Forgiveness for the love she has lost. She smiles at Stefano, she does not understand everything he said but he is so wonderful with his helpless affection and the awkward way he has about him that she wants to please him.

"I understand everything, *babbo*," she says.

"Aha! I knew you'd come on in leaps and bounds with your Venetian, I told them: With the nuns she'll make incredible progress, she'll be able to count and read and write and—"

"Have you seen her?"

"Who do you mean?"

"Mimmina."

Stefano is caught off guard. He gestures to Chiara and Melia to move aside. "What on earth are you two doing there? You're smothering her with your hugs and kisses, she can't even breathe, poor girl. Of course I've seen her, she's very well."

"Sad?"

"No. She's doing very well, I tell you."

"Does she cry?"

"Goodness, no! She's happy for you. She's thrilled, like all of us. We're all so happy, aren't we?"

"Stefano, stop." Clementina looks right into Bakhita's eyes and speaks gently, as if her tone of voice could lighten the load of her words. "Mimmina's gone. Mimmina's on her way to Suakin."

Bakhita understands. They have swapped countries. Given each other their homelands. And she can see it all: the train, the boat, the stops, the Red Sea, the island of Suakin, the shores of Africa in the mist, and the hotel. The men. The children at the gate driven away by the gardener. And Mimmina playing by the fountain where she learned to walk.

"That's good."

She has faith in Mimmina, knows her. Does not believe the child smiles all the time, knows she cries and calls for her because she can hear her. But she also knows that this little girl, this rich free white little girl who is inquisitive about everything, who is funny and affectionate, this little girl will bring a pretty burst of light to the martyred land of Sudan. And who knows? Perhaps one day, without even realizing, she will meet Kishmet. Or Binah. There is no knowing. There is never any knowing where life will take us.

Start again, Madre, please. Start again."

Madre Fabretti has never prepared an adult for baptism with such application. Every day Bakhita asks her to go over the words she will have to say, she is frightened of saying them wrong, as she did at the trial, and she repeats them to herself all day long: "Faith, eternal life, I renounce, I turn to, Credo, Credo, faith, eternal life, I turn to, I renounce." Madre Fabretti is worried Bakhita will scramble the words, then decides she must trust her. Now aged twenty-one, Bakhita has a combination of vulnerability and strength, a powerful energy, a deep-seated intelligence, and she is funny too, often risking a little joke that the others struggle to understand, but she smiles and the others think it must be affection, must be her good humor, to hide her inner turmoil.

Madre Fabretti has shown Bakhita which entrance she will use to come into the chapel and where the cardinal will stand, the things he will do, the words he will say, in what order and why. She has acted out every part—Bakhita, the cardinal, the chaplain, the godfather—and has warned her there will be a lot of people. In the chapel. At the institute. And out in the small square. She knows there is something fierce, avid about the way people stare at Bakhita, hopes she can enter the church as if entering her own home, in a mood of trust and peace. Will that be possible?

It is a clear morning in Venice on January 9, 1890, with generous sunshine, it is the day of her baptism, Bakhita knows it will be the opposite of the trial. There will be powerful men, the nuns, the Checchini family, the inquisitive crowd, but she also knows she will not be cursed ("You ingrate!"), she will be welcomed instead. But does she really have a right to this? She is still a slave. Slavery never fades. It is not an experience. Does not belong in the past. But if she has the right to be loved, then this day ahead of her is her reward. She has walked all the way to this day. Has been walking for years. Walking all the way to el Paron. So that she never has to obey other orders again, never has to prostrate herself before other masters again.

The small chapel has been decorated, adorned with flowers, lit up. It is very soon full. The institute's bell rings nonstop and the *portinaia* is overwhelmed by eager crowds, there are friends but also strangers, nobility, intellectuals, a few artists. Not all of them are Italian, they belong to the European intelligentsia who live in old palaces, patrician homes, and sumptuous private hotels. The rest, ordinary Venetians, jockey for space on the small square and spill out into the whole Dorsoduro neighborhood, and people who were once so afraid of the Moretta and laughed at her expense now boast that they know her. Impoverished local women are curious to see this girl from savage, faraway Africa, where men eat human flesh, children are sold, and villages burned, and they are reassured to know she is to be saved by *their* God, the one in whose name they accept so much unacceptable suffering. Today they love the Moretta with a fervor full of hope, she is poorer still than they are and look how famous she has become. The institute's bells ring, the basilica's bells ring, and it all starts again, the patriarch cardinal, and his retinue, and the authorities, all these important figures back in this *their* neighborhood, going into this institute full of abandoned children and uneducated young women, and the lives of these poor, lowly people are caught up in this dazzling event, as if catching the reflection of a bright light.

But who notices them? Who looks at them, the crowds who are left at the door? A thin, pushy little woman has barged past all of them to stand on the threshold of the chapel whose wooden doors have been opened wide, and, perched up on tiptoe, she sees how beautiful it is, *inside.* She turns toward the thronging crowd in the small square and shouts out what she can see. Tells the story, describes what is going on. *Mamma mia,* it's so beautiful. And how wonderful it is to have faith.

The little chapel has lost some of its humility, has grown opulent and flamboyant, magnified by candlelight and flowers, by the officiators' heavy colorful clothes and the Sunday best of the congregation. People turn to Stefano to ask what she was like *before,* when she arrived here from her own country. What was the black girl like? And how do you feel, having succeeded in saving her? One woman dares to step over to the men's side to ask whether it's true she was tortured. Was she boiled like Saint George or burned like Saint Joan? Will he make a pilgrimage to the Virgin to give thanks? But Stefano says nothing. He is choked with apprehension, is afraid for the Moretta, and happy, too. He has been fighting for this day for five years, and he remembers Bakhita on the day after she arrived in Zianigo, when he saw her at Augusto Michieli's house. He wonders whether the shock he felt was because of her color, that very dark, very fulsome black, or her presence. Paternal love at first sight. Does that happen? He looks at the font that is simply carved out of the brick wall and thinks it right that Bakhita should be baptized in a place where the children of ordinary people live—lost, unloved children. He stands very upright. So that she will see him alone when she steps inside the chapel.

She waits in the oratory. Kneeling, in private contemplation, private contemplation of her life. Thinks of her twin and speaks to her: Look at the clothes I'm wearing, they're as beautiful as the red paint on our mother's naked body. As beautiful as our beads and bracelets. As white ash. Tattooed eyelids. See what you would look like if you lived here, in Italy, a very long way beyond the Nile. You do live here, in Italy, a very long way beyond the Nile. You crossed the deserts and the seas with me, and I want to thank you for also being by our mother's side. Never leave her.

She hears Madre Fabretti come over to her and stands up. Her thigh hurts, a familiar, almost reassuring pain.

"I've come to fetch you, my darling." Then she adds quietly, "Heavenly Father, Bakhita...you're so beautiful..."

Bakhita hears this word, which is no longer acquisitive but respectful. And it is true, she is beautiful in her purple cloak, her face covered with a long black veil. She is tall, imposing, and Madre Fabretti gestures for her to hold her head high. It is difficult, she is not used to it. She crosses the cloisters where the institute's little orphans are waiting to see her. It is cold, and they stand there in their gray coats with thick socks peeping out of their clogs. She wants to tell them she loves them. But doesn't know how to say it in the plural. Wants to tell them she knows them. The frightened way they wait, and the feeling of hope mixed with so much apprehension, this too she knows. One child is bolder than the other girls, wishes her good luck, and the others tease her because she has dared speak to the Moretta. Bakhita lays her hand on the face of each of these little girls whom, when she arrived here, she mistook for slaves, like herself.

Madre Fabretti is next to her, standing by the chapel's side door. Bakhita knocks three times. Hard and slow. The door is opened. She stands in silence on the doorstep and remembers to lift her head. Her father is waiting for her, she will be reunited with her father today, with el Paron. The chapel is full. She cannot see Stefano but knows he is here with Clementina and their children. She remembers what she must do. Has now come to this intensely powerful moment in which nothing can happen but the event. Hears Domenica Agostini, the patriarch cardinal of Venice, praying, then he walks into the attentive crowd, all the way to her, and accompanies her to her godfather, Count Marco Soranzo, her godmother is unwell and he is representing her. She keeps her hands joined and can tell from the shaking in her legs that the fear is back, despite her best efforts. Her breathing makes the long veil quiver. The cardinal's voice reverberates around the brick walls, loud and clear.

"What is your name?"

The question pierces right through her, she was not expecting it. It is the greatest shame of her life, that she has forgotten her name. Does God not accept stolen children? Madre Fabretti did not make her rehearse this question. She flashes her a look of panic. The silence seems to go on forever. What her name is. What her name is... No. Impossible. *Asfa*. I'm sorry, all of you. She bows her head. It is over.

"She doesn't have a name!" The pushy little woman has turned to tell the crowd, and the rumor spreads, disappointing and toothsome. There is whispering and coughing in the chapel, the congregation is stunned. But the cardinal moves on to his second question.

"What do you ask of the Church of God?"

Is it still happening, then? She must pull herself together. Must look him in the eye to give her answer, Madre Fabretti told her so. She raises her veiled face and is careful to reply confidently.

"FAITH!"

"What does faith give you?"

She knows the answer. Has already said it. Said it again and again. She looks up to the heavens to show what faith gives her, it is up there: love and the healing power of love. The cardinal sighs.

"Yes, that's right," he says, "eternal life."

The congregation can breathe, the pushy little woman on the doorstep turns around toward the square and shouts out, "She gave the right answer! Eternal life!"

And now comes the moment everyone has been anticipating with apprehension and relish. The terrifying story they have known since their childhood. The story that frightens, and soothes. Sometimes.

"The exorcism! The exorcism!" shrieks the avid woman on the doorstep.

And the crowd prostrates itself, crosses itself. The Venice sun hides behind a cloud. Impressionable girls weep, lockets and rosaries are kissed. Men, women, the young, the old, all are united, all alike and humble, and inside the chapel the shadow of fear settles over the congregation. Who knows? The devil might win. Hasn't the Moretta been compared to a black devil? Who is she really, this foreigner with no name and no language, this foreigner people suddenly started to love? Some find this stage of the proceedings exotic, titillating, already eager to describe it, write about it, even draw it. The truth will erupt now or never. Everyone will know on which side the forces of evil lie. The cardinal comes up to Bakhita and blows on her face three times. Her veil shivers and her eyelids are closed. She waits. Something weighs on her shoulders, heavier than her cloak, an atmosphere of distrustful curiosity and rejection poised to explode.

"I exorcise thee, unclean spirit, in the name of the Father and of the Son, and of the Holy Spirit, that thou goest out and depart from this servant of God, Bakhita. For He commands thee, accursed one, Who walked upon the sea, and stretched out His right hand to Peter about to sink. Therefore, accursed devil, acknowledge thy sentence, and give honor to the living and true God: give honor to Jesus Christ His Son, and to the Holy Spirit; and depart from this servant of God, Bakhita, because God and our Lord Jesus Christ hath vouchsafed to call her to His holy grace and benediction and to the font of baptism."

The cardinal traces the sign of the cross on Bakhita's forehead, on her ears, her eyes, mouth, heart, shoulders. She is shaking and drives away images from the past, the expression in little boys' eyes when the cleric took them off for castration, the screams of that young mother whose baby was slammed against the rocks, little Yebit's body when she died during the torture of her tattooing, she could scream out loud, give a bestial howl to drive out this demon and restore the good in the lives of all these martyrs. But she makes no sound. Wants the cardinal to do it for her, drive out evil with the appropriate words, he alone knows how this ritual should be performed, and she trusts in him. She concentrates on the people who are there and who love her, the Checchinis, the nuns, forgets the insatiable crowd, the power of all those people gathered in public places who have always stared at the Negress she truly is.

Now that the devil has made room for the Holy Spirit, she can enter the God's Temple.

"Do you renounce the devil?" the cardinal asks her.

"I renounce him."

"And all his works and vanities?"

"I renounce them."

The cardinal anoints her forehead with the holy chrism.

"Do you believe in God the Father and His only son Jesus Christ and the Holy Spirit?"

"Credo! Credo! Credo!"

"Do you want to be baptized?"

"I want to be."

She is overcome and exhausted, as if she has run a long way to reach this moment. And she hears her baptized name, which includes the name of her baptismal godmother, her confirmation godmother, her slave name in Italian, the name of the Virgin, and her slave name in Arabic.

"Gioseffa Margherita Fortunata Maria Bakhita, I baptize you in the name of the Father, the Son, and the Holy Spirit."

Three times in succession the cardinal pours the baptismal water on her forehead, her purple cloak falls to the floor, she removes her long veil and emerges, a new creature, clothed in a white habit. Her face appears to everyone as an indelible truth above that habit filled with light. To their great shame, some think of the body that must be there, underneath, it is said to be black too, black and marked, could it possibly leave traces on the baptismal gown? And they predict, with some delectation, that this girl's story might disturb their sleep and transfix their souls.

A large candle is brought to her, and she lights it from the one her godfather holds. The final words are about to be pronounced. The order and the dispensation.

"Go in peace. The Lord is with you."

"Amen."

"Amen yes!" Mimmina is with her. She can hear her. "Amen yes!" Mimmina would almost certainly be playing with the veil that has fallen to the floor, dressing up as Saint Alice, the beautiful empress. Bakhita and her little girl are the same now, both daughters of God. Held within the same love, part of the same family. But who will tell her, tell her little Mimmina, that she now has a name? Who will tell her to stop calling her mama?

She is officially called Gioseffa, but people will always use the diminutive "Giuseppina." They will struggle to say it, concentrate on saying it, because to everyone, she will always be the Moretta. On the baptism certificate she is declared to have been born to unknown parents, a Mohammedan girl from Nubia. No one knows either her history or her geography. Her country has no name and her mother does not exist. Her childhood is not her childhood, it is a collective imagining, years summed up in a single word, "suffering," years that are now diluted in an Italy that represents "deliverance." Deliverance, and yet... It is a year since she was baptized, she has continued her catechism education, and those around her would like to see her glow, living proof of the love of Christ. She is destroyed. She is sometimes found alone in the small chapel, prostrated at the Virgin's feet, praying and weeping. The sisters talk to her and she does not listen, she is devastated, no one knows why. Stefano often invites her to spend a few days in Zianigo, in this family that is now hers. She has interludes of happiness with them, moments when she laughs at last, launches into impenetrable descriptions and waves her hands in every direction. The laughter they share with her is a surprise and a blessing. Stefano cherishes these moments. Bakhita has watched his children grow up, attended his son Giuseppe's wedding. Stefano's happiness, the bride's beauty, the white bride in her white dress, and the promise of children to come, children who will be her nephews and nieces too, he tells her this and she knows it is true.

Everything they say is true. They love her. And she would so love to reciprocate this love, would so love to be a Giuseppina who brings joy and gratitude to everyone. She cannot. She wants something *she cannot say*. She knows that her catechumen year is drawing to an end. She is twenty-three and will have to choose: living with the Checchinis, as Stefano has suggested, or going into service to a mistress, being a servant. When girls leave the institute, with their small "dowry," they have become true Christians, good housekeepers, and excellent embroiderers. They can read and write. They will work and marry, because without marriage they would simply not exist. But of course, in Bakhita's case, marriage is out of the question. The color of her skin is an insuperable natural barrier. No marriage or children.

One evening when they are taking their walk along the Zattere landing docks, Madre Fabretti asks her what memories she has of her childhood.

"I mean... your childhood before."

"Before slavery?"

"Yes, before you were a slave."

Bakhita was not expecting this. She has already been asked this, of course, by the Italian consul, by Stefano and his children... Why do they want to know the things she feels but cannot say? The things she remembers so obscurely. And yet so intimately. It is like asking her to understand the workings of her blood, her breathing, everything she is. The air is mild. The day waning in a faded pink light, cast tenderly over the sky. *Abda*... What was there before? *Abda*. A life that happened so long ago, rooted so deep inside her, where words do not exist. Describing the place she has never managed to revisit. The family she has never been able to find. Impossible. She looks at what lies in front of her, the sea and the sky. The expansive but somehow cozy scene in the gathering gloom. A large fishing net is attached to the banks of the canal, the posts are covered in moss and look so old, but these posts are in fact what hold Venice up on this powerful, living body of water.

The sky has widened, extended into fine blue and gray trails that cross over each other and disappear. It is so vast that the horizon is moving away. It is very beautiful. Almost too beautiful. Bakhita gazes at this devastating beauty and speaks, as if addressing the wonder of it.

"I don't leave. I stay."

Madre Fabretti does not understand. Is she talking about her childhood? But Bakhita turns to look her in the eye, her face glowing with emotion, astonished by her own boldness.

"I don't leave the institute, Madre. I stay."

It knocks the breath out of Madre Fabretti. But she admires the girl for this, this strength. This way she has of going to the furthest reaches of her pain and returning infallible. Of course, Madre Fabretti would like to keep Bakhita by her side for another year... She could teach her more Venetian, a language to help her understand more than other people's words, to understand their way of life, the way they think. She could protect her a little longer from everything that awaits her outside, and she is disappointed with herself for loving her so much, a nun forms no relationships, only with God. But this girl, this girl is different. Bakhita is quite different.

Madre Fabretti writes to the supervisors of the Charitable Congregation, asks for an extra year, Giuseppina needs more time than the others, she is a slow learner, still cannot write. The request is swiftly granted.

A year goes by, a year of patient teaching, difficult confidences, periods of respite, but also long phases of sadness. This time Bakhita does not need to look at the three hundred sixty-five suns drawn by Madre Fabretti to understand the passing time. She watches the sky and the days drawing in, growing icy and short-lived, the year coming to a close and showing her the door. This time, she must leave the institute once and for all. No more exceptions. No letters, no recourse. She cannot write, people still have trouble understanding her, but she is a peerless cook, she embroiders, knits, and darns better than anyone else, she uses beads to make things no other young woman can make: purses, strange belts, bunches of flowers. She would make an excellent servant. Perhaps not a nanny, she becomes too attached. But being a servant is exactly right for her.

Once again, she wants something she dare not say, and as time marches on it takes her to the edge of the abyss. Her life is made up of violent separations, abductions, escapes, she has survived it all... but still. When she tries to admit her innermost desire, she freezes. Mute and helpless. Madre Fabretti tries to soothe her, understand her, console her. In vain. Bakhita is overwhelmed by her anxiety. Imprisoned within it. She is cut off from those around her by a longing she cannot admit.

And then one morning she asks to see her confessor. She has had a dream that, yet again, took her back to the violence, to the days when she had nothing left to lose, when she threw herself at the consul's feet, begging him to take her to Italy, and persisting, despite his repeated refusals. In her dream the earth was red, and she could hear the laughter-like roar of camels, their teeth grinding and their hobbled legs, the sound of them clanking in the dark, a sound that woke her with a start. And the fear was right there, spreading out before her with no horizon. A vast naked fear. And in that moment, she decided to free herself of it.

Her confessor listens attentively. Through the wooden lattice, he can see only the whites of her eyes, and he likes the spark in them, likes the Moretta's voice too, reverberating in the confessional, her deep exotic voice, and her new convert's fervor.

"Padre, there is something I want."

"I'm listening, Giuseppina."

"It's very big."

"Hmm... very big, yes."

"And I'm small."

"Hmm..."

"Black."

"Keep going, keep going..."

"Well, there it is."

"No. Keep going. Don't be afraid."

"Padre."

"Don't be afraid, Giuseppina, keep going."

"I'm not leaving. I'm staying."

"Again?"

"No. Not again."

"Well, yes, Giuseppina, it's nearly two years since you were baptized, three since you arrived here!"

"Padre..."

"My poor Giuseppina..."

"Padre, I want something."

"Say it. Say it slowly and I'll understand."

"I want... to be... like... the others."

"White?"

He hears her laugh. Her throaty laugh, peals of it going on and on, and he wants to laugh too, with relief. For a moment he thought she was half-witted, but the truth is, he's the half-wit.

"But what do you mean by being like the others?"

"A nun."

It is raining in Venice, icy raindrops spattering passersby, pelting roofs, and lancing into the narrow canals. The rainy season here is short. A momentary hesitation. She remembers those days that felt just like the nights, enveloped in the same rain. Remembers stores of grain kept safe, frightened patient livestock, angry rivers, and her own fearful respect for the sky. Distantly remembers rain in her village, a choked color, a smell of mud and grilled maize. Strangely, a smell of skin too, perhaps her mother's skin as she held her close, or her twin's as they slept side by side. Remembers rain in masters' houses, and their anger, which amazed her at first and then stopped surprising her once she grasped that they despised anything that disobeyed them.

The rain beats down and swells into rivulets on the paving stones, she listens to the force of it, Venice resigned. She takes shelter, with two other women and some children, in a shed open to the street, where an old man is weaving baskets. He shows very little surprise at this intrusion from these women who do not look at him and, not daring to uncover themselves in front of him, keep their soaked scarves over their heads. They stand there looking out at the rain as it comes down even harder, while the children squelch their hands in the wet dirt on the beaten-earth floor. Bakhita knows that in the half-light she is less black. She keeps her head bowed, clutching to her the bread bought in the market. It feels good being in this semidarkness, this sustained silence. Not frightening anyone. Not being recognized, as she still so often is, with faces coming so close to hers she can smell the breath from their gap-toothed mouths, intrusive smiles that she reciprocates shyly, revealing her unusually white teeth. Sometimes wealthy passersby stop her. Once a painter wanted to paint her, one of the numberless artists, Venice is overflowing with them. She very rarely goes out alone, and the nuns ward off unwelcome intrusions for her. But when it rains as it is today, artists, noblemen, and rich traders stay indoors, having headed home the moment the sirocco picked up. She closes her eyes and can hear flies maddened by the rain, and the sound of the rain itself, endless and unrelenting. She feels good. She dared speak to her confessor yesterday. Dared to utter the word. Like something blasphemous. That she, Bakhita, Giuseppina, *she* should be a nun! Oh, if the priest understood her language, she'd have told him how surprised she was at first. Almost as much as he was. She didn't understand what was going on. Yes, it really is astonishing: having faith. Hearing God's sweet song, and knowing it is addressed to her, yes her! She is changing, she can feel it, changing in a world that is the same everywhere. Sudan, Italy, the beauty is the same, as is the evil. She used to weep because God knows everything, He can see her whole life, and then she realized that God is like a particular kind of love coming to rest. Would her confessor have accepted that? Would she have succeeded in being understood? She now has the strength to love others. Now that her life is in higher hands.

The nuns will forgive her. The bread is difficult to tear, but she goes about it carefully, her hands can do anything, always have been able to. She breaks off several hunks of bread and gives them to the children playing in the mud. They are untalkative, focused. And all at once she remembers. Can picture herself, she is sure of it, picture her sister and the children in her village stamping the churned-up dirt to make a smooth, soupy mud, exactly like, yes, exactly like the mud of their homes. That was what the rainy season meant too. New houses made with mud trampled by the children. This memory blows over her like a wind. Images like this surface more and more frequently. She remembers herself, so far back in her life and yet it feels so close, a wind buffeting her, reviving the embers of the child she once was. Her life.

Her childhood somewhere. When she was no different from anyone else. When being black was just being.

After her confession the priest reassured Giuseppina that "Jesus pays no attention to your race or the color of your skin." And then he ran to tell the news to Mother Superior and Madre Fabretti: Not only has the Moretta converted but what's more, she's asking to enter holy orders! In *their* order! You could say their institute is working miracles. Or at least wonders. They put the request before the Mother Superior in Verona, Primaria Anna Previta, and she studies it with Cardinal Luigi dei Marchesi di Canossa, the nephew of the order's founder. Can they admit a former slave as a novice? Right back to the twelfth century, Italy has a tradition for the redemption of slaves. Its Franciscan missionaries would return from Egypt, Sudan, and Ethiopia with former slaves whom they educated and converted. Now, in the nineteenth century, it is still very popular for Italian missionaries to go to Sudan. Which is how the priest Daniele Comboni came to set up the project called the Plan for the Rebirth of Africa and opened the Comboni Missionaries and Missionary Sisters in Cairo, where he trained former slaves who, once educated, would help him evangelize Sudan. This was the notion of "Save Africa with Africa," it being the continent considered "the part of the world most resistant to civilization." The primaria and the cardinal deem that this former slave's wish to take holy orders follows in this tradition, and Bakhita is accepted as a novice. She is neither a conquest nor a trophy but an affirmation: Catholic Italy saves slaves. And on December 7, 1893, the church opens its doors to this young woman whose spirit had no home.

Bakhita experiences this period as a novice, which lasts almost two years, as the opposite of what it is intended to be: a trial. For her it is, at last, a period of deliverance. Madre Fabretti is appointed mistress of the novitiate and helps her "girls" identify and broaden their vocation. But testing the spiritual and physical resilience of someone who has survived everything is superfluous. Bakhita asks only one thing: permission to love. She now has a right to this emotion that was for so long forbidden, dangerous, a bearer of much greater suffering than her mistreatment. She gives herself body and soul to el Paron, the master whose love redeems sins.

She is twenty-four and even though she follows the same teachings, says the same prayers, communicates, confesses, and wears the same uniform as the others, she is not like the others. She is set apart. And for all time. Exceptions will always be made for her. Dispensations requested. People hesitate to accept her or, conversely, they are vociferously self-congratulatory about accepting her. She is the one who chooses a seat but does not sit on it. The one who wants to say something but cannot manage it. She amazes, surprises, and often unnerves. Most of the novices admire her, her kindness, her tireless energy for work, up before anyone else and the last to go to bed, willing and talented, but others feel uncomfortable. Dare not look her in the eye. Do not understand a word she says. Are frightened of coming across her at night in a corridor. Do not like sleeping in the same dormitory. Washing in the same water or eating opposite her. The way she holds her fork, her guttural voice when she says the Benedicite, and the scars that peep out from her sleeve. They are embarrassed by their own disgust, mention it in confession, but there is nothing for it, they are afraid and would prefer that this particular trial, living alongside this black girl, had not been visited on them. Bakhita stays black under her uniform, like an unforgivable flaw, a sin with no remission.

Madre Fabretti sees all this, the fear in some of her "girls," and Bakhita's humiliation. One day she takes her to the church of Santa Maria della Salute. They climb the marble steps that seem to emerge straight from the water, and it feels like walking into a vast, cold white womb. This famous, proud, and honored church. The columns and domes and multiple chapels, the countless statues and paintings by great masters, Bakhita bows, crosses herself with water from the font, awed by the secular riches, the immemorial devotion. Madre Fabretti goes up to the high altar, and the two of them kneel before it in silence. Bakhita closes her eyes. She is aware, all around her, of the voices of visitors and the whispered prayers of people lighting tall, leaning candles. The air carries a damp chill, tiny drafts blow through the basilica. She ignores them, concentrates on her praying. But Madre Fabretti taps her arm.

"Look, Giuseppina, she's like you."

Bakhita does not understand. What should she be looking at? She thinks "like you" means a "novice" or "praying," "kneeling." "Like you." Words no one ever says to her.

"Look there, the icon."

Above the high altar is a Madonna covered in gold, she wears a crown set with precious stones, and the baby Jesus in her arms is equally richly adorned. Their faces are flat, their expressions impassive, their eyes distant. Bakhita did not know this Madonna existed. Would not have thought it possible. She has never seen her before. Not in any catechism book, any pious image, or even any dream. But Madre Fabretti is right, this Virgin and child are like her. *They have black skin.* She looks at them and does not understand. Where are they from? Are they really the Virgin and her son Jesus Christ?

"They have been loved by Venetians for centuries, Giuseppina. Do you see? Can you see now that you are like the others?"

"Is that the Madre?"

"Well, of course, it's the Madre. The black Madonna."

"And the angels too."

Madre Fabretti had never noticed them, but true enough, two little angels in the background have black faces.

"You see, Giuseppina, there are five of you black people: one, two, three, four, five. And meanwhile…I'm on my own. The only white person."

Bakhita smiles at her. "Well, I can protect you!"

And they try not to laugh too loudly in the imposing basilica that affords this unexpected relief.

They have come, eager and inquisitive, to Saint Joseph's convent in Verona to see her. She closes her eyes and it resounds next to her ears, swift and precise, and while the scissors snip and her hair falls, she feels profound relief, as well as great pain. She is losing something of herself, something of her mother's dexterity and great patience, when she braided her hair with those beads that made her so proud. Bakhita felt beautiful like that, and she was. And when she moved her head, the little beads knocked against her face, she liked it. She remembers this, the memory is clear, accurate, and hers alone.

She sits motionless, upright, with her eyes closed, cannot see what the others are watching: her tightly curled hair hovering momentarily before falling, indecisive, featherlight. They watch and know nothing. The dark cell, the hole high up in the earth wall that she tried to widen by rubbing it with her hair, she was seven and it was the start of her captivity, that great enduring nightmare. She remembers wild hope, remembers also what was only just beginning. They watch her, would like to touch the drifts of hair, take some and put it in a locket that they could show to their friends with blustering superstition, laughing as they said, "Touch the lucky charm!"

She thinks of Mimmina who could not get to sleep without fingering her hair, and she would say nothing when the child tugged too hard as she rolled over, because it felt good to be loved that much. So much that you stayed with the loved one all through the night. She can now feel the scissors against her scalp. Remembers her head being smacked against the floor, remembers Samir's violence, her own impurity. But today she is a bride. Today, June 21, 1895, is the first day of summer and the Feast of the Sacred Heart. She is to be the bride of someone who will never leave her and will love her so much that a single life will not be enough, there will be another afterward, a flawless eternal life. Today she will take on the habit of the Canossian sisters, similar to the clothes worn by ordinary women in the street, a brown robe and black headdress and shawl, because these nuns live alongside ordinary people to "console, teach, and heal" the poorest of them. She runs her hand over her hairless head, has no mirror and cannot see herself. But everyone else looks at her and recognizes her. With her shaven head, she looks like the slaves photographed in newspapers, illustrated in books by explorers, botanists, missionaries, and doctors. They picture her with a slave yoke around her neck, a chain on her ankle, and they weep with pity, coupled, in some cases, with a hint of inexplicable guilt. And they are all equally relieved not to be of "that race."

Next, dressed in clothes and a headdress like the other nuns, she will make her first vows, her habit will be the habit of penitence. This will take place in the house of the Madre, the big gold-and-marble church. She would have preferred the small chapel in Dorsoduro but obeys with the fervor of someone prepared to make any number of sacrifices, even secretly longs for them, proof of her unfailing commitment. After the vows of poverty, obedience, and chastity, she is called Sister Giuseppina Bakhita and is given the locket of the order of Canossian Daughters of Charity, marked with the initials MD, mater dolorosa. She is accepted into the community of sisters who take in lost and abandoned children.

When she returns to Venice, the locals swarm to the institute, prostrate themselves at her feet, kiss her locket, and ask her to pray for them. They have stopped calling her the Moretta. The black girl. But do not call her Sister Giuseppina either. To ordinary people she is Madre Moretta, and will be till the day she dies. Mother and black. Similar and different. Accepted and isolated.

Three years after taking her vows, when she is more than thirty, she still cannot write. Struggles to read. Talks Venetian a little better. She embroiders. Prays. Obeys instructions, and likes this reassuring framework, where the days are all alike, punctuated by prayer, vigils, lauds, sext, vespers, compline. She likes lauds best of all, the prayers at dawn. Never passes the black velvet drape without remembering that first morning when, standing barefoot in the doorway of her bedroom, she watched the nuns go through and was terrified. But was happy. Mimmina was asleep in bed. She will never know that happiness again, sharing every moment with a child who is discovering life and nudging you into discovering it too. That is over. Holding Mimmina in her arms, singing so the child puts her little hand on her reverberating chest, looking out for the first star and the moon making its appearance, sharing a unique language, affinity, and intimacy. It is over. The warm smell of her skin, her hand in hers, and the look in her eye that says, "I expect everything of you." It is over. She is where she wanted to be and has fought to become the nun she now is. No one will ever be her child again, and no one will replace Mimmina.

In fact, over the years, it is she who becomes Madre Fabretti's daughter. Madre Fabretti is an aging nun who grows happier and happier, as if amused by the endless movement of this vain, disoriented world.

They have kept up their regular *passeggiata*, their evening walks along the quay, walking more slowly now, with Madre Fabretti leaning on Bakhita's arm, and Bakhita thinks that perhaps her twin walks like this with their by now elderly mother. They speak little, look at the light of the sunset, the small marooned islands, the movement of the tides, squeeze each other's hand with swift tenderness. Sometimes Madre Fabretti asks Bakhita to remember. Now that she has more vocabulary, and her life is more peaceful. And it comes back to her. Such violent memories they do not seem to belong to her, and others she recognizes but dare not relate. For the sake of decency, and also for fear of shocking her Madre, this old lady from a well-to-do Italian family. Here, with this nun who has given her life to other people, Bakhita hesitates to describe what people did to slaves back there, but despite the suffering caused by retrieving images of her torment, it feels right to explain her experiences to the person she loves. Madre Fabretti waits for the silences and the tears, lets them come, unravels the incoherent sentences, listens with horrified love. And when she says, "My darling," Bakhita knows it is over. It is time to walk back. She will return to the convent, pray, and go to bed, will get up to pray again, will not wake in the night to howl out her memories of inhumanity.

It is a filial connection. And this is a happy time. But the ecclesiastical authorities deem these conditions too easy. Giuseppina's faith is clear for all to see, she is given everything, the time has come to see what is truly in her heart. The time has come to test her. One evening, after vespers, she is told that it is over. This house where she has lived for thirteen years, seven of them as a nun, is no longer her home. She must say a final goodbye to Madre Fabretti in the morning, does not even have time for a *passeggiata*. It will be in the morning, in the visiting room, in the presence of the whole community, no favoritism, no sentimentality. They are both astounded, almost reeling, and go their separate ways with no demonstration of weakness or affection. This wrench marked by no tears or rebellion is something they offer to God, the master who expects undivided love.

It is almost noon when Giuseppina climbs into the gondola that will take her to the station, heading for a town whose name she does not know.

She goes back to her former life, rejoins her ancestors and every pariah of her kind, slaves forever, their skin black for all time. Carrying within her the curse and fascination of everything people imagine of her but that she is not. She frightens children, disgusts the elderly, appeals to men, like an animal they want to master to test their own power and display their supremacy. She sits and holds her tongue, has been told in all circumstances to keep quiet, her voice is something they can discover later, they will be frightened by it, will mimic it among themselves, now and for centuries to come. She has been sitting for hours, pain tugs at her injured thigh, her leg with the phantom chain, she herself is merely a ghost, her image has been stolen. She does not look at them, keeps her eyes lowered and listens to them, speaking Venetian with a new accent, heavier, clipped, and hard, which gives every word the weight of condemnation. She is seated, they are standing, even children tower over her. Stooped old women's faces are on a level with hers, and they sign themselves with a grimace, once home they will perform the rituals that drive out evil spirits, will make sacrifices on the sly, when the younger generation is not there to scoff at or interfere with these supplications. She is seated and wears their fear and ignorance like a cloak, affording them the pleasure of gathering and sharing their aversion. And just this once, they are all the same, all of them, the oppressed, laborers since childhood, the sick, people with rickets, people exploited by masters they will never meet, bearing children who will die in infancy or will run away to the Americas, most of them illiterate, sniveling illegitimates due to be sent off to the seminary, rebels soon to be quashed by military service, timorous little people, shopkeepers deep in debt, shepherds wilder than their flocks, peasants hungrier than their dogs, all of them look at her and pity her. This is better than the harvest festival, the Feast of Saint John, or religious processions, better than the theater, better than fife-playing and dancing, better than the Virgin carried through the streets amid noisy weeping and wailing, this is a panacea for all, a wordless prayer and a unifying joke. They stifle the laughter that bubbles up in their throats, this Negress is a nun, they know it would be blasphemous to laugh at her and, who knows, she might curse them later, cast the devil's anger over them. But what on earth is she made of? Did she come from a woman's belly, and what did that woman look like, was she wholly human from head to foot, or perhaps...? Some thoughts are best cast out, some visions best not seen, and a few of these people kneel and fall into prayer in response to the turmoil, to everything dangerous and violent, provoked by this black woman sitting in the convent's courtyard.

She has been exhibited here for two days, certain visitors have come twice to tame their fear of her, as the sisters from the institute explained. "Getting used to her and not being so frightened," but all the same, you can't see her eyes, and it's hard to make out her face. Sometimes Mother Superior goes over to her and says something in her ear, then the black woman slowly looks up. The crowd gives a long "Ohhh" of unruffled disgust. Her black eyes swim in such pure white it might have been stolen from the Madonna's veil. A child throws a spattering of water at her and is slapped, he cries loudly, only wanted to see if the color came off when she's wet. He is chided but everyone understands. Would it rub off? She can't speak but can she cry? And what if it rains? Oh, sweet Jesus, the nuns could exhibit this woman again and again, and they still wouldn't understand a thing about her! Before long they resent her for making them feel so awkward, things were easier before, did they really need this here? And off they go, disappointed and embittered, but all the same they feel a shiver of horror run down their spine, a sweet sensation they had quite forgotten.

When it is over, she runs, body aching and soul stultified, runs as best she can, limping more than usual, until she reaches her room, and there, once the shock has subsided, she cries. Cries so much that her body is wracked with furious hurt, cries hoarse sobs like the wild animal she is, would tear her hair out if she had any, would scratch her face were she not restraining herself, teeters on the brink of madness because she knows she will have to see these people every day, all of them, will have to get to know them and, more than that, to love them. That is why she is here. To forget Madre Fabretti and open her heart to these people, the inhabitants of a town whose name she still cannot remember, a short name, like a snake slipping past, a name like a curt merciless order.

The door to her cell opens, Mother Superior puts a hand on her shoulder. Asks her to see sense. She had to exhibit her to bring an end to this nightmare. Since Bakhita arrived at the institute, everything has been turned upside down, the convent's orderly life is in disarray, no one can work or pray, and the pupils stopped wanting to come in for classes. Bakhita has shown herself once and for all, surely that's better than hearing howls every time someone comes across her? Can she understand that she frightens the younger nuns who've never seen a Negress before, who dare not touch a door after her for fear of being stained, dare not get up in the night for fear of running into her, and surely it's fair that the laundry sister has refused to deal with her sheets? How could she be sure the color wouldn't run out of them?

Bakhita is exhausted and wants to sleep, to dream she is somewhere else, where nothing is expected of her, a slave lost among slaves, a black girl in the midst of desert caravans, the child who is stolen and then thrown away, invisible, forgettable, a girl with no value, worth less than a bag of maize. And then she is ashamed, horribly ashamed of this longing that is so like death. She thinks of the slave Jesus Christ, didn't he suffer spitting and laughter from the crowd too? She doesn't want to compare her life to his. She is nothing, he is everything. She would just like to lie down for a while and for him to watch over her, then she will pray, will honor him, but tonight will be too long if she is not loved.

She dreams of fire. Of Binah who has a terrible toothache. Binah's face is buried in the ground and she cannot get out. Bakhita calls to her, tells her they must leave, the fire is coming closer, she must come with her, but Binah says she will not, her teeth hurt too much. Bakhita calls her again, and oddly, Binah becomes little Yebit who died, tortured by the tattooist. She is held prisoner by the woman, kept in place by a slave, Bakhita kneels next to her and feeds her with a huge spoon. The child's body bleeds and convulses, and still she eats calmly, opens her mouth for each spoonful, soon her head comes away from her body, and she keeps eating. Bakhita screams and wakes in a sweat, and immediately checks whether she has soiled her sheets. She hopes her scream woke no one, they are all so frightened of her already, what will they think? She gets up and opens the window. It is an autumn night, deep and cool. Schio is protected by mountains, edged by the torrent and rivers. There is a chill coming off the clear fast-flowing water. She can hear the bells on livestock in mountain pastures and, from time to time, a brief bark, and then silence closing over everything again. She looks for the stars and the moon, but it is a misty night, shrouded in slow clouds. She would like to see a star, just one. The wind blows gently through the trees in the courtyard, motionless cypresses, and the sweet chestnut tree makes a sound like ruffled fabric, she likes this sound, which reminds her of palm trees in the warm Sudanese wind. A colorless cloud moves away, purifying the night sky. The stars are as small as pinheads. Bakhita thinks el Paron created night for men and beasts to rest, but also for no reason. For the beauty of it. She pushes up her sleeve, reaches her arm toward the window, shakes it gently, and makes herself look at it. And this may be the first time. Her body is hidden from her, is no longer hers, it bears the deep scars of whips and the tattooing chosen by her Turkish mistresses, ugly welts like criss-crossing snakes, she's so frightened of snakes, and she can feel them distend and tear when she moves in her sleep or prostrates herself, claws trying to hold her back. Her arm is like the night, a star could alight on her wrist like a bird. She wants to forget her nightmare, forget Binah and little Yebit, forget the fire, but when she opens her hand to the night air, she realizes she is wrong. She must not run away from her dreams. Must listen to them. Binah is far away, while she herself is free. Why?

It is during lauds, the dawn prayers she so loves, that she understands the message in her dream of Binah and the hungry little Yebit. She is singing the Song of Zechariah: "...the oath he swore to our father Abraham: to set us free from the hands of our enemies, free to worship him..." Is so disturbed by these words that she cannot keep singing. Stands there, transfixed by the revelation. If she wants to serve el Paron, she must stop being frightened. He brought her here, among all those people who eyed her with wary curiosity. "They're called slaves," Binah told her. In the name of everyone with whom she grew up, all those she saw being born, suffering, and dying, the time had finally come for her to go fearlessly among the people.

She asks permission to light the fire before the pupils arrive. Says she likes doing it, fetching wood in the dawning light, and she would like to get the stoves going in the classrooms. Hopes that by doing this she will be there to see them arrive, the youngest pupils, little children of nursery-school age, some of whom will have walked for hours. She will help them put their freezing clothes to dry around the stove and to sit themselves down before their teacher arrives. But is told this is not her responsibility. She has been assigned to the kitchens, in the basement, and if she wants to light fires, there's plenty to keep her busy: The kitchen has three wood ovens and a main fireplace. More than two hundred meals are prepared there every day for the orphans, pupils in the nursery school and elementary classes, teachers and nuns. She works under the kitchen sister's orders, with two orphan girls of about fifteen. It is never-ending work, starting at dawn and finishing when everyone else is in bed. She puts so much zeal into making meals, attends to it with such reverence and care, that soon people are teasing, "Madre Moretta always looks as if she's in church!" They poke fun. And envy her a little. The darkie smiles as she lights ovens, peels potatoes, scours pans, scrubs the floor, and carries cooking pots. She works as if her life depended on it. It must be the Negro cheerfulness the newspapers are all talking about, these people are used to working and obeying. A race that won't rebel.

They do not know. That she understands what they are saying. And has the patience of the saved. They cannot guess at the joy she feels preparing food for the institute's orphans, and the little peasant girls who come such long way, but not every day, only when they are not helping in the fields. And if she could, she would even work at night, would give up her rest, all her hours of sleep, to ease a single child's hunger. The head cook watches her warming the younger children's bowls so their food is always hot, making special dishes for the sick and often doubling the rations, warns her, "That's too much, Madre Moretta! The children don't need to eat that much."

She is wrong. The children need a lot to eat, they just do not say so. The children are hungry, and no one realizes. She knows, though. She knows you can lose the habit of eating and of asking. Knows it takes time to win over an unhappy child. She will find a way to approach them. Does her job quickly and well, always making a spare few minutes to come up from the basement to the refectory, or sometimes the infirmary. Slips a hunk of bread or a chunk of cheese into the children's pockets, crouching on a level with them to talk to them, the youngest of them call her the "Mare Moretta," "Madle Moletta," or even "Moetta Bella," and it is not long before they look out for her, call for her by drumming their fists on the table and chanting her name, she comes up and scolds them for the noise they make, is gentle, has a calm authority, and very quickly becomes more than a kitchen assistant, becomes someone who is needed. She is loved for the same reasons she was rejected. Her differences are reassuring, because when it comes down to it, which of the children and teenagers at this institute feels she belongs? Which of them does not feel threatened? Schio is a prosperous town for those who work at the Cazzola spinning mill and, to a greater extent, at the Alta Fabbrica, as people call the huge building that towers over the town and keeps it alive, the Lanerossi wool factory. But what of the rest? Being employed by Lanerossi means being saved. Means having a job, living in a factory workers' village, sending your children to the factory's school, having medical care, attending schools for adults, going to the theater, and having access to reading clubs. But what of the rest? Being "a Lanerossi" means feeling pride in being part of this model factory, contributing to the prestige of this town, of Veneto and reunified Italy. Being "a Lanerossi" means being a living example of what a post-unification Italy has to offer the sick and the cowed: education and culture. The men, women, and children of the Lanerossi workforce are literate, educated, and their work is exported all over Europe. Being "a Lanerossi" is an opportunity. Of course, you must abide by the working hours, the regulations, not challenge the wages, but most important you must not fall ill or be injured. Because stopping work at that factory, leaving Lanerossi, means leaving the country, sending your wages and your lies of happiness to a family you will never see again, to a country that will forget you. In the heights of Schio is the prosperous and proud town begat by the Alta Fabbrica, and down below is the other, older town of peasants and servants, small shopkeepers, municipal staff, single women, the elderly, and the sick.

The children recognize themselves in Madre Moretta. Like her, they make themselves understood in a language of few words, and like her, they are trying to find where they belong. They study this world, the places to which they are sent: the institute or the fields, mountain pastures or school, family or absence of family. With the passing months, Moretta Bella comes up from the basement more and more frequently, comes out of the kitchen to join them in the yard. She tells stories of a little girl who sleeps in trees, wild animals that want to eat her, tells stories that end well, true stories, describing things with her hands, and she has that way of looking at you, with huge silences, her eyes locked onto yours, and the eye contact is as intimate as kisses. The children cluster around her in the schoolyard, they sit on the ground and she joins them, never wants to stay on the bench, and it's funny seeing a nun dirty her habit sitting on the ground. Before she leaves them she always asks them to hold hands and say softy, "I won't let go your hand." Then she stands up with a grimace because her thigh hurts, she claps her hands and the children disperse, slightly dazed, half daydreaming, some run back to her spontaneously, throw themselves at her legs, and then set off again, she rests her hand on their heads, that was all they wanted. She knows the things they cannot say. Knows about sickness and poverty, and the shame of poverty. Always has a needle and thread in her pocket and surreptitiously mends tears and holey pockets, sees the hidden bruises, guesses a child is in pain from how she holds herself, how she walks, how she refuses to play. Bakhita is not like other adults, does not teach, not personal cleanliness or the catechism, not reading or arithmetic. But she is the one summoned to feed a sick child who has stopped eating, to comfort a girl who has hurt herself and is calling for her, she is the one the children call to when she crosses the yard, she gives them a little wave and walks on with her hasty, slightly lopsided step, they shout out and blow her kisses that she can feel even when she does not see them. The children love her the way you love someone who will never betray you. She can feel the warmth of it, and her voice is slow and deep. She is as black as a warm night, she is the one you can pick out instantly from the others, the not-same, an overgrown child, and the girls who go home in the evenings do not mention her, keep their discovery, their Moretta Bella, to themselves, and clamp their lips when their parents ask if the Negress has the evil eye.

She knows she must not become attached to any of these pupils, the youngest of whom are only five. Knows she must not become attached to the orphans who grow up at the institute until they marry or have found work. Knows she must become attached to no one, only to God. This is what they say, but she does not believe it. What she believes is that she must love above and beyond her own abilities, and she is not afraid of separation, this woman who has lost so many people, who is so full of absences and loneliness. What she now does, helping in the kitchen and telling stories to the children, is exactly why she came into the world. The moment she is out of the kitchen or away from the children, she goes to pray in the sacristy, the refuge behind the church that opens onto the schoolyard. From here, she can hear the children's shrieks, and she collects her thoughts in this tide of voices absorbed into the silence of the sacristy, like sunlight in clear water. She speaks to el Paron, and He never rejects her, this love is forever, it is the wide meadow in which she can rest, and she feels her heart might burst with joy and pain. Is almost crippled by her gratitude and strives to give the best of herself, everything she can. The stories she tells the children are a sugar-coated version of her childhood, her misfortunes become adventures, her despair, a fearful adversary. But when she goes to bed at night, it is quite different. Having unwound the spool of memories, images come flooding in, brutal and truthful. Sometimes she can hardly breathe and fear rises within in her like a rush of heat, enveloping her, holding her tightly, she has to get up in the night to avoid succumbing to panic. Are these memories real? Her body bears witness to things her mind has buried, and she gradually reconciles the two, accepts what happened to her and cannot belong to anyone else, to any other life but hers. Slowly pieces together her family, her village, her life *before,* but her name, that she does not find. It stayed back there, a name that would be difficult to pronounce in Italy, would be a distortion of what only her mother can say. And so she accepts even this unforgivable lapse, and her shame becomes her mother's secret.

In 1907, five years after she arrived in Schio, the woman who was exhibited for two full days, like a wild animal brought to heel, is appointed head cook at the institute. Bakhita is thirty-eight, Mother Superior hands her the keys to the kitchen and appoints three orphans—Anna, Elena, and Elvira—to work under her. Keys to the kitchen, the cupboards, the storeroom, the cellar, the storehouse, a heavy bunch of keys, and an acknowledgment.

Anna and Elena emerge with stories that the other girls listen to with amused curiosity.

"Yesterday, the Moretta hid the cornmeal! We couldn't make the polenta. She wanted us to improvise, she said, 'Come on, girls, quickly, an idea!' We ran to find the gardener and picked and peeled so many zucchinis our hands are still green!"

"The other day when it was raining hard, she made us put cloves and onions in everything we cooked. She said, 'The little ones are cold.' She treats them *before* they get sick! Oh *Dio!* And there I was with all those onions, I spent the whole morning in tears!"

"Oh, Jesus, Mary, and Joseph, be nice, don't laugh!"

But they are not laughing, not the nuns or the orphans, they are happy to know they will be well-fed, there will be no waste or lack of foresight, and visitors, be they ecclesiastical or family, will admire the way the Schio institute's kitchens are run.

Elvira does not gossip about what happens in the kitchen. She asked to work there in order to be with the Moretta. She has no gift for cooking and does not intend to take a position as a servant when she leaves the orphanage. She likes drawing and painting. But in the kitchens she is with the Moretta, she has known her since she was ten years old and loves her dearly. She works in this dark basement with walls covered in deposits of soot, in this busy warmhearted atmosphere, and her every day is protected. Elvira is a tall, muscular girl, whose body is mismatched with the delicacy of her smooth, angular face, her lively brown eyes, and her pale lips. It is as if this face opted for the wrong body, or rather is protected by it, a fragile girl carried by an athlete. Elvira was sickly in nursery school, hollow-chested, with legs as thin as reeds, and she fell over so often her injured knees never had time to scab. With time she concentrated on building herself up, battling through childhood as if through a minefield, and she won. From the age of ten she has known the stories about the little black girl who is brought up with the words "If you scream, I'll kill you," and who does not scream, the little girl who sleeps in a tree and is not eaten by wild animals, the slave who walks through the desert and climbs into the enormous boat after begging the kind Italian consul to take her with him to the country that saves Africans. Like Madre Moretta, Elvira has no family, her childhood is a wasteland and it is difficult for her to untangle the real memories from the fable she has invented for herself, her childhood is mired in a distant past that wavers like a landscape seen through nearly closed lashes, that flickers and is gone. She knows her mother is still alive, not far away, on the other side of the Alps. Elvira waits for her without truly believing she will return, and perhaps not wanting her to. Her mother writes to say she will come but never does, every letter is an event and a disappointment. Why does she never come? Why does she write? Does she really remember her daughter?

"What about you," Bakhita asks, "do you remember?"

"I remember what I've been told. Not long after emigrating to Geneva, she realized she was pregnant, but immigrants in Switzerland weren't allowed to have children. So a few days after her confinement she gave me to my grandparents who'd stayed in their village. My grandfather brought me back to Posina, he used to say I weighed no more than a piglet and was as white as milk. I remember him saying that, about the piglet and the milk, and I always picture myself as a swaddled little pig. I was five when they died, him and my grandmother. I was very lucky."

"Lucky?"

"I had a good mother. She nursed me. She didn't put oil on her breasts, like the other women did."

"What oil?"

"Camphor oil, to stop the baby from sucking. Lots of immigrant women starved their babies and stopped just before they died. Then they took them to the orphanage."

"She loves you."

"I'm going to teach you to conjugate, Madre."

"What?"

"I'll teach you the tenses. You can't always talk in the present tense, because then what you're saying isn't true."

"But it is, what I'm saying is right. *I* think it is."

"No. You said my mother loves me. That's as wrong as saying 'your mother's coming.' You should say, 'your mother *loved* you' and 'your mother *will come*.'"

"Your mother *will* come. And she *will* still love you. But right now we need to get to work."

Bakhita dictates her orders to Elvira, anticipates quantities, plans ahead, and her life finds new points of reference. Her most tangible reference is Clementina and her children, whom she calls her nephews and nieces. Stefano died suddenly the year before. She wept a great deal for this good and providential man, but he kept his word and she now has a family, like the other nuns. She has visitors and parcels, and photographs on her nightstand next to pious images and a statuette of the Virgin. With Elvira's help she learns to talk in the future and past tense, and this changes events, ordering and classifying them. One day, Elvira shows her the drawings she has made of the little slave girl asleep in the trees. Bakhita is speechless. What she sees in these drawings is herself. She is so tiny, scrawny but with a capable look about her, and most important, she looks "gentle and good."

"How do you know? What I'm like?"

"What I *was* like, Madre, in the past."

"No, it's what I'm like, now. I recognize myself in that drawing, recognize myself now."

Elvira takes her face and kisses her cheeks with their smell of washing powder, would like to hug her but that is not acceptable. No shows of emotion and no favoritism. But in her mind, when she says "Madre," the word does not have the same meaning as for the other sisters.

"I'll bring you more drawings tomorrow. I'll draw the little girl watching the sheep."

"Not sheep. Cows."

"Sheep, cows, it doesn't make any difference. What I'm interested in is you."

"But for me, it's cows. They're harder. And, anyway…I don't like sheep. Someday I'll tell you why."

And word travels, tales are repeated, stories about the Moretta, and it feels to the community as if she is growing in some way, eluding them a little, taking shape as a complex individual. Human, just like them.

The kitchen is her domain and her pride. Rising every morning to feed children eases her guilt for being saved and for being so far from all the others. But one morning, Mother Superior, Madre Margherita Bonotto, tells her it is over. She is to stop working in the kitchen. It catches her like a tripwire, sending her falling slowly, and she wonders where she can now invest her love and joy.

"Madre Giuseppina, I'm appointing you to the sacristy. Do you understand what that means?"

"Yes, Madre. Thank you."

"Being a sacristan is more important than being a cook. You have made food for people, now you'll prepare meals in the House of our Lord, the host and the Eucharist wine."

"Thank you, Madre."

"You don't look very happy."

"I am."

"Of course, we'll all have to get used to not having such good food, we must all offer this...minor sacrifice to the Lord. Can I have the keys, Madre Giuseppina?"

Her hand shakes and the keys make the little metallic clinking sound she dislikes. She is annoyed with herself for experiencing this change of duties as a separation. Being sacristan is an honor and a great responsibility, she knows it is. She hands back the keys to the kitchen, feeling disoriented and hurt.

"I'll give these to the head cook, I'll be back in an hour to give you the other keys, the new set. An hour, do you understand how long that is?"

She looks out the window at the shadow of the big chestnut tree in the yard. "Yes. In an hour I'm...I'll be here, Madre."

She bows her head and leaves with her slow footsteps, she has kept her habit of hugging the walls to avoid being seen, avoid frightening anyone. She sits on a bench in the corridor and listens to the children reciting their catechism before their lessons start. They are taught in Italian, the language in all the books, they too must forget their dialects, and she knows how difficult it is to think calmly when speaking a language that is harder to pin down than water in the torrent. She keeps telling herself that she is doing God's will. Keeps telling herself she has been saved and is a joyful daughter of God. Keeps telling herself she has been given an honor. And does not know what to do with her irrational misery. They say she will soon be forty, and here she is crying outside a classroom, she looks at her gnarled hands and feels a loneliness she has no right to feel. So she stands up and goes to her cell, tries to walk as upright as possible, head held high and biting her lip, her breathing is loud, she is relieved not to meet anyone in the corridors or on the stairs. She wants to be alone to experience this heavy burden that, she knows, will be soothed only by tears whose vehemence, though customary, is still surprising. "When we're sad, we think we always will be, don't you find, Madre?" She struggled to understand this idea of Elvira's. Considered it at length and said she disagreed. When she is unhappy, she feels as if she is returning to a place, somewhere she left, someone whom she would like to bring along with her. But who does not come. She would have liked to add that when she is happy, she feels she always will be. But she got confused with the words and said simply, "When you're sad, you have to do one thing, just one. You have to have faith."

It will be difficult not feeding the children. Not joining them in the schoolyard anymore. Not tending to them, consoling them, telling them stories. She will miss the way they mispronounce her name, their kisses and their laughter, and their familiar manner that is such a boon in this convent life lived sensibly, with restraint and respect. The work she is to do in the sacristy is so momentous it feels fantastical to her. She will prepare the Master's House. She will be the one to open the church doors every day. Prepare for services, readying ecclesiastical robes, books, liturgical objects, sacred vases, chalices, wafer boxes, monstrances, bookstands, fonts, trays, she will ensure that they always have the host and wine, but also coal, incense, candles, candle protectors, matches, and boxwood, she will have to know by heart each service and the order of the services, she will be the guardian of el Paron's Temple. His servant.

She enjoys walking around the town. Enjoys going alone, which is exceptional for a Canossian sister, but on her own she can walk slowly, her legs hurt, and going slowly she sees more, watches, wanders through Schio as if in a garden, her tall silhouette leaning on her folded umbrella. She never mentions her physical suffering, works meticulously, faultlessly, puts passion into being sacristan. No one would guess that her knees are two blazing fires, that she has trouble walking, kneeling, standing up again, that she wakes every night with waves of pain under her skin and gnawing at her bones. She looks down as she walks on Schio's uneven cobblestones, and the world accosts her in all its mess and fury, boisterous with the sound of children playing among mules and dogs, carts, bicycles, tradesmen, foul water, and detritus, countless children, and just like in her village, as soon as they can walk they become responsible for those born after them. She looks at the yellow and pink walls of the closely packed houses, feels the damp in their cluttered yards, life bursts forth with overexcited urgency and occasionally abates, recedes into docile weariness. She walks cautiously through this living world. There are still, and always will be, people who are afraid of her, who call her the Negress, the devil, the monkey, she dreads this, protects herself in anticipation with the slightly weary smile of a never-ending fight. A few days ago Mother Superior asked her about the stories she used to tell the children when she worked in the kitchens. She did not know how to reply.

"Are they true stories?"

"Partly."

"Are these things that happened to you? Is it your life?"

She said no at first. Then she wiped away this lie, and said yes, but immediately regretted it. She would rather Madre Bonotto had not asked the question, because she remembered the trial in Venice, remembered the modest celebrations after her baptism, remembered all those inquisitive people who came to the catechumen institute, remembered them asking why she had not rebelled, why she had not taken revenge, and poor girl! Oh, poor thing! How they pitied her. And in the way they looked at her, she was in a cage, studied and condemned. But Mother Superior wanted to know. And Bakhita must obey. She would rather have melted into the convent's walls, disappeared into the oblique light in the church, offered her work up to el Paron and for Him to keep her forever. But Madre Bonotto asked her to go to Madre Teresa Fabris's office, and she went. She sat down opposite Madre Fabris and obeyed when she was asked to tell the stories from her life, clearly and calmly tell these stories that she used to tell the children.

She did not know that what she said would be written down. She talked and saw her stories transformed into written words, successions of black shapes, and she asked Madre Fabris to read it to her.

"My mother has lots of children. My mother is very beautiful. My mother watches the morning, every day, I mean she watches the rising sun every morning. And I remember that."

She was ashamed. Did she really talk like that? Like a little girl. She was forty-one, and in writing, her life sounded like a nursery rhyme. Naïve and commonplace. Her life is commonplace, her life as a slave is just like tens of thousands of others, over many centuries, but she was there in that office and her words were being written, her words, the girl who "neither rebelled nor took revenge." She wished she could be forgotten. Was almost in tears.

"I'm sorry for stirring up these memories, Madre Giuseppina."

But the nun was stirring nothing. Quite the opposite. She was making a written record of Bakhita's inability to describe things, to relate them. What should she do? Hitch up her sleeves and her dress, show her scars? Mime the events, the work, the violence and fear? Elvira was the one who knew, her drawings could tell the stories better than words.

"What's that for?" Bakhita asked, pointing to the page of writing.

"To know. About your life. And Africa."

"Africa?"

"Yes, of course."

"Madre, I'm sorry, but…I know the map. The consul shows me the map and Giuseppe Checchini shows me the map. And Africa…is big. And I…what do I say?"

"You must describe things, Madre Giuseppina, traditions, food, religion."

"Religion?"

"Of course. Before you met the one true God, what idols did you worship?"

"I like to go in the garden."

"Giuseppina, do you understand what I asked you?"

"I like to go in the garden."

They walked around the garden behind the church, the early-autumn light was clear and faltering, the bitter smell of windfall apples and rambling roses reminded Bakhita of the intimacy in private homes, something about their over-furnished old rooms. It was a little cold for Bakhita, and Madre Fabris had put a shawl around her shoulders. She was as gentle as she was ignorant, and her clumsy eagerness betrayed her lack of experience. Bakhita wondered how, with what words she could talk. She knew some of the questions in advance, about her captors, forgiveness, her conversion, and the answers she had to offer never seemed to be what was expected of her. It was different and also more straightforward. Her captors? She had long since entrusted them to el Paron, no longer burdened herself with them, except of course when they decided to pay her visits during her grueling nights of bad dreams. But she had been relieved of them, because God forgave on her behalf.

She was His daughter and He did this for her. Were her stories true? Were these memories her own? But nothing was true, only the way we navigated our way through it. How to tell them that? In Venetian? Italian? Latin? She had no language for this, not even a combination of African dialects and Arabic. Because what mattered was not in words. There was what we experienced and what we truly were. Deep inside. That was all. People often asked whether she missed her mother, missed her father and brothers and sisters, her village, and she wanted to say: As much as you do. Yes, as much as you do, because everyone loves someone they miss. But that is not what they wanted to hear. They wanted to hear the difference, they wanted to make an effort to love, to reach out to her as if discovering a dangerous landscape, an archaic Africa. They were sincere, oh so sincere. But she could only disappoint them because her life was simple, and her past suffering had no words.

The institute's doors open every morning to the pupils and teachers, and the world comes in with them. On November 3, 1911, the sisters cluster around Anna, the youngest teacher, who has a newspaper celebrating a national hero, Giulio Gavotti. They peer at the photograph, cannot understand what it depicts, what the young man is sitting on. There are metal bars, two canopies, and there he is in the middle of it, with his boots and hat. Mother Superior says that two years ago a man in France crossed the sea without touching the sea, her niece, who has emigrated to Paris, told her so. Anna says that the Frenchman, Blériot, flew over the sea.

"Over the sea?"

"Yes. In the sky."

"The sky?"

No one dares probe any further. It is beyond comprehension, almost blasphemous. But there the photograph is, with this seated man flying like a bird through the kingdom of heaven.

"He flies with this machine," Anna explains. "It's called an Etrich Taube, and the writing here says 'Etrich Taube Monoplane.'"

Put like that, it sounds even more aggressive. None of them knows how to pronounce the words. But the man's name, the hero's name, Giulio Gavotti, is so beautiful, and so Italian, that Gabriele D'Annunzio has written a poem. They cannot linger here any longer, lessons are about to start, and they go their separate ways. The newspaper stays at the doorkeeper's lodge, is soon forgotten in a corner. The teachers will chat about it among themselves briefly today. But the nuns never will. Their meals are taken in silence, their days are arduous, their relaxation time joyful, almost childish, and their nights punctuated with prayer. The words in that newspaper celebrate something that happened on

November 1, 1911: the first aerial bombing in history, four fragmentation grenades lobbed out over Libya by the pilot Gavotti. At the time no one suspects that this war, this brief easily won war, will arouse nationalistic feelings in the Balkans, because no one ever sees these things coming, these human catastrophes, these successions of events perpetuating mankind's savagery and shared disaster. The early years of the twentieth century are gearing up to the Great War, but these conflicts are far away and the dead of little importance. It is all happening in deserts and colonies, in dismantled empires, and there are dreams of expansion and territorial revenge. The Canossian sisters patiently teach the children their prayers and the alphabet, mathematics and embroidery. Meanwhile, it thunders on, advancing toward them like an avalanche on the mountain behind Schio. Their world will be turned upside down, they are living in a doomed present, because somewhere there are men dreaming dreams for them, and this heroism will be their martyrdom.

One day when Bakhita takes the priest's chasuble and alb to the laundry room, she happens to hear that grenades have been dropped on Africa. The laundress nun has never liked Madre Giuseppina and, even though her color does not run as the laundress first feared it would, the Moretta's sheets disgust her and she leaves the task of cleaning them to her helpers.

"They've dropped grenades on your home, Madre Giuseppina, do you know what that means?"

"My home?"

"Africa! Boom!"

"Which Africa?"

"Your Africa. Boom!"

Bakhita does not tell the laundress nun what she knows. Neither about Africa nor about the grenades. She learned long ago that to reassure others she must always be the one who knows nothing, and she remains impassive when people shout at her to make themselves understood or talk in staccato, unconnected words. She holds her tongue and smiles. Waits. Is very good at waiting. Has had so many masters, has been given so many bizarre orders, knows that keeping quiet is often the wisest stance. So today she does not reply to the laundress nun, simply brings the dirty washing and takes away the clean, does everything as usual. But when she leaves, her heart is thudding with panic and her breath whistles, churning in her throat, like the watery noise in the slave women's throats when they were yoked. She can feel the sweat running down her cheeks and she makes her way back to the sacristy as best she can, to put the clean laundry away in the linen press. Her hands make tiny movements, folding slowly, smoothing and stroking, separating the garments with a clean piece of cloth, her eyes are misted but she checks carefully, diligently that there are no signs of woodworm, mites, or mice in the drawers, that the garments do not touch the wood, that there is no dust, there are no loose threads on the sacred vestments, and then she starts again, takes out the albs, takes out the chasubles and stoles, unfolds them, piles them up, scrambles them together. And sits down. All the clean clothes are now in a mess and she cannot think what she should do with them. "Africa! Boom!" It doesn't sound like that. When Africa explodes. The threat is silent, and the explosions sound like cries from the earth itself, deep and unintelligible, their echo around the mountains has the racing tempo of a heart about to explode. She remembers the Mahdi's advances. For the first time clearly sees in her mind's eye the night when the Turkish master gathered his slaves before disbanding them so that he could flee Sudan as quickly as possible. She hears the wails of those who had been separated and the terror of people at the very limits of pain.

She was born of war. Has seen so many men and children bearing arms, so many wounded, so many raped women, that she must have lived several lives. She thinks of her village. Would anyone here have told her if grenades had been dropped on it? But for that to happen she would need to give names, need to understand maps and talk properly. She looks at the priests' clothes, crumpled and chaotic, an accumulation of bright colors and gold thread, like a child's drawing of a hill. What a disaster. She lets her tears flow. She should put away the clothes and clean the candleholders, it will soon be time for nones prayers, she can tell by the light coming in from the yard. But she is crying and can do nothing else. She looks up at the crucified slave who knows about war. "Blessed are those who mourn, for they will be comforted." She misses Madre Fabretti. She cries and thinks to herself that it takes a lot of tears and a long time to understand convent life. She kneels, bows down as she is not supposed to, Eastern-style, because it is like this, with her bare palms and forehead on the flagstones, with her chest bent forward and her arms outstretched, that she finds it easier to think of Africa.

She has been given permission to accompany Elvira to the train station. Has pluck enough for the two of them. Keeps her sorrow for later, does not show her sadness, only her confidence and pride. Would like to carry Elvira's suitcase but does not have the strength, her body is struggling, no longer has the resilience and endurance that saved her so many times, she walks in the same way she breathes, painstakingly, cautiously, and her unremitting suffering is becoming increasingly obvious. Elvira is a strapping girl, she carries her bag and forces herself to keep pace with Bakhita, even though she wishes she could run, briskly leave all this behind, without thinking, without pain.

It is a crisp, frosty morning, there is snow on the mountaintops, and the arid trails soon to be deserted by the flocks herald the imminent winter that will gobble up daylight hours, freeze the ground, and drive peasants to despair. The sun is white, shadows are pale, as if nothing has a real hold, everything is ready to fade and vanish. It is the fall of 1913, a time that no one will remember but that everyone should in fact be cherishing. For now the station is still a place for elective departures, individual journeys, and goodbyes are said without heartbreak. Bakhita stops to catch her breath, despite the chill, her forehead and eyelids are slick with sweat. She looks at Elvira, who seems so young but could be a mother already, strange the way time accelerates, as if the girls were all growing up suddenly.

"You're right to leave, Elvira. The right time to leave is when you really want it."

"I'll write you often, Madre. I'll send you postcards every week, all the time."

"Drawings. I'd prefer that."

"I won't be drawing in the streets but in studios. I told you. I'll be drawing beautiful young men, glorious models. Would you like me to send you drawings of beautiful boys? I'm sorry...I'm so dumb when I'm emotional."

"You must be careful. Very. Men don't understand girls' happiness."

"Parisians are very romantic."

"What does 'romantic' mean?"

"It means...gentle...kind...loving."

"Oh, I'll pray for you! You're so innocent..."

They walk on, and the only sound now is Bakhita's resolute breathing, her shoes hurt her, she could walk so much better without them, her feet are deformed and more and more swollen. Elvira feels like running and whooping. Crying, too, with frustration and joy. She is leaving Italy, escaping the never-ending wait for her mother, her need of her, she does not want to spend her whole life hoping for her mother's letters and does not want to go into service for a rich Schio housewife. She does not say that she is emigrating to France but that she is going to study painting in Paris, as so many other Italian artists do. She is giving herself an identity, a certain stature. They reach the station and have nothing left to say to each other. Are stranded in a time that no longer belongs to them, in this noisy, baffling place where everything is pointless. Everything is important.

"Do you have the ticket to Milan, too? Do you have everything?"

Elvira does not reply, looks at her Madre, eleven years they have known each other, and Elvira has drawn this thoughtful face so many times, knows its expressions by heart, its concentration at work, its flinches at the slightest sound—people calling to each other outside, footsteps, whistling—its happy surprise at the least sign of affection, her hand in front of her mouth before she breaks into a true laugh, the way she looks to the heavens and bites her lip when trying to find her words, Elvira loves her and likes to shake her up a little, to push her beyond propriety, to forget the nun and allow the unusual and passionate woman that she is to emerge. But Bakhita has never wanted her to keep the portraits, images of her laughing heartily, singing with her eyes closed, silently contemplating her own hands. Would like to live her life without anyone watching. Asked her to tear up these drawings. Elvira did not do so every time. Keeps these portraits as a privilege. The Moretta is now well-known in Schio, former pupils from the institute meet her in town and approach her with the contained enthusiasm of girls who have grown up, would no longer dare to call her Moretta Bella, would no longer dare to say "Come here!" to her, and are embarrassed to remember that they once licked her hands to get a taste of chocolate, once rubbed handkerchiefs on her cheeks, and she would let them put their hands on her face to feel her skin, saying, "Don't be frightened." And also, "Are you hungry? Tell me if you're hungry, always tell me." Elvira thinks she may perhaps have been her favorite, but knows that plenty of the boarders would have liked this honor as much as she, being the one Madre Moretta loved more than the others. Now she is about to leave them together, Bakhita will be all theirs, the pupils' and the orphans', and Elvira wonders whether there are black women in Paris, if people look at them the way they do at her Madre, as they do here on this platform, with that offended air of embarrassment.

Bakhita spots it before she does, the gray cloud cutting through the trees in the distance, growing, darkening, and the locomotive's thundering power, its earsplitting whistle, do they do this on purpose so you can finally scream everything you have been holding in, the fear of leaving and the constant feeling of loneliness? A small tuft of hair has snuck out from Madre's bonnet. Elvira tucks it back with a smile.

"You didn't tell me you had gray hair."

"Soon I'm white."

"I *will be.*"

"Yes. I will be white."

"Don't ever do that, Madre! I don't want you to be like the others. Never."

She snatches Bakhita into her arms, feels her heart next to her own, her thin bones, and the sweat running down her neck.

Elvira does not believe in God but says in all sincerity, "Pray for me, Madre. I'm not as innocent as you think, but still pray for me."

Bakhita closes her eyes, it is a yes, a very gentle, very heartfelt yes. Elvira walks away, leaves her with only the crowd and the smoke, the usual panicky excitement of travelers already mingling with regrets and guilt, with kisses blown and tears carried all the way home, with such courage that you are left wondering why life is this great mountain of renunciation and heartbreak.

Time passes, and its effects are seen only in the way bodies age and children come into the world. The war has started in France, on the far side of the mountains, and in Austro-Hungary, on the other side of the river. The newspapers talk of allied countries and enemy countries, of countries far away and countries coveted, Russia, Africa, nations argue and posture. Should they fight too, break the pact of neutrality, make war or not make war, and in which camp, with Germany and Austria, Italy's allies, or with France and England? Educated men read the papers, yell at each other in cafés, at home, in public squares, there is talk of revolution, of a republic, empire, democracy, and despotism. The socialists, including the popular Mussolini, urge factory workers and farm laborers to pacifism, unionists and intellectuals want the proletariat to fight at last, factory owners dream of mass production, nationalists want to wipe away the humiliation of emigration and rebuild the country, émigrés flee to France, Belgium, and Germany only to return home, and town criers in the streets no longer simply announce the times of funerals or the arrival of particular tradesmen but also call for gatherings outside the town hall where the *podestà* is to speak, will be louder and more passionate than the others; men come to life as they take sides, talk without a moment's silence, cling to news stories and become impassioned, attend demonstrations and fight for a war about which, deep down, they know nothing. So they change camps, change their minds. Mussolini, now barred from the Socialist Party, campaigns to go to war, is joined by anarchists and nationalists, sets up networks of revolutionary action, Italy becomes a nation divided, is already fighting on home territory, in a frenzy that nothing can contain, in a state of overwhelming exasperation and intoxication.

Bakhita prays in the convent's infirmary, prays all day without rest, all night without sleep. The world reaches her, she recognizes it, it is like a market, a bazaar where human lives are sold, always the same, a disoriented commotion. It is the winter of 1915, she has been in the infirmary for several weeks and is sitting up in bed, supported by piles of pillows and coughing nonstop, her skin is going purple, a dark, torn purple, she is choking to the burning pain of a crackling cough and feels she is being skinned on the inside, her lungs, the depths of her chest are being ripped apart, she is exhausted, as if she has been running under a blazing sun, her body sweats, and to her great shame her sheets are changed every day. She could go now, in the calm of this convent, with a crucifix over her bed and a visit from the priest every morning, but she wants to stay in this human chaos and battles against her bronchopneumonia. She knows that men want war and that they will have their war, family men and young lads, off they will go to war, to the massacre, to what they call "the great collective experience," and their wives and mothers will be inconsolable, irreparable, as her mother was. She remembers, after Samir's beatings, after the torture of being tattooed, those months spent fighting off death, lying on her mat on the bare earth, earth that kept traces of every martyr's blood, and she is aware of how things come around and leave their mark, all human suffering in the din of combat. She has difficulty breathing, has a fever, but has never been so lucid. This time spent in sickness feels unreal, but she can hear what is going on, can smell the smells and see the day dawning and fading outside the window, she is in a reality that confuses people and times, people whose paths have crossed hers, those with whom she has lived, she hears the haranguing of powerful leaders, the children's nursery rhymes, the nun's canticles, demonstrators' slogans, day laborers singing "Cornmeal polenta, water from the ditch, you work, boss, because I can't," she thinks of the pupils who have grown up, of the children she has watched being born, of these generations of soldiers. Will the men hide in the hills or come out of their houses, come out from caves and log cabins, from the remotest places, Eutichio the wolf charmer who lives up in the mountains, Angelo the charcoal burner who lives in the woods with his family, Tano the illiterate goatherd, peasants with no land of their own and those who hide in the fields and live off contraband tobacco? Will all these men who no longer know where to live or how to live join the great amassing armies? She must pray for the men who want to fight but do not want to die, who want to be unique but want to wear a uniform. Wishes she could tell them how fleeting life is, it is just an arrow, a slender searing arrow, life is a single gathering, frenzied and miraculous, we live, we love, and we lose what we love, so then we love again, and we are always looking for the same person in all the others. There is only one love. A single shared host. One bread multiplied. She wishes she could tell them, but with her *jumble,* and her shyness, who would understand her?

Night has fallen, the sky is deep, the blazing moon is cut in two, Bakhita wonders where in the world the other half lives, invisible in a bright sky. This half-moon as she sees it now, while she lies in this room with its smell of camphor, ether, and burning wood, is something she has in common with soldiers on the far side of the mountain, and the other side of the river, in warring lands whose names she cannot remember. She is safe, once again. Is sick and is being tended to. Her thirst is quenched and she is fed, is one of those to whom everything is given. She pushes back the sheets and blankets, and swings around her swollen legs, sits on the edge of the high bed and catches her breath, then stands and walks slowly to the window, opens it, as she normally does in the evening, and drinks in the metal cold of the night and the harsh light of the moon. She clings to the windowsill, her breathing gradually settles, she listens but hears nothing, not a single animal, not a breath of wind, as if over the convent and the town, over the mountains and streets, the factories and cowsheds, the night has laid the full weight of its scorching contempt. Showing no mercy and no succor. She would like to recite a Paternoster but her mind is hazy. Would like to kneel but her knees are stiff. Looks for her crucifix, around her neck or in her pocket, but finds nothing. Nothing but her old slave's body, black under her white nightdress, and before it, a world standing silent. A slave, yes, she is that. Bakhita. The Lucky One. The one that a priest teasingly nicknamed "Jesus's fly" because she was there in the sacristy, black and busy, black and buzzing, like a fly. She is an insect, perhaps less than an insect. And she will protect her life, however small it may be. And will recover in order to live on among men, the men who gather every day to wave flags and holler words that do not belong together, insane, determined perennial words: "Hooray for war!"

She likes being with children and teenage girls, because she likes those who are just beginning. Making their entrance into life, alert, credulous, and flamboyant. They understand her mongrel language, seek out her strength and protection, and laugh with her because to them she is nothing more or less than herself. She needs this. This recognition without hierarchy, this spontaneous tenderness and happy intimacy. But there are no pupils in the institute's classrooms today, and the orphans have left for Bergamo. On May 23, 1915, Italy went to war alongside France, England, and Russia. Its armies took up positions in the Julian March and the Alps. Schio took in northern Italians. Women, children, the elderly. The men, meanwhile, seemed to have multiplied, a plethora of busy, inventive strategists, nothing could resist them as they built wooden bridges across mountain precipices, tanks that swallowed up trees and houses, boats that lived underwater, insatiable airplanes, the war was a permanent fire, and confronted with its hallucinatory power, civilians fled, suddenly became wandering rootless creatures at the mercy of others.

In June 1916 Austrian troops marched on Veneto, as if to reclaim an asset unjustly lost, and the inhabitants of Schio fled. Having been hosts, they in turn became refugees. Bakhita watched them leave on foot and on bicycles, with livestock and heavy-laden little donkeys, with dogs following carts drawn by bone-thin oxen, carts topped with a mattress, covering a sewing machine or a mirror, a bucket, a hen, or the portrait of a dead loved one, the bric-a-brac that does not encapsulate a life but admits how impossible it is to know what makes up a life. The children seemed only mildly surprised, they were hungry anyway, and their eyes were bigger than their faces, they asked no questions, simply followed the course life was taking, left with their mothers, their grandparents, and all the other trusting, surprised creatures like themselves, a ragtag of babies, brothers and sisters, cousins. They headed away from the border with Austria, this empire to which—as inhabitants of Veneto—they had belonged for so long, and took refuge in Milan, Turin, Ferrara, and Cuneo, accommodated in hospices and schools, the sick sent to the civilian hospital in Vicenza, and on the bishop's orders all sacred objects, from the most sacred to the most punctilious, relics of saints right down to parish registers, were stowed safely in Venice. As if life were evaporating, becoming transparent, withdrawing.

A few months later shells fell on Schio's abandoned houses, and the streets turned into dusty ruins littered with broken crucifixes, copper cooking pots, and a few heartbreaking misspelled love letters. Bakhita walked through this transformed version of Schio, what was advancing on the town was death, borne in triumph by all those who survived, the slave traders whom the Italians called "kings," "emperors," "ministers," or "presidents," leaders who sent whole caravans of men into combat. She watched the sky grow light over those torn walls, over bedrooms in ripped-open houses, disemboweled shops, polluted streams, and then the streets of Schio were emptied even of these ruins, opened up to reveal truckloads of soldiers, Red Cross vehicles and officers' cars, mules carrying munitions cases, tractors towing canons, and, carried in on stretchers, the wounded were found space to rest in the convent's dormitories and the institute's classrooms. And to the fury of those who had stayed on here, the army requisitioned a house on the Via Rovereto to "serve" the soldiers, a place the locals would not look at, whose name they did not dare pronounce, a name as coarse as pleasure itself. A house in which to forget about death. Schio was transformed into a barracks.

She is no longer among children. No longer among youngsters starting out in life. Tends to men who have become ageless and, although amputated, mutilated, and disfigured, want to live. In their dogged determination she recognizes the terrible menacing strength of people who, like her, in a life so far away but also so close, have decided not to surrender one inch to the darkness.

When you are in pain. When you are hungry. You stop loving. No longer have the strength for it, she knows this. So she feeds the injured, hoping that as they rediscover their appetite for bread, they also find their lust for life. She brings them what she has managed to cook, replacing flour with potatoes, sugarless jellies with pear preserves, she keeps the eggs in limewater, the meat wrapped in ice and straw in the bottom of the well, she invents, improvises, and no one thinks to contradict her, she works in silence and when she comes up from the basement, she helps the sisters feed the soldiers. And she knows. What will happen when they see her for the first time. They will be frightened. A violent reaction, real terror, because anything people see for the first time frightens them, anything new is a threat. She is prepared for the looks of horror, the faces turned away, the rejection, the silent, paralyzing amazement. The dormitories are full of it, fear and neediness. She watches the experienced sisters tend to the men tirelessly, and others, younger ones, curbing the urge to vomit, to run away, a longing to be somewhere else, take refuge in the church to pray, close their eyes and pray, far removed from the inhumanity life has to offer, everything that should never happen but does happen simply presents itself, makes itself comfortable, is here to stay. She approaches soldiers with her face lowered, slowly, so they have time to get used to her.

Soon she is spending as much time in the infirmary as in the kitchen, hardly sleeping, just snoozing in an armchair in the dormitory, watching over them, and one night, in the lightning-flash brevity of a dream, she remembers a baby she cared for, born to a slave woman who died in childbirth in the "snake house," her first master's house. And then the child was sold or given away, she cannot remember, but she suddenly misses that child with ferocious intensity, she let him go, just as she did with Binah, did not hold on to him, the oppressive weight of it crushes her chest, Kishmet is an old woman trudging the streets of Khartoum, Mimmina has left Africa, her own mother has left the baobab trunk on the ground, where are you, where have you all gone? She wakes as if drowning, suffocating, gasping for breath, gripping the armrests of her chair, and the heavy putrid smell of the dormitory ricochets her back into her dream, it is the smell of nights spent in slave quarters, she gets up and kneels, right there, among the wounded. Speaks to her father, the African, the man who never managed to find her, and she asks el Paron to forgive him. Has only just grasped the guilt and terror felt by the man who fathered her and then lost her. She entrusts all of him, whether he is alive or dead, to the supreme infallible Father, entrusts his devastated soul, his love, and his defeat. And feels soothed. Gets back to her feet, walks slowly, her footsteps ponderous, uneven, swaying among the sleeping soldiers. Realizes that everything she learned as an *abda* is serving her now. She walks in the half-light between the rows of beds, and knows that in each of these men there is a part that is greatness and a part that wanders aimlessly. Some will die before dawn, without understanding, others will survive wounds that were thought fatal, there they lie, unequal in the face of pain and of death, and she hears their breathing, like frightened children.

It creeps up on her, almost in spite of herself, the tune of a song she did not even think she knew, and she sings it to the sleeping soldiers, who smell bad, are in pain. Sings and forgets some of the words, tripping up sometimes: "A little breeze blew by . . . the roses . . . the fragrance, while I, I dreamed and my soul dreamed too. But the threads...the threads," and one of the soldiers picks up the song for her, she can hear him at the far end of the dormitory, a hoarse halting voice: "My soul dreamed too. But while the threads ran through the loom, I heard the bell ring, like a gunshot to the heart. I felt a burning in my soul, I clenched my fists and shouted: curses on the factory with its smoking chimney, curses on the looms with their weaving and their shuttles, those machines are cursed monsters, they've been eating away at my life for twenty years."

She is at this man's bedside, amazed by the vehemence of the song. All she knew was the opening, the soul and the smell of roses.

"Are you a Lanerossi?"

"No, little sister, I'm from the other mill, Cazzola."

"And now you're here..."

"Yes. Back home. Life is strange..."

"Yes."

"I'll never go back there, to the factory...I'm only half a man now."

He gestures toward his one leg. She thinks that in Italy worthless men are not abandoned, and this man will draw his strength from another source, some part of himself he does not yet suspect.

"There's nothing to do for this bitter world. And nothing to do with what's left of me, either. Nothing..."

She looks at him, his anger and, more particularly, his disgust at what is happening to him. His contempt for himself.

"Look after your life."

"My life? What life? A *half* life, yes."

"Please, always look after it."

She smiles at him and dares to put a hand on his forehead, it is a long, chapped, very warm hand, a hand that soothes, she knows it does, and the soldier closes his eyes, his tears so sparse that they look old, ancient, like the very end of an exhausted sob.

"Why?" he asks.

"What?"

"Why are you so kind, little black sister?"

The soldier's breath comes in deep sighs, she still has her hand on his forehead, which is now sweating, burning under her palm, the fever is coming out, her arm aches, her shoulder is stiff, but she has not finished, this needs to go on longer, goes on and on, until the soldier turns his head, his lips parted, his face serene, succumbing to sleep. She returns to the armchair with her clumsy footsteps, would like to make no noise but does make some, hobbling and breathless, and she falls asleep for an hour or two in the chair, and when a soldier wakes from time to time, this woman sitting there sleeping reminds him that before this war started, he was just a child, just a little child.

A small black sun turns around and around, and the man's voice is right here beside her. She cannot see him, neither him nor the piano, does not understand what he is singing, but his song is so beautiful that she sits listening, attentive, wanting to join her gnarled hands in prayer. Dares not because this is not a sacred song, but still. It is the purest prayer she has ever heard. She does not know what this piece means, *The Pearl Fishers,* they are all fishers, and pearls too, but no one tells them, no one tells the men that they are divine. And they have come home from war bitter and tight-lipped, come home aged and full of resentment, Bakhita has seen their distrustful eyes watch everything as if to say, "So, it's like that now, is it? That's how you want things to be?" And she knows this is only the beginning. She listens to Caruso sing, his voice coming from the horn above the small box, and this is the most beautiful thing progress has produced. Caruso sings for all of Italy and for each individual Italian, his voice expresses all the devastation and pain offered up, his singing has the rhythm of life, willful and fragile but sustained like a victory of the human heart. If Bakhita dared, she would ask Elvira to put the phonograph in the church, so the crucified slave and the Madonna could take on the suffering of men contained within the tenor's singing. But she would never make such a decision, is here to obey, and obey she does, in humility and poverty. And yet how can she help these men? How can she heal them of so much pain? She anticipates what is still to come. The humiliation suffered is like a graft on a tree, one day there will be a new fruit, a fruit it will be impossible to ignore, because once rebellion has taken root it does not evaporate. The returning soldiers say nothing, but she recognizes the faces of animals ready to commit themselves passionately, knows it will not be long before they rally to the first cry and, with their heads lowered in determination, plow toward the powerful leaders, look them in the eye, and allow the leaders themselves to have a good look at them, see these returning armies.

During the war, thousands of Italian soldiers died of cold and hunger as prisoners of the Germans and Austrians. Bakhita knows this death, hunger that leaves you a husk, ruined on the inside, the cramps, the hiccuping, the dizziness, cold that freezes the heart, silting it up, choking it, till the eyes are blind, the mouth bleeding, the convulsions and the delirium, she remembers, saw so much of it in caravans, zarebas, and slave markets, hunger destroyed the mind long before the body gave way. Sometimes, in the still of the night, she finds herself wondering what point there is in prayer, and her doubts are still more violent than her suffering. She feels that everything hovers between uncertainty and belief, between beauty and the profanity of beauty. Today while she listens to Caruso sing her emotions are as raw as when she meets injured soldiers or soldiers' families. She learns new things, things that deep down are not new at all, immutable inhumanities, and an armistice does not mean amnesia. This war can be related without words, can be told with refusals and strikes, an accumulation of poverty and so much injustice. Madre Battiseli's nephew returned from Caporetto, where the Italian army was trapped in the mountains and defeated. He described how the soldiers retreated toward the river Piave, abandoning thousands of men to the enemy...along with the best part of Veneto. It was the fall of 1917, the disastrous fall. Everyone in Schio knew that Austro-German forces were twenty-five miles from Venice, and reverberating across the sky, around the mountains, and beside rivers was the sound of the cavalcade of death marching onward, a more powerful raiding party than the most vigorous slave dealers. When he returned from the camps, Luigi, the nun's nephew, explained in hushed secretive tones how the Italian prisoners' deaths had been planned by their commanding officers: orders for them to be kept starving, forced to work, sent neither private parcels nor Red Cross assistance while held in Austro-Hungarian camps. So they walked barefoot in the snow and died of pneumonia. Ate grass in the camp and died of dysentery. Rifled through garbage and died of hunger. But why speak so quietly? Why say all this as if it were confidential? Why did Luigi bear the burden of shame on behalf of the Italian general staff who had never hidden the truth, had actively campaigned to make it known, so that the "full horror of captivity" be brought home to the prisoners? Brought home to these insubordinate traitors. Luigi describes his purgatory, but it is news to no one. Italy went to war. War pulled the country apart, impoverished its people, and divided its population. Caruso may be singing of this too, a single language for a country that wanted to be unified but tore itself apart. Elvira had fled France, a country that was an ally in wartime but a traitor at the armistice, the country that stole peace from the Italians, who gained none of the territories, none of the expansion that had fueled their dreams. France is the new enemy. Everything changes camps so quickly.

Elvira did not draw in Paris, she survived by modeling, the naked girl on the dais, but she will not tell Bakhita this, Bakhita would not understand, could not understand that being the naked girl on the dais was not what she feared, she was not only *djamila,* not merely coveted. Being looked at by artists is in itself art. This is what she tells herself to keep intact her longing for something other than the factory floor or domestic service, but she now knows it will not be enough, painting, singing, and beauty will not be enough to rebuild a world. She has gone into service for the Caresinis in the big house on the edge of town. A hidden, protected residence, where she is simply passing through. She is not the sort to resign herself and serve, she came back here only to set off again and did not even recognize her hometown. Not just the gutted houses and fallow fields, destruction like that is the same everywhere. Rather than the ransacked houses, it was those left standing, those watched, guarded, that spoke to her of the newfound violence in her town. The carabinieri posted around the clock outside the family homes of soldiers accused of desertion and shot, a sentinel stopping anyone from coming to gape at the pariah's parents, but stopping no one from seizing their possessions, and the families are now nothing more than designated prey, caged in their homes and their shame.

In this mild afternoon, filled with the smell of figs, Elvira looks at her Madre Moretta, barely touched by the invention of the phonograph but devastated by this song she does not understand. If she were to draw her hands today, they would look like vine shoots, like twisted kindling wood.

"I'm going to interrupt Caruso, it makes you too sad. And you've stopped talking to me, too."

She lifts the tonearm, the singing stops, and the sudden silence feels like an affront.

"It's beautiful," Bakhita says.

"It makes you too sad. Look at me, Madre, even your hands are sad."

"My hands?"

"Yes. You could be a model for sad hands."

Bakhita laughs. Looks at her hands and waves them about like puppets.

"I'm happy, the children are coming back, the school's opening again."

"Wonderful! The school's opening again, the land has been promised to the peasants, and the bosses are going to give us an eight-hour day."

"The children are coming back, Elvira."

"The peasants are occupying the land, Madre."

"Occupying?"

"They're on the land but not working it. Things have changed. Nothing will be like before. Oh, no! Don't wring your hands! Come on, let's dance, let's dance!"

Elvira turns the handle on the phonograph, puts the stylus onto the second piece of music on the record.

"Tarantella Napolitana! Will you do me the honor of this dance, Moretta Bella!"

Bakhita glances around briefly. There is no one else in this shady courtyard next to the orchard. She takes the hand that Elvira offers and there on the dry earth they perform a few jubilant, ungainly dance steps. Bakhita closes her eyes and Elvira can see in her smile how much she loves life, a love that runs as deep as hope. A resistance.

Land. Factories. Mills. Workshops. They are all occupied. Strikes. Demonstrations. Riots. The proletariat is working up to a revolution, as it is in Russia. Socialist workers clash with the police. Throw officers—those lackeys of capitalism—out of windows on trains and trams. Clash with their bosses. With landowners. The idle rich and financiers. Enough of submission, destitution, unemployment, and exile. The order of things is turned on its head. After this war, which they never wanted, their country will be reborn, proud, indignant, and powerful. In the opposing camp are war veterans, now out of work, with no role in civilian life, taking issue with the socialists' pacifism and challenging their contempt. They are nationalists, futurists, unionists, republicans, Catholics, anarchists, elite soldiers, and they are forming a movement, the Italian Fasci of Combat. They take in anyone who believed in the war and is now choked with bitterness. Disappointment. Despair. Anger. Hate. Peace has been cut short. It has nothing to offer them. The Allies laughed at their country, carved up the world and left them only crumbs. These veterans did not go to hell and back to bow and scrape once again. Their leader is a journalist, the son of a lowly blacksmith and a nursery-school teacher, Benito Mussolini. He will restore the veterans' lost honor. Reinstate Italy's greatness. He has given his word.

That is how it started. With men who needed to band together. To fight. Be Italian. Proud, too. Virile. And, in many cases, violent. With a taste for war under their skin. And for revenge. To reign, in fact. In their own group, their camp, their village, their region. And to set themselves free. With fighting. Pillaging. Murder. Alcohol. Cocaine and sex. Their time had come. Time for a new Italy. Time for their youth. They sang "Giovinezza," and this song became an anthem. They dressed in black, and this color became a flag. They marched through the streets and sowed terror. They called themselves "Despair," "Fearless," "Lightning," "Satan." They had clubs, brass knuckles, daggers, revolvers, and grenades. Their blood was up, they moved quickly, like frenzied dogs, and their urge to live became confused with their urge to kill. They wanted to do away with all the others, anyone who was not with them. Anyone bogging down the country. Hampering their reign. The Reds. Peasant organizations. Catholic cooperatives. Unions. All those little people, the pathetic and the undesirable. They meanwhile were a fire consuming the country. A movement spreading its wings, casting its shadow, and forcibly instituting its laws. And then one day their movement was no longer a movement. It was a party. The National Fascist Party, set up by Mussolini. With deputies. Votes in parliament. Legitimacy and strength. The Bolshevik revolution was dead. The fascist revolution was up and running. Mussolini entered Rome. Was appointed prime minister. Established a militia. Restored order. Discipline and respect. War had created martyrdom and sacrifice, but it was now time to dominate the Mediterranean, find their own place in the sun at last. Reunification was the making of Italy. Now it was time to make the Italians.

The orphans return to the institute. More of them and younger than ever. Tiny little girls so thin that illnesses carried them off before the nuns even had time to tend to them. The white wooden coffins are light, adorned with a flower picked in the garden, followed by nuns dazed by their own impotence. The pupils arrive late, struggle to concentrate, and they too are hungry, as are the teachers, as is everyone. What to eat, where to find food, how to pay for it, with what? Inflation is at 450 percent, the weapons factories are emptying, unemployment breaks men's spirits, reduces families to despair, brings the country to its knees. But Il Duce points toward the sun.

Mother Superior asks to see Bakhita in her office. Bakhita feels an emotional response as she obeys what she always experiences as an order. She forces herself to calm down as she climbs the stairs to the office, clinging to the banisters without which she could not go any farther, and when she arrives, Mother Superior will be holding the handkerchief that she will inevitably need to wipe her brow. Mother Superior gestures to an armchair facing her and, with a wave of her hand, tells Bakhita to catch her breath. Bakhita smiles, one hand on her heart, embarrassed that it takes a while for her breathing to settle.

"I always make so much noise. I'm sorry."

"Madre Giuseppina, you know that many things have changed since the war—"

"Am I not staying?"

"Excuse me?"

"Am I being sent somewhere else, Madre?"

"Of course not."

"I'm staying?"

"Madre Giuseppina, you mustn't always talk as if you're going to be driven out. I'm here to tell you the exact opposite."

"The opposite?"

"You have worked in the kitchens, in the sacristy, and even in the infirmary. I would now like you to be at the institute's front door. Do you understand?"

Bakhita's heartbeat accelerates, as if any piece of news were a brutal shock, any change painful.

"Madre, do you mean that I am... sorry, that I will be the *portinaia*?"

"The doorkeeper, yes, that's right."

"Here? On the Via Fusinato?"

"Well, naturally, here, at the institute! Where else would it be?"

"But...Forgive me. Thank you, Madre. But...one question, if I may?"

"You may."

"I'm—"

"Very black, yes. They'll get used to it. You're patient. Kind. You can explain. You've already helped out a little at reception, you know what to do."

"A little..."

"It always went very well, I know it did."

Bakhita bites her lip, Mother Superior laughs out loud. "What I mean is, it always ended up all right. People see you, they're frightened, but after a few days, everything's fine."

"Well, yes..."

"You will greet the pupils, the orphans, the teachers, the nuns' families, church clerics, school inspectors, and even plumbers, decorators, delivery men, and the gardener! It's a big responsibility."

Bakhita bows her head as a sign of acquiescence. She should thank and obey. But being the institute's *portinaia* means being constantly exposed to the door, the first port of call for anyone from the outside world. Convent doors should be open to all people at all times. She knows this. And is frustrated with herself for feeling more fear than gratitude.

"Thank you, Madre," she says, and, because it is the only thought she finds reassuring, she adds, "It is el Paron's will..."

"Of course it's what the Lord wants, He's your 'boss,' Madre Moretta!"

It is strange how people always remind her she is the Moretta the moment she mentions el Paron. Even though the church uses the terms "master" and "servant" without intending any reference to slavery or skin color.

"When will I start?"

"Next week. In seven days."

"Thank you."

She leans on the arms of the chair to stand up, but Mother Superior has more to say.

"Do you remember when Madre Fabris started writing your story?"

"My story?"

"Your memories of Africa."

"Oh... of course."

"And when Madre Maria Turco pursued this with you, it helped you recover your memories, didn't it?"

"Yes..."

"We'd like to pick that up again."

"Oh, thank you, Madre, but... I have memories. Thank you."

"Well, that's good, but Madre Maria Cipolla is very interested in your... journey. In who you are. She asked for the notes Madre Fabris made to be sent to Venice, to Ida Zanolini, who writes for our periodical, *Vita canossiana*. Do you understand?"

"Yes."

"Signora Zanolini found your memories very... really very touching, but she thinks you could go further. Much further."

"Further?"

"With your recollections. Particularly of slavery."

The word is like a slap. This word that still defines her. But she cannot see what more she could say, what it is they need to hear. Perhaps her story is too wretched for this woman who writes in a periodical.

"Why, Madre? Why say more?"

"Because Signora Zanolini, who is a very cultured woman, a highly regarded teacher, and a good Christian, is going to write your story as a serial. Do you know what a serial is?"

"A story. A story several times."

"Exactly. It's an honor, Madre Giuseppina. But you must derive no pride from it. You will leave for Venice tomorrow morning. When you return you will take up your position as doorkeeper."

"Venice?"

"With the Canossians at the Sant'Alvise Institute. That's where Signora Zanolini will meet you. Madre Giuseppina... the Dorsoduro Institute now belongs to the Salesian sisters. There isn't a single Canossian sister left at the catechumen institute, did you know that? Don't expect to see anyone you know in Venice."

"But where are they? The sisters, where are they now?"

"Don't you worry about that. You go now."

Who else would be asked to tell their life story straight out like that? Who would be forced to have their confidences transcribed and made public? Who else but a former slave saved by Italy? A Negress converted to Catholicism? The year is 1930. Military operations have intensified in Libya. Women, children, and the elderly have been corralled in camps around Benghazi. Where they die of disease and malnutrition. Mussolini's army released mustard gas over the country. This is the "place in the sun," the "conquest of the Mediterranean." It is Africa that fuels Mussolini's dreams and the dreams of a nation brought to their knees, the Africa of barbarity and abject poverty, and conquering this Africa would restore the Italians' honor, and the power they have lost. The Africa featured in postcards, films, novels, songs, and even commercials for coffee, insurance, and beer. So why not have a serialization of the terrible life story of Madre Giuseppina, formerly Bakhita? Why hide what is a living testimony to the best that Italy can do?

She is back in Venice. And it is Mimmina she misses. Instantly. The baby clasped to her on those windy sun-sliced streets, captivated by the sudden beauty of a palace, a flower-decked terrace, a centenarian tree on a small square. Returning to Venice is like visiting it for the first time. She is more than sixty years old, but it is as if she were twenty with that child huddled against her, filling her with joy and a lust for life. One next to the other. This was where the two of them belonged. It was solid and happy. Since then, not a day has passed when she has not prayed for Mimmina, for el Paron to protect her, and, most important, for Him to tell her that she, Bakhita, loved her and still does with an indestructible love, bound to her life itself. She comes to the little square outside the convent in the heart of the Cannaregio district, and the red-brick church looks as imposing and weighty as a windowless palace. The sound of her lopsided footsteps rings on flagstones and bounces off houses caught in the sunlight. She is back in the city's salty, fishy smell, and the feeling of being protected, being on this island as if nestled in the crook of a hand, trusting, because the light is so beautiful, and men travel about in their gondolas like tribesmen in canoes, solitary and proud. Looking out over the nearby lagoon, she is back in a life lived openly under the sky, its uninterrupted horizon, and she smiles, because here in Venice she has found something of Africa's unconstrained spaces. She prayed a great deal the day before, has not slept, and knows that el Paron is asking her to talk of all the people she did not help, who she left to die in a ransacked land.

She meets Ida Zanolini in the cloisters of the Sant'Alvise convent. The young woman's surprise... Bakhita is the first black person she has met, and she is so taken aback she does not know how to greet her, bows, kisses the mater dolorosa of Bakhita's Canossian medallion, and smiles at her, emotional and embarrassed. She is a committed, exuberant woman, a lay teacher devoted to her profession and to Catholic action. She and Bakhita go to the convent's small visiting room to sit down, and Bakhita knows almost immediately that with Ida Zanolini she will be able to speak at her own pace, speak as she chooses, and she senses that she will tell her how it feels. How it feels to have come through it all. Without the others. She thinks she has said enough about the burned village, the abducted sister, and the captors' dagger against her neck. But Ida does not write anything down as she listens, does not ask her to repeat or explain any words, does not ask her to go back or rationalize the sequence of her account. Because she is listening not to Madre Giuseppina but to the woman who cannot remember her name and is now describing her past as she never has before. The pain. The defeats and the shame. And the loss that no fervor has succeeded in assuaging.

In her bedroom that evening, Ida writes down everything she has heard, at such speed that she struggles to read her own writing, which comes in a great tide, and it is the modest guttural words wrested from the little Daju girl that guide her hand. She has never experienced this. Never met anyone like Bakhita. Faltering, and yet filled with superhuman strength. Incandescent. Unclassifiable. Intelligent and restrained. She does not yet know where this narrative will take them both, and perhaps if she had known, she would never have dared. Had she been aware of the repercussions, the passions, the near madness this serialization in the Canossian periodical would provoke, perhaps she would have apologized to the woman who confided in her over the course of three full days, sometimes choked by sobs, and who pulled herself together like someone clinging to the last rock on the last mountain in order to describe the torture, the children, particularly the children, "you understand: the children, child slaves, child soldiers, do you understand, I did nothing and neither did you, and who could, who will, tell me who will do something someday?" This is what she said, in her *jumble*, in which there were flashes Ida understood so clearly.

On the last day Ida takes Bakhita to 108 Dorsoduro, the former catechumen institute. Twenty-eight years after leaving, she is back in this familiar place. The Salesian sisters have been warned, and, doing their best to disguise their surprise when they see the Moretta who is blacker than all the photographs and pictures they have seen of Africans, they open their door wide to her. The small cloister, the compact garden, a corner of silence under a calm sky, and a violent sensation of being at home. Here in this institute, the first place where she said no. She goes into the visiting room, vast and empty but still echoing to the sound of Mimmina's sobs and her mother's curse, "You ingrate!" This oppressively dark place is inhabited only by the shadows and echoes it still holds, and in this brutal concertinaing of time, she is struck by how achingly close the past is. Remembers Stefano, his impatience and commitment, she realized only much later how doggedly he had fought for her, all of this has been written down now. Justice has been done to him. Perhaps his children will read the serialization. And Mimmina? There is no news of her at all. She could so easily find out where her former nanny lives, she may even know but does not come.

Bakhita goes into the chapel, it is humble, almost bare. She walks over to the baptismal fonts, points them out to Ida.

"I became God's daughter. Here."

And Ida feels guilty that she will be writing down these words, these very intimate words, along with all the others. Bakhita sits facing the crucified slave, the man she knew without even knowing who he was. She can hear Madre Fabretti saying, "Blessed are those who mourn, for they will be comforted," and she feels as if she is returning to her very source, as if this place also kept watch over her childhood with her family, kept watch over the confusion and love she feels for it. She understands that Venice saved her because Venice belongs to the sea, it is a place of ebb and flow, of refugees and tradesmen, of intermixed people and dreamers, a city where she felt at home, drawn to and intrigued by the sisters singing at dawn, their hushed intoning behind a velvet drape.

Ida hangs back slightly, cannot help looking at her: What language does she speak to herself? Is there one language for Africa and one for Italy? One language for el Paron and another for the stars, stars she says she has looked at every evening since she was a child? Has she really forgotten her name, or is that her last secret? Ida is afraid of betraying her. Afraid of hurting her by writing about this childhood lived in another century, and quite immutable in its devastation. She looks at Bakhita and has an impression of theft. She is taking everything. There is what she does not see, what she intuits, and all the questions she has not asked. The savagery of her masters. Their boundless power over little girls and women. She can imagine. Will say nothing. Because nothing has been said. The dishonor. The dying inside. The part of her burned. She looks at Bakhita, slightly stooped now by tiredness, and feels uncomfortable knowing that her back is scarred by whipping, her skin tattooed, and especially uncomfortable because readers of the serial will soon know this too. She can see her own words, her sentences lined up like ropes, solid as chains, catching and confiscating confidences.

She has not told her. Must tell her. Absolutely must.

"People will read this, Madre Giuseppina, do you understand? They'll know. There aren't very many of them, and they are our kind. But they will know everything."

Vita canossiana does not have a vast readership. But deep down Ida knows. She will not accept it but knows it, the dishonesty of the written word, a spoken avowal written down, circulated, and replicated. "It could end up in anyone's hands," she thinks. Immediately brushes aside this premonition and masks it with a surprise, she has a surprise for Madre Giuseppina today, redeeming herself in advance for what might happen once the serial is published, things for which she knows she will be responsible.

They take the vaporetto together and the vigorous buffeting of the wind makes Bakhita laugh, she likes this short trip with the roar of the motor and the pitfalls of the swell, the Virgin's expansive gesture on the dome of the basilica, as if she were offering them the sky on this happy day, leaving Venice and watching it grow as they move away. "It's beautiful!" Bakhita cries, and Ida nods in agreement, holding her scarf over her wayward hair.

They come to the island of Giudecca, to the new institute for abandoned children. This is a surprise for Bakhita. And it will also be a surprise for the person she has come to see, Madre Fabretti. The *portinaia* who opens the door to them is young, seems like a child to Bakhita but says she has already been here fifteen years, as if this were an indicator of her rectitude, she blushes when Bakhita speaks to her, and her expression betrays a note of pride to be seeing with her own eyes this former slave whose conversion is described to every novice. She explains that Madre Fabretti no longer walks and calls for a sister to show them to her room. Bakhita sits down while they wait. Does a mother that old still recognize her child? Can you recognize someone after "nearly thirty years apart. Ten. Plus ten. And another ten," Ida explained with her outspread hands. She does not know. Has never been reunited with anyone.

She and Ida follow the sister who leads them down long corridors with waxed floors. They can hear the shrieks of children playing, shrieks that bounce off the countless windows. Ida takes Bakhita's arm, helping her to walk without appearing to, surprised by the weight of this body that has to peel itself away from the earth. She knows—and cannot help thinking of—the miles this body covered in deserts and on hills. Noticing the frightened expressions of those who come across Bakhita, she wonders whether anyone with a black body can ever be free.

Bakhita goes over to the armchair where Madre Fabretti is sitting, huddled, bowed as if in prayer, her chin on her chest, her neck fragile. Kneels to be on a level with her, and with the pain that this causes her, it is as if she is the same advanced age as the friend she has come to see. Their heads are so close, face-to-face, breath mingling with breath. They do not speak. But look at each other. For a long time. And then a slow gentle movement, Bakhita's forehead leans in and comes to rest on Madre Fabretti's lap. The old woman's misshapen hand strokes her headdress. And it wells up slowly, just a breath at first, rasping, obstructed, and then a cough, something trapped in her throat, and from Bakhita's buried face comes a powerful never-ending sob.

Ida tiptoes out, leaves the old nun and her protégée to renew their dependence on each other, renew a prohibited emotion, an attachment that, she understands, takes nothing away from God but gives these two women a taste of the elective, consensual, subjective love that makes us all unique.

"We'll need a photograph, Madre Giuseppina, a photograph of you on the cover of the book."

"What book?"

"After the serialization there'll be a book, you've been told that. *Have* you been told?"

"My hideous face? On a book?"

"Come on! The Italians are more and more accustomed to black faces. Show her the postcards, Ida, there are such pretty ones now. Do you know the one of the young Italians kneeling before the little black girl? You know, the one with the hammer. The Italian boy is kneeling and breaking the young slave's chains. My nephews showed it to me, it's so moving!"

A nun is taking Ida and Bakhita back to Venice from Giudecca, and her high-pitched voice can barely be heard over the noise of the vaporetto. Bakhita screws up her eyes as she looks at her.

"But you'll be on the book too, Madre," Bakhita says.

"Me? Why me?"

"Canossians are always in twos. So I can't be alone in the picture."

The nun laughs playfully to mean no. She has been told about Madre Moretta's sense of humor. She drops the two of them at the Cannaregio quay and heads straight back to the institute, happy to have met this black Madre whose story, as far as she can make out, is so exciting. As the vaporetto pulls away, she cups her hands around her mouth and calls out to Ida Zanolini, "And write us a nice serial, won't you!"

Bakhita has the photographs taken. Alone. Standing. Kneeling. Holding a book or with her hands together. Praying. Smile held in check. Eyes distant. She maintains an upright bearing, because she must look up and not move, she has a dignity and natural elegance that disconcerts the people choosing between the images, and they whisper that perhaps this is because her father was the village chief's brother, as she told Ida Zanolini. Who knows? What if she were an African princess? Oh... it's no laughing matter, the life she's had... the life! How to describe her? She's... well, yes, she really is a wonder just as the name implies, this "wonderful story," this *storia meravigliosa*. Every Italian child ought to know it, they'd see what children are subjected to in Africa, and they'd be twice as happy to live with Il Duce.

In January 1931 the first installment of Madre Giuseppina Bakhita's *Storia Meravigliosa* was published in the Canossian periodical. In December the book was on the shelves. It describes the hell of slavery, her lifesaving meeting with the Italian consul, and her time in Italy until she became a novice. The book's cover frightened no one: The illustration of Bakhita's smooth wise face with her Canossian headdress is set against a map of Italy, her face is light, almost mixed race. Inside the book, the photograph itself reveals the deep black of her skin, as if it would take Italian readers a while to come to terms with it. In the preface, after Ida Zanolini has described how moved she was by their meeting, the editor adds a few lines about God's wonderful ways, God who, in His goodness, wanted to "bring Bakhita from the distant desert mired in superstition and barbarity to the light of Christ and the glories of His grace, in religious perfection." These last words were for the missionary movement.

The book is not a success. It is a phenomenon. People fight over it. It is reprinted. Reprinted over the course of several years, up until 1937, at the end of the war in Ethiopia. At first Bakhita does not understand at all. Does not understand why people come ringing at the institute's door all day long and sometimes at night, but she opens up, she is the *portinaia*. They come from all over the place. Not just nearby villages, not just towns in Veneto, they come from Trieste, Fiume, Venice, Turin, come to see her, touch her and be touched by her, be blessed, healed, consoled. Some throw themselves at her feet sobbing. Others gaze at her in astonishment, touch her medallion, kiss the hem of her robes, ask her to pray for them. There are the homeless. The superstitious. The wounded souls. The inquisitive. The humiliated and the exalted. And beside the Madre, who is so black, so *moretta,* the sisters have put a collection box. After meeting Madre Giuseppina, people are encouraged to give money for the Canossian missionaries, every donation buys a slave's freedom, so the poor among these visitors feel they are contributing to their country's greatness, Italians are no longer mandolin-playing exiles, no longer illiterate alcoholic peasants, they are these generous souls who work to save other peoples that are not yet acquainted with civilization.

"It is el Paron's will . . ." When evening comes and she is alone in her cell, with the window open to the night air, she keeps telling herself this. It is God's wish. And she prays for Him to explain it to her. What are they all looking for? Mother Superior laughed when Bakhita asked why so many people wanted to see her, when they can look at the photo in the book. She laughed and did not answer. And ever since the serialization was published, long before the book came out, things have changed in the very heart of the convent. One day, during their leisure time, the sisters asked Bakhita to sing an African song. She could not remember a single one. They insisted, come on, couldn't she make an effort, an African song, just one. She closed her eyes, it was an April morning with pale light, a clear morning holding nothing back, she simply could not remember, this disappointed the sisters and left her feeling miserable and ashamed, as if she had lied to them, as if she was not really from "over there," and apart from her

devil skin, she had brought nothing from Africa, she could see some of them had their doubts and suspicions: She'd told her life story but couldn't even remember a song? This tormented her for several days, and she would go about her business, her brow furrowed, humming the beginnings of a melody that went nowhere, trying to whistle, to recall a sound from childhood, a snatch of music from her mother, who no longer visited her dreams now that she had been described in a book. Bakhita could find her nowhere now, as if she had definitively left that fallen baobab trunk (a detail Bakhita had kept to herself) and vanished into an inaccessible beyond, but perhaps her soul and Bakhita's father's soul resented her for telling the story of their failure. The little slave girl. That little slave girl was the daughter they failed to find. She prays for this too, for her family to forgive her. And when she hears money drop into the Canossian mission's collection box, she cannot help thinking of Binah, Kishmet, and all the others. So she agrees to be this "rare creature," as she puts it, but is sometimes just too tired, sometimes feels so awkward and anxious that it paralyzes her. "Two lira to buy the book, and how much to see me?" she asks. How much is she worth? How much has she ever cost? At more than sixty, she would not be much use now in Sudan, to slave masters, and she pictures herself in Khartoum's stifling, dusty streets, sitting against a bare wall, a beggar woman like the others, like those she sees in Italy, hounded and beaten by the Fascists, and then found half dead, with their manic smiles and their embarrassment for still being alive. These are the women for whom she feels an affinity. But el Paron wants something else. And the day she remembers her song "When children were born to the lioness," she announces the fact to the other nuns with the relief of a conscientious child. The nuns are delighted, and so curious that they ask her to sing it right here, right now, even though it isn't leisure time, here, in the refectory, where they have pushed the tables into place before sitting down to eat. They want to watch too: "You must clap your hands, Madre Giuseppina! And dance!" They have seen the films, they know how this goes. Bakhita sings her childish song. Even though she feels so old. The song for the children who sat around her, carefree and wide-eyed. It is in a combination of dialects, Arabic and Turkish, she does her best, has long since forgotten her mother tongue. At first the nuns are embarrassed, her full-bodied voice, lumpen words, clapping hands, swaying body, they dare not look at her, are ashamed that it makes them shudder, and when Bakhita closes her eyes at the end of the song, drops her arms by her side, motionless and serious, they are afraid someone will come in and see this, this pain they cannot begin to understand.

Subsequently, to atone for this awkward atmosphere, they decide to laugh about it. And it becomes a regular occurrence in their leisure time to ask Madre Moretta to sing her song. But without closing her eyes. "African style" to the very end: Clapping and dancing. Joyful. Always joyful! Afterward, Bakhita's legs and back and even her arms hurt so much she thinks she definitely wouldn't be any use to anyone in Khartoum now, she'd just be a beggar. Would no longer serve in anyone's house. No young mistress would ask her to sing or act like a monkey to entertain her guests.

Of course, all of these people who come to see her know what to expect, have read the book, are curious but not afraid. It is better now than in her early days as *portinaia*, when she frightened children. The first days of school were the worst, the children did not want her to touch them, some burst into tears at the sight of her and stood staring at her, rooted to the spot, helpless. Surely she was the wife of *l'uomo nero*, the babau, the bogeyman in fables, a horrifying black ghost that their parents threatened them with at the least misdemeanor. Does she have legs under her robes? Does the lower half of her body give off smoke? Does she hide under their beds at night? And the perennial fear that she would dirty them, contaminate them, steal them to eat them. The patience it took to calm them, these children who grew up with fear and whose parents replaced their clothes with Fascist Party uniforms, black dresses, skirts, and shirts, ever keen to do the right thing, be like everyone else, acceptable and identical.

She wants only one thing: to welcome them in as best she can, be the best possible doorkeeper, it matters, she knows it matters how each day starts. So she asks the children to sit down before the bell sounds for them to go in and tells them about the life of Christ. She would rather never talk of her own life again, never answer more questions about it, prefers talking about the crucified slave, how people wanted to follow him, listen to him, how he loved beggars and the sick and little children. But a lot of them prefer to have Mussolini's book explained specially for children, or the poems they recite at breathtaking speed, clapping their hands: "Rosa was her name, a name that's full of thorns, but he was her bloom, her little boy Benito. She kissed his brow and said, You're mine, oh you are mine! But she knew that he belonged to Italy. And God." It is a game. A new way of life. As a group. Gathered together. Surrounding the leader who is reviving the country after the Great War made it "worse than a lunatic asylum or an African tribe."

She will do this until 1933, usher in the institute's children, its visitors, and respond to the endless needs of those who have read her *storia meravigliosa.* Wherever she may be in the convent, the school, or the church, when the doorbell rings, she goes to it. Perhaps because she admitted to the terrible treatment, the blows, the torture of tattooing, perhaps because she talked of the long walks, the hunger, and the thirst, her body can take no more. It is failing. Just when she is in such demand, when she must run the moment she is needed, her body would like to stop. But she still has the same reflex response: Someone asks her to do something, she obeys. She does not always understand what is wanted of her. Why do they need to come so close to her? Why do they read her story with such passion? Can't they see what's going on here, in their own country? Don't they see the little peasant girls? Do they know how many children there are at the institute who don't know their birth dates? Why don't they ask the orphans to tell their "wonderful stories," these girls who come here with no underwear, dirty and silent, already abused and ashamed? She does not understand, and then accepts this lack of understanding, she is the nun who wears her story on her skin like stigmata, and does her best to disguise the pain shooting up her legs to her lower back, never asks for a doctor to examine her, and will never show the infirmary the strange little spots that appear on her scars, inflaming her skin.

One day she is told she must go. She is sixty-four years old, and will leave Schio. Mother Superior introduces her to Madre Leopolda Benetti who has returned from more than thirty years as a missionary in China.

"Do you know where China is, Madre Giuseppina?"

Bakhita shakes her head, she does not know China, and she smiles as appealingly as she can to Madre Benetti who is eyeing her with such curiosity.

"China's a very long way away. Farther than Africa," says Mother Superior, and Madre Benetti nods as if to say, Oh, yes, that *is* possible, somewhere farther away than Africa!

Madre Benetti tells Bakhita that she has read the book. Bakhita nods. The book, of course, why else would anyone want to talk to her, and what else does anyone talk to her about since its publication, yes, the book, and she listens while she herself is discussed, her childhood and her conversion, and then there is talk of missions which, as she knows, are more and more widespread in Africa, in Sudan and Libya. She listens and waits for the request that is bound to come next, because there is always a request at the end of these discourses.

"All those slaves whose freedom must be bought. All those lives to save."

"Yes."

"And you... the Italians love you so much."

"Me?"

"Our Madre Moretta is the personification of humility," Mother Superior says to apologize for Bakhita's innocence. "You could help our missionaries, Madre Giuseppina."

"How?"

"People come from all over Italy to see you, don't they? Well, now you shall go out to meet them."

"I'm leaving?"

"Yes. You're leaving."

"I'm not staying? I'm going?"

She is driven out once again, it is her fault, she said too much, chokes the place by taking up so much space, knows this, sometimes feels like a huge flag planted outside the institute, masking everything else, the humble, patient work of the other nuns, and she remembers how happy she was when she worked in the kitchens, and the sacristy, the happiness of those prewar times when the little girls called out to her in the schoolyard, "Moretta Bella, come here!" She should never have gathered them around her and told them about the escaped slave girl who sleeps in trees and isn't eaten by wild animals. That was how it all started.

"Are you listening, Madre Moretta? Will you help us buy the freedom of slaves? Save your brothers in Africa?"

"In Africa?"

Madre Benetti spreads a map of Italy on the desk. Bakhita has seen images of it since the war, this long country of mountains and seawater.

"You and I are going to set out to spread the word. You, me... and the book. We'll travel all over Italy, every Canossian institute in the country, and we'll collect money for our missionaries."

"I have to tell you, Madre. Sorry, but... I walk difficult. Really."

They do not understand straightaway. To Bakhita, leaving means walking. When they do understand, they are torn between laughing and hugging this Madre Moretta, protectively but also gratefully, because the idea that Madre Maria Cipolla, the overall Mother Superior, has had is very good: "increase the institute's standing" by taking Madre Giuseppina all over Italy. And this, this simpleminded innocence of hers, so perfectly represents the African people!

They will take trains. Dozens and dozens of trains across the entire country, for three years. Before leaving, Bakhita confides in Elvira. She is anxious at the thought of talking about a book she did not write and had trouble reading. Elvira reassures her: Madre Benetti ("the Chinawoman," as she calls her) will translate her Venetian dialect, everything will be fine, people love her so much, love her without even knowing her. She tries to soothe Bakhita when she would prefer to tell her not to go. Bakhita has a right to rest. A right to be like the others, a tired old nun, loved by former pupils, lay teachers, orphans, everyone who has grown up and grown old alongside her.

"I'll come to join you, Madre, I'll come to see you, I promise."

"Your mistress doesn't want you to."

"Don't you worry about my mistress."

"How long do you think I'm gone?"

"I don't know."

"Could I have a walking stick?"

"I'll ask them."

And then they sit in silence for moment. Elvira notices her sagging profile, so different from the drawings others now do of her, the image that is in general circulation, wise, so wise, her lips closed, her heart silent, and all her torments held in check. As if guessing what Elvira is thinking, Bakhita tells her this very private fact: "My mother is back, you know, Elvira. She forgives the book."

"Have you seen her? In a dream?"

"Not in a dream. She kissed me."

Elvira loves her so much when she is like a five-year-old, when she twists her mouth and raises her eyebrows, the little twinkle of blue in her astonished eyes.

"What do you mean she kissed you?"

"It's very cold, but when I sleep she kisses me, here, on my cheek. She forgives."

"Yes, my darling little Madre, she's forgiven you, and now she'll never leave you again."

"Do you think?"

"Who would want to leave you?" she asks and, taking her in her arms, adds quietly, "And let the Chinawoman carry your suitcase, won't you!"

Feeling Bakhita's laugh reverberate against her chest, Elvira realizes Bakhita has no idea what is expected of her. She is from a very real

Africa but will be expected to talk about an invented country, her mother kisses her at night, and she will be asked to describe an Abyssinia of savages. The official speech. It is what they do best in Italy, reassurance and hope transmitted along simplistic lines that speak directly to the fears of the general population, their fear of "other people." Of barbarians.

In their thousands, and over several years, they come. Groups. Schools. Universities. Sick children. Pilgrims. They come to listen to her and more particularly to see her. In churches, theaters, and schools. In the convent in Castenedolo, men who have never set foot in a church before kiss her hands and come away in tears. In Florence, Bologna, and Ancona she meets the cardinal, in Lodi the bishop grants her a special audience, in Trento more official photographs are taken, in Milan she meets the children in a Canossian establishment where they teach young deaf-mutes. The children run away at the sight of her. One little girl comes closer, touches Bakhita with a finger. Her finger does not come away dirty. The child waves the other children over, and they throw themselves in Bakhita's arms, asking for kisses. She spends the whole afternoon with them, they show her sign language, she responds with flailing gestures, with them she feels understood. In Venice she is invited to the centenary of the institute's foundation. At the Vimercate novitiate she is asked to perform the role of *portinaia* for a few days. The novices' parents refuse to enter the building until a white nun comes to the door. In one town there is such a crush to see her that the tram lines are blocked, four thousand people throng the streets. In other places people climb into the pulpit to have a better view of her and call for her to come up and preach. Crowds wait for her in stations, and when the train pulls in some start singing canticles while the more politically minded sing "Faccetta Nera": "Little black face, little Abyssinian, we'll take you to Rome a free woman, you will be kissed by our sun, and you will be pure in a black shirt." She is asked whether she knows Josephine Baker, who has a Sicilian lover and whose triumphant tour included Italy. Is asked whether she has read the scandalous book *Sambadù, amore negro,* which Mussolini has recently ordered to be taken out of circulation because it is an offense to the nation's dignity. (The cover features a white woman kissing a black man, but at the end of the novel the Italian heroine acknowledges her lover's barbarity and he returns to his tribe.) Bakhita is Africa. Some even say she is "the color of Africa." She herself, though, would admit later, much later, "I felt I was falling into the abyss."

What she is being asked to do is essentially fairly simple, and each appearance follows exactly the same format. The missionary sister, Madre Benetti, talks about Canossian missions, the lack of funds, conversions, freed slaves, missionaries' lives, and—emphatically—their deaths (through sickness, violence, or poverty), then asks Bakhita to join her. This is the moment everyone is waiting for. The reason they are here, overwhelmed with emotion before it even begins. She comes to the middle of the stage, steps into the light. And she always allows them a moment to look. Because this is what they want, she knows it is. Once the shock, the exquisite shock has passed, they try to recognize in her the little girl from the book, the half-naked slave in Khartoum's markets, they stare in silence and sometimes she remembers the white bird that sailed over El Obeid, when a buyer asked to have a closer look at the merchandise. Remembers what she then had to do, fetch a stick, run, crouch down, show her teeth, she could not do this now that she uses a stick to walk, but not here, not in public, the walking stick stays in the cloakroom, and she arrives on the stage with her cumbersome limp. Next, Madre Benetti asks her to "speak from the heart." She will talk and knows her voice will frighten them. And that they will enjoy their fear, which is also such a good expression of "Africa." She says hello to them and thanks them in her bad Veneto, she says, "I will remember you in my prayers," sometimes adding, "I hope to see you all in paradise." And then she climbs down from the stage. She does not want to, but it is an order and she obeys. ("Three things, Madre

Giuseppina: First, no walking stick during these gatherings; second, please don't hesitate to speak in your African dialect; and last, please feel free to go down among them, and do whatever they ask.") She signs books, grants forgiveness, sits down with those who want "more details," and even shows the scars on her arm to those who really insist. She blesses sick children with her medallion of the Virgin, and as she blesses them she prays for all those she has seen die, in Sudan and in Italy, and she feels boundless tenderness for these children who ask for nothing. The children themselves look at their mothers, hoping that they too, they in particular, will take comfort from Madre Giuseppina, and Bakhita wishes she could take these women in her arms, but that is not the accepted thing to do.

It is in doing this, mingling with crowds, talking to students, local journalists, the intrusive and the well-meaning, that she gleans news of events in Ethiopia.

On October 2, 1935, she attended a gathering on the main square in Bergamo where everyone was to listen to Il Duce's speech transmitted live on the radio. Madre Benetti showed her where the voice would come from, loudspeakers hung in trees.

"Il Duce is in Rome, in his palace, but he will speak here, and we will hear him. And so will people in town squares all over Italy. Everyone will hear him."

"Yes."

"You mustn't give any indication that you don't understand or you disagree."

"I know."

"You mustn't show anything at all. And anything you don't understand, I'll explain later."

"Yes."

"Let's find somewhere on the sidelines."

She understood later why Madre Benetti protected her from the crowd's prying eyes. With what he was to announce in this particular speech, it was better not to be black if listening to it among those jubilant masses, it was better to sit a little apart, on a bench, in the shade of a linden tree that went some way toward hiding her.

She heard the band play before the speech, the clamoring crowd, the announcement that Il Duce had arrived before he himself spoke, and she would never forget Mussolini's music. Listened with all the focus of someone trying to understand, and getting the gist of his words. Heard *"Rivoluzione!," "Tuta l'Italia!," "Unità della Patria!," "Destino!," "Determinazione!," "Tutti uniti!,"* heard the slow, halting tempo of the beginning, as if the story to come would build to a crescendo, weighed down at first by ponderous slowness, by short sentences interrupted by the roaring crowds, the crowd on the radio and its echo from the one in Bergamo, heard also the anger in Il Duce's voice because he carried all the anger of every Italian on every town square, and then the rhythm of the speech changed, the story built momentum, his deep voice went very low, like in an aria by Caruso, then suddenly swelled, rose to a shrill register, only to drop back down, hoarsely, laden with rebellion, his powerful rolled *r*'s like drumrolls, his sentences expansive and full of fury, at times it seemed Il Duce might cry, but he puffed himself up once more with the implacable anger that gave him such terrifying energy. And then Bakhita heard dates and numbers shouted, feeding the mood of rebellion in the exhausted exultant crowd, figures that inflamed them, seeming to rally them to head off to war. And this was the aim. *"La guerra!!!" "Italia proletaria e fascista!!!"* Men in the square identified themselves in these utterances, as if these words were what had been missing their whole lives. At the end of the speech, the cheering mingled with the crackling from the radio, Mussolini was inside them, his blood flowed in their veins, his voice rang in their ears long after the loudspeakers were unplugged. Bakhita did not know what Il Duce did once he had finished speaking to the whole of Italy, but on that square, from where she was on the bench on the sidelines, she witnessed an explosion of joy, in singing, shouting, tears, and hugs between people of all ages and both sexes, and children in their black shirts, who had understood still less than she had, were happy, because everyone else was. Fascist Italy was advancing in unison to claim the vital position it was due and to avenge the injustices it had been dealt for too long. It would no longer settle for the crumbs of the colonial feast. That was what this announcement was. And when Il Duce roared "Oh, Ethiopia, we've been waiting forty years, and it's enough now!," the Italians were as euphoric as if they had been reunited with someone they had missed terribly, someone without whom their lives were impossible. But they had in fact missed themselves. And thought they would find themselves again by fighting "those Abyssinian dogs," because colonization would make a wealthy respected people of them.

It is by talking to the countless hordes who come to listen to her (and to see her more than listen to her, to touch her rather than just see her), it is through contact with Italians that Bakhita grasps that Ethiopia, a country so close to her own, is an immoral nation but also a place of untapped wealth, with oil, gold and silver, platinum, nitrates, sulfur, iron, it has everything and they will devour it all, devour, invade, excavate, and dig in this exotic but barbaric country, a country they know well, they hear terrifying reports of infibulation and child sacrifices, and secretly exchange prohibited pornographic photographs, Africans with their devil skin tempting innocents as the devil does, Ethiopia not only has countless riches, it also fuels their fantasies and longings that have been repressed for too long, the steamboats to transport them there are groaning with soldiers, farmers, laborers, nuns, and missionaries, but also with Italian girls intended for Italian brothels, so that the white race does not become contaminated and all that virility is spent in the right place, without weakening itself.

Andrea Fabiani writes a simple parish newspaper and, like so many others, asks for an interview with Bakhita. He asks her to repeat what has already been written in the book and reiterate what she has just told the crowd. She speaks as if reciting, could almost tell the whole story in Italian having heard Madre Benetti relate it so many times in this official language, the language of the book. Nevertheless, she makes an effort to be involved in what she is saying, to relate events as if for the first time but without the pain of the first time. Fabiani makes the most of a moment when Madre Benetti slips out of the room to ask Bakhita a question, but so quietly, so quickly, that she does not fully understand and answers only with an apologetic smile that the journalist interprets as a discreet manifestation of her anguish.

She remembers the words. Her instincts tell her that they are dangerous. She must approach them cautiously. And so it is with caution that she asks Madre Benetti a question in the train taking them from one institute to another, asks what "arsenic" means.

"Arsenic? It's a poison. Why do you mention arsenic?"

Bakhita closes her eyes. She feels terribly hot, her hands shake as they clutch her rosary, Madre Benetti assumes she has drifted into prayer. Bakhita is walking through the fields of Ethiopia. Alongside lakes full of dead fish, poisoned rivers, and dead bodies frozen in their final convulsions. Fabiani's words encapsulate this murdered landscape: "They gassed the population. Do you understand gassed? Shells containing arsine and mustard gas. You must have heard of arsine? It's true. I heard it on a foreign radio station."

She tries to hold back her pain. Channels it. Steers it. Contains it. And later, in her cell in whichever institute welcomes them that evening, she weeps. She lives in the furious chaos of this world. And does not know where to put her own rebellion.

She heard it on the radio. Has seen photos and illustrations, newspapers, posters and postcards, seen him taming a lion, galloping on horseback, straddling canons, wielding a pickax, sowing grain, threshing corn bare-chested, and skiing, kissing children, inspecting armies. Seen his face set against a map of Africa as her own face is on the cover of *Storia Meravigliosa*. Ethiopia is now Italian. And she is to meet Il Duce at his private residence, the Palazzo Veneziano, from which he addresses the whole of Italy. It is cold on this December day in 1936, Rome is full of huge public squares and drafts, ruins and dark streets, her walking stick slips on the frozen cobblestones that make walking difficult for her. A stooped figure, she makes her way supported by two nuns who are emotional about helping her, as if they were close to her, and it is true that strangers know her now. People discuss her father with her, the night she escaped, the sheepfold, but the more people talk of her life, the farther away it feels. When she confided in Ida Zanolini, she did not know that what she said would become a book and that she would be asked to give a copy of this book to a warlord. Had she known, as she whispered in Sant'Alvise's tiny visiting room, that these words prized out of her would be sold for two lira all across the country, she would surely have kept intimate details to herself. Would have talked of children. Slaves. Numberless martyrs. But not the others. Not her brother. Her twin sister. Kishmet. Not the little kids to whom she told stories and sang songs. She would have protected the children in her village from this, from Mussolini's palace. She makes her way, whipped by the icy whistling wind that drives her forward, hunched over, seeing only her own feet and the walking stick, she has three idiotic legs moving so inadequately and cannot keep up with the valiant strides of the missionary nuns who are bound for Addis Ababa, missionaries full of curiosity and fear at the thought of seeing Ethiopia saved by Il Duce. And suddenly Bakhita stops. Catches her breath. Looks up. There it is, facing her, so tiny. The balcony. The one where he stands to talk. To yell. He is on the verge of tears, prepared to kill them all, she can sense it, this man with the voice of terror, and she knows terror, oh, she knows it so well. She almost collapses, the nuns hold her up: "Don't prostrate yourself now, Madre, wait until you're before him." Her eyes cloud. The wind snakes under her robes, stings her damaged legs, she is hiding with Binah, behind a towering acacia, they have run away and are listening to the guard's voice carried on the wind. And then, slowly, the sound of chains. The slaves' breathing. She looks at this ridiculously small balcony with two Italian flags flying on it.

"The first thing to do with the children..." she says, turning to one of the missionary nuns.

But the sister cannot hear her, there is too much wind and Bakhita is speaking too quietly.

"I DON'T UN-DER-STAND!" she shouts, enunciating her words. "LET'S HURRY."

Bakhita grasps her walking stick firmly, nods, and says quietly, to herself, "The first thing to do with the children is give them something to drink."

And, flanked by the missionaries, she steps into the vast snake house.

A few days later, still with the same missionaries, she will meet Pope Pius XI, it will be the pinnacle of her tour, and she thinks that after this she will return to Schio but is instead appointed *portinaia* at the institute of the Canossian Daughters of Charity in Vimercate, near Milan, where she has been before and where the novices are preparing to set out on a mission. She is put there like a bridge between two continents, reassuring parents who are anxious that their daughters are to travel abroad when they are so young, so exalted, and ignorant about so many things. Ethiopia may well be Italian, but the Ethiopians themselves are still African, and their revolts are subject to savage reprisals from a military power against which they are helpless. Of course, Italy must know nothing of this. But the facts cannot be kept silent for long, the murders, deportations, and concentration camps. Men change hands, like money and guns. There are cracks in the wall, for those prepared to see them, large clouds obscuring Il Duce's sun. And those who return to Italy, whether they speak or refuse to say anything, in fact admit the offenses, perhaps in spite of themselves. The missionaries' good intentions come face-to-face with the buying and selling of men, of children, little girls bought for fun, given as gifts and abandoned in the streets when their owners go home to Italy. On the one hand, a sincere commitment, on the other, pillage. Mussolini becomes drunk on his own power, engages his armies in supporting General Franco's nationalists, "to defend Christian civilization," he is hungry and the world belongs to him, he wants everything, is indestructible, intoxicated, and deranged. He soon makes an official trip to Germany, another balcony, another speech, the same furious enthusiasm for hard work and the young, the same hostility to communism, he crowingly highlights the similarities between Nazism and Fascism.

In May 1938, Hitler comes to Rome. Shortly afterward, the subject of race appears in the Italian press, alongside the Jewish question.

Bakhita stays in Vimercate for two years. From 1937 to 1939. She knows war never dies. War is everlasting. She is an old woman now and that is how she is addressed, as one *who knows.* In Vimercate she is no longer the object of fear and curiosity that she has previously been. She is from the country where the novices are heading. The novices themselves and their parents ask her things. To pray for them and, especially, to prepare them. She talks of the land of childhood, which is the same for everyone, tells them that over there daytime is blessed, nighttime respected, and nature thanked. "It's the same for you, isn't it?" With a father. A mother. The people who conceived you. And babies waiting to come into the world. "It's the same for you, isn't it?" And this is precisely what disturbs them. They are afraid of recognizing themselves in African lives, becoming confused with them. Losing themselves in the hopes and suffering of others, which are so similar to their own.

Bakhita has been given a priceless gift. Sometime earlier, in the monastery in Cremona, she came across her sister. That is what they decided to be to each other, the possibility that it could be true. Sister Maria Agostina is Kishmet's age, has the same black skin from the same part of Sudan, the same abduction and years of slavery, the same conversion as Bakhita, having been given her freedom by the priest Don Biagio Verri, "the girl slaves' apostle," "the *morette* apostle." It was fifty-three years since Bakhita had seen a man or woman her color. Fifty-three years in which she had been the terrifying oddity, the only one in the world. As she approached Maria, Bakhita could tell, from her skin, her hands, the way her body moved and her eyes watched, that the two of them were of the same beliefs, from the same landscapes and caravans, experienced the same slave traders and masters. Could tell that they were sisters. They had lost everything. Had had everything torn from them. Seen everything. And, inexplicably, their hearts continued to beat. They hugged each other for a long time, without a word, with a sense of recognition as if by holding each other close, they were in fact hugging themselves, an infallible, legitimate, unashamed black body. They talked in a language that came back to them, a fuddled, disparate, damaged language, they laughed and they cried with a relief that had all the violence of love and the longing for it harbored in each of them. They had so much to say to each other, and behind every word, every situation lay the same lost happiness, the same barbarity, the same beginning and end, what their lives could have been and what brought them to this, meeting here in an Italian monastery, with the cross of Jesus on their breasts and their medallions of the Madonna who protects stolen children. After two years of touring, her meeting with the Sudanese slave who became Sister Maria Agostina was a sign to Bakhita that she had worked well and el Paron was thanking her for it. And then her life was never really the same again. She felt, perhaps for the first time, worthy of Him, and knew nothing would ever frighten her now, nothing horrible or unforeseen could happen to her. She was protected from everything.

Three racial laws establishing the basis of Italy's fascist regime were published in July 1938. Shortly after this, Giulia, a friend of Elvira's, came to Vimercate to give Bakhita a letter that she was to burn once she had read it.

"Read it to me."

"But Madre... you've just read it."

"I don't understand it."

"Oh, you do. I'm afraid you understand it perfectly."

It was the start of a hot dry afternoon, the shutters were closed and the cell was filled with that half-light of siesta time when the sun is all-powerful. With her misshapen fingers, Bakhita stroked Elvira's letter again and again, as if trying to smooth creases out of fabric. Or erase the words.

"You must burn it, Madre, I promised her."

"How does she know?"

"That she's Jewish?"

"Yes."

"A friend of her grandmother's came to warn her. He told her that her maternal grandmother, you know, the one who raised her, was Jewish. That's what he said."

"But she grew up with us, in Schio. She grew up with Catholics."

Giulia said she had to go but would come back with news as soon as she had any, as soon as Elvira was safe in Switzerland, where, from what she said, her mother was waiting for her.

"Pray for her, Madre."

"Yes. And for the others."

Giulia stood to leave, Bakhita reached for her walking stick.

"Don't see me out, Madre."

Bakhita opened the door and took Giulia's arm. The convent was silent, they walked slowly along the corridor with its curtains faded by sunlight, could hear the buzz of flies and wasps trapped among their folds. Bakhita stopped to catch her breath, asked Giulia to open a window. The air was scorching, and it felt as if they had come into an overheated room rather than put their heads outside.

"Look, that's Milan. It's beautiful."

"Yes, Madre."

"But people are hiding. Can you see?"

Giulia looked for a long time but was much too far from Milan to make out anything other than the cathedral's spire and the city's terraces and hotchpotch of roofs.

"I'm sorry, Madre, I can't see anything."

"That's because they're well hidden." She smiled as if she had made a joke, but this was no laughing matter. She brought one hand to rest on Giulia's heart.

"This is where people hide. In strength. Tell Elvira that. Strength."

And then she returned to her cell, and her breathing mingled with the buzzing of wasps and flies. She knew. The world reached her here in Vimercate. Radio, newspaper, discussions on all sides. Everything was out in the open. These were impassioned times. *Il Giornale d'Italia* had published an article entitled "Fascism and the Problem of Race," in which scientists had established that the vast majority of Italians were of Aryan origin and constituted an Aryan civilization. The manifesto encouraged Italians to "declare in all honesty that they were racist," and stated that Jews were the only population that had never been assimilated in Italy. With this, fear reared its head once more. Fear from the "superior race" for "inferior races": Jews and Negroes. The former were depraved, the latter infantile, and both threatened the nation's purity. Italian children were to be taught that they were superior to blacks and racially distinct from Jews, and Italy's minister of education asserted the "eminently spiritual" nature of Fascist anti-Semitism. Newspapers and magazines relayed the message by publishing caricatures and satirical articles; the cover of the magazine *La difesa della razza* featured them together, Jews and Negroes in league against Italy; photographs of bare-breasted black women, of hook-nosed Jews skulking behind a white baby doing the Roman salute; a Roman statue sullied with a black handprint and affixed with the Star of David; and much more besides, Negro women and Jewish men always in cahoots. And while missionaries were sent off to Ethiopia, Jews were being excluded from universities, schools, most professions, and many public spaces.

Bakhita did not burn Elvira's letter that day. She kept it close to her, between her skin and her nun's habit, right where her heart beat with what strength she had left. And her prayer was addressed as much to el Paron as to His children, to that cruel, lost, brutally fractured family plowing forward into disaster and hatred.

She is seventy years old, the train she is on is the last one she will take, she knows this. It is taking her "home," to Schio, and she has been told that now she can rest. She does not believe this to be true. No one rests in a time of war. Italy is fighting alongside Germany in a war that the government is saying, once again, will be quick and easy. People read the time on watches and calendars, see the world in atlases and from airplanes. She thinks they are seeing everything from far too far away. Knows this will take a long time. Longer than the war itself. It will come and it will go down in history, the massacre of the living will bequeath their sorrow to their descendants, but who will console them, who will console these peacetime children carrying their fathers' invisible pain within them? There is a memory, a trace of it in the universe, and it cannot be erased. Nothing is invented. And nothing erased. She thinks of Elvira, has no more news of her, thinks of the young missionaries lost somewhere between the love of Christ and their fear of "barbarian" nations. She has come through many years and many countries, and has only ever seen the same landscape, a landscape of lost men, of dispossessed mothers, and of children robbed of innocence. The train brakes hard, screeches over quite some distance, and lurches to a halt. Her suitcase falls at her feet, the nun accompanying her hurries to pick it up, is concerned, is she all right?

"Yes. I'm fine."

The train does not set off again. People open windows. It is very hot. Very humid. The weather is about to turn. It would be good to have rain, for the sky to burst. The doors have been opened and passengers have climbed down into the fields. Bakhita can hear people calling to each other, rumors spreading.

"It's a deer..."

"Yes. It's taking long enough to get it off the track."

"What on earth are they waiting for?"

Everyone talks, gets involved. Bakhita stays seated. Her ears thrum, ring continuously. This happens more and more frequently, this interference between her and the world. Nothing to be done about it. And all of a sudden, it rains. Big hot raindrops that stir up smells from the soil. Children reach their arms outside. They are scolded, and the windows are closed. The air is stifling. And still the train does not start up again.

"For goodness' sake, move the wretched animal!"

"What the hell are they doing?"

The gunshot is sharp. It obliterates Bakhita's thrumming, and there is a sudden, astonished silence, immediately followed by a great commotion.

"What now?"

"Oh, my word, what's going on?"

And, slowly, the train sets off. The passengers have climbed back in hastily, soaked by the rain, laughing and shaking off their clothes, removing their hats. They were frightened but it was nothing. Impossible to get the deer out of the way without destroying it. Its legs were broken. A child starts to cry in distress, his mother gives him a kiss and a hunk of bread. Sitting on his mother's lap, the boy studies Bakhita. The old woman with the burned face. She smiles at this child who has just entered the war.

She herself is entering old age. Back in Schio she no longer has duties or a set schedule. Finds herself in the stark emptiness associated with sickness. Her fingers deformed by arthritis and synovitis, her wrists red, swollen with edema, her knees, hips, and shoulders seized up and tight, she is held together by pain, and under the effects of cataracts will progressively lose her sight. She wanders down corridors, clings to the walls, heads toward noises, but her ears whistle and everything becomes confused, her points of reference blurred. Her body is withdrawing, her mind looks on. In this convent she goes through the same experience as every sick elderly nun, praying and preparing herself for what is to come. By night. Or by day. She moves slowly about the institute, from one place to another. Makes a point of combing the hair and washing the hands of pupils who arrive dirty and neglected, hands out her share of bread, her piece of fruit to the hungry who take it and hide it, the tired children who hang back to watch the others play with the dreamy expression of aimless drifters. She hand-washes the altar cloth and other linen from the sacristy every day. Tidies the refectory. Knits, sews, darns, and embroiders, and no one dares tell her there is a newfound ugliness to her work, now that her sight is poor and her fingers so gnarled that they look ready to break, snap like twigs. People visit her in the hush of the visitor's room or her own cell, and they gradually realize that, although almost blind, she is remarkably insightful, announcing the recovery of a loved one, predicting a nun's next posting, or simply knowing where a mislaid letter can be found.

At seventy-three she falls for the first time. And then again. And yet again. When she collapses in front of a priest, he asks her never to do this again, prostrate herself before him Eastern-style. She asks him to help her up. Soon she is being pushed in a wheelchair, a hefty wooden chair rather like her, dark and stiff. Sometimes she is taken to mass but no one thinks to take her back, and she stays, hunched in her chair, forgotten in the church. In time her breath fails her. She has asthmatic bronchitis, and people know she is around from the sounds she makes, the creaking of her wheelchair, the whistle of her breathing, her cough, her spitting into a handkerchief that quivers in her hand. Her spells in the infirmary become increasingly frequent. She no longer knows how to get comfortable. Lying down is impossible. Sitting compresses her chest, her torso slips slowly, collapsing, the nurses support her legs on a chair outside the bed because she has elephantiasis. Nuns come to keep her company, she sends them away, too afraid the nurse will be upset, thinking she is not taking good enough care of her.

On December 8, 1943, her golden anniversary is celebrated, fifty years as a nun, and the convent grants itself an hour of peace amid the turmoil of war. After mass she stays sitting in silence, in a corner of the refectory, watching the gathered company. A great many people have come to mark her jubilee, and not only the institute but the whole town is celebrating. She has spent fifty years among sisters, and most of them now seem so young to her, what was it that made each of them turn around one day and say, "I'm not leaving. I'm staying"? They will never have children. Must form no close ties. Own nothing. Obey everything. "I'm not leaving. I'm staying." The prison is outside. Being in the convent means being free. There are rules, and they are sometimes difficult, stringent, and unfair. But they are reassuring, and the nuns' lives are underpinned by them, Bakhita realizes this: The convent is on the inside. Internal. Not immediately understood. It takes years to find one's place. She sees them, these novices and young nuns, those who have a few regrets and those who are already tired, those who are so radiant that their skin seems impregnated with light, they live together day and night, and sporadically struggle to tolerate one another, there are irritations, rivalries, and friendships that are not meant to blossom. Affection is expressed in the smallest considerations, the occasional confidence, like those Bakhita receives. The sisters talk to her, there are things that are more easily admitted to a woman than to a confessor, and the Moretta who has seen everything is equipped to hear everything. Bakhita looks at all these people who have come for her, she is both among them and withdrawn, imposing and unassuming. She would have liked Elvira to share in this occasion. She has no news but knows the Jews have already slipped away to the ends of the earth, and she can foresee what will happen. She is not clairvoyant, as people believe. But simply knows a little about the world. Knows that what will happen to us is engraved in us. And what will happen to the world is inscribed. She will never see Mimmina again, nor Elvira. They will be a part of that portion of herself ripped asunder like painful, inflamed skin lost forever.

The roundups start, and it is not the blacks who are being taken but the Jews. Before joining the Allies in Sicily, the Italian king had Mussolini arrested. Hitler released him and under the Führer's control he now rules over the Fascist-Nazi Republic of Salò in northern Italy. The first convoy left for Auschwitz in September.

Bombs fell on the world, fell on Italy and Schio. Bakhita never agreed to be taken to the shelters. Said no bomb would go falling on the institute, but the children must be protected. She meanwhile stayed in the house, like a caretaker, a broken old woman listening to the thunderous din of bombing raids. There were fatalities, injuries, and terrible destruction near Alta Fabbrica. Children were terrorized by the sky. How could she now demonstrate the beauty of the world through an open window? Darkness had invaded daytime. She prayed that the little ones would not be too frightened down in the cellars, would not become oversensitive or embittered at the thought of the lives that lay ahead of them. "Give them strength, Lord," she implored. And wondered who made the decision that children could be allowed to die. Who decided on those massacred motherhoods. And when the girls wailed at the sound of airplanes, she said, "That's just the sound of a cart, my darling, can you hear it?" And it was true, you could pick out the sound of horseshoes on cobblestones in the drone of the airplanes. "You mustn't be frightened of carts, because they always go away, you know that, my darling, don't you?" And the children did not answer, merely gazed at this wrinkled, twisted, black old lady who seemed so poor and so powerful. They believed her and went down to the shelters "until the cart has passed." After bombing raids, Bakhita would ask, "How did the girls take it? Did someone tell them stories? Did someone sing them songs?"

And then peace returned. To a world that had been erased. Fifty million dead. And as many missing. Bakhita sometimes dreamed of Elvira, confused her with other people, her twin, or slave girls she thought she had forgotten but who cropped up in her dreams with accurate names and faces she recognized. She knew they were coming for her. It was over. The end of her life had come this time. She was already living more intensely in her dreams than in that room in the infirmary where she was watched over day and night. Her tongue was swollen, her breathing dwindled, her water-bloated limbs stretched her scars, her body looked ready to tear open. An apotheosis of suffering after an entire life of fighting pain. Could she hear the murmured prayers and words of compassion? Did she know she was not alone?

One evening as she lay in bed, she felt her feet in sand, it was hot, shifting, soft. She had her thin legs back again, the legs of a child walking a long distance. Had the terror back again and the weight of that terror.

"The chains!" she screamed. "The chains!"

And her cry was so weak that the sister watching over her leaned closer.

"What did you say, Madre? What chains? Madre?"

"They're too heavy..."

The sister took her hand, a little frightened by these words. What could she do? What could she say? "She's feverish..." "She's leaving us..." "My God!"

The prayers started, two days and two nights, at Bakhita's bedside. The nuns moistened her lips with a dab of water, held her hand, as if giving to this old lady what the little girl had so desperately needed. Bakhita had been given extreme unction, the convent was in a state of vigil, lessons were suspended, people fasted, workers at Lanerossi took a break for a moment's private reflection, and the inhabitants of Schio went to the church in shifts to pray day and night. The whole town surrounded her, gathered to wait for what would inevitably happen. Word had been sent to the nuns in Venice, to Ida Zanolini, and to Stefano's children. Every institute she had visited. Orphanages, missions, and convents. Her imminent death made everyone feel like falling silent, like adopting her very particular rhythm for the first time, an internal rhythm connected to the world, and they realized that she had brought more with her than simply a life.

"*Mama!* Oh! Mama…"

The nuns came closer, Madre Giuseppina had cried out, but what did she say? Her rasping voice seemed to come from someone else, and no one could tell whether it was expressing joy or terror. Her death throes were her final struggle.

"I think she called the Madonna."

"What?"

"I said I think Madre called the Holy Virgin!"

Word spread through the convent, the institute, the town, and other towns: In her death throes, Madre Giuseppina had seen Santa Madonna. She was happy, already. And everyone bowed before this news. Candles were lit at the Virgin's feet. And the organ played "Ave Maria."

She could not hear it. Could no longer hear or see anything. Except her mother. Who was standing behind her. With her agile hands in Bakhita's braided hair, she added tiny colored beads given to her by her own mother, and from farther back still, every woman in this Daju family that had lived beside the river for so long. She felt her mother's mouth on the nape of her neck, cool moist lips, and before kissing her, they nibbled her brand-new skin and whispered in her ear, and what they whispered in their unique, joyful, and unerring way, was her birth name.

On Saturday, February 8, 1947, at the age of seventy-eight, Madre Gioseffa Margherita Fortunata Maria Bakhita died in Schio. The next day her body was taken to a chapel of rest. For two days a never-ending procession of people came to see her.

On Tuesday, February 11, after a mass in the institute's chapel, she was buried in Schio's cemetery, in the tomb of the wealthy Gasparella family, in recognition of who she had been.

In 1955 the church began proceedings toward having her beatified.

In 1969 her remains were exhumed and transferred to the chapel at the institute for the Canossian Daughters of Charity in Schio.

On December 1, 1978, Pope John Paul II signed the decree of her heroic virtues. After investigation, Bakhita was deemed venerable for her dauntless efforts to conform with the Gospel and be faithful to the church.

On July 6, 1991, Pope John Paul II signed the decree for her beatification.

On May 17, 1992, Pope John Paul II announced that Bakhita was blessed for leaving "a message of reconciliation and evangelical unity in a world so divided and wounded by hatred and violence."

In 1995, Pope John Paul II declared her the patron of Sudan.

On October 1, 2000, Pope John Paul II declared her a saint. This made Bakhita the first Sudanese saint and the first African woman to be raised to such religious glory without being martyred. In his address John Paul II said, "Only God can give hope to victims of ancient and modern forms of slavery."

In order to proclaim someone blessed or a saint, the church requires non-martyrs to perform one miracle for beatification and another for canonization. The first miracle attributed to Bakhita relates to Angela Silla, a Paduan Canossian sister who, the day before she was due to have her leg amputated, prayed to the late Madre Giuseppina Bakhita and was cured of her tuberculosis of the knee. The second relates to Eva da Costa, a diabetic Brazilian whose condition was deteriorating and who in 1992 was due to have her right leg amputated. She was healed by her prayers to the blessed Madre Giuseppina Bakhita.

Acknowledgments

Thank you to Odile Blandino who followed and encouraged my work with her vigilant, joyful, and unfailing friendship.

Thank you to Elena Vezzadini who so patiently answered my questions about slavery in Sudan in the late nineteenth century.

Thank you to the Canossian sisters in Schio and Venice for welcoming me and listening to me.

Thank you to the Salesian sisters in Venice for opening the doors of the Dorsoduro convent to me.

Thank you to Claire Delannoy, Richard Ducousset, and Francis Esménard for their faith in me and for being there.

Véronique Olmi is an actor, playwright, and stage director who has written several novels, including the critically acclaimed *Beside the Sea* anbd *Cet été-là,* for which she received the Prix Maison de la Presse in 2011. She has also published two plays, *Une séparation* and *Un autre que moi.*

Adriana Hunter studied French and Drama at the University of London. She has translated more than fifty books including Camille Laurens's *Who You Think I Am* and Hervé Le Tellier's *Eléctrico W,* winner of the French-American Foundation's 2013 Translation Prize in fiction. She lives in Kent, England.

OTHER PRESS

You might also enjoy these titles from our list:

THE HUNDRED WELLS OF SALAGA
by Ayesha Harruna Attah

"A skillful portrayal of life in precolonial Ghana emphasizes distinctions of religion, language, and status ... [Attah] has a careful eye for domestic and historical detail."
—*The Guardian*

"Compelling ... rich and nuanced ... Attah is adept at leading readers across the varied terrain of 19th-century Ghana and handles heavy subjects with aplomb. Two memorable women anchor this pleasingly complicated take on slavery, power, and freedom."
—*Kirkus Reviews*

NEVER ANYONE BUT YOU
by Rupert Thomson

A literary tour de force that traces the real-life love affair of two extraordinary women, recreating the surrealist movement in Paris and the horrors of the world wars with a singular incandescence and intimacy.

"A fascinating portrait of two women who challenged gender boundaries and society's norms in all they did, the book builds to a moving celebration of resistance, creativity, and self-reinvention."
—*The Guardian*, Best Books of the Year

"Gorgeous and heart-rending."
—*The Observer*, Best Books of the Year